The Power and the Glory

The Power and the Glory

Grace MacGowan Cooke

Introduction by Elizabeth S. D. Engelhardt

Northeastern University Press

BOSTON

Advisor to Northeastern University Press in American Literature and Culture
MARJORIE PRYSE

First published in 1909 by The Butterick Publishing Company
Published in 2003 by Northeastern University

Library of Congress Cataloging-in-Publication Data

Cooke, Grace MacGowan, 1863–1944.
The power and the glory / Grace MacGowan Cooke ; introduction by
Elizabeth S. D. Engelhardt.
p. cm.
ISBN 1-55553-553-4 (alk. paper)
1. Women—Appalachian Region—Fiction. 2. Working class
women—Fiction. 3. Mills and mill-work—Fiction. 4. Appalachian
Region—Fiction. 5. Social problems—Fiction. 6. Social
classes—Fiction. I. Title.
PS3505.05632P69 2003
813'.52—dc21   2002155914

Printed and bound by Maple Press in York, Pennsylvania. The paper
is Sebago Antique, an acid-free sheet.

MANUFACTURED IN THE UNITED STATES OF AMERICA
07   06   05   04   03   5   4   3   2   1

TO HELEN

INTRODUCTION

In 1910, Johnnie Consadine, the heroine of Grace MacGowan Cooke's novel *The Power and the Glory,* drove an automobile into the pages of American literature. Years before Nancy Drew piloted her roadster or F. Scott Fitzgerald's Daisy hopped into her convertible in *The Great Gatsby,* Johnnie climbed behind the wheel. Dodging buckshot flying around her head, worrying for an injured passenger, and facing a dangerous mountain road, Johnnie tries to bring the people she loves to safety, despite having had only one driving lesson in her life. She has, however, already faced dangerous machinery in her new job at a cotton mill—machines that cut off arms and fingers—and she has even invented safety equipment to make them better. A mere automobile is not going to defeat her: "Johnnie worked over her machine wildly. . . . her hand encountering the lever of the emergency brake, she grasped it at a hazard and shoved it forward. . . . The sudden, violent check . . . gave the girl a sense of power. If she could do that, they were fairly safe."[1] Navigating the hazards of switch-back curves, horses that spook at the sound of the vehicle, and deadly bullets replacing the buckshot, Johnnie Consadine becomes possibly the first female stunt driver in American literature. To find a self-assured young mountain woman driving into her very modern future in a novel about Appalachia, a place supposedly forever caught in the past, is only one of many surprises in *The Power and the Glory.*

Cooke, a writer who traveled across the United States and was friend to her era's literary lights, introduces readers to the world of Cottonville through Johnnie's eyes. Although she could have set the novel in any of the regions in which she lived, Cooke makes Johnnie a native of her childhood community. Soon after the novel begins, Johnnie, a young woman whose name is not the only unconventional element of her character, leaves her home deep in Tennessee's Unaka Mountains to take a job in a mill on the Tennessee-Georgia border because she is determined to rise beyond her family's (and Appalachia's) reputation for "borrowing" rather than working. Despite being stereotyped as ignorant and backward in other literature of the day, Cooke's Appalachians read the popular magazines, are educated (even the antagonists), invent and patent improvements to industrial machinery (even the women), debate women's rights and different forms of patriarchy, and face corporate environmental poisoning. Upper-class outsiders are alternately kind and cruel; they are similarly as well rounded as the mountain characters. Over the course of the book, Johnnie sends most of her wages back to her mother and siblings on the mountain; in the meantime, she joins the Uplift Club (a women's Progressive organization), is disturbed by women's exclusion from unions, and imagines a new grassroots settlement house, utopian mine, and mill village to help other women like herself. Against the background of Johnnie's coming of age and along with its in-depth look at cotton mill culture, the novel also includes a lost silver mine; a wandering chiropractor; a stolen patent that may be worth millions and may save countless arms, fingers, and other limbs; and an unlikely romance.

By making her story of industrialization and changing social roles an Appalachian one, Cooke raised questions that were largely unvoiced in other literature of the time. Another surprise of the book is how little those questions have changed from her era to today. They include: How does a community desperately in need of jobs nevertheless stand up to polluting employers? How young is too young for children to work and who should be held accountable: the hungry families that need their children's labor or the mills that hire them? What should a community do if it decides that women should not work the worst hours for the least pay or hand over all of their wages to the men in their lives? Should activism focus on federal laws, the national unions, or local "family values," all of which encourage the practices to continue? Can well-meaning, "do-gooder" ladies whose lifestyles are financed by a community's industry ever really "uplift" women who are being victimized by that industry—women who are starving, freezing, losing fingers, struggling with depression, and whose dreams are dying because the company thinks of them as disposable bodies? Can corporate medicine—with doctors paid by the company—ever fairly advocate for its patients? How does a person from a forgotten, small place become an American? If your status as a worker or an owner in a community makes the biggest difference in your quality of life, can people of different races or classes find real ways to talk with each other, work with one another, or fall in love with each other? While Cooke raises these questions throughout the novel, often in the voices of local mountain characters and in her narrative persona, she generally leads readers through humor, crises, and political asides to her conclusions. Ultimately, with Johnnie's optimism suggesting all is possible, Cooke has in mind nothing less than utopian social revolution.

A Writer Everywhere and Nowhere

So who was Grace MacGowan Cooke? Researching her is like uncovering a 1910 edition of "Who's Who" in United States literature. Cooke is connected to most Appalachian writers of her era and to a surprising number of well-remembered writers of the time. Yet, because she has been largely forgotten by the histories of literature, she is a writer at once everywhere and nowhere: an Appalachian, a Californian, a New York writer of American stories. While brief outlines of Cooke's life are known through Kay Baker Gaston's research and Cooke's own journal written between 1909 and 1915, in-depth research on her life is only just beginning.[2]

Cooke was born in 1863 in Grand Rapids, Ohio. During Reconstruction, her father took the family—including Cooke, her mother, and sister Alice—to Chattanooga, Tennessee. They settled in Appalachia after her father's military career for the Union; Cooke's parents lived in Chattanooga for the rest of their lives. Before embarking on her cross-country travels, Grace lived in Appalachia from age two until forty-three, longer than she lived anywhere else in her busy life.

As a young adult, Cooke joined the family vocation. Writing was the family business, although not all of her family members became published writers. Cooke's father worked for years as the editor of Chattanooga's prominent newspaper. His *New York Times* obituary in 1903 described him as "one of the best-known figures in Southern journalism of the past thirty years."[3] When Cooke married in 1887, her new husband,

William, and her younger brother Frank ran a printing firm in Chattanooga. Cooke was the company bookkeeper, but that was not her only employment. Cooke's writing was first published in the nation's magazines in 1888, when she was twenty-five. Both Cooke and her sister Alice MacGowan eventually supported themselves on proceeds from publishing short stories, poems, and novels. Cooke herself published almost until her death in 1944 at age eighty-one.

Cooke and her husband had two children, Helen and Katharine, who remained with Cooke through her travels. Although the marriage lasted two decades, it was not altogether a success. In her journal, to friends, and in print throughout her life, Cooke dropped hints that the housework associated with marriage was particularly frustrating to her, taking, as it did, time away from what she called her "real work" of writing. While feminists like Charlotte Perkins Gilman and Mary Johnston were imagining houses without kitchens to give women and men comparable freedoms, Cooke stayed for twenty years in a marriage that she ultimately found unworkable.[4]

In 1906, Cooke decided that her writing and personal freedom were more important than her married life. She left her husband and soon after they filed for divorce. As Gaston's research on William Cooke's divorce petition shows, "she has made it clear . . . that she will lead no other life than one of celibacy, retirement, and intellectual effort. Complainant avers that his marriage contract did not contemplate such a life."[5] After leaving her husband, Cooke headed to the East Coast, the seat of publishing and literary culture, to pursue her dreams. Her sister Alice joined her, and they set up housekeeping together. With custody of her children and, hence, the responsibility to support them, Cooke had to combine idealism with the realities of writing for pay. After her divorce, Cooke became more vocal in her nascent support for women's rights as she interacted with feminists who were as outspoken and committed as Gilman and Johnston.

Around that same year, writer Upton Sinclair made a reality out of his own idealism, as he invested the profits from *The Jungle,* his famous exposé of the meat-packing industry, in a new artists' colony he called Helicon Hall. Visual artists, writers, professors, suffragists, and other activists joined Sinclair in communal living. Because it matched so well with Cooke's desire for a life of intellectual effort, it is no surprise that she and Alice, along with Helen and Katharine, moved to Englewood, New Jersey, and Helicon Hall. Friendships she made in New Jersey would influence the rest of Cooke's life, even as events at the house propelled her across the country.

Along with Upton Sinclair, who had turned from researching the meat-packing industry to working on an exposé of the Steel Trust, Cooke met Edith Summers, who years later, as Edith Summers Kelley, wrote *Weeds*, another novel about the dreams and realities of working-class women living on the borders of Appalachia. For a while, Edith Summers's fiancé was Sinclair Lewis, author of novels such as *Elmer Gantry* and *Main Street,* who also became a good friend of Cooke's. Sinclair Lewis, Cooke, and Alice MacGowan soon hatched a plan to collaborate on a book—a plan that benefited the young, inexperienced writer Lewis more than Cooke or MacGowan. Although the book, *Ecce Homo,* never materialized, the sisters would, in fact, be the reason Sinclair Lewis also made his way across the country.[6]

Unfortunately, Helicon Hall came to a tragic end, and Cooke bore the brunt of it. On 16 March 1907, a fire broke out that destroyed the property, killed a man, and injured several women. Two of the injured were Cooke and MacGowan, who were forced to throw Cooke's daughters and then themselves from a second-story window to rescuers waiting on the ground. The media reported the day after the fire that both women received internal injuries and that "Miss MacGowan, it was thought, undoubtedly would recover, but those who were attending her sister were not so sure of Mrs. Cooke." Fortunately, the papers were wrong, and both recovered; however, by Upton Sinclair's estimate the sisters lost all of their possessions and ten thousand dollars worth of manuscripts.[7] As speculation of arson and conspiracy about the cause of the fire circulated, Cooke and Alice left the East Coast on a journey that would end at the Pacific Ocean, where Cooke would spend most of the rest of her life. On her way to California, Cooke completed the manuscript of *The Power and the Glory*.

By 1909, the novel was finished and Cooke had purchased a bungalow on the beach at another artists' colony, this time at Carmel-by-the-Sea. Sinclair Lewis recalls the influence of the sisters in "I'm an Old Newspaperman Myself," in which he says, "I was rescued by two women writers, sisters and collaborators, Grace Macgowan Cook [*sic*] and Alice Macgowan, bless their souls, who wired me from Carmel, California, asking whether I would care to consider going out as their secretary."[8] Although the employer-employee relationship failed, Lewis nevertheless joined the growing colony in Carmel. Founded by the poet George Sterling, the community of bungalows on the beach was one of the few developments in its corner of California. Cooke's neighbors in the community, though, were, like her, both worldly and well known to the larger world. Adventure writer Jack London joined feminist writer Mary Austin, Cooke's protégé Sinclair Lewis, and poets Robinson Jeffers and William Rose Benét in cabins and homes on the beach. Life at the colony included impromptu stagings of plays, long picnics, fierce debates, hikes, and automobile road trips. The colony's spirit of collaboration, as well as the sense that she could make herself over as an independent woman, suited Cooke well.

Even as she achieved economic independence, Cooke continued a practice she began early in her career of writing not only individually but also in collaboration with others, especially with women. Although some of her works acknowledge their co-authorship, it is an unsettled question how many others were also written in collaboration. She enjoyed the process of revision and discussion, and she often helped others refine their manuscripts. Cooke and her sister worked extremely closely together; their relationship was also marked by periods of separation, in which one or the other rejected their collaborative process. Around the time *The Power and the Glory* was published, she and MacGowan were not working together, and Cooke was reconsidering how much independence she wanted. Although Cooke proved that she could write on her own, she and her sister eventually reconciled and returned to their pattern of collaboration and communal living on the California coast.

While Cooke never left Appalachia behind as a setting for her writing, her life and some of her later novels fully embraced California and the West. The book immediately after *The Power and the Glory* was set in the deserts of California and

Arizona. Much like Mary Austin's *The Land of Little Rain,* Cooke's *The Joy Bringer* (1913) was written after spending months visiting with Native Americans, which in Cooke's case was the Hopi tribe in their desert homes. Cooke caught the independent spirit of California and celebrated liberal ideas about lifestyle and society. Somewhere on her journey to the West, she met Elizabeth Townes, editor of the *Nautilus,* a journal of "New Thought" on alternative health, vegetarianism, women's rights, and liberal politics—and Cooke began writing for it, too. As early as *The Power and the Glory,* readers can see Cooke questioning mainstream doctors and suggesting the importance of exercise, freedom, and fresh air for women.

Cooke's final novel was *The Fortunes of John Hawk* (1928), and although her publishing dropped off late in life, she continued to mentor other writers in her final decades. By the time she died in 1944, Cooke had published, often with collaborators, at least fifteen books. They include *A Gourd Fiddle* (1904), *The Grapple* (1905), *William and Bill* (1914), *The Straight Road* (1917), and *Wild Apples: A California Story* (1918). She also wrote children's books, short stories, and developed plays and screenplays. After her death, Cooke's writings fell out of print. With the exception of a 1976 reprint of *The Grapple,* her works have been unavailable for nearly seventy years.

The Life and Times of The Power and the Glory

At the beginning of the twentieth century, it was almost unthinkable that Cooke could fall into obscurity. She was established as a successful writer, publishing in *Harper's, Munsey's, Century,* and the *Atlantic Monthly.* Influential editor William Dean Howells, introducing his collection *Southern Lights and*

Shadows, in which one of Cooke's Appalachian short stories appeared, praised Cooke and the rest of the included writers for breathing new life into the short story form. Reviewers in the *New York Times* mentioned Cooke along with Oliver Wendell Holmes, Mark Twain, and O. Henry.[9]

As solid as her reputation was, the story of Johnnie Consadine, a woman dedicated to making it on her own, marks a watershed in Cooke's career. With the publication of *The Power and the Glory,* Cooke's dreams and aspirations as a writer, like Johnnie's as an inventor, were becoming realities. Although she notes in her journal that the story of switching publishers is not worth telling, *The Power and the Glory* was Cooke's first publication with Doubleday, Page and Company. She calls them the company "whom I prefer out of the whole list of them that make books" and is thrilled at the initial print run of fifteen thousand. Her journal alludes to frustration with her previous publishers around marketing her books, but Doubleday seems to have viewed Cooke as one of their significant authors.[10]

In the *New York Times* alone, *The Power and the Glory* appeared eight times from May to December of 1910, including one lengthy, positive review about its "undeniable charm" and celebration of "adventures to the adventurous and luck to the brave." Doubleday also took out at least three advertisements featuring the novel, two of which highlighted Cooke. The novel was reviewed in newspapers around the country; cities such as San Francisco, Chicago, and Richmond, Virginia, all took notice. By November, on the strength of the novel's sales, Cooke wrote, "I have got on a good base of living and feeling, a basis of poise and power. I am going to build up this home in Carmel, whoever goes or stays." Cooke was determined to make it on her own, but in a way that benefited the friends and family depending on her.[11]

Readers also were curious about Cooke's personal life—reports about where she was living after the Helicon Hall fire and about her family testify to her relative fame as an author. A short piece in the *New York Times* even speculates that her daughter Helen, to whom *The Power and the Glory* is dedicated, was the inspiration for Johnnie.[12] With her celebrity, Cooke joined a group of increasingly visible women writers.

Across the United States during Cooke's era, women writers were using their pens for provocative questions and rebellious acts. Authors who today are known as regionalists, such as Cooke's friend Mary Austin, were writing detailed, careful sketches of out-of-the-way places and in the process were challenging ideas of what makes up and who is included in the nation. Regionalists focused on women, children, the silences, and the taboos in society; they gave voice to the land, the marginalized, and the seemingly unimportant. Arguing that the nation was more diverse and more complicated than the "American dream" would have it, regionalists suggested that tapping forgotten people and places could strengthen the country as a whole. While the *New York Times* focused on her "mountain folk," most reviewers recognized Cooke's story as an "American" book and Johnnie as an "American girl."[13] Critics acknowledged the balance *The Power and the Glory* found between the local and the national, and in so doing put it with other regionalist works.

At the same time, immigrant authors like Anzia Yezierska or Progressive authors like Upton Sinclair tried to give voice to immigrant and working-class experiences. Their literature examined how the United States' rush to industrialization was crushing the bodies and the dreams of its underclass of workers while making a small group of industrialists very wealthy. African American and other antiracist women writers, such as Ida B. Wells-Barnett, were documenting the inhumanity of Jim Crow and other racist structures. They also insisted that class and gender deeply affected one's experiences in the United States. As authors, many of the same women were combining genres, mixing autobiography with fiction or essays with sketches; they violated traditional "rules" of plots and characters and in so doing created new ideas of what writing could be. Since Cooke's novel features working-class characters, includes African American and white citizens of Cottonville, and uses gender to analyze mill conditions, Cooke can be viewed as standing on a literary crossroads in which radical experiments and new questions were possible.[14]

Cooke's experiments are set in the most notorious mountain range in North America: Appalachia. At the turn of the twentieth century, the Appalachian Mountains and their residents were a literary fad. One could hardly find a national magazine that did not include a sketch of "this strange land and peculiar people," to paraphrase a common description of the region. Although often difficult to define precisely, Appalachia's boundaries stretched from Pennsylvania to Georgia, but most often centered on West Virginia, Kentucky, Tennessee, Virginia, and North Carolina. With her novel of industrialization and changing social roles set in Appalachia, Cooke participated in the literary fad, even while she struggled with fault lines in the common understandings of Appalachian people. The *New York Times* reviewer identified Cooke's portrait of mountain residents as a major issue in the book, saying, "She writes of the mountain folk both on the heights and in the valleys, in their nobler and their baser moods and characteristics, and she holds the reader with a firm grip to the very last page."[15] Through presenting a range of fully drawn Appalachian characters, Cooke uses her Appalachians frankly to confuse easy ideas of the American dream: they are not recent immigrants, but they have not assimilated (some people were not even sure they were the same race as other European Americans); they are industrialized, but they are known more by rural and isolated traditions than by their cities and factories; they are southern, but not privileged; they are close to the sophisticated centers of American culture such as Philadelphia, Boston, and New York, but are not wealthy like the most visible residents of those cities.

How Cooke conceives of the differences and similarities of Appalachians and people from outside the region is one of the most challenging questions in the novel. Turning to her contemporaries in Appalachian literature may shed light on Cooke's own vision. Recent scholarly attention has focused on other female writers, such as Mary Noailles Murfree, Rebecca Harding Davis, and Emma Bell Miles, who made careers speaking for and with Appalachians. All three published in their era's magazines, and all three have been brought back into print as early feminist and regionalist writers. At one point, Mary Noailles Murfree was viewed as everything wrong with turn-of-the-century portraits of Appalachians; scholars today are revisiting her Tennessee mountain stories and noticing her complex ideas of insider and outsider. Cooke's decision to make Johnnie both exceptional and normal among mountain mill workers suggests similar commitments to rethinking the fuzzy boundaries between mountain and American societies. Rebecca Harding Davis's *Life in the Iron Mills* is an earlier portrait of mill workers; while it was one of the first works recovered by modern feminist literary critics, few have analyzed its Wheeling, West Virginia, setting or discussed it as an Appalachian novel. Bringing *The Power and the Glory* back into print makes possible more questions about urban Appalachian literature, especially with our growing recognition of the long history of urbanization within Appalachia (in contrast to its reputation as wild and unsettled). Further, it highlights Cooke's commitment to making visible the social and class pressures pulling the United States together, often violently. Emma Bell Miles's *The Spirit of the Mountains* shares with Cooke's novel deep concerns about runaway industrial development in Appalachian Tennessee. Although the two friends, Cooke and Miles, reach different conclusions, they both dramatize the painful consequences and brave choices of Appalachian women in labor, social, and environmental protest. In Cooke's novel, some Appalachian characters fall into desperate poverty while others reap wild profits from the mills' intimate blending of new capital and old values.[16]

Contemporary reviews of *The Power and the Glory* recognized the challenges her novel posed to stereotypes about Appalachia. Even so, they focused even more on other issues within the book, especially on Cooke's treatment of child labor practices and changing gender roles. Cooke was writing at a time when conventional wisdom suggested labor politics divided along class and regional lines. Wealthier Americans on the one hand and southerners on the other were thought to be generally probusiness and antilabor. They often formed the opposition against legislation to get children out of the mills. Cooke, a woman who had lived in and was connected to the

South and to the class of people who formed the mill management and ownership, nevertheless gives a human face to the
children in the mills through Johnnie's younger brothers and
sisters. She violated conventional wisdom by unflinchingly
criticizing the mills' employment of children and the toll the
mills took on workers. Why did Cooke choose to voice such
strong criticisms of industrial capitalism? What is the effect of
having a female heroine who realizes the unfairness of the
mills' wage and work structures? Finally, how did Cooke's
criticisms reconcile with her utopian solutions and faith in
industrial altruism at the end of the novel?

For Cooke, the injustice of child labor is inseparable from
women's rights in the mountains, a theme picked up by the
book's original reviewer: "There is a deeper note to the book,
lent by the situation in the cotton mills and the bearing of the
child-labor question on the happiness of the heroine."[17]
Cooke's personal feminism becomes a major theme of the
novel as it spills into her portrait of adult women in the town.
Women are the primary caretakers of the mill children; their
own adult lives are shortened by worry and by their own childhood experiences in the mills. Because mill women are caught
in both the patriarchy of the mountains and the class and gender hierarchies of the mills, they are the most disempowered
and, therefore, the most thoughtful about the society in which
they live. But that does not mean Cooke is simply dogmatic
in her portrayal. Some characters, especially Lydia Sessions,
talk a good talk about helping other women, while others find
meaningful ways to make actual changes in women's lives,
such as the trio of Mandy Meacham (a fellow mill worker),
Mavity Bence (the midwife who birthed Johnnie and kept the

house in which she boards in Cottonville), and Johnnie. The combination in the novel makes for dynamic tension and sophisticated complexity against the backdrop of what was a broad-based United States movement for women's rights.

Although the right to vote for women was still more than ten years away when Cooke wrote *The Power and the Glory*, thousands of women across the United States were working in the political or public realm to expand women's freedoms. The Progressive movement had at its core the idea that the more fortunate should help "uplift" the less fortunate in United States society—whether those less fortunate lived in New York tenements, the Appalachian Mountains, Native American reservations, or on the outskirts of small towns in every state. For middle-class women, Progressive activism expanded the domestic sphere and traditional roles for women to include the public realm, making it both revolutionary and safe. Building on earlier benevolence work and gaining visibility from the 1880s on, Progressivism had started the settlement house movement (with Jane Addams's Hull House being the most famous), worked on clean air and water campaigns, started parks in towns and wilderness areas, promoted health and disease prevention, emphasized public education and libraries, and brought attention to labor issues for men, women, and children. Progressive crusaders like Upton Sinclair concentrated on uncovering dangerous practices in the country's new industries. *The Jungle* was one of many such exposés and Cooke surely drew on her friend's research. She also may have read books such as Marie Van Vorst's *Amanda of the Mill* (1905), a book that criticized working conditions in Appalachia's burgeoning cotton mills and was popular enough to garner a preface from President Theodore Roosevelt. Cooke's familiarity with and interest in Progressive and feminist activism are reflected in her careful portrait of Cottonville's women and children.[18]

In the novel, questions about feminism and activism come together within the doors of Lydia Sessions's Uplift Club. The struggle between Sessions and Johnnie epitomizes a larger national struggle only beginning to be voiced. Across the United States, the Progressive movement often relied on middle-class, domestic solutions to the social problems it wanted to address, and women's clubs stepped in to provide those solutions. In some women's clubs, teaching needy women how to waltz or how to choose the proper fork at a formal dinner stood in for more significant social services. Progressive women were faced with systemic structural inequalities forcing needy women even deeper into poverty and desperation; yet they often backed away from challenging class hierarchies and viewed poorer women's cultures as fundamentally inferior to their own. Domestic lessons proved insufficient in "uplifting" the needy and were one of the factors that ultimately crippled the movement. Working-class men and women like the mill women in *The Power and the Glory* or the Jewish shirtwaist workers ten years later in Anzia Yezierska's *Hungry Hearts* found the superficial activism of some charitable work empty. In both portrayals, working-class women demanded their own voices in the debate.[19] Although she was not a member of the working class in Appalachia, Cooke exposed the complicity of some middle-class activists in the oppression of Appalachia's mill workers.

Readers today may also be struck by Cooke's emphasis on

environmental pollution as a part of Appalachia's industrialization. From today's perspective of superfund sites, declining
air and water quality, and occupational illness, the environmental impact of industry seems a crucial line of inquiry. Yet
Cooke anticipates this perspective by sixty years. During her
era, East Coast middle-class lifestyles were celebrated by some
Progressive, feminist reformers and the movement's hangers-
on, such as the do-gooder, middle-class Uplift Club ladies in
Cottonville. Such lifestyles, however, were built on the large-
scale extraction of natural resources from regions like Appalachia. In many concrete ways, Appalachia powered the industrialization of the East Coast, by supplying coal, timber, and
other raw materials such as the novel's cotton fabric. In 1907,
logging reached its peak across Appalachia. States such as
West Virginia, Kentucky, Ohio, and Pennsylvania saw massive
amounts of coal mined from their mountains; the more southern Appalachian states such as North Carolina and Cooke's
Tennessee faced unprecedented growth of textile mills, paper
plants, and other industrial developments. Some of these
industries undeniably brought positive improvements to the
quality of life in Appalachia. But most relied on absentee ownership and exploitative labor practices; ordinary Appalachians
faced displacement from family land, unsafe working conditions, and relatively few profits as they supplied raw material
for the nation's middle-class consumption. Appalachians
witnessed massive changes to the land around them—animals dying, mountain peaks reshaped, rivers and springs poisoned.[20]

While activists and women's club members in other com-
munities across the United States were working to found

parks, historical sites, and national wilderness areas, Mandy Meacham joins Johnnie in worrying about the water in Cottonville. Johnnie and Mavity Bence point out the lack of green spaces for women and children in Cottonville's mills. And all three women worry about the air quality in and around Cottonville. In other words, instead of addressing pristine wilderness sites outside of Cottonville, Cooke considers how to clean up densely populated, already poisoned city land. Where does Cooke's environmentalism—with its emphasis on women's roles within it—fit in the history of Appalachian and environmental activism? What challenges does she pose to what we thought we knew about environmental literature? Here, Cooke's answers are embedded in the conversations tired mill women have as they walk to yet another shift in the dusty, hot, windowless rooms of the textile industry.

What makes *The Power and the Glory* especially gripping for readers today is that its themes—of Appalachian and American identity, Progressivism, women's rights, child labor, and environmentalism—are all filtered through vital, funny, tragically human female characters. Cottonville is a changing place; its dramas are not static or codified. It is rushing into the twentieth century, not at the pace of Johnnie's first walk down the mountain or at the speed of Lydia Sessions's horse-drawn carriage, but at the accelerating push of Johnnie in the automobile.

In *The Power and the Glory*, the auto becomes a symbol of all women's capabilities, as Johnnie harnesses technology to get herself and the people she loves out of dangerous situations. Cooke completely rewrites the conventional action plot when Johnnie becomes the rescuing hero, and she does it by putting her heroine in the driver's seat. Judging from the growth of the automobile industry in the United States, the time was right for literature to reflect America's adoption of the car into daily life. In 1911 alone, the industry produced 199,000 passenger cars. Car ownership was no longer confined to the ultra rich; it was becoming a part of America's mass culture (for comparison, the industry made 63,500 cars in 1908 and 356,000 in 1912). But if Cooke was in line with mainstream culture in her inclusion of an automobile in her novel, she was ahead of the trends with her portrait of a female driver. In an article originally appearing in a 1910 issue of *Outing Magazine,* Robert Sloss acknowledged that women most often played the role of a hood ornament in car advertisements—they looked pretty as they posed with the product, but they remained passive and certainly did not drive the vehicles. Joining Cooke in a belief that women drivers are more than a bad joke, Sloss dared "make the surprising statement that woman not only can do but has done with the automobile everything of which man can boast—in some respects she has done it better."[21] By the end of the novel, the reader is more reassured that Johnnie is at the wheel than if it were any other character.

If Johnnie is successful in driving safely down the mountain, she will drive herself and her lover into the new century and its new ideas of gender roles and marriage. Will she drive away from old models of patriarchy, violence, and women's economic and social submission (not just for Appalachia, but for all her readers)? Can she find a companionate marriage, economic freedom, and class mobility just by "a-bringin' him down in his own cyar!"? Can she overcome the economic poverty of the women and children in her extended family, and her own sense of responsibility to them? Will she drive into Cottonville or straight through it, and what will Cooke conclude about whether Appalachian and American identities can blend? All rests, ultimately, on Johnnie's "cool head."[22]

There is still much to discover about the creator of such an action hero, from the biographical (did Cooke own her own car?) to the theoretical (does her method of collaborative writing represent a new way of practicing her feminist values?). Closer exploration of Cooke's participation in and modification of literary trends such as regionalism should add a distinct Appalachian perspective. Her connections to other Appalachian writers, her influence on fellow artist colony participants (New Yorkers and Californians), her mentoring relationships, and her participation in alternative journals should be teased out. Cross-era comparisons to today's popular Appalachian writers such as Lee Smith, Adriana Trigiani, or Sharyn McCrumb could reveal surprising connections and differences. Perhaps a dialogue will begin about how Johnnie's ideal mill village might work, how loving the places in which we live leads to activism to save those places, how Johnnie driving down that mountain at break-neck speed might inspire all of our lives, and how everyone wins when women are allowed to achieve their dreams.

A few years after her move to California, on 4 January 1912, Cooke was thinking about her own dreams and happiness. She wrote in her journal:

> For oh, the work—the work—the work—the blessed
> work—the sacred work. . . . All other things go back on you

at times; but never work well done. Love passes by looking the other way, pleasure tricks you and turns out to be but sugar coated pain. For solace you may securely trust to the task well completed; even the feel of the tools in your hands will help some . . . the one pure joy, the draught that has no morning after to its blissful elation is that of creative work, whether one creates shoes or stories—pies or poetry.

Cooke may well have been looking out over the Pacific Ocean from her bungalow at Carmel-by-the-Sea as she thought about shoes, stories, pies, and poetry. She was sharing a house with her daughters and older sister, writing during the day, and having picnics of abalone and Spanish beans with the other artists and writers on Carmel's beaches.[23] *The Power and the Glory* had been published and was selling well. Although Johnnie and Cooke were quite different in many ways, Cooke, like her literary heroine, had achieved her own dreams from long ago in Chattanooga.

In 1918, *The Power and the Glory* was made into a feature-length film of the same title. The movie version, directed by the well-known Lawrence C. Windom, was filmed on location and included all of the major and minor characters in the novel. Grace MacGowan Cooke received writing credit on the film, which further diversified her writing career.[24] The 1910 story of Johnnie Consadine, indebted to the Progressivism of the nineteenth century and itself one of the resources exported from Appalachia, also belongs to the twentieth century. Like Johnnie in the automobile, the novel and film are thoroughly American; they are complicated, contradictory, spirited, and fun.

Elizabeth S. D. Engelhardt

Notes

Sincere thanks go to the staff of the Bancroft Library at the University of California, Berkeley, for their long-distance help with this project, and to Marjorie Pryse and Elizabeth Swayze for their insight and feedback, without which Johnnie and her car would still be confined to archives.

1. Carolyn Keene, Nancy Drew Mystery Stories, series (New York: Grosset and Dunlap, 1930–); F. Scott Fitzgerald, *The Great Gatsby* (1953; reprint, New York: Macmillan, 1988); Cooke, *The Power and the Glory*, this edition, 348–49.

2. For biographical information on Cooke, see Kay Baker Gaston, "The MacGowan Girls," *California History: The Magazine of the California Historical Society* 59, no. 2 (summer 1980): 116–25. Also, see Grace MacGowan Cooke Papers, journal 1909–1915, BANC MSS 71/248 c, Bancroft Library, University of California, Berkeley. Biographical information in the following paragraphs is gathered from these two sources except where otherwise noted.

3. "Col. John E. MacGowan Dead," *New York Times*, 13 April 1903.

4. Charlotte Perkins Gilman, *Herland and Selected Stories*, ed. Barbara H. Solomon (New York: Signet, 1992); Mary Johnston, *Hagar*, ed. Marjorie Spruill Wheeler (Charlottesville: University Press of Virginia, 1994).

5. Gaston, "MacGowan Girls," 119.

6. For biographical information on Summers and her memories of Cooke, see Matthew J. Bruccoli's afterword in Edith Summers Kelley, *Weeds* (1923; reprint, Carbondale: Southern Illinois University Press, 1972). Although he gets their names wrong, Richard Lingeman relates the story of the sisters and *Ecce Homo* in *Sinclair Lewis: Rebel from Main Street* (New York: Random House, 2002), 31.

7. The details of their escape and Sinclair's estimate of the sisters' losses are in "Fire Wipes Out Helicon Hall," *New York Times*, 17 March 1907, p. 1; the report of Cooke's injuries is in "To Investigate Helicon Fire," *New York Times*, 18 March 1907, p. 16; Grace and Alice

are proclaimed "out of danger" in "Sinclair Colony to Try Tent Life," *New York Times,* 19 March 1907, p. 16.

8. Sinclair Lewis, *The Man from Main Street: Selected Essays and Other Writings, 1904–1950,* ed. Harry E. Maule and Melville H. Cane (New York: Random House, 1953), 87. For the history of the Carmel colony, see Franklin Walker, *Sea Coast of Bohemia* (Santa Barbara: Peregrine Smith, 1973).

9. William Dean Howells speaks on Cooke's behalf in the volume *Southern Lights and Shadows,* ed. William Dean Howells and Henry Mills Alden (New York: Harper and Brothers, 1907). See Herbert S. Gorman, "Exotics, Not Classics, for Tired Business Men," *New York Times,* 1 August 1920, p. 43, for the ranking of Cooke with Holmes.

10. On her frustration with other presses and the switch to Doubleday, see Cooke journal, "April Mar close of month," 1910; on the print run, see 23 November 1910, Papers, Bancroft Library.

11. The book is reviewed in "Mrs. Cooke's Mountain Folk," *New York Times,* Book Review section, 3 September 1910, p. 3. The *New York Times* articles mentioning the book are "Among the Authors," Book Review section, 21 May 1910, p. 8; "Among the Authors," Book Review section, 27 August 1910, p. 5; "Mrs. Cooke's Lesson," Book Review section, 3 September 1910, p. 6; the review itself; "Mrs. Grace MacGowan Cooke dedicates 'To Helen' her new novel, 'The Power and the Glory,'" *New York Times,* Book Review section, 26 November 1910, p. 9. Cooke discusses her sense of "poise and power" in her journal, 23 November 1910, Papers, Bancroft Library.

12. "Mrs. Grace MacGowan Cooke dedicates," p. 9.

13. Doubleday, Page and Company advertisements in the *Times* on 3 July 1910, p. 12; 3 September 1910, p. 3; and 3 December 1910, p. 7. On regionalism, see, for instance, Judith Fetterley and Marjorie Pryse, eds., *American Women Regionalists, 1850–1910* (New York: W. W. Norton, 1992); Mary Austin, *The Land of Little Rain* (New York: Dover, 1996. On regionalists' challenges to "nation," see Fetterley, "'Not in the Least American': Nineteenth-Century Literary Regionalism as Un-

American Literature," in *Nineteenth-Century American Women Writers: A Critical Reader,* ed. Karen Kilcup (Oxford: Blackwell, 1998); Kate McCullough, *Regions of Identity: The Construction of America in Women's Fiction, 1885–1914* (Stanford: Stanford University Press, 1999).

14. Anzia Yezierska, *Hungry Hearts,* with an introduction by Blanche H. Gelfant (1920; reprint, New York: Penguin, 1997); Upton Sinclair, *The Jungle,* with an afterword by Robert B. Downs (New York: New American Library, 1988); Ida B. Wells-Barnett, "Lynch Law in America," in *Words of Fire: An Anthology of African-American Feminist Thought,* ed. Beverly Guy-Sheftall (New York: New Press, 1995). For a discussion of regionalists violating traditional "rules" of genre, see Pryse, "Writing Out of the Gap: Regionalism, Resistance, and Relational Reading," *Textual Studies in Canada* 9 (1997): 19–34; Stephanie Foote, *Regional Fictions: Culture and Identity in Nineteenth-Century American Literature* (Madison: University of Wisconsin Press, 2001).

15. "Mrs. Cooke's Mountain Folk," *New York Times,* Book Review section, 3 September 1910, p. 3.

16. Mary Noailles Murfree, *In the Tennessee Mountains,* with an introduction by Nathalia Wright (Knoxville: University of Tennessee Press, 1970); Rebecca Harding Davis, *Life in the Iron Mills and Other Stories,* ed. Tillie Olsen, 2d ed. (New York: Feminist Press at City University of New York, 1985); Emma Bell Miles, *The Spirit of the Mountains* (1905; reprint, with a foreword by Roger D. Abrahams and introduction by David E. Whisnant, Knoxville: University of Tennessee Press, 1975).

17. "Mrs. Cooke's Mountain Folk," p. 3.

18. On the Progressive movement, see Carroll Smith-Rosenberg, *Disorderly Conduct: Visions of Gender in Victorian America* (New York: Alfred A. Knopf, 1985); Dorothy Schneider and Carl J. Schneider, *American Women in the Progressive Era, 1900–1920* (New York: Facts on File, 1993); Marie Van Vorst, *Amanda of the Mill* (New York: Dodd, Mead and Company, 1905).

19. See, in particular, Yezierska, "The Free Vacation House," in *Hungry Hearts,* 62–71.

20. See, among others, Albert E. Cowdrey, *This Land, This South: An Environmental History* (Lexington: University Press of Kentucky, 1983), 103–24; Ronald L. Lewis, *Transforming the Appalachian Countryside: Railroads, Deforestation, and Social Change in West Virginia, 1880–1920* (Chapel Hill: University of North Carolina Press, 1998); and Benita J. Howell, ed., *Culture, Environment, and Conservation in the Appalachian South* (Urbana: University of Illinois Press, 2002).

21. Note that at this point in the automobile's history, few could imagine the environmental destruction automobiles would eventually cause—in fact, cars seemed like a cleaner environmental option over horses or trains. Floyd Clymer, *Those Wonderful Old Automobiles* (New York: Bonanza Books, 1953), 19, 32; Robert Sloss, "What a Woman Can Do with an Auto," in *Motoring in America: The Early Years,* ed. Frank Oppel (Secaucus, N.J.: Castle, 1989), 263.

22 Cooke, *Power and the Glory,* 349–51.

23. Cooke journal, 4 January 1912, Papers, Bancroft Library. Sinclair Lewis remembers the sisters' generous abalone and Spanish beans picnics in his essay "I'm an Old Newspaper Man Myself," in *The Man from Main Street,* 88.

24. Descriptions of the film can be found in J. W. Williamson, *Southern Mountaineers in Silent Films: Plot Synopses of Movies About Moonshining, Feuding and Other Mountain Topics, 1904–1929* (Jefferson, N.C.: McFarland and Company, 1994); also see "Internet Movie Database," http://us.imdb.com/credits?0009508 (1 August 2002) and "All Movie Guide," http://allmovie.com/cg/avg.dll?p=avg&sql=A153406, (1 August 2002). I have been unable to determine if a copy of the film still exists. The search is ongoing.

CONTENTS

CONTENTS

The Power and the Glory

CHAPTER I

THE BIRTH OF A WOMAN-CHILD

"WHOSE cradle's that?" the sick woman's thin querulous tones arrested the man at the threshold.

"Onie Dillard's," he replied hollowly from the depths of the crib which he carried upside down upon his head, like some curious kind of overgrown helmet.

"Now, why in the name o' common sense would ye go and borry a broken cradle?" came the wail from the bed. "I 'lowed you'd git Billy Spinner's, an' hit's as good as new."

Uncle Pros set the small article of furniture down gently.

"Don't you worry yo'se'f, Laurelly," he said enthusiastically. Pros Passmore, uncle of the sick woman and mainstay of the forlorn little Consadine household, was always full of enthusiasm. "Just a few nails and a little wrappin' of twine'll make it all right," he informed his niece. "I stopped a-past and borried the nails and the hammer from Jeff Dawes; I mighty nigh pounded my thumb off knockin' in nails with a rock an' a sad-iron last week."

"Looks like nobody ain't got no sense," returned Laurella Consadine ungratefully. "Even you, Unc'

3

Pros — while you borryin' why cain't ye borry whole things that don't need mendin'?"

Out of the shadows that hoarded the further end of the room came a woman with a little bundle in her arm which had evidently created the necessity for the borrowed cradle.

"Laurelly," the nurse hesitated, "I wouldn't name it to ye whilst ye was a-sufferin,' but I jest cain't find the baby's clothes nowhars. I've done washed the little trick and wrapped her in my flannen petticoat. I do despise to put anything on 'em that anybody else has wore — hit don't seem right. But I've been plumb through everything, an' cain't find none of her coats. Whar did you put 'em?"

"I didn't have no luck borryin' for this one," complained the sick woman fretfully. "Looks like everybody's got that mean that they wouldn't lend me a rag — an' the Lord knows I only ast a *wearin'* of the clothes for my chillen. Folks can make shore that I return what I borry — ef the Lord lets me."

"Ain't they nothin' to put on the baby?" asked Mavity Bence, aghast.

"No. Hit's jest like I been tellin' ye. I went to Tarver's wife — she's got a plenty. I knowed in reason she'd have baby clothes that she couldn't expect to wear out on her own chillen. I said as much to her, when she told me she was liable to need 'em befo' I did. I says, 'Ye cain't need more'n half of 'em, I reckon, an' half'll do me, an' I'll return 'em to ye when I'm done with 'em.' She acted jest as selfish — said

she'd like to know how I was goin' to inshore her that
it wouldn't be twins agin same as 'twas before. Some
folks is powerful mean an' suspicious."

All this time the nurse had been standing with the
quiet small packet which was the storm centre of
preparation lying like a cocoon or a giant seed-pod
against her bosom.

"She's a mighty likely little gal," said she finally.
"Have ye any hopes o' gittin' anything to put on her?"

The woman in the bed — she was scarcely more
than a girl, with shining dark eyes and a profusion of
jetty ringlets about her elfish, pretty little face —
seemed to feel that this speech was in the nature of
a reproach. She hastened to detail her further activities on behalf of the newcomer.

"Consadine's a poor provider," she said plaintively,
alluding to her absent husband. "Maw said to me
when I would have him that he was a poor provider;
and then he's got into this here way of goin' off like.
Time things gets too bad here at home he's got a big
scheme up for makin' his fortune somewhars else, and
out he puts. He 'lowed he'd be home with a plenty
before the baby come. But thar — he's the best man
that ever was, when he's here, and I have no wish to
miscall him. I reckon he thought I could borry what
I'd need. Biney Meal lent me enough for the little un
that died; but of course some o' the coats was buried
with the child; and what was left, Sis' Elvira borried
for her baby. I was layin' off to go over to the Deep
Spring neighbourhood when I could git a lift in that

direction — the folks over yon is mighty accommoda-
tive," she concluded, "but I was took sooner than I
expected, and hyer we air without a stitch. I've done
sont Bud an' Honey to Mandy Ann Foncher's —
mebby they'll bring in somethin'."

The little cabin shrank back against the steep side
of the mountain as though half terrified at the hollow
immensity of the welkin above, or the almost sheer
drop to the valley five hundred feet beneath. A sidling
mountain trail passed the front of its rail fence, and
stones continually rolled from the upper to the lower
side of this highway.

The day was darkening rapidly. A low line of red
still burned behind the massive bulk of Big Unaka,
and the solemn purple mountains raised their peaks
against it in a jagged line. Within the single-roomed
cabin the rich, broken light from the cavernous fire-
place filled the smoke-browned interior full of shadow
and shine in which things leaped oddly into life, or
dropped out of knowledge with a startling effect.
The four corners of the log room were utilized, three
of them for beds, made by thrusting two poles through
auger holes bored in the logs of the walls, setting a leg
at the corner where these met and lacing the bottom
with hickory withes. The fourth had some rude
planks nailed in it for a table, and a knot-hole in one
of the logs served the primitive purpose of a salt-cellar.
A pack of gaunt hounds quarrelled under the floor,
and the sick woman stirred uneasily on her bed and
expressed a wish that her emissaries would return.

Uncle Pros had taken the cradle to a back door to get the last of the evening sun upon his task. One would not have thought that he could hear what the women were saying at this distance, but the old hunter's ears were sharp.

"Never you mind, Laurelly," he called cheerfully. "Wrop the baby up some fashion, and I'll hike out and get clothes for her, time I mend this cradle."

"Ef that ain't just like Unc' Pros!" And the girlish mother laughed out suddenly. You saw the gypsy beauty of her face. "He ain't content with borryin' men's truck, but thinks he can turn in an' borry coats 'mongst the women. Well, I reckon he might have better luck than what I did."

As she spoke a small boy and girl, her dead brother's children, came clattering in from the purple mysteries of dusk outside, hand clasped in hand, and stopped close to the bed, staring.

"Mandy Ann, she wouldn't lend us a thing," Bud began in an aggrieved tone. "I traded for this — chopped wood for it — and hit was all she would give me." He laid a coarse little garment upon the ragged coverlet.

"That!" cried Laurella Passmore, taking it up with angrily tremulous fingers. "My child shain't wear no sech. Hit ain't fittin' for my baby to put on. Oh, I wisht I could git up from here and do about; I'd git somethin' for her to wear!"

"Son," said Mrs. Bence, approaching the bedside, "air ye afeared to go over as far as my house right now?"

"I ain't skeered ef Honey'll go with me," returned the boy doubtfully, as he interrogated the twilit spaces beyond the open cabin door.

"Well, you go ask Pap to look in the green chist and send me the spotted caliker poke that he'll find under the big bun'le. Don't you let him give you that thar big bun'le; 'caze that's not a thing but seed corn, and he'll be mad ef it's tetched. Tell Pap that what's in the spotted poke ain't nothin' that he wants. Tell him it's — well, tell him to look at it before he gives it to you."

The two little souls scuttled away into the gathering dark, and the neighbour woman sat down by the fire to nurse the baby and croon and await the clothing for which she had sent.

She was not an old woman, but already stiff and misshapen by toil and the lack of that saving salt of pride, the stimulation of joy, which keeps us erect and supple. Her broad back was bent; her hands as they shifted the infant tenderly were knotted and work-worn. Mavity Bence was a widow, living at home with her father, Gideon Himes; she had one child left, a daughter; but the clothing for which she had sent was an outfit made for a son, the posthumous offspring of his father; and the babe had not lived long enough to wear it.

Outside, Uncle Pros began to sing at his work. He had a fluty old tenor voice, and he put in turns and quavers that no ear not of the mountains could possibly follow and fix. First it was a hymn, all abrupt, odd, minor cadences and monotonous refrain. Then he shifted to a ballad — and the mountains are full of old ballads of Scotland and England, come down from the time of the first settlers, and with local names quaintly substituted for the originals here and there.

> " She's gwine to walk in a silken gownd,
>   An' ha'e plenty o' siller for to spare,"

chanted the old man above the little bed he was repairing.

"Who's that you're a-namin' that's a-goin' to have silk dresses?" inquired Laurella, as he entered and set the mended cradle down by the bedside.

"The baby," he returned. "Ef I find my silver mine — or ruther *when* I find my silver mine, for you know in reason with the directions Pap's Grandpap left, and that word from Great Uncle Billy that helped the Injuns work it, I'm bound to run the thing down one o' these days — when I find my silver mine this here little gal's a-goin' to have everything she wants — ain't ye, Pretty?"

And, having made a bed in the cradle from some folded covers, he lifted the baby with strange deftness and placed it in.

"See thar," he called their attention proudly. "As good as new. And ef I git time I'm a-goin' to give it a few licks o' paint."

Hands on knees, he bent to study the face of the new-born, that countenance so ambiguous to our eyes, scarce stamped yet with the common seal of humanity.

"She's a mighty pretty little gal," he repeated Mavity Bence's words. "She's got the Passmore favour, as well as the Consadine. Reckon I better be steppin' over to Vander's and see can I borry their cow. If it's with you this time like it was with the last one, we'll have to have a cow. I always thought if we'd had a fresh cow for that other one, hit would 'a' lived. I know in reason Vander'll lend the cow for a spell" — Uncle Pros always had unbounded confidence in the good will of his neighbours toward himself, since his own generosity to them would have been fathomless — "I know in reason he'll lend hit, 'caze they ain't got no baby to their house."

He bestowed one more proud, fond look upon the little face in the borrowed cradle, and walked out with as elated a step as though a queen had been born to the tribe.

In the doorway he met Bud and Honey, returning with the spotted calico poke clutched fast between them.

"I won't ask nothin' but a wearin' of em for my child," Laurella Consadine, born Laurella Passmore, reiterated when the small garments were laid out on the bed, and the baby was being dressed. "They're mighty fine, Mavity, an' I'll take good keer of 'em and always bear in mind that they're only borried."

"No," returned Mavity Bence, with unwonted firmness, as she put the newcomer into the slip intended for her own son. "No, Laurelly, these clothes ain't loaned to you. I give 'em to this child. I'm a widder, and I never look to wed again, becaze Pap he has to have somebody to do for him, an' he'd just about tear up the ground if I was to name sech a thing. I'm mighty glad to give 'em to yo' little gal. I only wisht," she said wistfully, "that hit was a boy. Ef hit was a boy, mebbe you'd give hit the name that should 'a' went with the clothes. I was a-goin' to call the baby John after hit's pappy."

Laurella Consadine lay quiescent for a moment, big black eyes studying the smoky logs that raftered the roof. Then all at once she laughed, with a flash of white teeth.

"I don't see why Johnnie ain't a mighty fine name for a gal," she said. "I vow I'm a-goin' to name her Johnnie!"

And so this one of the tribe of borrowing Passmores wore her own clothing from the first. No borrowed garment touched her. She rejected the milk from the borrowed cow, fiercely; lustily she demanded — and eventually received — her own legitimate, unborrowed sustenance.

Perhaps such a beginning had its own influence upon her future.

CHAPTER II

THE BIRTH OF AN AMBITION

ALL day the girl had walked steadily, her bare feet comforted by the warm dust, shunning the pebbles, never finding sharp stones in the way, making friends with the path — that would always be Johnnie. From the little high-hung valley in the remote fastnesses of the Unakas where she was born, Johnnie Consadine was walking down to Cottonville, the factory town on the outskirts of Watauga, to find work. Sometimes the road wound a little upward for a quarter of a mile or so; but the general tendency was persistently down.

In the gray dawn of Sunday morning she had stepped from the door of that room where the three beds occupied three corners, and a rude table was rigged in the fourth. It might almost seem that the same hounds were quarrelling under the floor that had scrambled there eighteen years before when she was born. At first the way was entirely familiar to her. It passed few habitations, and of those the dwellers were not yet abroad, since it was scarce day. As time went on she got to the little settlement at the foot of the first mountain, and had to explain to everybody her destination and ambition. Beyond this, she stopped occasionally for direction, she met more people; yet she was still in the heart of the mountains when noon found her, and she crept up a wayside bank and sat down alone to eat her bite of corn pone.

Guided by the instinct — or the wood-craft — of the mountain born and bred, she had sought out one of the hermit springs of beautiful freestone water that hide in these solitudes. When she had slaked her thirst at its little ice-cold chalice, she raised her head with a low exclamation of rapture. There, growing and blowing beside the cool thread of water which trickled from the spring, was a stately pink moccasin flower. She knelt and gazed at it with folded hands, as one before a shrine.

What is it in the sweeping dignity of these pointed, oval, parallel-veined leaves, sheathed one within another, the clean column of the bloom stalk rising a foot and a half perhaps above, and at its tip the wonderful pink, dreaming Buddha of the forest, that so commands the heart? It was not entirely the beauty of the softly glowing orchid that charmed Johnnie Consadine's eyes; it was the significance of the flower. Somehow the finding this rare, shy thing decking her path toward labour and enterprise spoke to her soul of success. For a long time she knelt, her bright uncovered head dappled by a ray of sunlight which filtered through the deep, cool green above her, her face bent, her eyes brooding, as though she prayed. When she had finished her dinner of corn pone and fried pork, she rose and parted with almost reverent fingers the pink wonder from its stalk, sought out a coarse, clean handkerchief from her bundle and, steeping it in the icy water of the spring, lapped it around her treasure. Not often in her eighteen summers had she found so fine a specimen. Then she took up her journey, comforted and strangely elated.

"Looks like it was waiting right there to tell me howdy," she murmured to herself.

The keynote of Johnnie Consadine's character was aspiration. In her cabin home the wings of desire were clipped, because she must needs put her passionate young soul into the longing for food, to quiet the cravings of a healthy stomach, which generally clamoured from one blackberry season to the other; the longing for shoes, when her feet were frost-bitten; the yet more urgent wish to feed the little ones she loved; the pressing demand, when the water-bucket gave out and they had to pack water in a tin tomato can with a string bail; the dull ache of mortification when she became old enough to understand their position as the borrowing Passmores. Yet all human desire is sacred, and of God; to desire — to want — to aspire — thus shall the individual be saved; and surely in this is the salvation of the race. And Johnnie felt vaguely that at last she was going out into a world where she should learn what to desire and how to desire it.

Now as she tramped she was conning over her present plans. Again she saw the cabin at home in that pitchy black which precedes the first leavening of dawn, and herself getting up to start early on the long walk. Her mother would get up too, and that was foolish. She saw the slight figure stooping to rake together the embers in the broad chimney's throat that the coffee-pot might be set on. She remonstrated with the little mother, saying that she aimed not to disturb anybody — not even Uncle Pros.

"Uncle Pros!" Laurella echoed from the hearthstone, where she sat on her heels, like a little girl playing at mud-pies. Johnnie smiled at the memory of how her mother laughed over the suggestion, with a drawing of slant brows above big, tragic dark eyes, a look of suffering from the mirth which adds the crown to joyousness. "Your Uncle Pros he got a revelation 'long 'bout midnight as to just whar that thar silver mine is that's been dodgin' him for more'n forty year. He come a-shakin' me by the shoulder — like I reckon he's done fifty times ef he's done it once — and telling me that he's off to make all our fortunes inside of a week. He said if you still would go down to that thar old fool cotton mill and hire out, to name it to you that Shade Buckheath would stand some watchin'. Your Uncle Pros has got sense — in streaks. Why in the world you'll pike out and go to work in a cotton mill is more than I can cipher."

"To take care of you and the children," the girl had said, standing tall and straight, deep-bosomed and red-lipped, laughing back at her little mother. "Somebody's got to take care of you-all, and I just love to be the one."

Laurella Consadine, commonly called in mountain fashion by her maiden name of Laurella Passmore, scrambled to her feet and tossed the dark curls out of her eyes.

"Aw — law — huh!" she returned carelessly. "We'll get along; we always have. How do you reckon I made out before you was born, you great big some-body? What's the matter with you? Did you fail to borry a frock for the dance over at Rainy Gap? Try again, honey — I'll bet S'lomy Buckheath would lend you one o' her'n."

That was it; borrowing — borrowing — borrowing till they were known as the borrowing Passmores and became the jest of the neighbourhood.

"No, I couldn't stand it," the girl justified herself. "I had obliged to get out and go where money could be earned — me, that's big and stout and able."

And sighingly — yet light-heartedly, for with Laurella Consadine and Johnnie there was always the quaint suggestion of a little girl with a doll quite too big for her — the mother let her go. It had been just so when Johnnie would have her time for every term of the "old field hollerin' school," where she learned to read and write; even when she persisted in going to Rainy Gap where some charitably inclined northern church maintained a little school, and pushed her education to dizzy heights that to mountain vision appeared "plumb foolish."

That morning she had cautioned her mother to be careful lest they waken the children, for if the little ones roused and began, as the mountain phrase has it, "takin' on," she scarcely knew how she should find heart to leave them. The children — there was the thing that drove. Four small brothers and sisters there were; with little Deanie, the youngest, to make the painfully strong plea of recent babyhood. Consadine, who never could earn money, and used to be from home following one wild scheme or another most of the time, was gone these two years upon his last dubious, adventurous journey; there was not even his intermittent assistance to depend upon. Johnnie was the man of the family, and she shouldered her burden bravely, declaring to herself that she would yet have a chance, which the little ones could share.

She had kissed her mother, picked up her bundle and got as far as the door, when there came a spat of bare feet meeting the floor, a pattering rush, and Deanie's short arms went around her knees, almost tripping her up.

"I wasn't 'sleep — I was 'wake the whole time," whispered the baby, lifting a warm, pursed mouth for a kiss. "Deanie'll be good an' let you go, Sis' Johnnie. An' then when you get down thar whar it's all so sightly, you'll send for Deanie, 'cause deed and double you couldn't live without her, now could ye?" And she looked craftily up into the face bent above her, bravely choking back the tears that wanted to drown her long speech.

Johnnie dropped her bundle and caught up the

child, crushing the warm, soft, yielding little form against her breast in a very passion of tenderness.

"Deed and double I couldn't," she whispered back. "Sister's goin' to earn money, and Deanie shall have plenty of good things to eat next winter, and some shoes. She shan't be housed up every time it snows. Sis's goin' to ——"

She broke off abruptly and kissed the small face with vehemence.

"Good-bye," she managed to whisper, as she set the baby down and turned to her mother. The kindling touch of that farewell warmed her resolution yet. She was not going down to Cottonville to work in the mill merely; she was going into the Storehouse of Possibilities, to find and buy a chance in the world for these poor little souls who could never have it otherwise.

Before she kissed her mother, took up her bundle and trudged away in the chill, gray dawn, she declared an intention to come home and pay back every one to whom they were under obligations. Now her face dimpled as she remembered the shriek of dismay Laurella sent after her.

"Good land, Johnnie Consadine! If you start in to pay off all the borryin's of the Passmore family since you was born, you'll ruin us — that's what you'll do — you'll ruin us."

These things acted themselves over and over in Johnnie's mind as, throughout the fresh April afternoon, her long, free, rhythmic step, its morning vigour undiminished, swung the miles behind her; still present in thought when, away down in Render's Gap, she settled herself on a rock by the wayside where a little stream crossed the road, to wash her feet and put on the shoes which she had up to this time carried with her bundle.

"I reckon I must be near enough town to need 'em," she said regretfully, as she drew the big, shapeless, cowhide affairs on her slim, brown, carefully washed and dried feet, and with a leathern thong laced down a wide, stiff tongue. She had earned the money for these shoes picking blackberries at ten cents the gallon, and Uncle Pros had bought them at the store at Bledsoe according to his own ideas. "Get 'em big enough and there won't be any fussin' about the fit," the old man explained his theory: and indeed the fit of those shoes on Johnnie's feet was not a thing to fuss over — it was past considering.

The sun was westering; the Gap began to be in shadow, although the point at which she sat was well above the valley. The girl was all at once aware that she was tired and a little timid of what lay before her. She had written to Shade Buckheath, a neighbour's boy with whom she had gone to school, now employed as a mechanic or loom-fixer in one of the cotton mills, and from whom she had received a reply saying that she could get work in Cottonville if she would come down.

Mavity Bence, who had given Johnnie her first clothes, was a weaver in the Hardwick mill at Cottonville, Watauga's milling suburb; her father, Gideon

Himes, with whom Shade Buckheath learned his trade, was a skilled mechanic, and had worked as a loom-fixer for a while. At present he was keeping a boarding-house for the hands, and it was here Johnnie was to find lodging. Shade himself was reported to be doing extremely well. He had promised in his letter that if Johnnie came on a Sunday evening he would walk up the road a piece and meet her. She now began to hope that he would come. Then, waiting for him, she forgot him, and set herself to imagine what work in the cotton mill and life in town would be like.

To Shade Buckheath, strolling up the road, in the expansiveness of his holiday mood and the dignity of his Sunday suit, the first sight of Johnnie came with a little unwelcome shock. He had left her in the mountains a tall, thin, sandy-haired girl in the growing age. He got his first sight of her profile relieved against the green of the wayside bank, with a bunch of blooming azaleas starring its verdure behind her bright head. He was not artist enough to appreciate the picture at its value; he simply had the sudden resentful feeling of one who has asked for a hen and been offered a bird of paradise. She was tall and lithe and strong; her thick, fair hair, without being actually curly, seemed to be so vehemently alive that it rippled a bit in its length, as a swift-flowing brook does over a stone. It rose up around her brow in a roll that was almost the fashionable coiffure. Those among whom she had been bred, laconically called the colour red; but in fact it was only too deep a gold to be quite yellow. Johnnie's face, even in repose, was always potentially joyous. The clear, wide, gray eyes, under their arching brows, the mobile lips, held as it were the smile in solution; when one addressed her it broke swiftly into being, the pink lips lifting adorably above the white teeth, the long fringed eyes crinkling deliciously about the corners. Johnnie loved to laugh, and the heart of any reasonable being was instantly moved to give her cause.

For himself, the young man was a prevalent type among his people. Brown, well built, light on his feet, with heavy black hair growing low on his forehead, and long blackish-gray eyes, there was something Latin in the grace of his movements and in his glance. Life ran strong in Shade Buckheath. He stepped with an independent stride that was almost a swagger, and already felt himself a successful man; but that one of the tribe of borrowing Passmores should presume to such opulence of charm struck him as well-nigh impudent. The pure outlines of Johnnie's features, their aristocratic mould, the ruddy gold of her rich, clustering hair, those were things it seemed to him a good mill-hand might well have dispensed with. Then the girl turned, saw him, and flashed him a swift smile of greeting.

"It's mighty kind of you to come up and meet me," she said, getting to her feet a little awkwardly on account of the shoes, and picking up her bundle.

"I 'lowed you might get lost," bantered the young

fellow, not offering to carry the packet as they trudged away side by side. "How's everybody back on Unaka? Has your Uncle Pros found his silver mine yet?"

"No," returned Johnnie seriously, "but he's lookin' for it."

Shade threw back his head and laughed so long and loud that it would have been embarrassing to any one less sound and sweet-natured than this girl.

"I reckon he is," said Buckheath. "I reckon Pros Passmore will be lookin' for that silver mine when Gabriel blows. It runs in the family, don't it?"

Johnnie looked at him and shook her head.

"You've been learnin' town ways, haven't you?" she asked simply.

"You mean my makin' game of the Passmores?" he inquired coolly. "No, I never learned that in the settlement; I learned it in the mountains. I just forgot your name was Passmore, that's all," he added sarcastically. "Are you goin' to get mad about it?"

Johnnie had put on her slat sunbonnet and pulled it down so he could not see her face.

"No," she returned evenly, "I'm not goin' to get mad at anything. And my name's not Passmore, either. My name is Consadine, and I aim to be called that. Uncle Pros Passmore is my mother's uncle, and one of the best men that ever lived, I reckon. If all the folks he's nursed in sickness or laid out in death was numbered over it would be a-many a one; and I never heard him take any credit to himself for anything he did. Why, Shade, the last three years of your father's life Uncle Pros didn't dare hunt his silver mine much, because your father was paralysed and had to have close waitin' on, and — and there wasn't nobody but Uncle Pros, since all his boys was gone and ——"

"Oh, say it. Speak out," urged Shade hardily. "You mean that all us chaps had cut out and left the old man, and there wasn't a cent of money to pay anybody, and no one but Pros Passmore would 'a' been fool enough to do such hard work without pay. Well, I reckon you're about right. You and me come of a mighty poor nation of folks; but I'm goin' to make my pile and have my share, if lookin' out for number one 'll do it."

Johnnie turned and regarded him curiously. It was characteristic of the mountain girl, and of her people, that she had not on first meeting stared, village fashion, at his brave attire; and she seemed now concerned only with the man himself.

"I reckon you'll get it," she said meditatively. "I reckon you will. Sometimes I think we always get just what we deserve in this here world, and that the only safe way is to try to deserve something good. I hope I didn't say too much for Uncle Pros; but he's so easy and say-nothin' himself, that I just couldn't bear to hear you laughin' at him and not answer you."

"I declare, you're plenty funny!" Buckheath burst out boisterously. "No, I ain't mad at you. I kind o' like you for stickin' up for the old man. You and me 'll get along, I reckon."

As they moved forward, the man and the girl fell into more general chat, the feeling of irritation at Johnnie's beauty, her superior air, growing rather than diminishing in the young fellow's mind. How dare Pros Passmore's grandniece carry a bright head so high, and flash such glances of liquid fire at her questioner? Shade looked sidewise sometimes at his companion as he asked the news of their mutual friends, and she answered. Yet when he got, along with her mild responses, one of those glances, he was himself strangely subdued by it, and fain to prop his leaning prejudices by contrasting her scant print gown, her slat sunbonnet, and cowhide shoes with the apparel of the humblest in the village which they were approaching.

CHAPTER III

SO WALKING, and so desultorily talking, they came out on a noble white highway that wound for miles along the bluffy edge of the upland overlooking the valley upon the one side, fronted by handsome residences on the other.

It was Johnnie's first view of a big valley, a river, or a city. She had seen the shoestring creek bottoms between the endless mountains among which she was born and bred, the high-hung, cup-like depressions of their inner fastnesses; she was used to the cool, clear, boulder-checked mountain creeks that fight their way down those steeps like an armed man beating off assailants at every turn; she had been taken a number of times to Bledsoe, the tiny settlement at the foot of Unaka Old Bald, where there were two stores, a blacksmith shop, the post-office and the church.

Below her, now beginning to glow in the evening light, opened out one of the finest valleys of the southern Appalachees. Lapped in it, far off, shrouded with rosy mist which she did not identify as transmuted coal smoke, a city lay, fretted with spires, already sparkling with electric lights, set like a glittering boss of jewels in the broad curve of a shining river.

Directly down the steep at their feet was the cotton-mill town, a suburb clustered about a half-dozen great factories, whose long rows of lighted windows defined their black bulk. There was a stream here, too; a small, sluggish thing that flowed from tank to tank among the factories, spanned by numerous hand-rails, bridged in one place for the wagon-road to cross. Mills, valley, town, distant rimming mountains, river and creek, glowed and pulsed, dissolved and relimned themselves in the uprolling glory of sunset.

"Oh, wait for me a minute, Shade," pleaded the girl, pulling off her sunbonnet. . . . "I want to look. . . . Never in my life did I see anything so sightly!"

"Good land!" laughed the man, with a note of impatience in his voice. "You and me was raised on mountain scenery, as a body may say. I should think we'd both had enough of it to last us."

"But this — this is different," groped Johnnie, trying to explain the emotions that possessed her. "Look at that big settlement over yon. I reckon it's a city. It must be Watauga. It looks like the — the mansions of the blest, in the big Bible that preacher Drane has, down at Bledsoe."

"I reckon they're blest — they got plenty of money," returned Shade, with the cheap cynicism of his kind.

"So many houses!" the girl communed with herself. "There's bound to be a-many a person in all them houses," she went on. One could read the loving outreach to all humanity in her tones.

"There is," put in Shade caustically. "There's many a rogue. You want to look out for them tricky town folks — a girl like you."

Had he been more kind, he would have said, "a pretty girl like you." But Johnnie did not miss it; she was used to such as he gave, or less.

"Come on," he urged impatiently. "We won't get no supper if you don't hurry."

Supper! Johnnie drew in her breath and shook her head. With that scene unrolled there, as though all the kingdoms of earth were spread before them to look upon, she was asked to remember supper! Sighing, but submissively, she moved to follow her guide, a reluctant glance across her shoulder, when there came a cry something like that which the wild geese make when they come over in the spring; and a thing with two shining, fiery eyes, a thing that purred like a giant cat, rounded a curve in the road and came to a sudden jolting halt beside them.

Shade stopped immediately for that. Johnnie did not fail to recognize the vehicle. Illustrated magazines go everywhere in these days. In the automobile rode a man, bare-headed, dressed in a suit of white flannels, strange to Johnnie's eyes. Beside him sat a woman in a long, shimmering, silken cloak, a great, misty, silver-gray veil twined round head and hat and tied in a big bow under the chin. Johnnie had as yet seen nothing more pretentious than the starched and ruffled flummeries of a small mountain watering-place. This beautiful, peculiar looking garb had something of the picturesque, the poetic, about it, that appealed to her as the frocks worn at Chalybeate Springs or Bledsoe had never done. She had not wanted them. She wanted this. The automobile was stopped, the young fellow in it calling to Shade:

"I wonder if you could help me with this thing, Buckheath? It's on a strike again. Show me what you did to it last time."

Along the edge of the road at this point, for safety's sake, a low stone wall had been laid. Setting down her bundle, Johnnie leaned upon this, and shared her admiration between the valley below and these beautiful, interesting newcomers. Her bonnet was pushed far back; the wind ruffled the bright hair about her forehead; the wonder and glory and delight of it all made her deep eyes shine with a child's curiosity and avid wishfulness. Her lips were parted in unconscious smiles. White and red, tremulous, on tiptoe, the eager soul looking out of her face, she was very beautiful. The man in the automobile observed her kindly; the woman's features she could not quite see, though the veil was parted.

Neither Johnnie nor the driver of the car saw the quick, resentful glance her companion shot at the city man as Shade noted the latter's admiring look at the girl. Buckheath displayed an awesome familiarity with the machine and its workings, crawling under the body, and tapping it here and there with a wrench its driver supplied. They backed it and moved it a little, and seemed to be debating the short turn which would take them into the driveway leading up to a house on the slope above the road.

Johnnie continued to watch with fascinated eyes; Shade was on his feet now, reaching into the bowels of the machine to do mysterious things.

"It's a broken connection," he announced briefly.

"Is the wire too short to twist together?" inquired the man in the car. "Will you have to put in a new piece?"

"Uh-huh," assented Buckheath.

"There's a wire in that box there," directed the other.

Shade worked in silence for a moment.

"Now she'll go," I reckon," he announced, and once more the driver started up his car. It curved perilously near the bundle she had set down, with the handkerchief containing her cherished blossom lying atop; the mud-guard swept this latter off, and Buckheath set a foot upon it as he followed the machine in its progress.

"Take care — that was a flower," the man in the auto warned, too late.

Shade answered with a quick, backward-flung glance and a little derisive laugh, but no words. The young fellow stopped the machine, jumped down, and picked up the coarse little handkerchief which showed a bit of drooping green stem at one end and a glimpse of pink at the other.

"I'm sorry," he said, presenting it to Johnnie with exactly the air and tone he had used in speaking to the lady who was with him in the car. "If I had seen it in time, I might have saved it. I hope it's not much hurt."

Buckheath addressed himself savagely to his work at the machine. The woman in the auto glanced uneasily up at the house on the slope above them. Johnnie looked into the eyes bent so kindly upon her, and could have worshipped the ground on which their owner trod. Kindness always melted her heart utterly, but kindness with such beautiful courtesy added — this was the quality in flower.

"It doesn't make any differ," she said softly, turning to him a rapt, transfigured face. "It's just a bloom I brought from the mountains — they don't grow in the valley, and I found this one on my way down."

The man wondered a little if it were only the glow of the sunset that lit her face with such shining beauty; he noted how the fires of it flowed over her bright, blown hair and kindled its colour, how it lingered in the clear eyes, and flamed upon the white neck and throat till they had almost the translucence of pearl.

"I think this thing 'll work now — for a spell, anyhow," Shade Buckheath's voice sounded sharply from the road behind them.

"Are you afraid to attempt it, Miss Sessions?" the young man called to his companion. "If you are, we'll walk up, I'll telephone at the house for a trap and we'll drive back — Buckheath will take the machine in for us."

The voice was even and low-toned, yet every word came to Johnnie distinctly. She watched with a sort of rapture the movements of this party. The man's hair was dark and crisp, and worn a little long about the temples and ears; he had pleasant dark eyes and an air of being slightly amused, even when he did not smile. The lady apparently said that she was not afraid, for her companion got in, the machine negotiated the turn safely and began to move slowly up the steep ascent. As it did so, the driver gave another glance toward where the mountain girl stood, a swift, kind glance, and a smile that stayed with her after the shining car had disappeared in the direction of the wide-porched building where people were laughing and calling to each other and moving about — people dressed in beautiful garments which Johnnie would fain have inspected more closely.

Buckheath stood gazing at her sarcastically.

"Come on," he ordered, as she held back, lingering. "They ain't no good in you hangin' 'round here. That was Mr. Gray Stoddard, and the lady he's beauin' is Miss Lydia Sessions, Mr. Hardwick's sister-in-law. He's for such as her — not for you. He's the boss of the bosses down at Cottonville. No use of you lookin' at him."

Johnnie scarcely heard the words. Her eyes were on the wide porch of the house above them.

"What is that place?" she inquired in an awestruck whisper, as she fell into step submissively, plodding with bent head at his shoulder.

"The Country Club," Shade flung back at her. "Did you 'low it was heaven?"

Heaven! Johnnie brooded on that for a long time. She turned her head stealthily for a last glimpse of the portico where a laughing girl tossed a ball to a young fellow on the terrace below. After all, heaven was not so far amiss. She had rather associated it with the abode of the blest. The people in it were happy; they moved in beautiful raiment all day long; they spoke to each other kindly. It was love's home, she was sure of that. Then her mind went back to the dress of the girl in the auto.

"I'm a-going to have me a frock like that before I die," she said, half unconsciously, yet with a sudden passion of resolution. "Yes, if I live I'm a-goin' to have me just such a frock."

Shade wheeled in his tracks with a swift narrowing of the slate-gray eyes. He had been more stirred than he was willing to acknowledge by the girl's beauty, and by a nameless power that went out from the seemingly helpless creature and laid hold of those with whom she came in contact. It was the open admiration of young Stoddard which had roused the sullen resentment he was now spending on her.

"Ye air, air ye?" he demanded sharply. "You're a-goin' to have a frock like that? And what man's a-goin' to pay for it, I'd like to know?"

Such talk belonged to the valley and the settlement. In the mountains a woman works, of course, and earns her board and keep. She is a valuable industrial possession or chattel to the man, who may profit by her labour; never a luxury — a bill of expense. As she walked, Johnnie nodded toward the factory in the valley, beginning to blaze with light — her bridge of toil, that was to carry her from the island of Nowhere to the great mainland of Life, where everything might be had for the working, the striving.

"I didn't name no man," she said mildly. "I don't reckon anybody's goin' to give me things. Ain't there the factory where a body may work and earn money for all they need?"

"Well, I reckon they might, if they was good and careful to need powerful little," allowed Shade.

At the moment they came to the opening of a small path which plunged abruptly down the steep side of the ridge, curving in and out with — and sometimes across — a carriage road. As they took the first steps on this the sun forsook the valley at last, and lingered only on the mountain top where was that Palace of Pleasure into which He and She had vanished, before which the strange chariot waited. And all at once the little brook that wound, a golden thread, between the bulk of the mills, flowed, a stream of ink, from pool to pool of black water. The way down turned and turned; and each time that Shade and Johnnie got another sight of the buildings of the little village below, they had changed in character with the changing point of view. They loomed taller, they looked darker in spite of the pulsing light from their many windows.

And now there burst out a roar of whistles, like the bellowing of great monsters. Somehow it struck cold upon the girl's heart. They were coming down from that wonderful highland where she had seemed to see all the kingdoms of earth spread before her, hers for the conquering; they were descending into the shadow.

As they came quite to the foot they saw groups of women and children, with here and there a decrepit man, leaving the cottages and making their way toward the lighted mills. From the doors of little shanties tired-faced women with boys and girls walking near them, and, in one or two cases, very small ones clinging to their skirts and hands, reinforced the crowd which set in a steady stream toward the bridges and the open gates in the high board fences.

"What are they a-goin' to the factory for on Sunday evening?" Johnnie inquired.

"Night turn," replied Buckheath briefly. "Sunday's over at sundown."

"Oh, yes," agreed Johnnie dutifully, but rather disheartened. "Trade must be mighty good if they have to work all night."

"Them that works don't get any more for it," retorted Shade harshly.

"What's the little ones goin' to the mill for?" Johnnie questioned, staring up at him with apprehensive eyes.

"Why, to play, I reckon," returned the young fellow ironically. "Folks mostly does go to the mill to play, don't they?"

The girl ran forward and clasped his arm with eager fingers that shook.

"Shade!" she cried; "they can't work those little babies. That one over there ain't to exceed four year old, and I know it."

The man looked indifferently to where a tiny boy trotted at his mother's heels, solemn, old-faced, unchild-ish. He laughed a little.

"That thar chap is the oldest feller in the mills," he said. "That's Benny Tarbox. He's too short to tend a frame, but his maw lets him help her at the loom — every weaver has obliged to have helpers wait on 'em. You'll get used to it."

Get used to it! She pulled the sunbonnet about her face. The gold was all gone from the earth, and from her mood as well. She raised her eyes to where the last brightness lingered on the mountain-top. Up there they were happy. And even as her feet carried her forward to Pap Himes's boarding-house, her soul went clamouring, questing back toward the heights, and the sunlight, the love and laughter, she had left behind.

"The power and the glory — the power and the glory," she whispered over and over to herself. "Is it all back there?" Again she looked wistfully toward the heights. "But maybe a body with two feet can climb."

CHAPTER IV

THE suburb of Cottonville bordered a creek, a starveling, wet-weather stream which offered the sole suggestion of sewerage. The village was cut in two by this natural division. It clung to the shelving sides of the shallow ravine; it was scattered like bits of refuse on the numerous railroad embankments, where building was unhandy and streets almost impossible, to be convenient to the mills. Six big factories in all, some on one side of the state line and some on the other, daily breathed in their live current of operatives and exhaled them again to fill the litter of flimsy shanties.

The road which wound down from the heights ran through the middle of the village and formed its main street. Across the ravine from it, reached by a wooden bridge, stood a pretentious frame edifice, a boarding-house built by the Gloriana mill for the use of its office force and mechanics. Men were lounging on the wide porches of this structure in Sabbath-afternoon leisure, smoking and singing. The young Southern male of any class is usually melodious. Across the hollow came the sounds of a guitar and a harmonica.

"Listen a minute, Shade. Ain't that pretty? I

know that tune," said Johnnie, and she began to hum softly under her breath, her girlish heart responding to the call.

"Hush," admonished Buckheath harshly. "You don't want to be runnin' after them fellers. It's some of the loom-fixers."

In silence he led the way past the great mill buildings of red brick, square and unlovely but many-windowed and glowing, alight, throbbing with the hum of pent industry. Johnnie gazed steadily up at those windows; the glow within was other than that which gilded turret and pinnacle and fairy isle in the Western sky, yet perchance this light might be a lamp to the feet of one who wished to climb that way. Her adventurous spirit rose to the challenge, and she said softly, more to herself than to the man:

"I'm a-goin' to be a boss hand in there. I'm goin' to get the highest wages of any girl in the mill, time I learn my trade, because I'm goin' to try harder 'n anybody."

Shade looked around at her, curiously. Her beauty, her air of superiority, still repelled him — such fancy articles were not apt to be of much use — but this sounded like a woman who might be valuable to her master.

Johnnie returned his gaze with the frank good will of a child, and suddenly he forgot everything but the adorable lift of her pink lip over the shining white teeth.

The young fellow now halted at the step of a big frame

house. The outside was of an extent to seem fairly
pretentious; yet so mean was the construction, so sparing of window and finish, that the building showed itself
instantly for what it was — the cheap boarding-house
of a mill town. A group of tired-looking girls sitting
on the step in blessed Sunday idleness and cheap
Sunday finery stared as he and Johnnie ascended and
crossed the porch. One of these, a tall lank woman
of perhaps thirty years, got up and followed a few hesitating paces, apparently more as a matter of curiosity
than with any hospitable intent.

A man with a round red face and a bald pate whose
curly fringe of grizzled, reddish hair made him look like
a clown in a pantomime, motioned them with a surly
thumb toward the back of the house, where clattering
preparations for supper were audible and odoriferous.
The old fellow sat in a splint-bottomed chair of extra
size and with arms. This he had kicked back against
the wall of the house, so that his short legs did not
reach the floor, the big carpet-slippered feet finding
rest on the rung of the chair. His attitude was one
of relaxation. The face, broad, flat, small of eye
and wide of mouth, did indeed suggest the clown countenance; yet there was in it, and in the whole personality,
something of the Eastern idol, the journeyman attempt
of crude humanity to represent power. And the potential
cruelty of the type slept in his placid countenance as
surely as ever in the dreaming face of Shiva, the destroyer.

"Mrs. Bence — Aunt Mavity," called Shade, advancing into the narrow hall. In answer a tired-faced

woman came from the kitchen, wiping her hands on her checked apron.

"Good Lord, if it ain't Johnnie! I was 'feared she wouldn't git here to-night," she ejaculated when she saw the girl. "Take her out on the porch, Shade; I ain't got a minute now. Pap's poorly again, and I'm obliged to put the late supper on the table for them thar gals — the night shift's done eat and gone. I'll show her whar she's to sleep at, after while. I don't just rightly know whar Pap aimed to have her stay," she concluded hastily, as something boiled over on the stove. Johnnie set her bundle down in the corner of the kitchen.

"I'll help," she said simply, as she drew the excited coffee-pot to a corner of the range and dosed it judiciously with cold water.

"Well, now, that's mighty good of you," panted worried Mavity Bence. "How queer things comes 'round," she ruminated as they dished up the biscuits and fried pork. "I helped you into the very world, Johnnie. I lived neighbour to your maw, and they wasn't nobody else to be with her when you was born, and I went over. I never suspicioned that you would be helpin' me git supper down here in the settlement inside o' twenty year."

Johnnie ran and fetched and carried, as though she had never done anything else in her life, intent on the one task. She was alive in every fibre of her young body; she saw, she heard, as these words cannot always be truthfully applied to people.

"Did Shade tell you anything about Louvania?"
inquired the woman at length.

"No," replied Johnnie softly, "but I seen it in the paper."

Louvania Bence, the only remaining child of the widow, had, two weeks before, left her work at the mill, taken the trolley in to Watauga, walked out upon the county bridge across the Tennessee and jumped off. Johnnie had read the published account, passed from hand to hand in the mountains where Pap Himes and Mavity Bence had troops of kin and where Louvania was born. The statement ran that there was no love affair, and that the girl's distaste for her work at the cotton mill must have been the reason for the suicide.

"That there talk in the newspaper wasn't right," Louvania's mother choked. "They wasn't a word of truth in it. You know in reason that if Louvany hated to work in the mill as bad as all that she'd have named it to me — her own mother — and she never did. She never spoke a word like it, only to say now and ag'in, as we all do, that it was hard, and that she'd — well, she did 'low she'd ruther be dead, as gals will; but she couldn't have meant it. Do you think she could have meant it, Johnnie?"

The faded eyes, clouded now by tears, stared up into Johnnie's clear young orbs.

"Of course she couldn't have meant it," Johnnie comforted her. "Why, I'm sure it's fine to work in the mill. If she didn't feel so, she'd have told you the first thing. She must have been out of her mind. People always are when they — do that."

"That's what I keep a-thinkin'," the poor mother said, clinging pathetically to that which gave her consolation and cheer. "I say to myself that it must have been some brain disease took her all of a sudden and made her crazy that-a-way; because God knows she had nothing to fret her nor drive her to such."

By this time the meal was on the table, and the girls trooped in from the porch. The old man with the bald pate was seating himself at the head of the board, and Johnnie asked the privilege of helping wait on table.

"No, you ain't a-goin' to," Mrs. Bence said hospitably, pushing her into a seat. "If you start in to work in the morning, like I reckon you will, you ain't got no other time to get acquainted with the gals but right now. You set down. We don't take much waitin' on. We all pass things, and reach for what we want."

In the smoky illumination of the two ill-cleaned lamps which stood one at each end of the table, Johnnie's fair face shone out like a star. The tall woman who had shown a faint interest in them on the porch was seated just opposite. Her bulging light-blue eyes scarcely left the newcomer's countenance as she absent-mindedly filled her mouth. She was a scant, stringy-looking creature, despite her height; the narrow back was hooped like that of an old woman and the shoulders indrawn, so that the chest was cramped, and sent forth a wheezy, flatted voice that

sorted ill with her inches; her round eyes had no
speculation in them; her short chin was obstinate without power; the thin, half-gray hair that wanted to
curl feebly about her lined forehead was stripped
away and twisted in a knot no bigger than a walnut,
at the back of a bent head.

For some time the old man at the end of the table
stowed himself methodically with victuals; his air was
that of a man packing a box; then he brought his
implements to half-rest, as it were, and gave a divided
attention to the new boarder.

"What did I hear them call yo' name?" he inquired
gruffly.

Johnnie repeated her title and gave him one of
those smiles that went with most of her speeches.
It seemed to suggest things to the old sinner.

"Huh," he grunted; "I riccollect ye now. Yo'
pap was a Consadine, but you're old Virgil Passmore's
grandchild. One of the borryin' Passmores," he
added, staring coolly at Johnnie. "Virge was a fine,
upstandin' old man. You've got the favour of him
— if you wasn't a gal."

He evidently shared Schopenhauer's distaste for
"the low-statured, wide-hipped, narrow-shouldered
sex."

The girls about the table were all listening eagerly.
Johnnie had the sensation of a freshman who has
walked out on the campus too well dressed.

"Virge was a great beau in his day," continued Pap,
reminiscently. "He liked to wear good clothes, too.

I mind how he borried Abner Wimberly's weddin'
coat and wore it something like ten year — showed it off
fine — it fitted him enough sight better than it ever
fitted little old Ab. Then he comes back to Wimberly
at the end of so long a time with the buttons. He says,
says he, 'Looks like that thar cloth yo' coat was made
of wasn't much 'count, Ab,' says he. 'I think Jeeters
cheated ye on it. But the buttons was good. The
buttons wore well. And them I'm bringin' back,
'caze you may have use for 'em, and I have none,
now the coat's gone. Also, what I borry I return, as
everybody knows.' That was your granddaddy."

There was a tremendous giggling about the board
as the old man made an end. Johnnie herself smiled,
though her face was scarlet. She had no words to tell
her tormentor that the borrowing trait in her tribe
which had earned them the name of the borrowing
Passmores proceeded not from avarice, which ate
into Pap Himes's very marrow, but from its reverse
trait of generosity. She knew vaguely that they would
have shared with a neighbour their last bite or dollar,
and had thus never any doubt of being shared with
nor any shame in the asking.

"Yes," pursued Himes, surveying Johnnie chucklingly, "I mind when you was born. Has your Uncle
Pros found his silver mine yet?"

"My mother has often told me how good you and
Mrs. Bence was to us when I was little," answered
Johnnie mildly. "No, sir, Uncle Pros hasn't found
his silver mine yet — but he's still a-hunting for it."

The reply appeared to delight Himes. He laughed immoderately, even as Buckheath had done.

"I'll bet he is," he agreed. "Pros Passmore's goin' to hunt that there silver mine till he finds another hole in the ground about six feet long and six feet deep — that's what he's a-goin' to do."

The hasty supper was well under way now. Mrs. Bence brought the last of the hot bread, and shuffled into a seat. The old man at the head of the board returned to his feeding, but with somewhat moderated voracity. At length, pretty fully gorged, he raised his head from over his plate and looked about him for diversion. Again his attention was directed to the new girl.

"Air ye wedded?" he challenged suddenly.

She shook her head and laughed.

"Got your paigs sot for to git any one?" he followed up his investigations.

Johnnie laughed more than ever, and blushed again.

"How old air ye?" demanded her inquisitor. "Eighteen? 'Most nineteen? Good Lord! You're a old maid right now. Well, don't you let twenty go by without gittin' your hooks on a man. My experience is that when a gal gits to be twenty an' ain't wedded — or got her paigs sot for to wed — she's left. Left," he concluded impressively.

That quick smile of Johnnie's responded.

"I reckon I'll do my best," she agreed reasonably; "but some folks can do that and miss it."

Himes nodded till he set the little red curls all bobbing around the bare spot.

"Uh-huh," he approved, "I reckon that's so. Women is plenty, and men hard to git. Here's Mandy Meacham, been puttin' in her best licks for thirty year or more, an' won't never make it."

Johnnie did not need to be told which one was Mandy. The sallow cheek of the tall woman across from her reddened; the short chin wabbled a bit more than the mastication of the biscuit in hand demanded; a moisture appeared in the inexpressive blue eyes; but she managed a shaky laugh to assist the chorus which always followed Pap Himes's little jokes.

The old man held a sort of state among these poor girls, and took tribute of admiration, as he had taken tribute of life and happiness from daughter and granddaughter. Gideon Himes was not actively a bad man; he was as without personal malice as malaria. When it makes miserable those about it, or robs a girl of her pink cheeks, her bright eyes, her joy of life, wearing the elasticity out of her step and making an old woman of her before her time, we do not fly into a rage at it — we avoid it. The Pap Himeses of this world are to be avoided if possible.

Mandy stared at her plate in mortified silence. Johnnie wished she could think of something pleasant to say to the poor thing, when her attention was diverted by the old man once more addressing herself.

"You look stout and hearty; if you learn to weave as fast as you ort, and git so you can tend five or six looms, I'll bet you git a husband," he remarked in a burst of generosity. "I'll bet you do; and what's more, I'll speak a good word for ye. A gal that's a peart weaver's mighty apt to find a man. You learn your looms if you want to git wedded — and I know in reason you do — it's about all gals of your age thinks of."

When supper was over Johnnie was a little surprised to see the tall woman approach Pap Himes like a small child begging a favour of a harsh taskmaster.

"Can't that there new girl bunk with me?" she inquired earnestly.

"I had the intention to give her Louvany's bed," Pap returned promptly. "As long as nobody's with you, I reckon I don't care; but if one comes in, you take 'em, and she goes with Mavity, mind. I cain't waste room, poor as I am."

Piloted by the tall girl, Johnnie climbed the narrow stair to a long bare room where a row of double beds accommodated eight girls. The couch she was to occupy had been slept in during the day by a mill hand who was on night turn, and it had not been remade. Deftly Johnnie straightened and spread it, while her partner grumbled.

"What's the use o' doin' that?" Mandy inquired, stretching herself and yawning portentously. "We'll jist muss it all up in about two minutes. When you've worked in a mill as long as I have you'll git over the notion of makin' your bed, for hit's *but* a notion."

Johnnie laughed across her shoulder.

"I'd just as soon do it," she reassured her companion. "I do love smooth bedclothes; looks like I dream better on 'em and under 'em."

Mandy sat down on the edge of the bed, interfering considerably with the final touches Johnnie was putting to it.

"You're a right good gal," she opined patronizingly, "but foolish. The new ones always is foolish. I can put you up to a-many a thing that'll help you along, though, and I'm willin' to do it."

Again Johnnie smiled at her, that smile of enveloping sweetness and tenderness. It made something down in the left side of poor Mandy's slovenly dress-bodice vibrate and tingle.

"I'll thank you mightily," said Johnnie Consadine, "mightily." And knew not how true a word she spoke.

"You see," counselled Mandy from the bed into which she had rolled with most of her clothes on, "you want to get in with Miss Lydia Sessions and the Uplift ladies, and them thar swell folks."

Johnnie nodded, busily at work making a more elaborated night toilet than the others, who were going to bed all about them, paying little attention to their conversation.

"Miss Lyddy she ain't as young as she once was, and the boys has quit hangin' 'round her as much as they used to; so now she has took up with good works," the girl on the bed explained with a directness which Miss Sessions would not perhaps have appreciated. "Her and some other of the nobby folks has started what they call a Uplift club amongst the mill girls. Thar's a big room whar you dance — if you can — and whar they give little suppers for us with not much to eat; and thar's a place where they sorter preach to ye — lecture she calls it. I don't know what-all Miss Lyddy hain't got for her club. But you jist go, and listen, and say how much obliged you are, an she'll do a lot for you, besides payin' your wages to get you out of the mill any day she wants you for the Upliftin' business."

Mandy had a gasp, which occurred between sentences and at the end of certain words, with grotesque effect. Johnnie was to find that this gasp was always very much to the fore when Mandy was being uplifted. It then served variously as the gasp of humility, gratitude, admiration; the gasp of chaste emotion, the gasp of reprobation toward others who did not come forward to be uplifted.

"Did you say there was books at that club ?" inquired Johnnie out of the darkness — she had now extinguished the light. "Can a body learn things from the lectures ?"

"Uh-huh," agreed Mandy sleepily; "but you don't have to read 'em — the books. They lend 'em to you, and you take 'em home, and after so long a time you take 'em back sayin' how much good they done you. That's the way. If Mr. Stoddard's 'round, he'll ask you questions about 'em; but Miss Lyddy won't — she hates to find out that any of her plans ain't workin'."

For a long time there was silence. Mandy was just

dropping off into her first heavy sleep, when a whispering voice asked,

"Is Mr. Stoddard — has he got right brown eyes and right brown hair, and does he ride in one of these — one of these ——"

"Good land!" grumbled the addressed, "I thought it was mornin' and I had to git up! You ort to been asleep long ago. Yes, Mr. Stoddard's got sorter brown eyes and hair, and he rides in a otty-mobile. How did you know?"

But Mandy was too tired to stay awake to marvel over that. Her rhythmic snores soon proved that she slept, while Johnnie lay thinking of the various proffers she had that evening received of a lamp to her feet, a light on her path. And she would climb — yes, she would climb. Not by the road Pap Himes pointed out; not by the devious path Mandy Meacham suggested; but by the rugged road of good, honest toil, to heights where was the power and the glory, she would certainly strive.

She conned over the new things which this day had brought. Again she saw the auto swing around the curve and halt; she got the outline of the man's bent head against the evening sky. They were singing again over at the mechanics' boarding-house; the sound came across to her window; the vibrant wires, the chorus of deep male voices, even the words she knew they were using but could not distinguish, linked themselves in some fashion with memory of a man's eyes, his smile, his air of tender deference as he cherished her broken flower. Something caught in her throat and choked. Her mind veered to the figures on the porch of that Palace of Pleasure; the girl with the ball tossing it to the young fellow below on the lawn. In memory she descended the hill, coming down into the shadows with each step, looking back to the heights and the light. Well, she had said that if one had feet one might climb, and to-night the old man had tried to train her to his pace for attaining heart's desire. In the midst of a jumble of autos and shining mill windows, she watched the room grow ghostly with the light of a late-risen moon. Suddenly afar off she heard the "honk! honk! honk!" which had preceded the advent of the car on the ridge road.

Getting up, she stole to the one window which the long room afforded. It gave upon the main street of the village. "Honk! honk! honk!" She gazed toward the steep from which the sounds seemed to come. There, flashing in and out of the greenery, appeared half a dozen pairs of fiery eyes. A party of motorists were going in to Watauga, starting from the Country Club on the Ridge crest. Johnnie watched them, fascinated. As the foremost car swept down the road and directly beneath her window, its driver, whom she recognized with a little shiver, by the characteristic carriage of his head, swerved the machine out and stopped it at the curb below. The others passed, calling gay inquiries to him.

"We're all right," she heard a well-remembered voice reply. "You go ahead — we'll be there before you."

The slim, gray-clad figure in the seat beside him laughed softly and fluttered a white handkerchief as the last car went on.

"Now!" exulted the voice. "I'll put on my goggles and cap and we'll show them what running is.

> ' It's they'll take the high road and we'll take the low,
> And we'll be in Watauga befo-o-ore them!' "

Even as he spoke he adjusted his costume, and Johnnie saw the car shoot forward like a living creature eager on the trail. She sighed as she looked after them.

Feet — of what use were feet to follow such a flight as that?

CHAPTER V

JOHNNIE was used to hardship and early rising, but in an intermittent fashion; for the Passmores and Consadines were a haggard lot that came to no lure but their own pleasure. They might — and often did — go hungry, ill-clad, ill-housed; they might sometimes — in order to keep soul and body together — have to labour desperately at rude tasks unsuited to them; but these times were exceptions, and between such seasons, down to the least of the tribe, they had always followed the Vision, pursuing the flying skirts of whatever ideal was in their shapely heads. The little cabin in the gash of the hills owned for domain a rocky ravine that was the standing jest of the mountain-side.

"Sure, hit's good land — fine land," the mountaineers would comment with their inveterate, dry, lazy humour. "Nothing on earth to hender a man from raisin' a crap off 'n it — ef he could once git the leathers on a good stout, willin' pa'r o' hawks or buzzards, an' a plough hitched to 'em." And Johnnie could remember the other children teasing her and saying that her folks had to load a gun with seed corn and shoot it into the sky to reach their fields. Yet, the unmended roof covered much joy and good feeling. They were light feet that trod the unscoured puncheons. The Passmores were tender of each other's eccentricities, admiring of each other's virtues. A wolf race nourished on the knees of purple kings, how should they ever come down to wearing any man's collar, to slink at heel and retrieve for him?

One would have said that to the daughter of such the close cotton-mill room with its inhuman clamour, its fetid air, its long hours of enforced, monotonous, mechanical toil, would be prison with the torture added. But Johnnie looked forward to her present enterprise as a soldier going into a new country to conquer it. She was buoyantly certain, and determinedly delighted with everything. When, the next morning after her arrival, Mandy Meacham shook her by the shoulder and bade her get up, the room was humming with the roar of mill whistles, and the gray dawn leaking in at its one window in a churlish, chary fashion, reminded her that they were under the shadow of a mountain instead of living upon its top.

"I don't see what in the world could 'a' made me sleep so!" Johnnie deprecated, as she made haste to dress herself. "Looks like I never had nothing to do yesterday, except walking down. I've been on foot that much many a time and never noticed it."

The other girls in the room, poor souls, were all cross and sleepy. Nobody had time to converse with Johnnie. As they went down the stairs another contingent began to straggle up, having eaten a hasty meal after their night's work, and making now for certain of the just-vacated beds.

Johnnie ran into the kitchen to help Mrs. Bence get breakfast on the table, for Pap Himes was bad off this morning with a misery somewhere, and his daughter was sending word to the cotton mill to put a substitute on her looms till dinner time. Almost as much to her own surprise as to that of everybody else, Mandy Meacham proposed to stay and take Johnnie in to register for a job.

When the others were all seated at table, the new girl from the mountains took her cup of coffee and a biscuit and dropped upon the doorstep to eat her breakfast. The back yard was unenclosed, a litter of tin cans and ashes running with its desert disorder into a similar one on either side. But there were no houses back of the Himes place, the ground falling away sharply to the rocky creek bed. Across the ravine half a dozen strapping young fellows were lounging, waiting for breakfast; loom-fixers and mechanics these, whose hours were more favourable than those of the women and children workers.

"It's lots prettier out here than it is in the house," she returned smilingly, when Mavity Bence offered to get her a chair. "I do love to be out-of-doors."

"Huh," grunted Mandy with her mouth full of biscuit, "I reckon a cotton mill'll jest about kill you. What makes you work in one, anyhow? I wouldn't if I could help it."

Johnnie eyed the tall girl gravely. "I've got to earn some money," she said at length. "Ma and the children have to be taken care of. I don't know of any better way than the mill."

"An' I don't know of any worse," retorted Mandy sourly, as they went out together.

Johnnie began to feel timid. There had been a secret hope that she would meet Shade on the way to the mill, or that Mrs. Bence would finally get through in time to accompany her. She was suddenly aware that there was not a soul within sound of her voice who had belonged to her former world. With a little gasp she looked about her as they entered the office.

The Hardwick mill to which they now came consisted of a number of large, red brick buildings, joined by covered passage-ways, abutting on one of those sullen pools Johnnie had noted the night before, the yard enclosed by a tight board fence, so high that the operatives in the first- and second-floor rooms could not see the street. This for the factory portion; the office did not front on the shut-in yard, but opened out freely on to the street, through a little grassy square of its own, tree-shadowed, with paved walks and flower beds. As with all the mills in its district, the suggestion was dangerously apt of a penitentiary, with its high wooden barrier, around all the building, the only free approach from the world to its corridors through the seemly, humanized office, where abided the heads, the bosses, the free men, who came and went at will. The walls were already beginning to wear that garment of green which the American ivy flings over so many factory buildings.

As the two girls came up, Johnnie looked at the wide, clear, plate windows, the brass railing that guarded the heavy granite approach, the shining name "Hardwick" deep-set in brazen lettering on the step over which they entered. Inside, the polished oak and metal of office fittings carried on the idea of splendour, if not of luxury. Back of the crystal windows were the tempering shades, all was spacious, ordered with quiet dignity, and there was no sense of hurry in the well-clad, well-groomed figures of men that sat at the massive desks or moved about the softly carpeted floors. The corridor was long, but cleanly swept, and, at its upper portion, covered with a material unfamiliar to Johnnie, but which she recognized as suited to its purpose. Down at the further end of that corridor, something throbbed and moaned and roared and growled — the factory was awake there and working. The contrast struck cold to the girl's heart. Here, yet more sharply defined, was the same difference she had noted between the Palace of Pleasure on the heights and the mills at the foot of the mountain.

Would the people think she was good enough? Would they understand how hard she meant to try? For a minute she had a desperate impulse to turn and run. Then she heard Mandy's thin, flatted tones announcing:

"This hyer girl wants to git a job in the mill. Miz Bence, she cain't come down this morning — you'll have to git somebody to tend her looms till noon;

Pap, he's sick, and she has obliged to wait on him —
so I brung the new gal."

"All right," said the man she addressed. "She
can wait there; you go on to your looms."

Johnnie sat on the bench against the wall where
newcomers applying for positions were placed. The
man she was to see had not yet come to his desk, and
she remained unnoticed and apparently forgotten for
more than an hour. The offices were entered from
the other side, yet a doorway close by Johnnie commanded a view of a room and desk. To it presently
came one who seated himself and began opening and
reading letters. Johnnie caught her breath and leaned
a little forward, watching him, her heart in her eyes,
hands locked hard together in her lap. It was the
young man of the car. He was not in white flannels
now, but he looked almost as wonderful to the girl
in his gray business suit, with the air of easy command, and the quiet half-smile only latent on his face.
Shade Buckheath had spoken of Gray Stoddard as
the boss of the bosses down at Cottonville. Indeed,
his position was unique. Inheritor of large holdings
in Eastern cotton-mill stock, he had returned from
abroad on the death of his father, to look into this
source of his very ample income. The mills in which
he was concerned were not earning as they should,
so he was told; and there was discussion as to whether
they be moved south, or a Southern mill be established which might be considered in the nature of a
branch, and where the coarser grades of sheeting

would be manufactured, as well as all the spinning done.

But Stoddard was not of the blood that takes opinions second-hand. Upon his mother's side he was the grandson of one of the great anti-slavery agitators. The sister of this man, Gray's great-aunt, had stood beside him on the platform when there was danger in it; and after the Negro was freed and enfranchised, she had devoted a long life to the cause of woman suffrage. The mother who bore him died young. She left him to the care of a conservative father, but the blood that came through her did not make for conservatism.

Perhaps it was some admixture of his father's traits which set the young man to investigating the cotton-mill situation in his own fashion. To do this as he conceived it should be done, he had hired himself to the Hardwick Spinning Company in an office position which gave him a fair outlook on the business, and put him in complete touch with the practical side of it; yet the facts of the case made the situation evident to those under him as well as his peers. Whatever convictions and opinions he was maturing in this year with the Hardwicks, he kept to himself; but he was supposed to hold some socialistic ideas, and Lydia Sessions, James Hardwick's sister-in-law, made her devoir to these by engaging zealously in semi-charitable enterprises among the mill-girls. He was a passionate individualist. The word seems unduly fiery when one remembers the smiling, insouciant manner of his divergences from the conventional type; yet he was inveterately himself, and not some schoolmaster's or tailor's or barber's version of Gray Stoddard; and in this, though Johnnie did not know it, lay the strength of his charm for her.

The moments passed unheeded after he came into her field of vision, and she watched him for some time, busy at his morning's work. It took her breath when he raised his eyes suddenly and their glances encountered. He plainly recognized her at once, and nodded a cheerful greeting. After a while he got up and came out into the hall, his hands full of papers, evidently on his way to one of the other offices. He paused beside the bench and spoke to her.

"Waiting for the room boss? Are they going to put you on this morning?" he asked pleasantly.

"Yes, I'm a-going to get a chance to work right away," she smiled up at him. "Ain't it fine?"

The smile that answered hers held something pitying, yet it was a pity that did not hurt or offend.

"Yes — I'm sure it's fine, if you think so," said Stoddard, half reluctantly. Then his eye caught the broken pink blossom which Johnnie had pinned to the front of her bodice. "What's that?" he asked. "It looks like an orchid."

He was instantly apologetic for the word; but Johnnie detached the flower from her dress and held it toward him.

"It is," she assented. "It's an orchid; and the

little yellow flower that we-all call the whippoorwill's shoe is an orchid, too."

Stoddard thrust his papers into his coat pocket, and took the blossom in his hand.

"That's the pink moccasin flower," Johnnie told him. "They don't bloom in the valley at all, and they're not very plenty in the mountains. I picked this one six miles up on White Oak Ridge yesterday. I reckon I haven't seen more than a dozen of them in my life, and I've hunted flowers all over Unaka."

"I never had the chance to analyze one," observed Stoddard. "I'd like to get hold of a good specimen."

"I'm sorry this one's broken," Johnnie deprecated. Then her clouded face cleared suddenly with its luminous smile. "If it hadn't been for you I reckon it would have been knocked over the edge of the road," she added. "That's the flower I had in my handkerchief yesterday evening."

Stoddard continued to examine the pink blossom with interest.

"You said it grew up in the mountains — and didn't grow in the valley," he reminded her.

She nodded. "Of course I'm not certain about that," and while she spoke he transferred his attention from the flower to the girl. "I really know mighty little about such things, and I've not been in the valley to exceed ten times in my life. Miss Baird, that taught the school I went to over at Rainy Gap, had a herbarium, and put all kinds of pressed flowers in it. I gathered a great many for her, and she taught me to analyze them — like you were speaking of — but I never did love to do that. It seemed like naming over and calling out the ways of your friends, to pull the flower all to pieces and press it and paste it in a book and write down all its — its — ways and faults."

Again she smiled up at him radiantly, and the young man's astonished glance went from her dusty, cowhide shoes to the thick roll of fair hair on her graceful head. What manner of mill-girls did the mountains send down to the valley?

"But I —" began Stoddard deprecatingly, when Johnnie reddened and broke in hastily.

"Oh, I don't mean that for you. Miss Baird taught me for three years, and I loved her as dearly as I ever could any one. You may keep this flower if you want to; and, come Sunday, I'll get you another one that won't be broken."

"Why Sunday?" asked Stoddard.

"Well, I wouldn't have time to go after them till then, and the ones I know of wouldn't be open before Sunday. I saw just three there by the spring. That's the way they grow, you know — two or three in a place, and not another for miles."

"You saw them growing?" repeated Stoddard. "I should like to see one on its roots, and maybe make a little sketch of it. Couldn't you just as well show me the place Sunday?"

For no reason that she could assign, and very much against her will, Johnnie's face flushed deeply.

"I reckon I couldn't," she answered evasively. "Hit's a long ways up — and — hit's a long ways up."

"And yet you're going to walk it — after a week's work here in the mill?" persisted Stoddard. "You'd better tell me where they grow, and let me go up in my car."

"I wish't I could," said Johnnie, embarrassed. "But you'd never find it in the world. They isn't one thing that I could tell you to know the place by: and you have to leave the road and walk a little piece — oh, it's no use — and I don't mind, I'd just love to go up there and get the flowers for you."

"Are you the new girl?" inquired a voice at Johnnie's shoulder.

They turned to find a squat, middle-aged man regarding them dubiously.

"Yes," answered Johnnie, rising. "I've been waiting quite a while."

"Well, come this way," directed the man and, turning, led her away. Down the hall they went, then up a flight of wooden stairs which carried them to a covered bridge, and so to the upper story of the factory.

"That's an unusual-looking girl." Old Andrew MacPherson made the comment as he received the papers from Stoddard's hands.

"The one I was speaking to in the hall?" inquired Stoddard rather unnecessarily. "Yes; she seems to have an unusual mind as well. These mountain people are peculiar. They appear to have no idea of class, and therefore are in a measure all aristocrats."

"Well, that ought to square with your socialistic notions," chaffed MacPherson, sorting the work on his desk and pushing a certain portion of it toward Stoddard. "Sit down here, if you please, and we'll go over these now. The girl looked a good deal like a fairy princess. I don't think she's a safe topic for susceptible young chaps like you and me," the grizzled old Scotchman concluded with a chuckle. "Your socialistic hullabaloo makes you liable to foregather with all sorts of impossible people."

Gray shook his head, laughing, as he seated himself at the desk beside the other.

"Oh, I'm only a theoretical socialist," he deprecated.

"Hum," grunted the older man. "A theoretical socialist always seemed to me about like a theoretical pickpocket — neither of them stands to do much harm. For example, here you are, one of the richest young fellows of my acquaintance, living along very contentedly where every tenet you profess to hold is daily outraged. You're not giving away your money. You take a healthy interest in a good car, a good dinner, the gals; I'm even told you have a fad for old porcelains — and yet you call yourself a socialist."

"These economic conditions are not a pin," answered Gray, smiling. "I don't have to jump and say 'ouch!' the minute I find they prick me. Worse conditions have always been, and no doubt bad ones will survive for a time, and pass away as mankind outgrows them. I haven't the colossal conceit to suppose that I can reform the world — not even push it much faster toward the destination of good to which it is rolling. But I want to know — I want to understand, myself; then if there is anything for me to do I shall do it. It may be that the present conditions are the best possible for the present moment. It may be that if a lot of us got together and agreed, we could better them exceedingly. It is not certain in my mind yet that any growth is of value to humanity which does not proceed from within. This is true of the individual — must it not be true of the class?"

"No doubt, no doubt," agreed MacPherson, indifferently. "Most of the men who are loud in the leadership of socialism have made a failure of their own lives. We'll see what happens when a man who is a personal and economic success sets up to teach."

"If you mean that very complimentary description for me," said Gray with sudden seriousness, "I will say to you here and now that there is no preacher in me. But when I am a little clearer in my own mind as to what I believe, I shall practise. The only real creed is a manner of life. If you don't live it, you don't really believe it."

CHAPTER VI

THE Hardwick mill was a large one; to the mountain-bred girl it seemed endless, while its clamour and roar was a thing to daunt. They passed through the spinning department, in which the long lines of frames were tended by children, and reached the weaving-rooms whose looms required the attention of women, with here and there a man who had failed to make a success of male occupations and sunk to the ill-paid feminine activities. In a corner of one of these, Johnnie's guide stopped before two silent, motionless looms, and threw on the power. He began to instruct her in their operation, all communication being in dumb show; for the clapping thunder of the weaving-room instantly snatches the sound from one's lips and batters it into shapelessness. Johnnie had been an expert weaver on the ancient foot-power looms of the mountains; but the strangeness of the new machine, the noise and her surroundings, bewildered her. When the man saw that she was not likely to injure herself or the looms, he turned away with a careless nod and left her to her fate.

It was a blowy April day outside, with a gay blue

sky in which the white clouds raced, drawing barges of shadow over the earth below. But the necessity of keeping dust out of the machinery, the inconvenience of having flying ends carried toward it, closed every window in the big factory, and the operatives gasped in the early heat, the odour of oil, the exhausted air. There was a ventilating system in the Hardwick mill, and it was supposed to be exceptionally free from lint; but the fagged children crowded to the casements with instinctive longing for the outdoor air which could not of course enter through the glass; or plodded their monotonous rounds to tend the frames and see that the thread was running properly to each spool, and that the spools were removed, when filled.

By noon every nerve in Johnnie's body quivered with excitement and overstrain; yet when Mandy came for her at the dinner hour she showed her a face still resolute, and asked that a snack be brought her to the mill.

"I don't see why you won't come along home and eat your dinner," the Meacham woman commented. "The Lord knows you get time enough to stay in the mill working over them old looms. Say, I seen you in the hall — did you know who you was talking to?"

The red flooded Johnnie's face as she knelt before her loom interrogating its workings with a dexterous hand; even the white nape of her neck showed pink to Mandy's examining eye; but she managed to reply in a fairly even tone:

"Yes, that was Mr. Stoddard. I saw him yesterday evening when I was coming down the Ridge with Shade."

"But did you know 'bout him? Say — Johnnie Consadine — turn yourself round from that old loom and answer me. I was goin' a-past the door, and when I ketched sight o' you and him settin' there talkin' as if you'd knowed each other all your lives, why you could have — could have knocked me down with a feather."

Johnnie sat up on her heels and turned a laughing face across her shoulder.

"I don't see any reason to want to knock you down with anything," she evaded the direct issue. "Go 'long, Mandy, or you won't have time to eat your dinner. Tell Aunt Mavity to send me just a biscuit and a piece of meat."

"Good land, Johnnie Consadine, but you're quare!" exclaimed Mandy, staring with bulging light eyes. "If it was me I'd be all in a tremble yet — and there you sit and talk about meat and bread!"

Johnnie did not think it necessary to explain that the tremor of that conversation with Stoddard had indeed lasted through her entire morning.

"There was nothing to tremble about," she remarked with surface calm. "He'd never seen a pink moccasin flower, and I gave him the one I had and told him where it grew."

"Well, he wasn't looking at no moccasin flower when I seed him," Mandy persisted. "He was lookin' at you. He jest eyed you as if you was Miss Lydia Sessions herself — more so, if anything."

Johnnie inwardly rebuked the throb of joy which greeted this statement.

"I reckon his looks are his own, Mandy," she said soberly. "You and me have no call to notice them."

"Ain't got no call to notice 'em? Well, I jest wish't I could get you and him up in front of Miss Sessions, and have her see them looks of his'n," grumbled Mandy as she turned away. "I bet you there'd be some noticin' done then!"

When in the evening Mandy came for Johnnie, she found the new mill hand white about the mouth with exhaustion, heavy-eyed, choking, and ready to weep.

"Uh-huh," said the Meacham woman, "I know just how you feel. They all look that-a-way the first day or two — then after that they look worse."

Nervelessly Johnnie found her way downstairs in the stream of tired girls and women. There was more than one kindly greeting for the new hand, and occasionally somebody clapped her on the shoulder and assured her that a few days more would get her used to the work. The mill yard was large, filled with grass-plots and gravel walks; but it was shut in by a boarding so tall that the street could not be seen from the windows of the lower floor. To Johnnie, weary to the point where aching muscles and blood charged with uneliminated waste spelled pessimism, that high board fence seemed to make of the pretty place a prison yard.

A man was propping open the big wooden gates, and

through them she saw the street, the sidewalk, and a carriage drawn up at the curb. In this vehicle sat a lady; and a gentleman, hat in hand, talked to her from the sidewalk.

"Come on," hissed Mandy, seizing her companion's arm and dragging her forward. "Thar's Miss Lydia Sessions right now, and that's Mr. Stoddard a-talkin' to her. I'll go straight up and give you a knock-down — I want to, anyway. She's the one that runs the Uplift Club. If she takes a shine to you it'll be money in your pocket."

She turned over her shoulder to glance at Johnnie, who was pulling vigorously back. There was no hint of tiredness or depression in the girl's face now. Her deep eyes glowed; red was again in the fresh lips that parted over the white teeth in an adorable, tremulous smile. Mandy stared.

"Hurry up — he'll be gittin' away," she admonished.

"Oh, no," objected the new girl. "Wait till some other time. I — I don't want to ——"

But her remonstrance came too late; Mandy had yanked her forward and was performing the introduction she so euphoniously described.

Gray Stoddard turned and bowed to both girls. He carried the broken orchid in his hand, and apparently had been speaking of it to Miss Sessions. Mandy eyed him narrowly to see if any of the looks she had apprehended as offensive to Miss Sessions went in Johnnie's direction. And she was not disappointed.

Stoddard's gaze lingered long on the radiant countenance of the girl from Unaka. Not so the young women looked after a few months of factory life. He was getting to know well the odd jail-bleach the cotton mill puts on country cheeks, the curious, dulled, yet resentful expression of the eyes, begotten by continuous repetition of excessive hours of trivial, monotonous toil. Would this girl come at last to that favour? He was a little surprised at the strength of protest in his own heart. Then MacPherson, coming down the office steps, called to him; and, with courteous adieux, the two men departed in company.

Johnnie was a bit grieved to find that the removal from Miss Sessions of the shrouding, misty veil revealed a countenance somewhat angular in outline, with cheekbones a trifle hard and high, and a lack of colour. She fancied, too, that Miss Sessions was slightly annoyed about something. She wondered if it was because they had interrupted her conversation with Mr. Stoddard and driven him away. Yet while she so questioned, she was taking in with swift appreciation the trim set of the driving coat Miss Lydia wore, the appropriate texture of the heavy gloves on the small hands that held the lines, and a certain indefinable air of elegance hard to put into words, but which all women recognize.

"Ain't she swell?" inquired Mandy, as they passed on. "She's after Mr. Stoddard now — it used to be the preacher that had the big church in Watauga, but he moved away. I wish I had her clothes."

"Yes," returned Johnnie absently. She had already forgotten her impression of Miss Sessions's displeasure. Gone was the leaden weariness of her day's toil. Something intimate and kind in the glance Stoddard had given her remained warm at her heart, and set that heart singing.

Meantime, Stoddard and MacPherson were walking up the ridge toward the Country Club together, intending to spend the night on the highlands. The Scotchman returned once more to the subject he had broached that morning.

"This is a great country," he opened obliquely, "a very great country. But you Americans will have to learn that generations of blood and breeding are not to be skipped with impunity. See the sons and daughters of your rich men. If the hope of the land lay in them it would be a bad outlook indeed."

"Is that peculiar to America?" asked Stoddard mildly. They were coming under the trees now. He took off his hat and ran his fingers through his hair to enjoy the coolness. "My impression was that the youthful aristocracy of every country often made of itself a spectacle unseemly."

The Scotchman laughed. Then he looked sidewise at his companion. "I'm not denying," he pursued, again with that odd trick of entering his argument from the side, "that a young chap like yourself has my good word. A man with money who will go to work to find out how that money was made, and to live as his father did, carries an old head on young shoulders. I put aside your socialistic vapourings of course — every fellow to his fad — I see in you the makings of a canny business man."

It was Stoddard's turn to laugh, and he did so unrestrainedly, throwing back his head and uttering his mirth so boyishly that the other smiled in sympathy.

"You talk about what's in the blood," Gray said finally, "and then you make light of my socialistic vapourings, as you call them. My mother's clan — and it is from the spindle side that a man gets his traits — are all come-outers as far back as I know anything about them. They fought with Cromwell — some of them; they came over and robbed the Indians in true sanctimonious fashion, and persecuted the Quakers; and down the line a bit I get some Quaker blood that stood for its beliefs in the stocks, and sacrificed its ears for what it thought right. I'm afraid the socialistic vapourings are the true expression of the animal."

MacPherson grunted incredulously.

"I give you ten years to be done with it," he said. "It is a disease of youth. But don't let it mark your affairs. It is all right to foregather with these workingmen, and find out about their trades-unions and that sort of thing — such knowledge will be useful to you in your business. But when it comes to women" — MacPherson paused and shook his gray head — "to young, pretty women — a man must stick to his own class."

"You mean the girl in the corridor," said Stoddard

with that directness which his friends were apt to find disconcerting. "I haven't classified her yet. She's rather an extraordinary specimen."

"Well, she's not in your class, and best leave her alone," returned MacPherson doggedly. "It wouldn't matter if the young thing were not so beautiful, and with such a winning look in her eyes. This America beats me. That poor lass would make a model princess — according to common ideals of royalty — and here you find her coming out of some hut in the mountains and going to work in a factory. Miss Lydia Sessions is a well-bred young woman, now; she's been all over Europe, and profited by her advantages of travel. I call her an exceedingly well-bred person."

"She is," agreed Stoddard without enthusiasm.

"And I'm sure you must admire her altruistic ideas — they'd just fall in with yours, I suppose, now."

Stoddard shook his head.

"Not at all," he said briefly. "If you were enough interested in socialism to know what we folks are driving at, I could explain to you why we object to charitable enterprises — but it's not worth while."

"Indeed it is not," assented MacPherson hastily. "Though no doubt we might have a fine argument over it some evening when we have nothing better to talk about. I thought you and Miss Sessions were fixing up a match of it, and it struck me as a very good thing, too. The holdings of both of you are in cotton-mill property, I judge. That always makes for harmony and stability in a matrimonial alliance."

Stoddard smiled. He was aware that Miss Lydia's holdings consisted of a complaisant brother-in-law in whose house she was welcome till she could marry. But he said nothing on this head.

"MacPherson," he began very seriously, "I wonder a little at you. I know you old-world people regard these things differently; but could you look at Mrs. Hardwick's children, and seriously recommend Mrs. Hardwick's sister as a wife for a friend?"

Old MacPherson stopped in the way, thrust his hands deep in his pockets and stared at the younger man.

"Well!" he ejaculated at last; "that's a great speech for a hot-headed young fellow! Your foresight is worthy of a Scotchman."

Gray Stoddard smiled. "I am not a hot-headed person," he observed. "Nobody but you ever accused me of such a thing. Marriage concerns the race and a man's whole future. If the children of the marriage are likely to be unsatisfactory, the marriage will certainly be so. We moderns bedeck and bedrape us in all sorts of meretricious togas, till a pair of fine eyes and a dashing manner pass for beauty; but when life tries the metal — when nature applies her inevitable test — the degenerate or neurotic type goes to the wall."

Again MacPherson grunted. "No doubt you're sound enough; but it is rather uncanny to hear a young fellow talk like his grandfather," the Scotchman said finally. "Are there many of your sort in this astonishing land?"

"A good many," Stoddard told him. "The modern young man of education and wealth is doing one of two things — burning up his money and going to the dogs as fast as he can; or putting in a power of thinking, and trying, while he saves his own soul, to do his part in the regeneration of the world."

"Yes. Well, it's a big job. It's been on hand a long time. The young men of America have their work cut out for them," said MacPherson drily.

"No doubt," returned Stoddard with undisturbed cheerfulness. "But when every man saves his own soul, the salvation of the world will come to pass."

CHAPTER VII

ALL week in Johnnie the white flame of purpose burned out every consciousness of weariness, of bodily or mental distaste. The preposterously long hours, the ill-ventilated rooms, the savage monotony of her toil, none of these reached the girl through the glow of hope and ambition. Physically, the finger of the factory was already laid upon her vigorous young frame; but when Sunday morning came, though there was no bellowing whistle to break in on her slumbers, she waked early, and while nerve and muscle begged achingly for more sleep, she rose with a sense of exhilaration which nothing could dampen. She had seen a small mountain church over the Ridge by the spring where her moccasin flowers grew; and if there were preaching in it to-day, the boys and girls scouring the surrounding woods during the intermissions would surely find and carry away the orchids. There was no safety but to take the road early.

The room was dark. Mandy slept noisily beside her. All the beds were full, because the night-turn workers were in. She meant to be very careful to waken nobody. Poor souls, they needed this one day of rest when they could all lie late. Searching for something, she cautiously struck a match, and in the flaring up of its small flame got a glimpse of Mandy's face, open-mouthed, pallid, unbeautiful, against the tumbled pillow. A great rush of pity filled her eyes with tears, but then she was in a mood to compassionate any creature who had not the prospect of a twelve-mile walk to get a flower for Gray Stoddard.

It was in that black hour before dawn that Johnnie let herself out the front door, finding the direction by instinct rather than any assistance from sight, since fences, trees, houses, were but vague blots of deeper shadow in the black. She was well on her way before a light here and there in a cabin window showed that, Sunday morning as it was, the earliest risers were beginning to stir. Her face was set to the east, and after a time a pallid line showed itself above the great bulk of mountains which in this quarter backed up the ramparts of the circling ridges about Watauga. The furthest line was big Unaka, but this passionate lover of her native highlands gave it neither thought nor glance, as she tramped steadily with lifted face, following unconsciously the beckoning finger of Fate.

It was a dripping-sweet spring morning, dew-drenched, and with the air so full of moisture that it gathered and pattered from the scant leafage. She was two miles up, swinging along at that steady pace her mountain-bred youth had given her, when the sky began to flush faintly, and the first hint of dawn rested on her upraised countenance.

Rain-laden mists swept down upon her from the heights, and she walked through them unnoting; the pale light from the eastern sky shone on an aspect introverted, rapt away from knowledge of its sur-roundings. She was going to get something for him. She had promised him the flowers, and he would be pleased with them. He would smile when he thanked her for them, and look at her as he had when she gave him the broken blossom. A look like that was to the girl in her present mood as the sword's touch on the shoulder of the lad who is being knighted by his king — it made her want to rise up and be all that such a man could ever demand of her. Twelve miles of walking after a week's toil in the mill was a very small offering to put before so worshipful a divinity. She sought vaguely to conjecture just what his words would be when next they spoke together. Her lips formed themselves into tender, reminiscent half-smiles as she went over the few and brief moments of her three interviews with Stoddard.

Johnnie was not inexperienced in matters of the heart. Mating time comes early in the mountains. Had her dreams been of Shade Buckheath, or any of the boys of her own kind and class, she would have been instantly full of self-consciousness; but Gray Stoddard appeared to her a creature so apart from her sphere that this overwhelming attraction he held for her seemed no more than the admiration she might have given to Miss Lydia Sessions. And so the dream lay undisturbed under her eyelashes, and she breasted the slope of the big mountain with a buoyant step, oblivious of fatigue.

She reached the little wayside spring before even the early-rising mountain folk were abroad, found three pink blossoms in full perfection, plucked them and wrapped them carefully in damp cloths disposed in a little hickory basket that Uncle Pros had made for her years ago. It was a tiny thing, designed to hold a child's play-pretties or a young girl's sewing, but shaped and fashioned after the manner of mountain baskets, and woven of stout white hickory withes shaved down to daintier size and pliancy by the old man's jack-knife. Life was very sweet to Johnnie Consadine as she straightened up, basket in hand, and turned toward the home journey.

It was nearly nine o'clock when she reached the gap above Cottonville. She was singing a little, softly, to herself, as she footed it down the road, and wishing that she might see Gray's face when he got her flowers. She planned to put them in a glass on his desk Monday morning, and of course she would be at her loom long before he should reach the office. She was glad they were such fine specimens — all perfect. Lovingly she pulled aside the wet cloth and looked in at them. She began to meet people on the road, and the cabins she passed were open and thronged with morning life. The next turn in the road would bring her to the spring where she had rested that evening just a week ago, and where Shade had met her.

Suddenly, she caught the sheen of something down the road between the scant greenery. It was a carriage or an automobile. Now, it was more likely to be the former than the latter; also, there were a half-dozen cars in Cottonville; yet from the first she knew, and was prepared for it when the shining vehicle came nearer and showed her Gray Stoddard driving it. They looked at each other in silence. Stoddard brought the machine to a halt beside her. She came mutely forward, a hesitating hand at her basket covering, her eyes raised to his. With the mountaineer's deathless instinct for greeting, she was first to speak.

"Howdy," she breathed softly. "I — I was looking for — I got you ——"

She fell silent again, still regarding him, and fumbling blindly at the cover of the basket.

"Well — aren't you lost?" inquired Stoddard with a rather futile assumption of surprise. He was strangely moved by the direct gaze of those clear, wide-set gray eyes, under the white brow and the ruffled coronet of bright hair.

"No," returned Johnnie gently, literally. "You know I said I'd come up here and get those moccasin flowers for you this morning. This is my road home, anyhow. I'm not as near lost on it as I am at a loom, down in the factory."

Stoddard continued to stare at the hand she had laid on the car.

"It'll be an awfully long walk for you," he said at last, choosing his words with some difficulty. "Won't you get in and let me take you up to the spring?"

Johnnie laughed softly, exultantly.

"Oh, I picked your flowers before day broke. I'll

bet there have been a dozen boys over from Sunday-school to drink out of that spring before this time. You wouldn't have had any blooms if I hadn't got up early."

Again she laughed, and, uncovering the orchids, held them up to him.

"These are beauties," he exclaimed with due enthusiasm, yet with a certain uneasy preoccupation in his manner. "Were you up before day, did you tell me, to get these? That seems too bad. You needed your sleep."

Johnnie flushed and smiled.

"I love to do it," she said simply. "It was mighty sweet out on the road this morning, and you don't know how pretty the blooms did look, standing there waiting for me. I 'most hated to pick them."

Stoddard's troubled eyes raised themselves to her face. Here was a royal nature that would always be in the attitude of the giver. He wanted to offer her something, and, as the nearest thing in reach, sprang down from the automobile and, laying a hand on her arm, said, almost brusquely:

"Get in. Come, let me help you. I want to go up and see the spring where these grow. I'll get you back to Cottonville in time for church, if that's what you're debating about."

Both of them knew that Johnnie's reluctance had nothing to do with the question of church-time. Stoddard himself was well aware that a factory girl could not with propriety accept a seat in his car; yet when once they were settled side by side, and the car resumed that swift, tireless climb which is the wonder and delight of the mechanical vehicle, it was characteristic that both put aside definitely and completely all hesitations and doubts. The girl was freely, innocently, exultantly blissful. Stoddard noticed her intent examination of the machine, and began explaining its workings to her.

"Was that what you were doing," she asked, alluding to some small item of the operating, "when you stopped by the side of the road, Sunday night, when Miss Lydia was with you?"

He looked his astonishment.

"You were right under my window when you stopped," Johnnie explained to him. "I watched you-all when you started away. I was sure you would beat."

"We did," Stoddard assured her. "But we came near missing it. That connection Buckheath put in for me the evening you were with him on the Ridge worked loose. But I discovered the trouble in time to fix it."

Remembrance of that evening, and of the swift flight of the motors through the dusk moonlight, made Johnnie wonder at herself and her present position. She was roused by Stoddard's voice asking:

"Are you interested in machinery?"

"I love it," returned Johnnie sincerely. "I never did get enough of tinkerin' around machines. If I was ever so fortunate as to own a sewing machine

I could take it all apart and clean it and put it together again. I did that to the minister's wife's sewing machine down at Bledsoe when it got out of order. She said I knew more about it than the man that sold it to her."

"Would you like to run the car?" came the next query.

Would she like to! The countenance of simple rapture that she turned to him was reply sufficient.

"Well, look at my hands here on the steering-wheel. Get the position, and when I raise one put yours in its place. There. No, a little more this way. Now you can hold it better. The other one's right."

Smilingly he watched her, like a grown person amusing a child.

"You see what the wheel does, of course — guides. Now," when they had run ahead for some minutes, "do you want to go faster?"

Johnnie laughed up at him, through thick, fair lashes.

"Looks like anybody would be hard to suit that wanted to go faster than this," she apologized. "But if the machine can make a higher speed, there wouldn't be any harm in just running that way for a spell, would there?"

It was Stoddard's turn to laugh.

"No manner of harm," he agreed readily. "Well, you advance your spark and open the throttle — that speeds her up. This is the spark and this the gas, here. Then you shove your shifting lever — see, here it is — over to the next speed. Remember that, any time you shift the gears, you'll have to pull the clutch. The machine has to gain headway on one speed before it can take the next."

Johnnie nodded soberly. Her intent gaze studied the mechanism before her intelligently.

"We're going a heap faster now," she suggested in a moment. "Can I move that — whatever it is — over to the third speed?"

"Yes," agreed Stoddard. "Here's a good, long, straight stretch of road for us to take it on. I'll attend to the horn when we come to the turn up there. We mustn't make anybody's horse run away."

So the lesson proceeded. He showed her brake and clutch. He gave her some theoretical knowledge of cranking up, because she seemed to enjoy it as a child enjoys exploiting the possibilities of a new toy.

Up and up they went, the sky widening and brightening above them. Hens began to lead forth their broods. Overhead, a hawk wheeled high in the blue, uttering his querulous cry.

"I'm mighty glad I came," the girl said, more to herself than to the man at her side. "This is the most like flying of anything that ever chanced to me."

From time to time Stoddard had sent swift, sidelong glances at his companion, noting the bright, bent head, the purity of line in the profile above the steering-wheel, the intelligent beauty of the intent, down-dropped eyes, with long lashes almost on the flushed cheeks. He wondered at her; born amid these wide, cool spaces, how had she endured for a week the fetid atmosphere of the factory rooms? How, having tested it, could she look forward to a life like that? Something in her innocent trust choked him. He began some carefully worded inquiries as to her experience in the mill and her opinion of the work. The answers partook of that charm which always clung about Johnnie. She told him of Mandy and, missing no shade of the humour there was in the Meacham girl, managed to make the description pathetic. She described Pap Himes and his boarding-house, aptly, deftly, and left it funny, though a sympathetic listener could feel the tragedy beneath.

Presently they met the first farm-wagon with its load of worshippers for the little mountain church beyond. As these came out of a small side road, and caught sight of the car, the bony old horses jibbed and shied, and took all the driver's skill and a large portion of his vocabulary to carry them safely past, the children staring, the women pulling their sunbonnets about their faces and looking down. Something in the sight brought home to Johnnie the incongruity of her present position. On the instant, a drop of rain splashed upon the back of her hand.

"There!" she cried in a contrite voice. "I knew mighty well and good that it was going to rain, and I ought to have named it to you, because you town folks don't understand the weather as well as we do. I ought not to have let you come on up here."

"We'll have to turn and run for it," said Stoddard,

laughing a little. "I wish I'd had the hood put on this morning," as he surveyed the narrow way in which he had to turn. "Is it wider beyond here, do you remember?"

"There's a bluff up about a quarter of a mile that you could run under and be as dry as if you were in the shed at home," said Johnnie. "This won't last long. Do you want to try it?"

"You are the pilot," Stoddard declared promptly, resigning the wheel once more to her hands. "If it's a bad place, you might let me take the car in."

Rain in the mountains has a trick of coming with the suddenness of an overturned bucket. Johnnie sent the car ahead at what she considered a rapid pace, till Stoddard unceremoniously took the wheel from her and shoved the speed clutch over to the third speed.

"I'm mighty sorry I was so careless and didn't warn you about the rain," she declared with shining eyes, as her hair blew back and her colour rose at the rapid motion. "But this is fine. I believe that if I should ever be so fortunate as to own an automobile I'd want to fly like this every minute of the time I was in it."

As she spoke, they swept beneath the overhanging rocks, and a great curtain of Virginia creeper and trumpet-vine fell behind them, half screening them from the road, and from the deluge which now broke more fiercely. For five minutes the world was blotted out in rain, with these two watching its gray swirls and listening to its insistent drumming, safe and dry in their cave.

Nothing ripens intimacy so rapidly as a common mishap. Also, two people seem much to each other as they await alone the ceasing of the rain or the coming of the delayed boat.

"This won't last long," Johnnie repeated. "We won't dare to start out when it first stops; but there'll come a little clearing-up shower after that, and then I think we'll have a fair day. Don't you know the saying, 'Rain before seven, quit before eleven?' Well, it showered twice just as day was breaking, and I had to wait under a tree till it was over."

The big drops lengthened themselves, as they came down, into tiny javelins and struck upon the rocks with a splash. The roar and drumming in the forest made a soft, blurring undertone of sound. The first rain lasted longer than Johnnie had counted on, and the clearing-up shower was slow in making its appearance. The two talked with ever-growing interest. Strangely enough Johnnie Consadine, who had no knowledge of any other life except through a few well-conned books, appreciated the values of this mountain existence with almost the detached view of an outsider. Her knowledge of it was therefore more assorted and available, and Stoddard listened to her eagerly.

"But what made you think you'd like to work in a cotton mill?" he asked suddenly. "After all, weren't you maybe better off up in these mountains?"

And then and there Johnnie strove to put into exact

and intelligent words what she had possessed and what she had lacked in the home of her childhood. Unconsciously she told him more than was in the mere words.   He got the situation as to the visionary, kindly father with a turn for book learning and a liking for enterprises that appealed to his imagination.   Uncle Pros and the silver mine were always touched upon with the tender kindness Johnnie felt for the old man and his life-long quest.   But the little mother and the children — ah, it was here that the listener found Johnnie's incentive.

"Mr. Stoddard," she concluded, "there wasn't a bit of hope of schooling for the children unless I could get out and work in the factory.   I think it's a splendid chance for a girl.   I think any girl that wouldn't take such a chance would be mighty mean and poor-spirited."

Gray Stoddard revolved this conception of a chance in the world in his mind for some time.

"I did get some schooling," she told him.   "You wouldn't think it to hear me talk, because I'm careless, but I've been taught, and I can do better.   Yet if I don't see to it, how am I to know that the children will have as much even as I've had?   Mountain air is mighty pure and healthy, and the water up here is the finest you ever drank; but that's only for the body. Of course there's beauty all about you — there was never anything more sightly than big Unaka and the ridges that run from it, and the sky, and the big woods — and all.   And yet human beings have got to have more than that. I aim to make a chance for the children."

"Are you going to bring them down and let them work in the mills with you?" Stoddard asked in a perfectly colourless tone.

Johnnie looked embarrassed. Her week in the cotton mill had fixed indelibly on her mind the picture of the mill child, straggling to work in the gray dawn, sleepy, shivering, unkempt; of the young things creeping up and down the aisles between the endlessly turning spools, dully regarding the frames to see that the threads were not fouled or broken; of the tired little groups as they pressed close to the shut windows, neglecting their work to stare out into a world of blue sky and blowing airs — a world they could see but not enter, and no breath of which could come in to them. And so she looked embarrassed. She was afraid that memory of those tired little faces would show in her own countenance. Her hands on the steering-wheel trembled. She remembered that Mr. Stoddard was, as Shade had said, one of the bosses in the Hardwick mill. It seemed too terrible to offend him. He certainly thought no ill of having children employed; she must not seem to criticize him; she answered evasively:

"Well, of course they might do that. I did think of it — before I went down there."

"Before you went to work in the mills yourself," supplied Stoddard, again in that colourless tone.

"Ye — yes," hesitated Johnnie; "but you mustn't

get the idea that I don't love my work — because I do. You see the children haven't had any schooling yet, and — well, I'm a great, big, stout somebody, and it looks like I'm the one to work in the mill."

She turned to him fleetingly a countenance of appeal and perplexity. It seemed indeed anything but certain that she was one to work in the mill. There was something almost grotesque in the idea which made Stoddard smile a little at her earnestness.

"I'd like to talk it over with you when you've been at work there longer," he found himself saying. "You see, I'm studying mill conditions from one side, and you're studying them from the opposite — perhaps we could help each other."

"I sure will tell you what I find out," agreed Johnnie heartily. "I reckon you'll want to know how the work seems to me at the side of such as I was used to in the mountains; but I hope you won't inquire how long it took me to learn, for I'm afraid I'm going to make a poor record. If you was to ask me how much I was able to earn there, and how much back on Unaka, I could make a good report for the mill on that, because that's all that's the matter with the mountains — they're a beautiful place to live, but a body can't hardly earn a cent, work as they may."

Johnnie forgot herself — she was always doing that — and she talked freely and well. It was as inevitable that she should be drawn to Gray Stoddard as that she should desire the clothing and culture Miss

Lydia possessed. For the present, one aspiration struck her as quite as innocent as the other. Stoddard had not yet emerged from the starry constellations among which she set him, to take form as a young man, a person who might indeed return her regard. Her emotions were in that nebulous, formative stage when but a touch would be needed to show her whither the regard tended, yet till that touch should come, she as unashamedly adored Gray as any child of five could have done. It was not till they were well down the road to Cottonville that she realized the bald fact that she, a mill girl, was riding in an automobile with one of the mill owners.

She was casting about for some reasonable phrase in which to clothe the statement that it would be better he should stop the car and let her out; she had parted her lips to ask him to take the wheel, when they rounded a turn and came upon a company of loom-fixers from the village below. Behind them, in a giggling group, strolled a dozen mill girls in their Sunday best. Johnnie had sight of Mandy Meacham, fixing eyes of terrified admiration upon her; then she nodded in reply to Shade Buckheath's angry stare, and a rattle of wheels apprized her that a carriage was passing on the other side. This vehicle contained the entire Hardwick family, with Lydia Sessions turning long to look her incredulous amazement back at them from her seat beside her brother-in-law.

It was all over in a moment. The loom-fixers had debouched upon the long, wooden bridge which crossed the ravine to their quarters; the girls were going on, Mandy Meacham hanging back and staring; a tree finally shut out Miss Sessions's accusing countenance.

"Please stop and let me out here," said Johnnie, in a scarcely audible voice.

When Stoddard would have remonstrated, or asked why, his lips were closed by sight of her daunted, miserable face. He knew as well as she the mad imprudence of the thing which they had done, and blamed himself roundly with it all.

"I'll not forget to bring the books we were talking of," he made haste to say. He picked up the little basket from the floor of the car.

"You'd better keep the flowers in that," Johnnie told him lifelessly. Her innocent dream was broken into by a cruel reality. She was struggling blindly under the weight of all her little world's disapprobation.

"You'll let me return the basket when I bring you the books," Gray suggested, helplessly.

"I don't know," Johnnie hesitated. Then, as a sudden inspiration came to her, "Mandy Meacham said she'd try to get me into a club for girls that Miss Sessions has. She said Miss Sessions would lend me books. Maybe you might just leave them with her. I'm sure I should be mighty proud to have them. I know I'll love to read them; but — well, you might just leave them with her."

A little satiric sparkle leaped to life in Stoddard's eyes. He looked at the innocent, upraised face in wonder. The most experienced manœuverer of Society's legion could not have handled a difficult situation more deftly.

"The very thing," he said cheerily. "I'll talk to Miss Sessions about it to-morrow."

CHAPTER VIII

OF THE USE OF WINGS

I TOLD you I'd speak a good word for you," shouted Mandy Meacham, putting her lips down close to Johnnie's ear where she struggled and fought with her looms amid the deafening clamour of the weaving room.

The girl looked up, flushed, tired, but eagerly receptive.

"Yes," her red lips shaped the word to the other's eyes, though no sound could make itself heard above that din except such eldritch shrieks as Mandy's.

"I done it. I got you a invite to some doin's at the Uplift Club a-Wednesday."

Again Johnnie nodded and shaped "Yes" with her lips. She added something which might have been "thank you"; the adorable smile that accompanied it said as much.

Mandy watched her, fascinated as the lithe, strong young figure bent and strained to correct a crease in the web where it turned the roll.

"They never saw anything like you in their born days, I'll bet," she yelled. "I never did. You're awful quare — but somehow I sorter like ye." And she scuttled back to her looms as the room boss came in. A weaver works by the piece, but Mandy had been reproved too often for slovenly methods not to know that she might be fined for neglect. Her looms stood where she could continually get the newcomer's figure against the light, with its swift motion, its supple curves, and the brave carriage of the well-formed head. The sight gave Mandy a curious satisfaction, as though it uttered what she would fain have said to the classes above her. Hers was something the feeling which the private in the ranks has for the standard-bearer who carries the colours aloft, or the dashing officer who leads the charge. Johnnie was the challenge she would have flung in the face of the enemy.

"I'll bet if you'd put one of Miss Lyddy's dresses on her she'd look nobby," Mandy ruminated, addressing her looms. "That's what she would. She'd have 'em all f —fa—faded away, as the feller says."

And so it came about that the next day Johnnie Consadine did not go to the mill at all, but spent the morning washing and ironing her one light print dress. It was as coarse almost as flour-sacking, and the blue dots on it had paled till they made a suspicious speckle not unlike mildew; yet when she had combed her thick, fair hair, rolled it back from the white brow and braided it to a coronet round her head as she had seen that of the lady on the porch at the Palace of Pleasure; when, cleansed and smooth, she put the frock on, one forgot the dress in the youth of her, the hope, the glorious expectation there was in that eager face.

The ladies assisting in Miss Lydia Sessions's Uplift

Club for work among the mill girls, were almost all young and youngish women. The mothers in Israel attacked the more serious problems of orphanages, winter's supplies of coal, and clothing for the destitute.

"But their souls must be fed, too," Miss Lydia asserted as she recruited her helpers for the Uplift work. "Their souls must be fed; and who can reach the souls of these young girls so well as we who are near their own age, and who have had time for culture and spiritual growth?"

It was a good theory. Perhaps one may say that it remains a good theory. The manner of uplifting was to select a certain number of mill girls whom it was deemed well to help, approach them on the subject, and, if they appeared amenable, pay a substitute to take charge of their looms while those in process of being uplifted attended a meeting of the Club. The gathering to which Johnnie was bidden was held in honour of a lady from London who had written a book on some subject which it was thought ought to appeal to workingwomen. This lady intended to address the company and to mingle with them and get their views. Most of those present being quite unfurnished with any views whatever on the problem she discussed, her position was something that of a pick-pocket in a moneyless crowd; but of this she was fortunately and happily unaware.

Mandy Meacham regarded Johnnie's preparation for the function with some disfavour.

"Ef you fix up like that," she remonstrated, "you're

bound to look too nice to suit Miss Lyddy. They won't be no men thar. I'm goin' to wear my workin' dress, and tell her I hadn't nary minute nor nary cent to do other."

Johnnie laughed a little at this, as though it were intended for a joke.

"But I did have time," she objected. "Miss Sessions would pay a substitute for the whole day though I told her I'd only need the afternoon for the party. I think it was mighty good of her, and it's as little as I can do to make myself look as nice as I can."

"You ain't got the sense you was born with!" fretted Mandy. "Them thar kind ladies ain't a-carin' for you to look so fine. They'll attend to all the fine lookin' theirselves. What they want is to know how bad off you air, an' to have you say how much what they have did or give has helped you."

Such interchange of views brought the two girls to the door of the little frame chapel, given over for the day to Uplift work. Within it rose a bustle and clatter, a hum of voices that spoke, a frilling of nervous, shrill laughter to edge the sound, and back of that the clink of dishes from a rear room where refreshments were being prepared.

Miss Sessions, near the door, had a receiving line, quite in the manner of any reception. She herself, in a blouse of marvellous daintiness and sweeping skirts, stood beside the visitor from London to present her. To this day Johnnie is uncertain as to where the wonderful blue silk frock of that lady from abroad was fastened, though she gave the undivided efforts of sharp young eyes and an inquiring mind to the problem a good portion of the time while it was within her view. The Englishwoman was called Mrs. Archbold, and on her other hand stood a tall, slim lady with long gray-green eyes, prematurely gray hair which had plainly been red, and an odd little twist to her smile. This was Mrs. Hexter, wife of the owner of the big woollen mills across the creek, and only bidden in to assist the Uplift work because the position of her husband gave her much power. These, with the Misses Burchard, daughters of the rector, formed the reception committee.

"I am so charmed to see you here to-day," Miss Lydia smiled as they entered. It was part of her theory to treat the mill girls exactly as she would members of her own circle. Mandy, being old at the business, possessed herself of the high-held hand presented; but Johnnie only looked at it in astonishment, uncertain whether Miss Lydia meant to shake hands or pat her on the head. Yet when she did finally divine what was intended, the quality of her apologetic smile ought to have atoned for her lapse.

"I'm sure proud to be here with you-all," she said. "Looks like to me you are mighty kind to strangers."

The ineradicable dignity of the true mountaineer, who has always been as good as the best in his environment, preserved Johnnie from any embarrassment, any tendency to shrink or cringe. Her beauty, in the fresh-washed print gown, was like a thing released and, as Miss Sessions might have put it, rampant.

Gray Stoddard had gone directly to Lydia Sessions, with his proffers of books, and his suggestions for Johnnie. The explanation of how the girl came to be riding in his car that Sunday morning was neither as full nor as penitent as Miss Lydia could have wished; yet it did recognize the impropriety of the act, and was, in so far, satisfactory. Miss Sessions made haste to form an alliance with the young man for the special upliftment of Johnnie Consadine. She would have greatly preferred to interest him in Mandy Meacham, but beggars can not be choosers, and she took what she could get.

"Whom have we here?" demanded the lady from London, leaning across and peering at Johnnie with friendly, near-sighted eyes. "Why, what a blooming girl, to be sure! You haven't been long from the country, I'll venture to guess, my dear."

Johnnie blushed and dimpled at being so kindly welcomed. The mountain people are undemonstrative in speech and action; and that "my dear" seemed wonderful.

"I come from away up in the mountains," she said softly.

"From away up in the mountains," repeated the Englishwoman, her smiling gaze dwelling on Johnnie's radiant face. "Why yes — so one would conceive. Well, you mustn't lose all those pretty roses in the mill down here." She was a visitor, remember; residents of Cottonville never admitted that roses, or anything else desirable, could be lost in the mills.

"I'll not," said Johnnie sturdily. "I'm goin' to earn my way and send for Mother and the children, if hard work'll do it; but I'm a mighty big, stout, healthy somebody, and I aim to keep so."

Mrs. Archbold patted the tall young shoulder as she turned to Mandy Meacham whom Miss Lydia was eager to put through her paces for the benefit of the lady from London.

"Isn't that the girl Mr. Stoddard was speaking to me about?" she inquired in a whisper as Johnnie moved away. "I think it must be. He said she was such a beauty, and I scarcely believe there could be two like her in one town."

"'Such a type,' were Mr. Stoddard's exact words I believe," returned Miss Sessions a little frostily. "Yes, John Consadine is quite a marked type of the mountaineer. She is, as she said to you, a stout, healthy creature, and, I understand, very industrious. I approve of John."

She approved of John, but she addressed herself to exploiting Mandy; and the lady in the blue silk frock learned how poor and helpless the Meacham woman had been before she got in to the mill work, how greatly the Uplift Club had benefited her, with many interesting details. Yet as the English lady went from group to group in company with Miss Lydia and T. H. Hexter's wife, her quick eyes wandered across the room to where a bright head rose a little taller than its fellows, and occasional bursts of laughter told that Johnnie was in a merry mood.

The threadbare attempt at a reception was gotten through laboriously. The girls were finally settled in orderly rows, and Mrs. Archbold led to the platform. The talk she had prepared for them was upon aspiration. It was an essay, in fact, and she had delivered it successfully before many women's clubs. She is not to be blamed that the language was as absolutely above the comprehension of her hearers as though it had been Greek. She was a busy woman, with other aims and activities than those of working among the masses; Miss Lydia had heard her present talk, fancied it, and thought it would be the very thing for the Uplift Club.

For thirty minutes Johnnie sat concentrating desperately on every sentence that fell from the lips of the lady from London, trying harder to understand than she had ever tried to do anything in her life. She put all her quick, young mind and avid soul into the struggle to receive, though piercingly aware every instant of the difference between her attire and that of the women who had bidden her there, noting acutely variations between their language and hers, their voices, their gestures and hers. These were the women of Gray Stoddard's world. Such were his feminine associates; here, then, must be her models.

Mandy and her likes got from the talk perhaps nothing at all, except that rich people might have what they liked if they wanted it — that at least was Miss Meacham's summing up of the matter when she went home that night.   But to Johnnie some of the sentences remained.

"You struggle and climb and strive," said Mrs. Archbold earnestly, "when, if you only knew it, you have wings. And what are the wings of the soul? The wings of the soul are aspiration. Oh, that we would spread them and fly to the heights our longing eyes behold, the heights we dream of when we cannot see them, the heights we foolishly and mistakenly expect to climb some day."

Again Johnnie saw herself coming down the ridge at Shade's side; descending into the shadow, stepping closer to the droning mills; while above her the Palace of Pleasure swam in its golden glory, and these who were privileged to do so went out and in and laughed and were happy. Were such heights as that what this woman meant? Johnnie had let it typify to her the heights to which she intended to climb. Was it indeed possible to fly to them instead? The talk ended. She sat so long with bent head that Miss Sessions finally came round and took the unoccupied chair beside her.

"Are you thinking it over, John?" she inquired with that odd little note of hostility which she could never quite keep out of her voice when she addressed this girl.

"Yes'm," replied Johnnie meekly.

Several who were talking together in the vicinity relinquished their conversation to listen to the two. Mrs. Hexter shot one of her quaint, crooked smiles at the lady from London and, with a silent gesture, bade her hearken.

"I think these things are most important for you girls who have to earn your daily bread," Miss Sessions condescended.

"Daily bread," echoed Johnnie softly. She loved fine phrases as she loved fine clothes. "I know where that comes from. It's in the prayer about 'daily bread,' and 'the kingdom and the power and the glory.' Don't you think those are beautiful words, Miss Lydia — the 'power and the glory'?"

Miss Sessions's lips sucked in with that singular, half-reluctant expression of condemnation which was becoming fairly familiar to Johnnie.

"Oh, John!" she said reprovingly, 'Daily bread' is all we have anything to do with. Don't you remember that it says 'Thine be the kingdom and the power and the glory'? Thine, John — Thine."

"Yes'm," returned Johnnie submissively. But it was in her heart that certain upon this earth had their share of kingdoms and powers and the glories. And, although she uttered that submissive "Yes'm," her high-couraged young heart registered a vow to achieve its own slice of these things as well as of daily bread.

"Didn't you enjoy Mrs. Archbold's talk? I thought it very fine," Miss Sessions pursued.

"It sure was that," sighed Johnnie. "I don't know as I understand it all — every word. I tried to, but maybe I got some of it wrong."

"What is it you don't understand, John?" inquired

Miss Lydia patronizingly. "Ask me. I'll explain anything you care to know about."

Johnnie turned to her, too desperately in earnest to note the other listeners to the conversation.

"Why, that about stretching out the wings of your spirit and flying. Do you believe that?"

"I certainly do," Miss Sessions said brightly, as delighted at Johnnie's remembering part of the visitor's words as a small boy when he has taught his terrier to walk on its hind legs.

"Then if a body wants a thing bad enough, and keeps on a-wanting it — Oh, just awful — is that aspiration? Will the thing you want that-a-way come to pass?"

"We-e-ell," Miss Sessions deemed it necessary to qualify her statement to this fiery and exact young questioner. "You have to want the right thing, of course, John. You have to want the right thing."

"Yes'm," agreed Johnnie heartily. "And I'd 'low it was certainly the right thing, if it was what good folks — like you — want."

Miss Sessions flushed, yet she looked pleased, aware, if Johnnie was not, of the number of listeners. Here was her work of Uplift among the mill girls being justified.

"I — Oh, really, I couldn't set myself up as a pattern," she said modestly.

"But you are," Johnnie assured her warmly. "There ain't anybody in this room I'd rather go by as by you." The fine gray eyes had been travelling from neck to belt, from shoulder to wrist of the lady who was enlightening her. "I think I never in all my life seen anything more sightly than that dress-body you're a-wearin'," she murmured softly. "Where — how might a person come by· such a one? If you thought that my wishing and — aspiring — would ever bring me such as that, I'd sure try."

There rose a titter about the two. It spread and swelled till the whole assembly was in a gale of laughter. Miss Sessions's becoming blush deepened to the tint of angry mortification. She looked about and assumed the air of a schoolmistress with a room full of noisy pupils; but Johnnie, her cheeks pink too, first swept them all with an astonished gaze which flung the long lashes up in such a wide curve of innocence as made her eyes bewitching, then joined it, and laughed as loud as any of them at she knew not what. It was the one touch to put her with the majority, and leave her mentor stranded in a bleak minority. Miss Sessions objected to the position.

"Oh, John!" she said severely, so soon as she could be heard above the giggles. "How you have misunderstood me, and Mrs. Archbold, and all we intended to bring to you! What is a mere blouse like this to the uplift, the outlook, the development we were striving to offer? I confess I am deeply disappointed in you."

This sobered Johnnie, instantly.

"I'm sorry," she said, bending forward to lay a wistful, penitent hand on that of Miss Sessions. "I'll try to understand better. I reckon I'm right dumb, and you'll have to have a lot of patience with me.   I don't rightly know what to aspire after."

The amende was so sweetly made that even Lydia Sessions, still exceedingly employed at being pictorially chagrined over the depravity of her neophyte, could but be appeased.

"I'll try to furnish you more suitable objects for your ambition," she murmured virtuously.

But the lady with the gray hair and the odd little twist to her smile now leaned forward and took a hand in the conversation.

"See here, Lydia," Mrs. Hexter remonstrated in crisp tones, "what's the matter with the girl's aspiring after a blouse like yours? You took a lot of trouble and spent a lot of money to get that one. I noticed you were careful to tell me it was imported, because I couldn't see the neck-band and find out that detail for myself. That blouse is a dream — it's a dream. If it's good enough aspiration for you or me, why not for this girl?"

"Oh, but Mrs. Hexter," murmured the mortified Miss Sessions, glancing uneasily toward the mill-girl contingent which was listening eagerly, and then at the speaker of the day, "I am sure Mrs. Archbold will agree with me that it would be a gross, material idea to aspire after blouses and such-like, when the poor child needs — er — other things so much more."

"Yes'm, I do that," conceded Johnnie dutifully, those changeful eyes of hers full of pensive, denied de-

sire, as they swept the dainty gowns of the women before her. "I do — you're right. I wouldn't think of
spending my money for a dress-body like that when
I'm mighty near as barefoot as a rabbit this minute,
and the little 'uns back home has to have every cent
I can save. I just thought that if beautiful wishes
was ever really coming true — if it was right and
proper for a person to have beautiful wishes — I'd
like ——"

Her voice faltered into discouraged silence. Tears
gathered and hung thick on her lashes. Miss Sessions
sent a beseeching look toward the lady from London.
Mrs. Archbold stepped accommodatingly into the
breach.

"All aspiration is good," she said gently. "I
shouldn't be discouraged because it took a rather
concrete form."

Johnnie's eyes were upon her face, trying to understand. A "concrete form" she imagined might allude
to the fact that Miss Sessions had a better figure than
she.

Mrs. Hexter, glad of an ally, tossed that incorrigible
gray head of hers and dashed into the conversation
once more.

"If I were you, Johnnie, I'd just aspire as hard as
I could in that direction," she said recklessly, her
mischievous glance upon the flowing lines of Johnnie's
young shoulders and throat. "A blouse like that would
be awfully fetching on you. You'd look lovely in it.
Why shouldn't you aspire to it? Maybe you'll have

one just as pretty before the style changes. I am sure you're nice enough, and good-looking enough, for the best in the way of purple and fine linen to come to you by the law of attraction — don't you believe in the law of attraction, Mrs. Archbold?"

Lydia Sessions got up and moved away in shocked silence. Mrs. Hexter was a good deal of a thorn in her flesh, and she only tolerated her because of Mr. Hexter and his position. After the retreating and disaffected hostess came Mrs. Archbold's voice, with a thread of laughter in it.

"I believe in the law of such attraction as this girl has," she said kindly. "What is it your Walt Whitman says about the fluid and attaching character? That all hearts yearn toward it, that old and young must give it love. That is, my dear," turning explainingly to Johnnie, "the character which gives much love, takes much interest in those about it, makes itself one with other people and their affairs — do you get my meaning?"

"I think I understand," half whispered Johnnie, glowing eyes on the face of the speaker. "Do you mean that I am anything like that? I do love everybody — most. But how could I help it, when everybody is so good and kind to me?"

The glances of the older women met across the bright head.

"She won't have much use for feet to climb with," Mrs. Hexter summed it up, taking her figure from the talk earlier in the afternoon. "She's got wings."

And puzzled Johnnie could only smile from one to the other.

"Wings!" whispered Mandy Meacham to herself. Mandy was not only restricted to the use of spiritual feet; she was lame in the soul as well, poor creature, "Wings — air they callin' her a angel?"

CHAPTER IX

A BIT OF METAL

IN THE valleys of Tennessee, spring has a trick of dropping down on the world like a steaming wet blanket. The season that Johnnie Consadine went to work in the mills at Cottonville, May came in with warm rains. Stifling nights followed sultry, drenching days, till vegetation everywhere sprouted unwholesomely and the mountain slopes had almost the reek of tropic jungles.

Yet the girl performed the labours of a factory weaver with almost passionate enthusiasm and devotion. Always and always she was looking beyond the mere present moment. If tending loom was the road which led to the power and the glory, what need to complain that it — the mere road — was but dull earth ?

She tried conscientiously, to do and be exactly what Lydia Sessions seemed to want. Gray Stoddard's occasional spoken word, or the more lengthy written messages he had taken to putting in the books he sent her, seemed to demand of her nothing, but always inspired to much. For all his disposition to keep hands off the personal development of his friends, perhaps on account of it, Gray made an excellent teacher, and these writings — the garnered grain, the gist, of his own wide culture — were the very sinews for the race Johnnie was setting out on. She began to intelligently guard her speech, her manner, her very thoughts, conforming them to what she knew of his ideals. Miss Session's striving to build up an imitation lady on the sincere foundation Johnnie offered appealed less to the girl, and had therefore less effect; but she immediately responded to Stoddard's methods, tucking in to the books she returned written queries or records of perplexity, which gradually expanded into notes, expressions of her own awakened thought, and even fancies, which held from the first a quaint charm and individuality.

The long, hot days at the foot of the hills did seem to the mountain-bred creature interminable and stifling. Perspiration dripped from white faces as the operatives stood listlessly at their looms, or the children straggled back and forth in the narrow lanes between the frames, tending the endlessly turning spools.

The Hardwick Mill had both spinning and weaving departments. Administrative ability is as much a native gift as the poet's voice or the actor's grace, and the managers of any large business are always on the lookout for it. Before Johnnie Consadine had been two months in the factory she was given charge of a spinning room. But the dignity of the new position — even the increase of pay — had a cloud upon it. She was beginning to understand the enmity there is between the soulless factory and the human tide that feeds its life. She knew now that the tasks of the little spinners, which seemed less than child's play, were deadly in their monotony, their long indoor hours, and the vibrant clamour amid which they were performed. Her own vigorous young frame resisted valiantly; yet the Saturday half-holiday, the Sunday of rest, could scarcely renew her for the exorbitant hours of mechanical toil.

As she left the mill those sultry evenings, with the heat mists still tremulous over the valley and heat lightnings bickering in the west, she went with a lagging step up the village street, not looking, as had been her wont, first toward the far blue mountains, and then at the glorious state of the big valley. The houses of the operatives were set up haphazard and the village was denied all beauty. Most of the yards were unfenced, and here and there a row of shanties would be crowded so close together that speech in one could be heard in the other.

"And then if any ketchin' disease does break out, like the diptchery did last year," Mavity Bence said one evening as she walked home with Johnnie, "hit's sartin shore to go through 'em like it would go through a family."

Johnnie looked curiously at the dirty yards with their débris of lard buckets and tin cans. Space — air, earth and sky — was cheap and plentiful in the mountains. It seemed strange to be sparing of it, down here where people were so rich.

"What makes 'em build so close, Aunt Mavity?" she asked.

"Hit's the Company," returned Mrs. Bence lifelessly. "They don't want to spend any more than they have to for land. Besides they want everything to be nigh to the mill. Lord — hit don't make no differ. Only when a fire starts in a row of 'em hit cleans up the Company's property same as it does the plunder of the folks that lives in 'em. You just got to be thankful if there don't chance to be one or more baby children locked up in the houses and burned along with the other stuff. I've knowed that to happen more than oncet."

Johnnie's face whitened.

"Miss Lydia says she's going to persuade her brother-in-law to furnish a kindergarten and a day nursery for the Hardwick Mill," she offered hastily. "They have one at some other mill down in Georgia, and she says it's fine the way they take care of the children while the mothers are at work in the factory."

"Uh-uh," put in Mandy Meacham slowly, speaking over the shoulders of the two, "but I'd a heap ruther take care of my own child — ef I had one. An' ef the mills can afford to pay for it the one way, they can afford to pay for it t'other way. Miss Liddy's schemes is all for the showin' off of the swells and the rich folks. I reckon that, with her, hit'll end in talk, anyhow — hit always does."

"Aunt Mavity," pursued Johnnie timidly, "do you reckon the water's unhealthy down here in Cottonville? Looks like all the children in the mill have the same white, puny look. I thought maybe the water didn't agree with them."

Mavity Bence laughed out mirthlessly. "The water!" she echoed in a tone of amused contempt. "Johnnie, you're mighty smart about some things; cain't you see that a cotton mill is bound to either kill or cripple a child? Them that don't die, sort o' drags along and grows up to be mis'able, undersized, sickly somebodies. Hit's true the Hardwick Mill won't run night turn; hit's true they show mo' good will about hirin' older children; but if you can make a cotton mill healthy for young-uns, you can do more than God A'mighty." She wiped her eyes furtively.

"Lou was well growed before ever she went in the mill. I know in reason hit never hurt her. I mean these here mammies that I see puttin' little tricks to work that ort to be runnin' out o' doors gettin' their strength and growth — well, po' souls, I reckon they don't know no better, God forgive 'em!"

"But if they got sick or anything, there's always the hospital," Johnnie spoke up hopefully, as they passed the clean white building standing high on its green slope.

"The hospital!" echoed Mandy, with a half-terrified glance over her shoulder. "Yes, ef you want to be shipped out of town in a box for the student doctors to cut up, I reckon the hospital is a good place. It's just like everything else the rich swells does — it's for their profit, not for our'n. They was a lot of big talk when they built that thar hospital, and every one of us was axed to give something for beds and such. We was told that if we got hurt in the mill we could go thar free, and if we fell sick they'd doctor us for little or nothin'. They can afford it — considerin' the prices they git for dead bodies, I reckon."

"Now, Mandy, you don't believe any such as that," remonstrated Johnnie, with a half-smile.

"Believe it — I know it to be true!" Mandy stuck to her point stubbornly. "Thar was Lura Dawson; her folks was comin' down to git the body and bury hit, and when they got here the hospital folks couldn't tell 'em whar to look — no, they couldn't. Atlas Dawson 'lows he'll git even with 'em if it takes him the rest of his natural life. His wife was a Bushares and her whole tribe is out agin the hospital folks and the mill folks down here. I reckon you live too far up in the mountains to hear the talk, but some of these swells had better look out."

As the long, hot days followed each other, Johnnie noticed how Mandy failed. Her hand was forever at her side, where she had a stitch-like pain, that she called "a jumpin' misery." Even broad, seasoned Mavity Bence grew pallid and gaunt. Only Pap Himes thrived. His trouble was rheumatism, and the hot days were his best. Of evenings he would sit on the porch in his broad, rush-bottomed chair, the big yellow cat on his knees, and smoke his pipe and, if he cared to do so, banter unkindly with the girls on the steps. Early in the season as it was, the upstairs rooms were terribly hot; and sometimes the poor creatures sat or lay on the porch till well past midnight. Across the gulch were songs and the strumming of banjos or guitars, where the young fellows at the inn waked late.

The rich people on top of the hill were beginning to make their preparations to flit to the seashore or mountains. Lydia Sessions left for two weeks, promising to return in June, and the Uplift work drooped, neglected. There seems to be an understanding that people do not need uplifting so much during hot weather. Gray Stoddard was faithful in the matter of books. He carried them to Lydia Sessions and discussed with that young lady a complete course of reading for Johnnie. Lydia was in the position of one taking bad medicine for good results. She could not but delight in any enterprise which brought Stoddard intimately to her, yet the discussion of Johnnie Consadine, the admiration he expressed for the girl's character and work, were as so much quinine.

Johnnie herself was dumb and abashed, now, in his presence. She sought vainly for the poise and composure which were her natural birthright in most of the situations of life. Yet her perturbation was not that of distress. The sight of him, the sound of his voice, even if he were not saying good morning to her, would cheer her heart for one whole, long, hot day: and if he spoke to her, if he looked at her, nothing could touch her with sadness for hours afterward. She asked no questions why this was so; she met it with a sort of desperate bravery, accepting the joy, refusing to see the sorrow there might be in it. And she robbed herself of necessary sleep to read Stoddard's books, to study them, to wring from them the last precious crumb of help or information that they might have for her. The mountain dweller is a mental creature. An environment which builds lean, vigorous bodies, is apt to nourish keen, alert minds. Johnnie crowded into her few months of night reading a world of ripening culture.

Ever since the Sunday morning of the automobile ride, Shade Buckheath had been making elaborate pretense of having forgotten that such a person as Johnnie Consadine existed. If he saw her approaching, he turned his back; and when forced to recognize her, barely growled some unintelligible greeting. Then one evening she came suddenly into the machine room. She walked slowly down the long aisle between pieces of whirring machinery, carrying all eyes with her. It was an offence to Buckheath to note how the other young fellows turned from their tasks to look after her. She had no business down here where the men were. That was just like a fool girl, always running after ——. She paused at his bench.

"Shade," she said, bending close so that he might hear the words, "I got leave to come in and ask you to make me a thing like this — see?" showing a pattern for a peculiarly slotted strip of metal.

Buckheath returned to the surly indifference of demeanour which was natural to him. Yet he smiled covertly as he examined the drawing she had made of the thing she wanted. He divined in this movement of Johnnie's but an attempt to approach himself, and, as she explained with some particularity, he paid more attention to the girl than to her words.

"I want a big enough hole here to put a bolt through," she repeated. "Shade — do you understand? You're not listening to one word I say."

Buckheath turned and grinned broadly at her.

"What's the use of this foolishness, Johnnie?" he inquired, clinking the strips of metal between his fingers. "Looks like you and me could find a chance to visit without going to so much trouble."

Johnnie opened her gray eyes wide and stared at him.

"Foolishness!" she echoed. "Mr. Stoddard didn't call it foolishness when I named it to him. He said I was to have anything I wanted made, and that one of the loom-fixers could attend to it."

"Mr. Stoddard — what's he got to do with it?" demanded Shade.

"He hasn't anything; but that I spoke to him about it, and he told me to try any plan I wanted to."

"Well, the less you talk to the bosses — a girl like you, working here in the mill — the better name you'll bear," Shade told her, twisting the drawing in his hands and regarding her from under lowered brows.

"Don't tear that," cautioned Johnnie impatiently. "I have to speak to some of the people in authority sometimes — the same as you do. What's the matter with you, Shade Buckheath?"

"There's nothing the matter with me," Buckheath declared wagging his head portentously, and avoiding her eye. Then the wrath, the sense of personal injury, which had been simmering in him ever since he saw her sitting beside Stoddard in the young mill owner's car, broke forth. "When I see a girl riding in an automobile with one of these young bosses," he growled, close to her ear, "I know what to think — and so does everybody else."

It was out. He had said it at last. He stared at her fiercely. The red dyed her face and neck at his words and look. For a desperate moment she took counsel with herself. Then she lifted her head and looked squarely in Buckheath's face.

"Oh, *that's* what has been the matter with you all this time, is it?" she inquired. "Well, I'm glad you spoke and relieved your mind." Then she went on evenly, "Mr. Stoddard had been up in the mountains that Sunday to get a flower that he wanted, like the one you stepped on and broke the day I came down. I was up there and showed him where the things grow. Then it rained, and he brought me down in his car. That's all there was to it."

"Mighty poor excuse," grunted Shade, turning his shoulder to her.

"It's not an excuse at all," said Johnnie. "You have no right to ask excuses for what I do — or explanations, either, for that matter. I've told you the truth about it because we were old friends and you named it to me; but I'm sorry now that I spoke at all. Give me that drawing and those patterns back. Some of the other loom-fixers can make what I want."

"You get mad quick, don't you?" Buckheath asked, turning to her with a half-taunting, half-relenting smile on his face. "Red-headed people always do."

"No, I'm not mad," Johnnie told him, as she had told him long ago. "But I'll thank you not to name Mr. Stoddard to me again. If I haven't the right to speak to anybody I need to, why it certainly isn't your place to tell me of it."

"Go 'long," said Buckheath, surlily; "I'll fix 'em for you." And without another word the girl left him.

After Johnnie was gone, Buckheath chewed for some time the bitter cud of chagrin. He was wholly mistaken, then, in the object of her visit to the mechanical department? Yet he was a cool-headed fellow, always alert for that which might bring him gain. Pushing, aspiring, he subscribed for and faithfully studied a mechanics' journal which continually urged upon its readers the profit of patenting small improvements on machinery already in use. Indeed everybody, these days, in the factories, is on the lookout for patentable improvements. Why might not Johnnie have stumbled on to something worth while? That Passmore and Consadine tribe were all smart fools. He made the slotted strips she wanted, and delivered them to her the next day with civil words. When, after she had them in use on the spinning jennies upstairs for a week, she came down bringing them for certain minute alterations, his attitude was one of friendly help-fulness.

"You say you use 'em on the frames? What for? How do they work?" he asked her, examining the little contrivance lingeringly.

"They're working pretty well," she told him, "even the way they are — a good deal too long, and with that slot not cut deep enough, I'm right proud of myself when I look at them. Any boy or girl tending a frame can go to the end of it and see if anything's the matter without walking plumb down. When you get them fixed the way I want them, I tell you they'll be fine."

The next afternoon saw Shade Buckheath in the spooling room, watching the operation of Johnnie Consadine's simple device for notifying the frame-tender if a thread fouled or broke.

"Let me take 'em all down to the basement," he said finally when he had studied them from every point of view for fifteen minutes. "They ain't as well polished as I'd like to have 'em and I think they might be a little longer in the shank. There ought to be a ring of babbit metal around that slot, too — I reckon I could get it in Watauga. If you'll let me take 'em now, I'll fix 'em up for you soon as I can, so that they'll do fine."

Johnnie remonstrated, half-heartedly, as he gathered the crude little invention from the frames; but his proposition wore a plausible face, and she suffered him to take them.

"They ain't but five here," he said to her sharply.

"I know I made you six. Where's the other one?"
He looked so startled, he spoke so anxiously, that she
laughed.

"I think that must be the one I carried home," she
said carelessly. "I had a file, and was trying to fix
it myself one evening, and I reckon I never brought
it back."

"Johnnie," said Shade, coming close, and speaking
in a low confidential tone that was almost affectionate,
"if I was you I wouldn't name this business to anybody.
Wait till we get it all fixed right," he pursued, as he
saw the rising wonder in her face. "No need to tell
every feller all you know — so he'll be jest as smart
as you are. Ain't that so? And you git me that
other strip. I don't want it layin' round for somebody
to get hold of and — you find me that other strip.
Hunt it up, won't you?"

"Well, you sure talk curious to-day!" Johnnie told
him. "I don't see anything to be ashamed of in my
loving to fool with machinery, if I *am* a girl. But
I'll get you the strip, if I can find it. I'm mighty
proud of being a room boss, and I aim to make my
room the best one in the mill. Shade, did you know
that I get eight dollars a week? I've been sending
money home to mother, and I've got a room to myself
down at Pap Himes's. And Mr. Sessions says they'll
raise me again soon. I wanted 'em to see this thing
working well."

"Look here!" broke in Shade swiftly; "don't you
say anything to the bosses about this" — he shook

the strips in his hand — "not till I've had a chance to talk to you again. You know I'm your friend, don't you Johnnie?"

"I reckon so," returned truthful Johnnie, with unflattering moderation. "You get me those things done as quick as you can, please, Shade."

After this the matter dropped. Two or three times Johnnie reminded Shade of his promise to bring the little strips back, and always he had an excuse ready for her: he had been very busy — the metal he wanted was out of stock — he would fix them for her just as soon as he could. With every interview his manner toward herself grew kinder — more distinctly that of a lover.

The loom-fixers and mechanics, belonging, be it remembered, to a trades-union, were out of all the mills by five o'clock. It was a significant point for any student of economic conditions to note these strapping young males sitting at ease upon the porches of their homes or boarding houses, when the sweating, fagged women weavers and childish spinners trooped across the bridges an hour after. Johnnie was surprised, therefore, one evening, nearly two weeks later, to find Shade waiting for her at the door of the mill.

"I wish't you'd walk a piece up the Gap road with me, I want to have speech with you," the young fellow told her.

"I can't go far; I 'most always try to be home in time to help Aunt Mavity put supper on the table, or anyway to wash up the dishes for her," the girl replied to him.

"All right," agreed Buckheath briefly. "Wait here a minute and let me get some things I want to take along."

He stopped at a little shed back of the offices, sometimes called the garage because Stoddard's car stood in it. Johnnie dropped down on a box at the door and the young fellow went inside and began searching the pockets of a coat hanging on a peg. He spoke over his shoulder to her.

"What's the matter with you here lately since you got your raise? 'Pears like you won't look at a body."

"Haven't I seemed friendly?" Johnnie returned, with a deprecating smile. "I reckon I'm just tired. Seems like I'm tired every minute of the day — and I couldn't tell you why. I sure don't have anything hard to do. I think sometimes I need the good hard work I used to have back in the mountains to get rested on."

She laughed up at him, and Buckheath's emotional nature answered with a dull anger, which was his only reply to her attraction.

"I was going to invite you to go to a dance in at Watauga, Saturday night," he said sullenly; "but I reckon if you're tired all the time, you don't want to go."

He had hoped and expected that she would say she was not too tired to go anywhere that he wished her to. His disappointment was disproportionate when she sighingly agreed:

"Yes, I reckon I hadn't better go to any dances. I wouldn't for the world break down at my work, when I've just begun to earn so much, and am sending money home to mother."

Inside the offices Lydia Sessions stood near her brother's desk. She had gone down, as she sometimes did, to take him home in the carriage.

"Oh, here you are, Miss Sessions," said Gray Stoddard coming in. "I've brought those books for Johnnie. There are a lot of them here for her to make selection from. As you are driving, perhaps you wouldn't mind letting me set them in the carriage, then I won't go up past your house."

Miss Sessions glanced uneasily at the volumes he carried.

"Do you think it's wise to give an ignorant, untrained girl like that the choice of her own reading?" she said at length.

Stoddard laughed.

"It's as far as my wisdom goes," he replied promptly. "I would as soon think of getting up a form of prayer for a fellow creature as laying out a course of reading for him."

"Well, then," suggested Miss Sessions, "why not let her take up a Chatauqua course? I'm sure many of them are excellent. She would be properly guided, and — and encroach less on your time."

"My time!" echoed Stoddard. "Never mind that feature. I'm immensely interested. It's fascina-

ting to watch the development of so fine a mind which
has lain almost entirely fallow to the culture of schools.
I quite enjoy looking out a bunch of books for her, and
watching to see which one will most appeal to her.
Her instinct has proved wholly trustworthy so far.
Indeed, if it didn't seem exaggerated, I should say her
taste was faultless."

Miss Sessions flushed and set her lips together.

"Faultless," she repeated, with an attempt at a
smile. "I fancy Johnnie finds out what you admire
most, and makes favourites of your favourites."

Stoddard looked a bit blank for an instant. Then,

"Well — perhaps — she does," he allowed, hesitatingly. His usual tolerant smile held a hint of indul-
gent tenderness, and there was a vibration in his voice
which struck to Lydia Sessions's heart like a knife.

"No, you are mistaken," he added after a moment's
reflection. "You don't realize how little I've talked
to the child about books — or anything else, for that
matter. It does chance that her taste is mine in very
many cases; but you underrate our protégé when you
speak of her as ignorant and uncultured. She knows
a good deal more about some things than either of us.
It is her fund of nature lore that makes Thoreau and
White of Selborne appeal to her. Now I love them
because I know so little about what they write of."

Lydia Sessions instantly fastened upon the one point.
She protested almost anxiously.

"But surely you would not call her cultured — a
factory girl who has lived in a hut in the mountains all

her life? She is trying hard, I admit; but her speech is — well, it certainly is rather uncivilized."

Stoddard looked as though he might debate that matter a bit. Then he questioned, instead:

"Did you ever get a letter from her? She doesn't carry her quaint little archaisms of pronunciation and wording into her writing. Her letters are delicious."

Miss Sessions turned hastily to the window and looked out, apparently to observe whether her brother was ready to leave or not. Johnnie Consadine's letters — her letters. What — when — ? Of course she could not baldly question him in such a matter; and the simple explanation of a little note of thanks with a returned book, or the leaf which reported impressions from its reading tucked in between the pages occurred to her perturbed mind.

"You quite astonish me," she said finally. "Well — that *is* good hearing. Mr. Stoddard," with sudden decision, "don't you believe that it would be well worth while, in view of all this, to raise the money and send John Consadine away to a good school? There are several fine ones in New England where she might partially work her way; and really, from what you say, it seems to me she's worthy of such a chance."

Stoddard glanced at her in surprise.

"Why, Miss Sessions, doesn't this look like going squarely back on your most cherished theories? If it's only to bestow a little money, and send her away to some half-charity school, what becomes of your argument that people who have had advantages should give of themselves and their comradeship to those they wish to help?" There was a boyish eagerness in his manner; his changeful gray-brown eyes were alight; he came close and laid a hand on her arm — quite an unusual demonstration with Gray Stoddard. "You mustn't discourage me," he said winningly. "I'm such a hopeful disciple. I've never enjoyed anything more in my life than this enterprise you and I have undertaken together, providing the right food for so bright and so responsive a mind."

Miss Lydia looked at him in a sort of despair.

"Yes — oh, yes. I quite understand that," she agreed almost mechanically. "I don't mean to go back on my principles. But what John needs is a good, sound education from the beginning. Don't you think so?"

"No," said Stoddard promptly. "Indeed I do not. Development must come from within. To give it a chance — to lend it stimulus — that's all a friend can do. A ready-made education plastered on the outside cultivates nobody. Moreover, Johnnie is in no crying need of mere schooling. You don't seem to know how well provided she has been in that respect. But the thing that settles the matter is that she would not accept any such charitable arrangement. Unless you're tired of our present method, I vote to continue it."

Lydia Sessions had been for some moments watching Johnnie Consadine who sat on her box at the door of the little garage. She had refrained from mentioning this fact to her companion; but now Shade Buckheath stepped out to join Johnnie, and instantly Lydia turned and motioned Stoddard to her.

"Look there," she whispered. "Don't they make a perfect couple? You and I may do what we choose about cultivating the girl's mind — she'll marry a man of her own class, and there it will end."

"Why should you say that?" asked Stoddard abruptly. "Those two do not belong to the same class. They ——"

"Oh, Mr. Stoddard! They grew up side by side; they went to school together, and I imagine were sweethearts long before they came to Cottonville."

"Do you think that makes them of the same class?" asked Stoddard impatiently. "I should say the presumption was still greater the other way. I was not alluding to social classes."

"You're so odd," murmured Lydia Sessions. "These mountaineers are all alike."

The village road was a smother of white dust; the weeds beside it drooped powdered heads; evil odours reeked through the little place; but when Shade and Johnnie had passed its confines, the air from the mountains greeted them sweetly; the dusty white road gave place to springy leaf-mould, mixed with tiny, sharp stones. A young moon rode low in the west. The tank-a-tank of cowbells sounded from homing animals. Up in the dusky Gap, whip-poor-wills were beginning to call.

"I'm glad I came," said Johnnie, pushing the hair

off her hot forehead. She was speaking to herself, aware that Buckheath paid little attention, but walked in silence a step ahead, twisting a little branch of sassafras in his fingers. The spicy odour of the bark was afterward associated in Johnnie's mind with what he had then to say.

"Johnnie," he began, facing around and barring her way, when they were finally alone together between the trees, "do you remember the last time you and me was on this piece of road here—do you?"

He had intended to remind her of the evening she came to Cottonville: but instead, recollection built for her once more the picture of that slope bathed in Sabbath sunshine. There was the fork where the Hardwick carriage had turned off; to this side went Shade and his fellows, with Mandy and the girls following; and down the middle of the road she herself came, seated in the car beside Stoddard.

For a moment memory choked and blinded Johnnie. She could neither see the path before them, nor find the voice to answer her questioner. The bleak pathos of her situation came home to her, and tears of rare self-pity filled her eyes. Why was it a disgrace that Stoddard should treat her kindly? Why must she be ashamed of her feeling for him? Shade's voice broke in harshly.

"Do you remember? You ain't forgot, have you? Ever since that time I've intended to speak to you — to tell you ——"

"Well, you needn't do it," she interrupted him passionately. "I won't hear a word against Mr. Stoddard, if that's what you're aiming at."

Buckheath fell back a pace and stared with angry eyes.

"Stoddard — Gray Stoddard?" he repeated. "What's a swell like that got to do with you and me, Johnnie Consadine? You want to let Gray Stoddard and his kind alone — yes, and make them let you alone, if you and me are going to marry."

It was Johnnie's turn to stare.

"If we're going to marry!" she echoed blankly — "going to marry!" The girl had had her lovers. Despite hard work and the stigma of belonging to the borrowing Passmore family, Johnnie had commanded the homage of more than one heart. She was not without a healthy young woman's relish for this sort of admiration; but Shade Buckheath's proposal came with so little grace, in such almost sinister form, that she scarcely recognized it.

"Yes, if we're going to wed," reiterated Buckheath sullenly. "I'm willin' to have you."

Johnnie's tense, almost tragic manner relaxed. She laughed suddenly.

"I didn't know you was joking, Shade," she said good-humouredly. "I took you to be in earnest. You'll have to excuse me."

"I am in earnest," Buckheath told her, almost fiercely. "I reckon I'm a fool; but I want you. Any day" — he spoke with a curious, half-savage reluctance — "any day you'll say the word, I'll take you."

His eyes, like his voice, were resentful, yet eager. He took off his hat and wiped the perspiration from his brow, looking away from her now, toward the road by which they had climbed.

Johnnie regarded him through her thick eyelashes, the smile still lingering bright in her eyes. After all, it was only a rather unusual kind of sweethearting, and not a case of it to touch her feelings.

"I'm mighty sorry," she said soberly, "but I ain't aimin' to wed any man, fixed like I am. Mother and the children have to be looked after, and I can't ask a man to do for 'em, so I have it to do myself."

"Of course I can't take your mother and the children," Buckheath objected querulously, as though she had asked him to do so. "But you I'll take; and you'd do well to think it over. You won't get such a chance soon again, and I'm apt to change my mind if you put on airs with me this way."

Johnnie shook her head.

"I know it's a fine chance, Shade," she said in the kindest tone, "but I'm hoping you will change your mind, and that soon; for it's just like I tell you."

She turned with evident intention of going back and terminating their interview. Buckheath stepped beside her in helpless fury. He knew she would have other opportunities, and better. He was aware how futile was this threat of withdrawing his proposition. Hot, tired, angry, the dust of the way prickling on his face and neck, he was persistently conscious of a letter in the pocket of his striped shirt, over his heavily beating heart, warm and moist like the shirt itself, with the sweat of his body. Good Lord! That letter which had come from Washington this morning informing him that the device this girl had invented was patentable, filled her hands with gold. It was necessary that he should have control of her, and at once. He put from him the knowledge of how her charm wrought upon him — bound him the faster every time he spoke to her. Cold, calculating, sluggishly selfish, he had not reckoned with her radiant personality, nor had the instinct to know that, approached closely, it must inevitably light in him unwelcome and inextinguishable fires.

"Johnnie," he said finally, "you ain't saying no to me, are you? You take time to think it over — but not so very long — I'll name it to you again."

"Please don't, Shade," remonstrated the girl, walking on fast, despite the oppressive heat of the evening. "I wish you wouldn't speak of it to me any more; and I can't go walking with you this way. I have obliged to help Aunt Mavity; and every minute of time I get from that, and my work, I'm putting in on my books and reading."

She stepped ahead of him now, and Buckheath regarded her back with sullen, sombre eyes. What was he to do? How come nearer her when she thus held herself aloof?

"Johnnie Consadine!" The girl checked her steps a bit at a new sound in his voice. "I'll tell you just one

thing, and you'd better never forget it, neither.   I ain't
no fool.   I know mighty well an' good your reason for
treating me this-a-way.   Your reason's got a name.
Hit's called Mr. Gray Stoddard.   You behave yo'self
an' listen to reason, or I'll get even with him for it.
Damn him — I'll fix him!"

CHAPTER X

THE SANDALS OF JOY

"COME in here, Johnnie," Mavity Bence called one day, as Johnnie was passing a strange little cluttered cubbyhole under the garret stairs and out over the roof of the lean-to kitchen. It was a hybrid apartment, between a large closet and a small room; one four-paned window gave scant light and ventilation; all the broken or disused plunder about the house was pitched into it, and in the middle sat a tumbled bed. It was the woman's sleeping place and her dead daughter had shared it with her during her lifetime. Johnnie stopped at the door with a hand on each side of its frame.

"Reddin' up things, Aunt Mavity?" she asked, adding, "If I had time I'd come in and help you."

"I was just puttin' away what I've got left that belonged to Lou," said the woman, sitting suddenly down on the bed and gazing up into the bright face above her with a sort of appeal. Johnnie noticed then that Mrs. Bence had a pair of cheap slippers in her lap. It came back vividly to the girl how the newspapers had said that Louvania Bence had taken off her slippers and left them on the bridge, that she might climb the netting more easily to throw herself into the water. The mother stared down at these, dry-eyed.

"She never had 'em on but the once," Mavity Bence breathed. "And I — and I r'ared out on her for buyin' of 'em. I said that with Pap so old and all, we hadn't money to spend for slippers. Lord God!" — she shivered — "We had to find money for the undertaker, when he come to lay her out."

She turned to Johnnie feverishly, like a thing that writhes on the rack and seeks an easier position.

"I had the best for her then — I jest would do it — there was white shoes and stockin's, and a reg'lar shroud like they make at Watauga; we never put a stitch on her that she'd wore — hit was all new-bought. For once I said my say to Pap, and made him take money out of the bank to do it. He's got some in thar for to bury all of us — he says — but he never wanted to use any of it for Lou."

Johnnie came in and sat down on the bed beside her hostess. She laid a loving hand over Mavity's that held the slippers.

"What pretty little feet she must have had," she said softly.

"Didn't she?" echoed the mother, with a tremulous half-smile. "I couldn't more'n get these here on my hand, but they was a loose fit for her. They're as good as new. Johnnie, ef you ever get a invite to a dance I'll lend 'em to you. Hit'd pleasure me to think some gal's feet was dancin' in them thar slippers. Lou, she never learned to dance — looked like she could never find time." Louvania, be it remembered had found time in which to die.

So Johnnie thanked poor Mavity, and hurried away, because the warning whistle was blowing.

The very next Wednesday Miss Sessions gave a dance to the members of her Uplift Club. These gaieties were rather singular and ingenious affairs, sterilized dances, Mrs. Hexter irreverently dubbed them. Miss Lydia did not invite the young men employed about the mill, not having as yet undertaken their uplifting; and feeling quite inadequate to cope with the relations between them and the mill girls, which would be something vital and genuine, and as such, quite foreign — if not inimical — to her enterprise. She contented herself with bringing in a few well-trained young males of her own class, who were expected to be attentive to the girls, treating them as equals, just as Miss Lydia did. For the rest, the members were encouraged to dance with each other, and find such joy as they might in the supper, and the fact that Miss Sessions paid for a half-day's work for them on the morrow, that they might lie late in bed after a night's pleasuring.

Johnnie Consadine had begun to earn money in such quantities as seemed to her economic experience extremely large. She paid her board, sent a little home to her mother, and had still wherewith to buy a frock for the dance. She treated herself to a trolley ride in to Watauga to select this dress, going on the Saturday half-holiday which the mills gave their workers, lest the labour laws regulating the hours per week which women and children may be employed be infringed upon. There was grave debate in Johnnie's mind as to what she should buy. Colours would fade — in cheap goods, anyhow — white soiled easily. "But then I could wash and iron it myself any evening I wanted to wear it," she argued to Mandy Meacham, who accompanied her.

"I'd be proud to do it for you," returned Mandy, loyally. Ordinarily the Meacham woman was selfish; but having found an object upon which she could centre her thin, watery affections, she proceeded to be selfish for Johnnie instead of toward her, a spiritual juggle which some mothers perform in regard to their children.

The store reached, Johnnie showed good judgment in her choice. There was a great sale on at the biggest shopping place in Watauga, and the ready-made summer wear was to be had at bargain rates. Not for her were the flaring, coarse, scant garments whose lack of seemliness was supposed to be atoned for by a profusion of cheap, sleazy trimming. After long and somewhat painful inspection, since most of the things she wanted were hopelessly beyond her, Johnnie carried home a fairly fine white lawn, simply tucked, and fitting to perfection.

"But you've got a shape that sets off anything," said the saleswoman, carelessly dealing out the compliments she kept in stock with her goods for purchasers.

"You're mighty right she has," rejoined Mandy,

sharply, as who should say, "My back is not a true expression of my desires concerning backs. Look at this other — she has the spine of my dreams."

The saleswoman chewed gum while they waited for change and parcel, and in the interval she had time to inspect Johnnie more closely.

"Working in the cotton mill, are you?" she asked as she sorted up her stock, jingling the bracelets on her wrists, and patting into shape her big, frizzy pompadour. "That's awful hard work, ain't it? I should think a girl like you would try for a place in a store. I'll bet you could get one," she added encouragingly, as she handed the parcel across the counter. But already Johnnie knew that the spurious elegance of this young person's appearance was not what she wished to emulate.

The night of the dance Johnnie adjusted her costume with the nice skill and care which seem native to so many of the daughters of America. Mandy, dressing at the same bureau, scraggled the parting of her own hair, furtively watching the deft arranging of Johnnie's.

"Let me do it for you, and part it straight," Johnnie remonstrated.

"Aw, hit'll never be seen on a gallopin' hoss," returned Mandy carelessly. "Everybody'll be so tuck up a-watchin' you that they won't have time to notice is my hair parted straight, nohow."

"But you're not a galloping horse," objected Johnnie, laughing and clutching the comb away from her. "You've got mighty pretty hair, Mandy, if you'd give it a chance. Why, it's curly! Let me do it up right for you once."

So the thin, graying ringlets were loosened around the meagre forehead, and indeed Mandy's appearance was considerably ameliorated.

"There — isn't that nice?" inquired Johnnie, turning her companion around to the glass and forcing her to gaze in it — a thing Mandy always instinctively avoided.

"I reckon I've looked worse," agreed the tall woman unenthusiastically; "but Miss Lyddy ain't carin' to have ye fix up much. I get sort of feisty and want to dav-il her by makin' you look pretty. Wish't you would wear that breas'-pin o' mine, an' them rings an' beads I borried from Lizzie for ye. You might just as well, and then nobody'd know you from one o' the swells."

Johnnie shook her fair head decidedly. Talk of borrowing things brought a reminiscent flush to her cheek.

"I'm just as much obliged," she said sweetly. "I'll wear nothing but what's my own. After a while I'll be able to afford jewellery, and that'll be the time for me to put it on."

Presently came Mavity Bence bringing the treasured footwear.

"I expect they'll be a little tight for me," Johnnie remarked somewhat doubtfully; the slippers, though cheap, ill-cut things, looked so much smaller than her heavy, country-made shoes. But they went readily upon the arched feet of the mountain girl, Mandy and the poor mother looking on with deep interest.

"I wish't Lou was here to see you in 'em," whispered Mavity Bence. "She wouldn't grudge 'em to you one minute. Lord, how pretty you do look, Johnnie Consadine! You're as sightly as that thar big wax doll down at the Company store. I wish't Lou *could* see you."

The dance was being given in the big hall above a store, which Miss Lydia hired for these functions of her Uplift Club. The room was half-heartedly decorated in a hybrid fashion. Miss Lydia had sent down a rose-bowl of flowers; and the girls, being encouraged to use their own taste, put up some flags left over from last Fourth of July. When Johnnie and Mandy Meacham — strangely assorted pair — entered the long room, festivities were already in progress; Negro fiddlers were reeling off dance music, and Miss Lydia was trying to teach some of her club members the two-step. Her younger brother, Hartley Sessions, was gravely piloting a girl down the room in what was supposed to be that popular dance, and two young men from Watauga, for whom he had vouched, stood ready for Miss Sessions to furnish them with partners, when she should have encouraged her learners sufficiently to make the attempt. Round the walls sat the other girls, and to Johnnie's memory came those words of Mandy's, "You dance — if you can."

Johnnie Consadine certainly could dance. Many a time back in the mountains she had walked five miles after a hard day's work to get to a dance that some one of her mates was giving, tramping home in the dawn and doing without sleep for that twenty-four hours. The music seemed somehow to get into her muscles, so that she swayed and moved exactly in time to it.

"That's the two-step," she murmured to her partner. "I never tried it, but I've seen 'em dance it at the hotel down at Chalybeate Springs.   I can waltz a little; but I love an old-fashioned quadrille the best — it seems more friendly."

Gray Stoddard was talking to an older woman who had come with her daughter — a thin-bodied, deep-eyed woman of forty, perhaps, with a half-sad, tolerant smile, and slow, racy speech.   A sudden touch on his shoulder roused him, as one of the young men from town leaned over and asked him excitedly:

"Who's that girl down at the other end of the room, Gray? — the stunning blonde that just came in? She's got one of the mill girls with her."

Gray looked, and laughed a little.   Somehow the adjectives applied to Johnnie did not please him.

"Both of them work in the mill," he said briefly. "The one you mean is Johnnie Consadine.   She's a remarkable girl in more ways than merely in appearance."

"Well, take me down there and give me an introduction," urged the youth from Watauga, in a tone of animation which was barred from Uplift affairs.

"All right," agreed Gray, getting to his feet with a

twinkle in his eye. "I suppose you want to meet the tall one. I've got an engagement for the first dance with Miss Consadine myself."

"Say," ejaculated the other, drawing back, "that isn't fair. Miss Sessions," he appealed to their hostess as umpire. "Here's Gray got the belle of the ball mortgaged for all her dances, and won't even give me an introduction. You do the square thing by me, won't you?"

Lydia Sessions had got her neophites safely launched, and they were making a more or less tempestuous progress across the floor. She turned to the two young men a flushed, smiling countenance. In the tempered light and the extremely favouring costume of the hour, she looked almost pretty.

"What is it?" she asked graciously. "The belle of the ball? I don't know quite who that is. Oh!" with a slight drop in her tone and the temperature of her expression; "do you mean John Consadine? Really, how well she is looking to-night!"

"Isn't she!" blundered the Watauga man with ill-timed enthusiasm. "I call her a regular beauty, and such an interesting-looking creature. What is she trying to do? Good Lord, she's going to attempt the two-step with that Eiffel tower she brought along!"

These frivolous remarks, suited well enough to the ordinary ballroom, did not please Miss Lydia for an Uplift dance.

"The girl with John is one in whom I take a very deep interest," she said with a touch of primness.

"John Consadine is young, and exceptionally strong and healthy. But Amanda Meacham has — er — disabilities and afflictions that make it difficult for her to get along. She is a very worthy case."

The young man from Watauga, who had not regarded Johnnie as a case at all, but had considered her purely as an exceptionally attractive young woman, looked a trifle bewildered. Then Gray took his arm and led him across to where the attempt at two-stepping had broken up in laughing disorder. With that absolutely natural manner which Miss Sessions could never quite achieve, good as her intentions were, he performed the introduction, and then said pleasantly:

"Mr. Baker wants to ask you to dance, Miss Johnnie. I'll carry on Miss Amanda's teaching, or we'll sit down here and talk if she'd rather."

"No more two-steppin' for me," agreed Miss Meacham, seating herself decidedly. "I'll take my steps one at a time from this on. I'd ruther watch Johnnie dance, anyhow; but she would have me try for myself."

Johnnie and the young fellow from Watauga were off now. They halted once or twice, evidently for some further instructions, as Johnnie got the step and time, and then moved away smoothly. Gray took the seat beside Mandy.

"Ain't she a wonder?" inquired the big woman, staring fondly after the fluttering white skirts.

"She is indeed," agreed Gray quietly. And then, Mandy being thus launched on the congenial theme

— the one theme upon which she was ever loquacious
— out came the story of the purchase of the dress, the
compliments of the saleswoman, the refusal of the
borrowed jewellery.

"Johnnie's quare — she is that — I'll never deny
it; but I cain't no more help likin' her than as if she
was my own born sister."

"That's because she is fond of you, too," suggested Gray, thinking of the girl's laborious attempts
to teach poor Mandy to dance.

"Do you reckon she is?" asked the tall woman,
flushing. "Looks like Johnnie Consadine loves every
livin' thing on the top side of this earth. I ain't never
seen the human yet that she ain't got a good word for.
But I don't know as she cares 'specially 'bout *me*."

Stoddard could not refuse the assurance for which
Mandy so naively angled.

"You wouldn't be so fond of her if she wasn't fond
of you," he asserted confidently.

"Mebbe I wouldn't," Mandy debated; "but I don't
know. Let Johnnie put them two eyes o' hern on
you, and laugh in your face, and you feel just like you'd
follow her to the ends of the earth — or I know I do.
Why, she done up my hair this evening and" — the
voice sank to a half-shamed whisper — "she said it
was pretty."

Gray turned and looked into the flushed, tremulous
face beside him with a sudden tightening in his throat.
How cruel humanity is when it beholds only the
grotesque in the Mandys of this world. Her hair

was pretty — and Johnnie had the eyes of love to see it.

He stared down the long, lighted room with unseeing gaze. Old Andrew MacPherson's counsel that he let Johnnie Consadine alone appealed to him at that moment as cruel good sense. He was recalled from his musings by Mandy's voice.

"Oh, look thar!" whispered his companion excitedly. "The other town feller has asked for a knock-down to Johnnie, too. Look at him passin' his bows with her just like she was one of the swells!"

Stoddard looked. Charlie Conroy was relieving Baker of his partner. Johnnie had evidently been asked if she was tired, for they saw her laughingly shake her head, and the new couple finished what was left of the two-step and seated themselves a moment at the other side of the room to wait for the next dance to begin.

"These affairs are great fun, aren't they?" inquired Conroy, fanning his late partner vigorously.

"I love to dance better than anything else in the world, I believe," returned Johnnie dreamily.

"Oh, a dance — I should suppose so. You move as though you enjoyed it; but I mean a performance like this. The girls are great fun, don't you think? But then you wouldn't get quite our point of view on that."

He glanced again at her dress; it was plain and simple, but good style and becoming. She wore no jewellery, but lots of girls were rather affecting that now, especially the athletic type to which this young beauty seemed to belong. Surely he wa ot mistaken in guessing her to be one of Miss Sessions's friends. Of course he was not. She had dressed herself in this simple fashion for a mill-girl's dance, that she might not embarrass the working people who attended. Yes, by George! that was it, and it was a long ways better taste than the frocks Miss Sessions and Mrs. Hexter were wearing.

Johnnie considered his last remark, her gaze still following the movements of the Negro fiddler at the head of the room. Understanding him to mean that, being a mill-hand herself, she could not get a detached view of the matter, and thus see the humour of this attempt to make society women of working-girls, Johnnie was yet not affronted. Her clear eyes came back from watching Uncle Zeke's manœuvres and looked frankly into the eyes of the man beside her.

"I reckon we are right funny," she assented. "But of course, as you say, I wouldn't see that as quick as you would. Sometimes I have to laugh a little at Mandy — the girl I was dancing with first this evening — but — but she's so good-natured it never hurts her feelings. I don't mind being laughed at myself, either."

"Laughed at — you?" inquired Conroy, throwing an immense amount of expression into his glance. He was rather a lady's man, and fancied he had made pretty fair headway with this beautiful girl whom he still supposed to be of the circle of factory owners. "Oh, you mean your work among the mill girls here.

Indeed, I should not laugh at that. I think it's noble for those more fortunate to stretch a hand to help their brothers and sisters that haven't so good a chance. That's what brought me over here to-night. Gray Stoddard explained the plan to me. He doesn't seem to think much of it — but then, Gray's a socialist at heart, and you know those socialists never believe in organized charity. I tell him he's an anarchist."

"Mr. Stoddard is a mighty good man," agreed Johnnie with sudden pensiveness. "They've all been mighty good to me ever since I've been here; but I believe Mr. Stoddard has done more for me than any one else. He not only lends me books, but he takes time to explain things to me."

Conroy smiled covertly at the simplicity of this young beauty. He debated in his mind whether indeed it was not an affected simplicity. Of course Gray was devoting himself to her and lending her books; of course he would be glad to assume the position of mentor to a girl who bade fair to be such a pronounced social success, and who was herself so charming.

"How long have you been in Cottonville, Miss Consadine?" he asked. "Do tell me who you are visiting — or are you visiting here?"

"Oh, no," Johnnie corrected him. "I believe you haven't understood from the first that I'm one of the mill girls. I board at — well, everybody calls it Pap Himes's boarding-house."

There was a moment's silence; but Conroy managed not to look quite as deeply surprised as he felt.

"I — of course I knew it," he began at length, after having sorted and discarded half a dozen explanations. "There — why, there's our dance!" And he stood up in relief, as the fiddlers began on an old-fashioned quadrille.

Johnnie responded with alacrity, not aware of having either risen or fallen in her companion's estimation. She danced through the set with smiling enjoyment. prompting her partner, who knew only modern dances. On his part Conroy studied her covertly, trying to adjust his slow mind to this astonishing new state of things, and to decide what a man's proper attitude might be toward such a girl. In the end he found himself with no conclusion.

"They say they're going to try a plain waltz," he began as he led her back to a seat. He hesitated, glanced about him, and finally placed himself uneasily in the chair beside her. Good Lord! The situation was impossible. What should he say if anybody — Gray Stoddard, for instance — chaffed him about being smitten in this quarter?

"A waltz?" echoed Johnnie helpfully when he did not go on. "I believe I could dance that — I tried it once."

"Then you'll dance it with me?" Conroy found himself saying, baldly, awkwardly, but unable, for the life of him, to keep the eagerness out of his voice.

Upon the instant the music struck up. The two rose and made ready for the dance; Conroy placing Johnnie in waltzing position, and instructing her solicitously.

Gray Stoddard looking on, was amazed at the naïf simple jealousy that swept over him at the sight. She had danced with Conroy twice already — he ought to be more considerate than to bring the girl into notice that way — a chump like Charlie Conroy, what would he understand of such a nature as Johnnie Consadine's? Before he fully realized his own intentions, he had paused in front of the two and was speaking.

"I think Miss Johnnie promised me a dance this evening. I'll have to go back to the office in twenty minutes, and — I hate to interrupt you, but I guess I'll have to claim my own."

He became suddenly aware that Conroy was signalling him across Johnnie's unconscious head with Masonic twistings of the features. Stoddard met these recklessly inconsiderate grimacings with an impassive stare, then looked away.

"I want to see you before you go," the man from Watauga remarked, as he reluctantly resigned his partner. "Don't you forget that there's a waltz coming to me, Miss Johnnie. I'm going to have it, if we make the band play special for us alone."

Lydia Sessions, passing on the arm of young Baker, glanced at Johnnie, star-eyed, pink-cheeked and smiling, with a pair of tall cavaliers contending for her favours, and sucked her lips in to that thin, sharp line of reprobation Johnnie knew so well. Dismissing her escort graciously, she hurried to the little supper room and found another member of the committee.

"Come here, Mrs. Hexter. Just look at that, will

you?" She called attention in a carefully suppressed, but fairly tragic tone, to Stoddard and Johnnie dancing together, the only couple on the floor. "None of the girls know how to waltz. I am not sure that it would be suitable if they did. When I came past, just now, there were two of the men — two — talking to John Consadine, and they were all three laughing. I can't think how it is that girls of that sort manage to stir things up so and get all the men around them."

"Neither can I," said Mrs. Hexter wickedly. "If I did know how, I believe I'd do it sometimes myself. What is it you want of me, Miss Sessions? I must run back and see to supper, if you don't need me."

"But I do," fretted Lydia. "I want your help. This waltzing and — and such things — ought to be stopped."

"All right," rejoined practical Mrs. Hexter. "The quickest way to do it is to stop the music."

She had meant the speech as a jeer, but literal-minded Lydia Sessions welcomed its suggestion. Hurrying down the long room, she spoke to the leader of their small orchestra. The Negro raised to her a brown face full of astonishment. His fiddle-bow faltered — stopped. He turned to his two fellows and gave hasty directions. The waltz measure died away, and a quadrille was announced.

"That was too bad," said Stoddard as they came to a halt; "you were just getting the step beautifully."

The girl flashed a swift, sweet look up at him. "I do love to dance," she breathed.

"John, would you be so kind as to come and help in the supper room," Miss Sessions's hasty tones broke in.

She was leaning on Charlie Conroy's arm, and when she departed to hide Johnnie safely away in the depths of their impromptu kitchen, it left the two men alone together. Conroy promptly fastened upon the other.

Charlie Conroy was a young man who had made up his mind to get on socially. Such figures are rarer in America than in the old world. Yet Charlie Conroy with his petty ambitions does not stand entirely alone. He seriously regarded marriage as a stepping-stone to a circle which should include "the best people." That this term did not indicate the noblest or most selfless, need hardly be explained. It meant only that bit of froth which in each community rides high on the top of the cup, and which, in Watauga, was augmented by the mill owners of its suburb of Cotton-ville. Conroy had been grateful for the opportunity to make an entry into this circle by means of assisting Miss Sessions in her charitable work. That lady herself, as sister-in-law of Jerome Hardwick and a descendant of an excellent New England family, he regarded with absolute veneration, quite too serious and profound for anything so assured as mere admiration.

"I tried to warn you," he began: "but you were bound to get stung."

"I beg your pardon?" returned Stoddard in that civil, colourless interrogation which should always check over-familiar speech, even from the dullest.

But Conroy was not sensitive.

"That big red-headed girl, you know," he said, leaning close and speaking in a confidential tone. "I mistook her for a lady. I was going my full length — telling her what fun the mill girls were, and trying to do the agreeable — when I found out."

"Found out what?" inquired Stoddard. "That she was not a lady?"

"Aw, come off," laughed Conroy. "You make a joke of everything."

"I knew that she was a weaver in the mill," said Stoddard quietly.

Conroy glanced half wistfully over his shoulder in the direction where Johnnie had vanished.

"She's a good-looker all right," he said thoughtfully. "And smile — when that girl smiles and turns those eyes on you — by George! if she was taken to New York and put through one of those finishing schools she'd make a sensation in the swagger set."

Stoddard nodded gravely. He had not Conroy's faith in the fashionable finishing school; but what he lacked there, he made up in conviction as to Johnnie's deserts and abilities.

"There she comes now," said Conroy, as the door swung open to admit a couple of girls with trays of coffee cups. "She walks mighty well. I wonder where a girl like that learned to carry herself so finely. By George, she *is* a good-looker! She's got 'em all beaten; if she was only —. Queer about the accidents of birth, isn't it? Now, what would you say, in her heredity, makes a common girl like that step and look like a queen?"

Gray Stoddard's face relaxed. A hint of his quizzical, inscrutable smile was upon it as he answered.

"Nature doesn't make mistakes. I don't call Johnnie Consadine a common girl — it strikes me that she is rather uncommon."

And outside, a young fellow in the Sunday suit of a workingman was walking up and down, staring at the lighted windows, catching a glimpse now and again of one girl or another, and cursing under his breath when he saw Johnnie Consadine.

"Wouldn't go with me to the dance at Watauga — oh no! But she ain't too tired to dance with the swells!" he muttered to the darkness. "And I can't get a word nor a look out of her. Lord, I don't know what some women think!"

CHAPTER XI

THE NEW BOARDER

PAP HIMES was sitting on the front gallery, dozing in the westering sunshine. On his lap the big, yellow cat purred and blinked with a grotesque resemblance in colouring and expression to his master. It was Sunday afternoon, when the toilers were all out of the mills, and most of them lying on their beds or gone in to Watauga. The village seemed curiously silent and deserted. Through the lazy smoke from his cob pipe Pap noticed Shade Buckheath emerge from the store and start up the street. He paid no more attention till the young man's voice at the porch edge roused him from his half-somnolence.

"Evenin', Pap," said the newcomer.

"Good evenin' yourself," returned Himes with unusual cordiality. He liked men, particularly young, vigorous, masterful men. "Come in, Buck, an' set a spell. Rest your hat — rest your hat."

It was always Pap's custom to call Shade by the first syllable of his second name. Buck is a common by-name for boys in the mountains, and it could not be guessed whether the old man used it as a diminutive of the surname, or whether he meant merely to nickname this favourite of his.

Shade threw himself on the upper step of the porch and searched in his pockets for tobacco.

"Room for another boarder?" he asked laconically. The old man nodded.

"I reckon there's always room, ef it's asked for," he returned. "Hit's the one way I got to make me a livin', with Louvany dyin' off and Mavity puny like she is. I have obliged to keep the house full, or we'd see the bottom of the meal sack."

"All right," agreed Buckheath, rising, and treating the matter as terminated. "I'll move my things in a-Monday."

"Hold on thar — hold on, young feller," objected Pap, as Shade turned away. It was against all reason- able mountain precedent to trade so quickly; but indeed Shade had merely done so with a view to forcing through what he well knew to be a doubtful proposition.

"I'm a-holding on," he observed gruffly at last, as the other continued to blink at him with red eyes and say nothing. "What's the matter with what I said? You told me you had room for another boarder and I named it that I was comin' to board at your house. Have you got any objections?"

"Well, yes, I have," Himes opened up ponderously. "You set yourself down on that thar step and we'll have this here thing out. My boardin'-house is for gals. I fixed it so when I come here. There ain't scarcely a rowdy feller in Cottonville that hain't at one time or another had the notion he'd board with Pap Himes; but I've always kep' a respectable house, and I always aim to. I am a old man, and I bear a good name, and I'm the only man in this house, and I aim to stay so. Now, sir, there's my flatform; and you may take it or leave it."

Buckheath glanced angrily and contemptuously into the stupid, fatuous countenance above him; he appeared to curb with some difficulty the disposition to retort in kind. Instead, he returned, sarcastically:

"The fellers around town say you won't keep anything but gals because nothin' but gals would put up with your hectorin' 'em, and crowdin' ten in a room that was intended for four. That's what folks say; but I've got a reason to want to board with you, Pap, and I'll pay regular prices and take what you give me."

Himes looked a little astonished; then an expression of distrust stole over his broad, flat face.

"What's bringin' you here?" he asked bluntly.

"Johnnie Consadine," returned Shade, without evasion or preamble. "Before I left the mountains, Johnnie an' me was aimin' to wed. Now she's got down here, and doin' better than ever she hoped to, and I cain't get within hand-reach of her."

"Ye cain't?" inquired Pap scornfully. "Why anybody could marry that gal that wanted to. But Lord! anybody can marry *any* gal, if he's got the sense he was born with."

"All right," repeated Shade grimly. "I come to you to know could I get board, not to ask advice. I aim to marry Johnnie Consadine, and I know my own business — air you goin' to board me?"

The old man turned this speech in his mind for some time.

"Curious," he muttered to himself, "how these here young fellers will get petted on some special gal and break their necks to have her."

"Shut up — will you?" ejaculated Buckheath, so suddenly and fiercely that the old man fairly jumped, rousing the yellow cat to remonstrative squirmings. "I tell you I know my business, and I ask no advice of you — will you board me?"

"I cain't do it, Buck," returned Himes definitely. "I ain't got such a room to give you by yourself as you'd be willin' to take up with; and nobody comes into my room.   But I'll tell you what I'll do for you — I'll meal you, ef that will help your case any.   I'll meal you for two dollars a week, and throw in a good word with Johnnie."

Buckheath received the conclusion of this speech with a grin.

"I reckon your good word 'd have a lot to do with Johnnie Consadine," he said ironically, as he picked up his hat from the floor.

"Uh-huh," nodded Pap.   "She sets a heap of store by what I say.   All of 'em does; but Johnnie in particular.   I don't know but what you're about right. Ain't no sense in bein' all tore up concernin' any gal or woman; but I believe if I was pickin' out a good worker that would earn her way, I'd as soon pick out Johnnie Consadine as any of 'em."

And having thus paid his ultimate compliment to

Johnnie, Himes relapsed into intermittent slumber as Shade moved away down the squalid, dusty street under the fierce July sun.

Johnnie greeted the new boarder with a reserve which was in marked contrast to the reception he got from the other girls. Shade Buckheath was a handsome, compelling fellow, and a good match; this Adamless Eden regarded him as a rival in glory even to Pap himself. When supper was over on the first night of his arrival, Shade walked out on the porch and seated himself on the steps. The girls disposed themselves at a little distance — your mountain-bred young female is ever obviously shy, almost to prudery.

"Whar's Johnnie Consadine?" asked the newcomer lazily, disposing himself with his back against a post and his long legs stretched across the upper step.

"Settin' in thar, readin' a book," replied Beulah Catlett curtly. Beulah was but fourteen, and she belonged to the newer dispensation which speaks up more boldly to the masculine half of creation. "Johnnie! Johnnie Consadine!" she called through the casement. "Here's Mr. Buckheath, wishful of your company. Better come out."

"I will, after a while," returned Johnnie absently. "I've got to help Aunt Mavity some, and then I'll be there."

"Hit's a sight, the books that gal does read," complained Beulah. "Looks like a body might get enough stayin' in the house by workin' in a cotton mill, without humpin' theirselves up over a book all evenin'."

"Mr. Stoddard lends 'em to her," announced Mandy

importantly. "He used to give 'em to Miss Lyddy Sessions, and she'd give 'em to Johnnie; but now when Miss Lyddy's away, he'll bring one down to the mill about every so often, and him an' Johnnie'll stand and gas and talk over what's in 'em — I cain't understand one word they say. I tell you Johnnie Consadine's got sense."

Her pride in Johnnie made her miss the look of rage that settled on Buckheath's face at her announcement. The young fellow was glad when Pap Himes began to speak growlingly.

"Yes, an' if she was my gal I'd talk to her with a hickory about that there business. A gal that ain't too old to carry on that-a-way ain't too old to take a whippin' for it. Huh!"

For her own self Mandy would have been thoroughly scared by this attack; in Johnnie's defence she rustled her feathers like an old hen whose one chick has been menaced.

"Johnnie Consadine is the prettiest-behaved gal I ever seen," she announced shrilly. "She ain't never said nor done the least thing that she hadn't ort. Mr. Stoddard he just sees how awful smart she is, and he loves to lend her books and talk with her about 'em afterward. For my part I ain't never seen look nor motion about Mr. Gray Stoddard that wasn't such as a gentleman ort to be. I know he never said nothin' he ort not to *me*."

The suggestion of Stoddard's making advances of unseemly warmth to Mandy Meacham produced a subdued snicker. Even Pap smiled, and Mandy herself, who had been looking a bit terrified after her bold speaking, was reassured.

Buckheath had been a week at the Himes boarding-house, finding it not unpleasant to show Johnnie Consadine how many of the girls regarded him with favour, whether she did or not, when he came to supper one evening with a gleam in his eye that spoke evil for some one. After the meal was over, he followed Pap out on the porch and sat down beside the old man, the girls being bunched expectantly on the step, for he was apt to delay for a bit of chat with one or another of them before leaving.

"You infernal old rascal, I've caught up with you," he whispered, leaning close to his host.

Himes clutched the pipe in his teeth till it clicked, and stared in helpless resentment at his mealer.

"What's the matter with you?" he demanded.

"Speak lower, so the gals won't hear you, or you'll wish you had," counselled Shade. "I sent that there thing on to Washington to get a patent on it, and now I find that they was a model of the same there in the name of Gideon Himes. What do you make of that?"

Pap stared at the thin strips of metal lying in Shade's hard, brown palm.

"The little liar!" he breathed. "She told me she got it up herself." He glared at the bits of steel with protruding eyes, and breathed hard.

"Well, she didn't," Shade countered swiftly, taking advantage of the turn things were showing. "I made

six of 'em; and when I told her to bring 'em back
and I'd give her some that would wear better, she
only brought me five. She said she'd lost one here
at home, she believed. I might have knowed then that
you'd get your claws on it ef I wasn't mighty peart."

Old Gideon was not listening; he had fallen into a
brown study, turning the piece of metal in his skilful,
wonted, knotty fingers, with their spade tips.

"Put it out of sight — quick — here she comes!"
whispered Shade; and the old man looked up to see
Johnnie Consadine in the doorway. A grin of tri-
umph grew slowly upon his face, as he gazed from one
to the other.

"She did get it up!" he returned in Buckheath's
face. "You liar! You're a-aimin' to steal it from
her. You filed out the pieces like she told you to, and
when you found it would work, you tried to get a patent
on it for yo'se'f. Yes, sir, I'm onto *you!*"

Shade looked over his shoulder. The girls had
forsaken the steps. Despairing of his coming, they were
strolling two-and-two after Johnnie on the sidewalk.

"It's you and me for it, Pap," he said hardily.
"What was *you* tryin' to do? Was you gettin' the
patent for Johnnie? Shall I call her up here and ask
her?"

"No, no," exclaimed the old man hastily. "They
ain't no use of puttin' sich things in a fool gal's hands.
She never heard of a patent — wouldn't know one
from a hole in the ground. Hit's like you say, Buck
— you and me for it."

The two men rose and stood a moment, Shade smiling a bit to think what he would do with Pap Himes and his claim if he could only once get Johnnie to say yes to his suit. The thick wits of the elder man apparently realized this feature of the matter not at all.

"Why that thar girl is crazy to get married," he argued, half angrily. "You know in reason she is — they all are. The fust night when you brung her here I named it to her that she was pretty well along in years, and she'd better be spry about gettin' her hooks on a man, or she was left. She said she'd do the best she could — I never heered a gal speak up pearter — most of 'em would be 'shamed to name it out so free. Why, if it was me, I'd walk her down to a justice's office an' wed her so quick her head'd swim."

"Who's that talking about getting married?" called Johnnie's voice from the street, and Johnnie herself ran up the steps.

"Hit was me," harangued Pap Himes doggedly. "I was tellin' Shade how bad you wanted to git off, and that I 'lowed you'd be a good bargain for him."

He looked hopefully from one to the other, as though he expected to see his advice accepted and put into immediate practice. Johnnie laughed whole-heartedly.

"Pap," she said with shining eyes, "if you get me a husband, I'll have to give you a commission on it. Looks like I can't noways get one for myself, don't it?"

She passed into the house, and Shade regarded his ally in helpless anger.

"That's the way she talks, here lately," he growled. "Seems like it would be easy enough to come to something; and by the Lord, it would, with any other gal I ever seed — or with Johnnie like she was when she first came down here! But these days and times she's got a way of puttin' me off that I can't seem to get around."

Neither man quite understood the power of that mental culture which Johnnie was assimilating so avidly. That reading things in a book should enable her — a child, a girl, a helpless woman — to negative their wishes smilingly, this would have been a thing quite outside the comprehension of either.

"Aunt Mavity wants me to go down to the store for her," Johnnie announced, returning. "Any of you girls like to come along?"

Mandy had parted her lips to accept the general invitation, when Shade Buckheath rose to his feet and announced curtly, "I'll go with you."

His glance added that nobody else was wanted, and Mandy subsided into a seat on the steps and watched the two walk away side by side.

"Looks like you ain't just so awful pleased to have me boardin' with Pap," Shade began truculently, when it appeared that the girl was not going to open any conversation with him. "Maybe you wasn't a-carin' for my company down street this evenin'."

"No," said Johnnie, bluntly but very quietly. "I wish you hadn't come to the house to board. I have told you to let me alone."

Shade laughed, an exasperated, mirthless laugh. "You know well enough what made me do it," he said sullenly. "If you don't want me to board with Pap Himes you can stop it any day you say the word. You promise to wed me, and I'll go back to the Inn. The Lord knows they feed you better thar, and I believe in my soul the gals at Pap Himes's will run me crazy. But as long as you hang off the way you do about our marryin', and I git word of you carryin' on with other folks, I'm goin' to stay where I can watch you."

"Other folks!" echoed Johnnie, colour coming into her cheeks. "Shade, there's no use of your quarrelling with me, and I see it's what you're settin' out to do."

"Yes, other folks — Mr. Gray Stoddard, for instance. I ain't got no auto to take you out ridin' in, but you're a blame sight safer with me than you are with him; and if I was to carry word to your mother or your uncle Pros about your doin's they'd say ——"

"The last word my uncle Pros left with ma to give me was that you'd bear watchin', Shade Buckheath," laughed Johnnie, her face breaking up into sweet, sudden mirth at the folly of it all. "You're not aimin' for my good. I don't see what on earth makes you talk like you wanted to marry me."

"Because I do," said Buckheath helplessly. He wondered if the girl did not herself know her own attractions, forgetful that he had not seen them plainly till a man higher placed in the social scale set the cachet of a gentleman's admiration upon them.

CHAPTER XII

THE CONTENTS OF A BANDANNA

IT WAS a breathless August evening; all day the land had lain humming and quivering beneath the glare of the sun. It seemed that such heat must culminate in a thunder shower. Even Pap Himes had sought the coolest corner of the porch, his pipe put out, as adding too much to the general swelter, and the hot, yellow cat perched at a discreet distance.

The old man's dreamy eyes were fixed with a sort of animal content on the winding road that disappeared in the rise of the gap. If was his boast that God Almighty never made a day too hot for him, and to the marrow of them his rheumatic bones felt and savoured the comfort of this blistering weather. High up on the road he had noted a small moving speck that appeared and disappeared as the foliage hid it, or gaps in the trees revealed it. It was not yet time for the mill operatives to be out; but as he glanced eagerly in the direction of the buildings, the gates opened and the loom-fixers streamed forth. Pap had matters of some importance to discuss with Shade Buckheath, and he was glad to see the young man's figure come swinging down the street. The two were soon deep in a whispered discussion, their heads bent close together.

The little speck far up the road beteween the trees announced itself to the eye now as a moving figure, walking down toward Cottonville.

"Well, I'll read it again, if you don't believe me," Buckheath said impatiently. "All that Alabama mill wants is to have me go over there and put this trick on their jennies, and if it works they'll give us a royalty of — well, I'll make the bargain."

"Or I will," countered Pap swiftly.

"You?" inquired Shade contemptuously. "Time they wrote some of the business down and you couldn't read it, whar'd you be, and whar'd our money be?"

The moving speck on the road appeared at this time to be the figure of a tall man, walking unsteadily, reeling from side to side of the road, yet approaching the village.

"Shade," pacified Himes, with a truckling manner that the younger man's aggressions were apt to call out in him, "you know I don't mean anything against you, but I believe in my soul I'd ruther sell out the patent. That man in Lowell said he'd give twenty thousand dollars if it was proved to work — now didn't he?"

"Yes, and by the time it's proved to work we'll have made three times that much out of it. There ain't a spinning mill in the country that won't save money by putting in the indicator, and paying us a good royalty on it. If Johnnie and me was wedded, I'd go to work to-morrow advertising the thing."

"The gal ain't in the mill this afternoon, is she?" asked old Himes.

"No, She's gone off somewheres with some folks Hardwick's sister-in-law has got here. If you want to find her these days, you've got to hunt in some of the swell houses round on the hills."

He spoke with bitterness, and Pap nodded comprehendingly; the subject was an old one between them. Then Shade drew from his pocket a letter and prepared to read it once more to the older man.

"Whar's Johnnie?"

Himes started so violently that he disturbed the equilibrium of his chair and brought the front legs to the floor with a slam, so that he sat staring straight ahead. Shade Buckheath whirled and saw Pros Passmore standing at the foot of the steps — the moving speck come to full size. The old man was a wilder-looking figure than usual. He had no hat on, and a bloody cloth bound around his head confined the straggling gray locks quaintly. The face was ghastly, the clothing in tatters, and his hands trembled as they clutched a bandanna evidently full of some small articles that rattled together in his shaking grasp.

"Good Lord — Pros! You mighty nigh scared me out of a year's growth," grumbled Pap, hitching vainly to throw his chair back into position. "Come in. Come in. You look like you'd been seein' trouble."

"Whar's Johnnie?" repeated old Pros hollowly.

It was the younger man who answered this time,

with an ugly lift of the lip over his teeth, between a sneer and a snarl.

"She's gone gaddin' around with some of her swell friends. She may be home before midnight, an' then again she may not," he said.

The old man collapsed on the lower step.

"I wish't Johnnie was here," he said querulously. "I —" he looked about him confusedly — "I've found her silver mine."

At the words the two on the porch became suddenly rigid. Then Buckheath sprang down the steps, caught Passmore under the arm-pits and half led, half dragged him up to a chair, into which he thrust him with little ceremony.

He stood before the limp figure, peering into the newcomer's face with eyes of greed and hands that clenched and unclenched themselves automatically.

"You've found the silver mine!" he volleyed excitedly. "Whose land is it on? Have you got options yet? My grandpappy always said they was a silver mine ——"

"Hush!" Pap Himes's voice hissed across the loud explosive tones. "No need to tell your business to the town. I'll bet Pros ain't thought about no options yit. He may need friends to he'p him out on such matters; and here's you and me, Buck — God knows he couldn't have better ones."

The old man stared about him in a dazed fashion.

"I've got my specimens in this here bandanner," he explained quaveringly. "I fell over the ledge,

was the way I chanced upon it at the last, and I lay
dead for a spell. My head's busted right bad. But
the ore specimens, they're right here in the bandanner,
and I aimed to give 'em to Johnnie — to put 'em right
in her lap— the best gal that ever was — and say to
her, 'Here's your silver mine, honey, that your good-
for-nothin' old uncle found for ye; now you can live
like a lady!' That's what I aimed to say to Johnnie.
I didn't aim that nobody else should tetch them samples
till she'd saw 'em."

Himes and Buckheath were exchanging glances
across the old man's bent, gray head. Common
humanity would have suggested that they offer him
rest or refreshment, but these two were intent only
on what the bandanna held.

What is it in the thought of wealth from the ground
that so intoxicates, so ravishes away from all reasonable
judgment, the generality of mankind? People never
seem to conceive that there might be no more than
moderate repayal for great toil in a mine of any sort.
The very word mine suggests to them tapping the vast
treasure-house of the world, and drawing an unlimited
share — wealth lavish, prodigal, intemperate. These
two were as mad with greed at the thought of the silver
mine in the mountains as ever were forty-niners in
the golden days of California, or those more recent
ignoble martyrs who strewed their bones along the
icy trails of the Klondike.

"Ye better let me look at 'em Pros," wheedled
Pap Himes. "I know a heap about silver ore. I've

worked in the Georgia gold mines — and you know you never find gold without silver. I was three months in the mountains with a feller that was huntin' nickel; he l'arned me a heap."

The old man turned his disappointed gaze from one face to the other.

"I wish't Johnnie was here," he repeated his plaintive formula, as he raised the handkerchief and untied the corners.

Pap glanced apprehensively up and down the street; Buckheath ran to the door and shut it, that none in the house might see or overhear; and then the three stared at the unpromising-looking, earthy bits of mineral in silence. Finally Himes put down a stubby forefinger and stirred them meaninglessly.

"Le' me try one with my knife," he whispered, as though there were any one to hear him.

"All right," returned the old man nervelessly. "But hit ain't soft enough for lead — if that's what you're meanin'. I know that much. A lead mine is a mighty good thing. Worth as much as silver maybe; but this ain't lead."

A curious tremor had come over Pap Himes's face as he furtively compared the lump of ore he held in his hand with something which he took from his pocket. He seemed to come to some sudden resolution.

"No, 'tain't lead — and 'tain't nothin'," he declared contemptuously, flinging the bit he held back into the handkerchief. "Pros Passmore — ye old fool — you come down here and work us all up over some truck that wasn't worth turnin' with a spade! You might as well throw them things away. Whar in the nation did you git 'em, anyhow?"

Passmore stumbled to his feet. He had eaten nothing for three days, The fall over the ledge had injured him severely. He was scarcely sane at the moment.

"Ain't they no 'count?" he asked pitifully. "Why, I made shore they was silver. Well" — he looked aimlessly about — "I better go find Johnnie," and he started down the steps.

"Leave 'em here, Pros, and go in. Mavity'll give you a cup of coffee," suggested Pap, in a kinder tone.

The bandanna slipped rattling from the old man's relaxed fingers. The specimens clattered and rolled on the porch floor. With drooping head he shambled through the door.

A woman's face disappeared for a moment from the shadowy front-room window, only to reappear and watch unseen. Mavity was listening in a sort of horror as she heard her father's tones.

"Git down and pick 'em up — every one! Don't you miss a one. Yo' eyes is younger'n mine. Hunt 'em up! hunt 'em up," hissed Pap, casting himself upon the handkerchief and its contents.

"What is it?" questioned Buckheath keenly. "I thort you had some game on hand." And he hastened to comply. "Air they really silver?"

"No — better'n that. They're nickel. The feller that was here from the North said by the dips and

turns of the stratagems an' such-like we was bound
to have nickel in these here mountains somewhar.
A nickel mine's better'n a gold mine — an' these is
nickel. I know 'em by the piece o' nickel ore from
the Canady mines that I carry constantly in my pocket.
We'll keep the old fool out of the knowin' of it, and
find whar the mine is at, and we'll ——"

The two men squatted on the floor, tallying over the
specimens they had already collected, and looking about
them for more. In the doorway behind them appeared
a face, gaunt, grimed, a blood-stained bandage around
the brow, and a pair of glowing, burning eyes looking
out beneath. Uncle Pros had failed to find Mavity
Bence, and was returning. Too dazed to comprehend mere words, the old prospector read instantly
and aright the attitude and expression of the two.
As they tied the last knot in the handkerchief, he
loomed above them, white and shaking.

"You thieves!" he roared. "Give me my bandanner! Give me Johnnie's silver mine!"

"Yes — yes — yes! Don't holler it out that-a-
way!" whispered Pap Himes from the floor, where
he crouched, still clutching the precious bits of
ore.

"We was a-goin' to give 'em to you, Uncle Pros.
We was just foolin'," Buckheath attempted to reassure
him.

The old man bent forward and shot down a long
arm to recover his own. He missed the bandanna,
and the impetus of the movement sent him staggering

a pace or two forward. At the porch edge he strove to recover himself, failed, and with a short, coughing groan, pitched down the steps and lay, an inert mass, at their foot.

"Cover that handkecher up," whispered Himes before either man moved to his assistance.

CHAPTER XIII

A PATIENT FOR THE HOSPITAL

WHEN the Hardwick carriage drove up in the heavy, ill-odoured August night, and stopped at the gate to let Johnnie Consadine out, Pap Himes's boarding-house was blazing with light from window and doorway, clacking and humming like a mill with the sound of noisy footsteps and voices. Three or four men argued and talked loudly on the porch. Through the open windows of the front room, Johnnie had a glimpse of a long, stark figure lying on the lounge, and a white face which struck her with a strange pang of vague yet alarming resemblance. She made her hasty thanks to Miss Sessions and hurried in. Gray Stoddard's horse was standing at the hitching post in front, and Gray met her at the head of the steps.

Stoddard looked particularly himself in riding dress. Its more unconventional lines suited him well; the dust-brown Norfolk, the leathern puttees, gave an adventurous turn to the expression of a personality which was only so on the mental side. He always rode bareheaded, and the brown hair, which he wore a little longer than other men's, was tossed from its masculine primness to certain hyacinthine lines which were

becoming.   Just now his clear brown eyes were luminous with feeling.   He put out a swift, detaining hand
and caught hers, laying sympathetic fingers over the
clasp and retaining it as he spoke.

"I'm so relieved that you've come at last," he said.
"We need somebody of intelligence here.   I just happened to come past a few minutes after the accident.
Don't be frightened; your uncle came down to see you,
and got a fall somehow.   He's hurt pretty badly,
I'm afraid, and these people are refusing to have him
taken to the hospital."

On the one side Himes and Buckheath drew back
and regarded this scene with angry derision.   In the
carriage below Lydia Sessions, who could hear nothing
that was said, stared incredulously, and moved as
though to get down and join Johnnie.

"You'll want him sent to the hospital?" Stoddard
urged, half interrogatively.   "Look in there.   Listen
to the noise.   This is no fit place for a man with a
possible fracture of the skull."

"Yes — oh, yes," agreed Johnnie promptly.   "If
I could nurse him myself I'd like to — or help; but of
course he's got to go to the hospital, first of everything."

Stoddard motioned the Hardwick driver to wait,
and called down to the carriage load, "I want you
people to drive round by the hospital and send the
ambulance, if you'll be so kind.   There's a man hurt
in here."

Lydia Sessions made this an immediate pretext for
getting down and coming in.

"Did you say they didn't want to send him to the hospital?" she inquired sharply and openly, in her tactless fashion, as she crossed the sidewalk. "That's the worst thing about such people; you provide them with the best, and they don't know enough to appreciate it. Have they got a doctor, or done anything for the poor man?"

"I sent for Millsaps, here — he knows more about broken bones than anybody in Cottonville," Pap offered sullenly, mopping his brow and shaking his bald head. "Millsaps is a decent man. You know what *he's* a-goin' to do to the sick."

"Is he a doctor?" asked Stoddard sternly, looking at the lank, shuffling individual named.

"He can doctor a cow or a nag better'n anybody I ever saw," Pap put forward rather shamefacedly.

"A veterinarian," commented Stoddard. "Well, they've gone for the ambulance, and the surgeon will soon be here now."

"I don't know nothin' about veterinarians and surgeons," growled Pap, still alternately mopping his bald head and shaking it contemptuously; "but I know that Millsaps ain't a-goin' to box up any dead bodies and send 'em to the medical colleges; and I know he made as pretty a job of doctoring old Spotty as ever I seen. To be shore the cow died, but he got the medicine down her when it didn't look as if human hands could do it — that's the kind of doctor he is."

"I aim to give Mr. Passmore a teaspoonful of lamp oil — karosene," said the cow doctor, coming forward, evidently feeling that it was time he spoke up for himself. "Lamp oil is mighty rousin' to them as lays like he's doin'. I've used copperas for such — but it takes longer. Some say a dose of turpentine is better'n lamp oil — but I 'low both of 'em won't hurt."

Johnnie pushed past them all into the front room where the women were running about, talking loud and exclaiming. A kerosene lamp without a chimney smoked and flared on the table, filling the room with evil odours. Pros Passmore's white face thrown up against the lounge cushion was the only quiet, dignified object in sight.

"Mandy," said Johnnie, catching the Meacham woman by the elbow as she passed her bearing a small kerosene can, "you go up to my room and get the good lamp I have there. Then take this thing away. Where's Aunt Mavity?"

"I don't know. She's been carryin' on somethin' turrible. Yes, Johnnie, honey—I'll get the lamp for ye."

When Johnnie turned to her uncle, she found Millsaps bending above him, the small can in his hands, its spout approached to the rigid blue lips of the patient with the unconcern of a man about to fill a lamp. She sprang forward and caught his arm, bringing the can away with a clatter and splash.

"You mustn't do that," she said authoritatively. "The doctors will be here in a minute. You mustn't give him anything, Mr. Millsaps."

"Oh, all right — all right," agreed Millsaps, with decidedly the air that he considered it all wrong.

"There is some people that has objections to having their kin-folks cyarved up by student doctors. Then agin, there is others that has no better use for kin than to let 'em be so treated. I 'low that a little dosin' of lamp oil never hurt nobody — and it's cured a-many, of most any kind of disease. But just as you say — just as you say." And he shuffled angrily from the room.

Johnnie went and knelt by the lounge. With deft, careful fingers she lifted the wet cloths above the bruised forehead. The hurt looked old. No blood was flowing, and she wondered a little. Catching Shade Buckheath's eye fixed on her from outside the window, she beckoned him in and asked him to tell her exactly how the trouble came about. Buckheath gave her his own version of the matter, omitting, of course, all mention of the bandanna full of ore which lay now carefully hidden at the bottom of old Gideon Himes's trunk.

"And you say he fell down the steps?" asked Johnnie. "Who was with him? Who saw it?"

"Nobody but me and Pap," Shade answered, trying to give the reply unconcernedly.

"I — I seen it," whispered Mavity Bence, plucking at Johnnie's sleeve. "I was in the fore room here — and I seen it all."

She spoke defiantly, but her terrified glance barely raised itself to the menacing countenances of the two men on the other side of the lounge, and fell at once. "I never heard nothin' they was sayin'," she made haste to add. "But I seen Pros fall, and I run out and helped Pap and Shade fetch him in."

Peculiar as was the attitude of all three, Johnnie felt a certain relief in the implied assurance that there had been no quarrel, that her uncle had not been struck or knocked down the steps.

"Why, Pap," she said kindly, looking across at the old man's perturbed, sweating face, "you surely ain't like these foolish folks round here in Cottonville that think the hospital was started up to get dead bodies for the student doctors to cut to pieces. You see how bad off Uncle Pros is; you must know he's bound to be better taken care of there in that fine building, and with all those folks that have learned their business to take care of him, than here in this house with only me. Besides, I couldn't even stay at home from the mill to nurse him. Somebody's got to earn the money."

"I wouldn't charge you no board, Johnnie," fairly whined Himes. "I'm willin' to nurse Pros myself, without he'p, night and day. You speak up mighty fine for that thar hospital. What about Lura Dawson? Everybody knows they shipped her body to Cincinnati and sold it. You ort to be ashamed to put your poor old uncle in such a place."

Johnnie turned puzzled eyes from the rigid face on the lounge — Pros had neither moved nor spoken since they lifted and laid him there — to the old man at the window. That Pap Himes should be concerned, even slightly, about the welfare of any living being save himself, struck her as wildly improbable. Then, swiftly, she reproached herself for not being readier to believe good of him. He and Uncle Pros had been boys together, and she knew her uncle one to deserve affection, though he seldom commanded it.

There was a sound of wheels outside, and Gray Stoddard's voice with that of the doctor's. Shade and Pap Himes still hovered nervously about the window, staring in and hearkening to all that was said. Mavity Bence had wept till her face was sodden. She herded the other girls back out of the way, but watched everything with terrified eyes.

"He'll jest about come to hisself befo' he dies," the older conspirator muttered to Shade as the stretcher passed them, and the skilled, white-jacketed attendants laid Pros Passmore in the vehicle without so much as disturbing his breathing. "He'll jest about come to hisself thar, and them pesky doctors 'll have word about the silver mine. Well, in this world, them that has, gits, mostly. Ef Johnnie Consadine had been any manner o' kin to me, I vow I'd 'a' taken a hickory to her when she set up her word agin' mine and let him go out of the house. The little fool! she didn't know what she was sendin' away."

And so Pros Passmore was taken to the hospital. His bandanna full of ore remained buried at the bottom of Gideon Himes's trunk, to be fished up often by the old sinner, fingered and fondled, and laid back in hiding; while the man who had carried it down the mountains to fling it in Johnnie's lap lay with locked lips, and told neither the doctors nor Himes where the silver mine was. August sweated itself away; September wore on into October in a procession of sun-robed, dust-sandalled days, and still Uncle Pros gave no sign of actual recovery.

Johnnie was working hard in the mill. Hartley Sessions had become, in his cold, lifeless fashion, very much her friend. Inert, slow, he had one qualification for his position: he could choose an assistant, or delegate authority with good judgment; and he found in Johnnie Consadine an adjutant so reliable, so apt, and of such ability, that he continually pushed more work upon her, if pay and honours did not always follow in adequate measure.

For a time, much as she disliked to approach Shade with any request, Johnnie continued to urge him whenever they met to finish up the indicators and let her have them back again. Then Hartley Sessions promoted her to a better position in the weaving department, and other cares drove the matter from her mind.

The condition of Uncle Pros added fearfully to the drains upon her time and thought. The old man lay in his hospital cot till the great frame had wasted fairly to the big bones, following her movements when she came into the room with strange, questioning, unrecognizing eyes, yet always quieted and soothed by her presence, so that she felt urged to give him every moment she could steal from her work. The hurts on his head, which were mere scalp wounds, healed over; the surgeon at the hospital was unable to find any indentation or injury to the skull itself which would account for the old man's condition. They talked for a long time of an operation, and did finally trephine, without result. They would make an X-ray photograph, they said, when he should be strong enough to stand it, as a means of further investigation.

Meantime his expenses, though made fairly nominal to her, cut into the money which Johnnie could send to her mother, and she was full of anxiety for the helpless little family left without head or protector up in that gash of the wind-grieved mountains on the flank of Big Unaka.

In these days Shade Buckheath vacillated from the suppliant attitude to the threatening. Johnnie never knew when she met him which would be uppermost; and since he had wearied out her gratitude and liking, she cared little. One thing surprised and touched her a bit, and that was that Shade used to meet her of an evening when she would be coming from the hospital, and ask eagerly after the welfare of Uncle Pros. He finally begged her to get him a chance to see the old man, and she did so, but his presence seemed to have such a disturbing effect on the patient that the doctors prohibited further visits.

"Well, I done just like you told me to, and them cussed sawboneses won't let me go back no more," Shade reported to Pap Himes that evening. "Old Pros just swelled hisself out like a toad and hollered

at me time I got in the room. He's sure crazy all
right. He looks like he couldn't last long, but them
that heirs what he has will git the writin' that tells
whar the silver mine's at. Johnnie's liable to find
that writin' any day; or he may come to hisself and
tell her."

"Well, for God's sake," retorted Pap Himes testily,
"why don't you wed the gal and be done with it?
You wed Johnnie Consadine and get that writin',
and I'll never tell on you 'bout the old man and such;
and you and me'll share the mine."

Shade gave him a black look.

"You're a good talker," he said sententiously.
"If I could *do* things as easy as you can *tell* 'em, I'd
be president."

"Huh!" grunted the old man. "Marryin' a fool
gal — or any other woman — ain't nothin' to do. If
I was your age I'd have her Miz Himes before sundown."

"All right," said Buckheath, "if it's so damn' easy
done — this here marryin' — do some of it yourself. Thar's Laurelly Consadine; she's a widow;
and more kin to Pros than Johnnie is. You go up in
the mountains and wed her, and I'll stand by ye in
the business."

A slow but ample grin dawned on the old man's
round, foolish face. He looked admiringly at Shade.

"By Gosh!" he said finally. "That ain't no bad
notion, neither. 'Course I can do it. They all want
to wed. And thar's Laurelly — light-minded fool —

ain't got the sense she was born with — up thar without Pros nor Johnnie — I could persuade her to take off her head and play pitch-ball with it — Lord, yes!"

"Well, you've bragged about enough," put in Buckheath grimly. "You git down in the collar and pull."

The old man gave him no heed. He was still grinning fatuously.

"It 'minds me of Zack Shalliday, and the way he got wedded," came the unctuous chuckle. "Zack was a man 'bout my age, and his daughter was a-keepin' house for him. She was a fine hand to work; the best butter maker on the Unakas; Zack always traded his butter for a extry price. But old as Sis Shalliday was — she must 'a' been all of twenty-seven — along comes a man that takes a notion to her. She named it to Zack. 'All right,' says he, 'you give me to-morrow to hunt me up one that's as good a butter maker as you air, and I've got no objections.' Then he took hisself down to Preacher Blaylock, knowin' in reason that preachers was always hungry for weddin' fees, and would hustle round to make one. He offered the preacher a dollar to give him a list of names of single women that was good butter makers. Blaylock done so. He'd say, 'Now this 'n's right fine-looking, but I ain't never tasted her butter. Here's one that ain't much to look at, but her butter is prime — jest like your gal's; hit allers brings a leetle extry at the store. This 'n's fat, yet I can speak well of her workin' qualifications.' He named 'em all out to Zack, and

Zack had his say for each one. 'The fat ones is easy keepers,' he says for the last one, 'and looks don't cut much figger in this business — it all depends on which one makes the best butter anyhow.'

"Well, he took that thar string o' names, and he left. 'Long about sundown, here he is back and hollerin' at the fence. 'Come out here, preacher — I've got her.' He had a woman in his buggy that Blaylock had never put eyes on in all his born days. 'Wouldn't none o' them I sent ye to have ye?' the preacher asked Zack in a kind of whisper, when he looked at that thar snaggle-toothed, cross-eyed some-body that Shalliday'd fetched back. 'I reckon they would,' says Zack. 'I reckon any or all of 'em would 'a' had me,' he says. 'I had only named it to three o' the four, and I hadn't closed up with none o' them, becaze I wasn't quite satisfied in my mind about the butter makin'. And as I was goin' along the road toward the last name you give me, I come up with this here woman. She was packin' truck down to the store for to trade it. I offered her a lift and she rid with me a spell. I chanced to tell her of what I was out after, and she let on that she was a widder, and showed me the butter she had — hit was all made off of one cow, and the calf is three months old. I wasn't a-goin' to take nobody's word in such a matter, and hauled her on down to the store and seed the store-keeper pay her extry for that thar butter — and here we air. Tie the knot, preacher; yer dollar is ready for ye, and we must be gittin' along home — it's 'most milkin' time.' The preacher he tied the knot, and Shalliday and the new Miz. Shalliday they got along home." The old man chuckled as he had at the beginning of this tale.

"Well, that was business," agreed Shade impatiently. "When are you goin' to start for Big Unaka?"

The old man rolled his great head between his shoulders.

"Ye-ah," he assented; "business. But it was bad business for Zack Shalliday. That thar woman never made a lick of that butter she was a packin' to the settlement to trade for her sister that was one o' them widders the preacher had give him the name of. Seems Shalliday's woman had jest come in a-visitin' from over on Big Smoky, and she turned out to be the laziest, no-accountest critter on the Unakas. She didn't know which end of a churn-dasher was made for use. Aw — law — huh! Business — there's two kinds of business; but that was a bad business for Zack Shalliday. I reckon I'll go up on Unaka to-morrow, if Mavity can run the house without me."

CHAPTER XIV

WEDDING BELLS

A VINE on Mavity Bence's porch turned to blood crimson. Its leaves parted from the stem in the gay Autumn wind, and sifted lightly down to joint he painted foliage of the two little maples which struggled for existence against an adverse world, crouching beaten and torn at the curb.

In these days Johnnie used to leave the mill in the evening and go directly to the hospital. Gray Stoddard was her one source of comfort — and terror. Uncle Pros's injuries brought these two into closer relations than anything had yet done. So far, Johnnie had conducted her affairs with a judgment and propriety extraordinary, clinging as it were to the skirts of Lydia Sessions, keeping that not unwilling lady between her and Stoddard always. But the injured man took a great fancy to Gray. Johnnie he had forgotten; Shade and Pap Himes he recognized only by an irritation which made the doctors exclude them from his presence; but something in Stoddard's equable, disciplined personality, appealed to and soothed Uncle Pros when even Johnnie failed.

The old mountaineer had gone back to childhood. He would lie by the hour murmuring a boy's woods lore to Gray Stoddard, communicating deep secrets of where a bee tree might be found; where, known only to him, there was a deeply hidden spring of pure freestone water, "so cold it'll make yo' teeth chatter"; and which one of old Lead's pups seemed likely to turn out the best coon dog.

When Stoddard's presence and help had been proffered to herself, Johnnie had not failed to find a gracious way of declining or avoiding; but you cannot reprove a sick man — a dying man. She could not for the life of her find a way to insist that Uncle Pros make less demand on the young mill owner's time.

And so the two of them met often at the bedside, and that trouble which was beginning to make Johnnie's heart like lead grew with the growing love Gray Stoddard commanded. She told herself mercilessly that it was presumption, folly, wickedness; she was always going to be done with it; but, once more in his presence, her very soul cried out that she was indeed fit at least to love him, if not to hope for his love in turn.

Stoddard himself was touched by the old man's fancy, and showed a devotion and patience that were characteristic.

If she was kept late at the hospital, Mavity put by a bite of cold supper for her, and Mandy always waited to see that she had what she wanted. On the day after Shade Buckheath and Gideon Himes had come to their agreement, she stopped at the hospital for a briefer stay than usual. Her uncle was worse, and an opiate had been administered to quiet him, so that she only sat a while at the bedside and finally took her way homeward in a state of utter depression for which she could scarcely account.

It was dusk — almost dark — when she reached the gate, and she noted carelessly a vehicle drawn up before it.

"Johnnie," called her mother's voice from the back of the rickety old wagon as the girl was turning in toward the steps.

"Sis' Johnnie — Sis' Johnnie!" crowed Deanie; and then she was aware of sober, eleven-year-old Milo climbing down over the wheel and trying to help Lissy, while Pony got in his way and was gravely reproved. She ran to the wheel and put up ready arms.

"Why, honeys!" she exclaimed. "How come you-all never let me know to expect you? Oh, I'm so glad, mother. I didn't intend to send you word to come; but I was feeling so blue. I sure wanted to. Maybe Uncle Pros might know you — or the baby — and it would do him good."

She had got little Deanie out in her arms now, and stood hugging the child, bending to kiss Melissa, finding a hand to pat Milo's shoulder and rub Pony's tousled poll.

"Oh, I'm so glad! — I'm so glad to see you-all," she kept repeating. "Who brought you?" She looked closely at the man on the driver's seat and recognized Gideon Himes.

"Why, Pap!" she exclaimed. "I'll never forget you for this. It was mighty good of you."

The door swung open, letting out a path of light. "Aunt Mavity!" cried the girl. "Mother and the children have come down to see me. Isn't it fine?"

Mavity Bence made her appearance in the doorway, her faded eyes so reddened with weeping that she looked like a woman in a fever. She gulped and stared from her father, where in the shine of her upheld lamp he sat blinking and grinning, to Laurella Consadine in a ruffled pink-and-white lawn frock, with a big, rose-wreathed hat on her dark curls, and Johnnie Consadine with the children clinging about her.

"Have ye told her?" she gasped. And at the tone Johnnie turned quickly, a sudden chill falling upon her glowing mood.

"What's the matter?" she asked, startled, clutching the baby tighter to her, and conning over with quick alarm the tow-heads that bobbed and surged about her waist. "The children are all right — aren't they?"

Milo looked up apprehensively. He was an old-faced, anxious-looking, little fellow, already beginning to have a stoop to his thin shoulders — the bend of the burden bearer.

"I — I done the best I could, Sis' Johnnie," he hesitated apologetically. "You wasn't thar, and Unc' Pros was gone, an' I thest worked the farm and took care of mother an' the little 'uns best I knowed how. But when she — when he — oh, I wish't you and Unc' Pros had been home to-day."

Johnnie, her mind at rest about the children, turned to her mother.

"Was ma sick?" she asked sympathetically. Then, noticing for the first time the unwonted gaiety of Laurella's costume, the glowing cheeks and bright eyes, she smiled in relief.

"You don't look sick. My, but you're fine! You're as spick and span as a bride."

The old man bent and spat over the wheel, preparatory to speaking, but his daughter took the words from his mouth.

"She is a bride," explained Mavity Bence in a flatted, toneless voice. "Leastways, Pap said he was a-goin' up on Unaka for to wed her and bring her down — and I know in reason she'd have him."

Johnnie's terror-stricken eyes searched her mother's irresponsible, gypsy face.

"Now, Johnnie," fretted the little woman, "how long air you goin' to keep us standin' here in the road? Don't you think my frock's pretty? Do they make em that way down here in the big town? I bought this lawn at Bledsoe, with the very first money you sent up. Ain't you a bit glad to see us?"

The lip trembled, the tragic dark brows lifted in their familiar slant.

"Come on in the house," said Johnnie heavily, and she led the way with drooping head.

Called by the unusual disturbance, Mandy left the supper she was putting on the table for Johnnie and ran into the front hall. Beulah Catlett and one or two of the other girls had crowded behind Mavity Bence's shoulders, and were staring. Mandy joined them in time to hear the conclusion of Mavity's explanation.

She came through the door and passed the new Mrs. Himes on the porch.

"Why, Johnnie Consadine!" she cried. "Is that there your ma?"

Johnnie nodded. She was past speech.

"Well, I vow! I should've took her for your sister, if any kin. Ain't she pretty? Beulah — she's Johnnie's ma, and her and Pap has just been wedded."

She turned to follow Johnnie, who was mutely starting the children in to the house.

"Well," she said with a sigh, "some folks gits two, and some folks don't git nary one." And she brought up the rear of the in-going procession.

"Ain't you goin' to pack your plunder in?" inquired the bridegroom harshly, almost threateningly, as he pitched out upon the path a number of bundles and boxes.

"I reckon they won't pester it till you git back from puttin' up the nag," returned Laurella carelessly as she swung her light, frilled skirts and tripped across the porch. "You needn't werry about me," she called down to the old fellow where he sat speechlessly glaring. "Mavity'll show me whar I can sit, and git me a nice cool drink; and that's all I'll need for one while."

Pap Himes's mouth was open, but no words came.

He finally shut it with that click of the ill-fitting false teeth which was familiar — and terrible — to everybody at the boarding-house, shook out the lines over the old horse, and jogged away into the dusk.

"And this here's the baby," admired Mandy, kneeling in front of little Deanie, when the newcomers halted in the front room. "Why, Johnnie Consadine! She don't look like nothin' on earth but a little copy of you. If she's dispositioned like you, I vow I'll just about love her to death."

Mavity Bence was struggling up the porch steps loaded with the baggage of the newcomers.

"Better leave that for your paw," the bride counselled her. "It's more suited to a man person to lift them heavy things."

But Mavity had not lived with Pap Himes for nearly forty years without knowing what was suited to him, in distinction, perhaps, from mankind in general. She made no reply, but continued to bring in the baggage, and Johnnie, after settling her mother in a rocking-chair with the cool drink which the little woman had specified, hurried down to help her.

"Everybody always has been mighty good to me all my life," Laurella Himes was saying to Mandy, Beulah and the others. "I reckon they always will. Uncle Pros he just does for me like he was my daddy, and my children always waited on me. Johnnie's the best gal that ever was, ef she does have some quare notions."

"Ain't she?" returned Mandy enthusiastically, as Johnnie of the "quare notions" helped Mavity Bence upstairs with the one small trunk belonging to Laurella.

"Look out for that trunk, Johnnie," came her mother's caution, with a girlish ripple of laughter in the tones. "Hit's a borried one. Now don't you roach up and git mad. I had obliged to have a trunk, bein' wedded and comin' down to the settlement this-a-way. I only borried Mildred Faidley's. She won't never have any use for it. Evelyn Toler loaned me the trimmin' o' this hat — ain't it sightly?"

Johnnie's distressed eyes met the pale gaze of Aunt Mavity across the little oilcloth-covered coffer.

"I would 'a' told you, Johnnie," said the poor woman deprecatingly, "but I never knowed it myself till late last night, and I hadn't the heart to name it at breakfast. I thort I'd git a chance this evenin', but they come sooner'n I was expectin' 'em."

"Never mind, Aunt Mavity," said Johnnie. "When I get a little used to it I'll be glad to have them all here. I — I wish Uncle Pros was able to know folks."

The children were fed, Milo, touchingly subdued and apologetic, nestling close to his sister's side and whispering to her how he had tried to get ma to wait and come down to the Settlement, and hungrily begging with his pathetic childish eyes for her to say that this thing which had come upon them was not, after all, the calamity he feared. Snub-nosed, nine-year-old Pony, whose two front teeth had come in quite too large for his mouth, Pony, with the quick-expanding pupils, and the temperament that would cope ill with disaster, addressed himself gaily to his supper and saw no sorrow anywhere. Little Melissa was half asleep; and even Deanie, after the first outburst of greeting, nodded in her chair.

"I got ready for 'em," Mavity told Johnnie in an undertone, after her father returned. "I knowed in reason he'd bring her back with him. Pap always has his own way, and gits whatever he wants. I 'lowed you'd take the baby in bed with you, and I put a pallet in your room for Lissy."

Johnnie agreed to this arrangement, almost mechanically. Is it to be wondered at that her mind was already busy with the barrier this must set between herself and Gray Stoddard? She had never been ashamed of her origin or her people; but this — this was different.

Next morning she sent word to the mill foreman to put on a substitute, and took the morning that she might go with her mother to the hospital. Passmore was asleep, and they were not allowed to disturb him; but oa the steps they met Gray Stoddard, and he stopped so decidedly to speak to them that Johnnie could not exactly run away, as she felt like doing.

"Your mother!" echoed Stoddard, when Johnnie had told him who the visitor was. He glanced from the tall, fair-haired daughter to the lithe little gypsy at her side. "Why, she looks more like your sister," he said.

Laurella's white teeth flashed at this, and her big, dark eyes glowed.

"Johnnie's such a serious-minded person that she favours older than her years," the mother told him. "Well, I give her the name of the dead, and they say that makes a body solemn like."

It was very evident that Stoddard desired to detain them in conversation, but Johnnie smilingly, yet with decision, cut the interview short.

"I don't see why you hurried me a-past that-a-way," the little mother said resentfully, when they had gone a few steps. "I wanted to stay and talk to the gentleman, if you didn't. I think he's one of the nicest persons I've met since I've been in Cottonville. Mr. Gray Stoddard — how come you never mentioned him to me Johnnie?"

She turned to find a slow, painful blush rising in her daughter's face.

"I don't know, ma," said Johnnie gently. "I reckon it was because I didn't seem to have any concern with a rich gentleman such as Mr. Stoddard. He's got more money than Mr. Hardwick, they say — more than anybody else in Cottonville."

"Has he?" inquired Laurella vivaciously. "Well, money or no money, I think he's mighty nice. Looks like he ain't studying as to whether you got money or not. And if you was meaning that you didn't think yourself fit to be friends with such, why I'm ashamed of you, Johnnie Consadine. The Passmores and the Consadines are as good a family as there is on Unaka mountains. I don't know as I ever met up with anybody that I found was too fine for my company. And whenever your Uncle Pros gets well and finds his silver mine, we'll have as much money as the best of 'em."

The tears blinded Johnnie so that she could scarcely find her way, and the voice wherewith she would have answered her mother caught in her throat. She pressed her lips hard together and shook her head, then laughed out, a little sobbing laugh.

"Poor ma — poor little mother!" she whispered at length. "You ain't been away from the mountains as I have. Things are — well, they're a heap different here in the Settlement."

"They're a heap nicer," returned Laurella blithely. "Well, I'm mighty glad I met that gentleman this morning. Mr. Himes was talking to me of Shade Buckheath a-yesterday. He said Shade was wishful to wed you, Johnnie, and wanted me to give the boy my good word. I told him I wouldn't say anything — and then afterward I was going to. But since I've seen this gentleman, and know that his likes are friends of your'n, well — I — Johnnie, the Buckheaths are a hard nation of people, and that's the truth. If you wedded Shade, like as not he'd mistreat you."

"Oh mother — don't!" pleaded Johnnie, scarlet of face, and not daring to raise her eyes.

"What have I done now?" demanded Laurella with asperity.

"You mustn't couple my name with Mr. Stoddard's that way," Johnnie told her. "He's never thought of me, except as a poor girl who needs help mighty bad; and he's so kind-hearted and generous he's ready

to do for each and every that's worthy of it. But —
not that way — mother, you mustn't ever suppose
for a minute that he'd think of me in that way."

"Well, I wish't I may never!" Laurella exclaimed.
"Did I mention any particular way that the man was
supposed to be thinking about you? Can't I speak a
word without your biting my head off for it? As for
what Mr. Gray Stoddard thinks of you, let me tell you,
child, a body has only to see his eyes when he's looking
at you."

"Mother — Oh, mother!" protested Johnnie.

"Well, if he can look that way I reckon I can speak
of it," returned Laurella, with some reason.

"I want you to promise never to name it again,
even to me," said Johnnie solemnly, as they came to
the steps of the big lead-coloured house. "You surely
wouldn't say such a thing to any one else. I wish
you'd forget it yourself."

"We-ell," hesitated Laurella, "if you feel so strong
about it, I reckon I'll do as you say. But there ain't
anything in that to hinder me from being friends with
Mr. Stoddard. I feel sure that him and me would
get on together fine. He favours my people, the
Passmores. My daddy was just such an upstanding,
dark-complected feller as he is. He's got the look in
the eye, too."

Johnnie gasped as she remembered that the grandfather of whom her mother spoke was Virgil Passmore,
and called to mind the story of the borrowed wedding
coat.

CHAPTER XV

THE FEET OF THE CHILDREN

THE mountain people, being used only to one class, never find themselves consciously in the society of their superiors. Johnnie Consadine had been unembarrassed and completely mistress of the situation in the presence of Charlie Conroy, who did not fail after the Uplift dance to make some further effort to meet the "big red-headed girl," as he called her. She was aware that social overtures from such a person were not to be received by her, and she put them aside quite as though she had been, according to her own opinion, above rather than beneath them. The lover-like pretensions of Shade Buckheath, a man dangerous, remorseless, as careless of the rights of others as any tiger in the jungle, she regarded with negligent composure. But Gray Stoddard — ah, there her treacherous heart gave way, and trembled in terror. The air of perfect equality he maintained between them, his attitude of intimacy, flattering, almost affectionate, this it was which she felt she must not recognize.

The beloved books, which had seemed so many steps upon which to climb to a world where she dared acknowledge her own liking and admiration for Stoddard, were now laid aside. It took all of her heart and mind and time to visit Uncle Pros at the hospital, keep the children out of Pap's way in the house, and do justice to her work in the factory. She told Gray, haltingly, reluctantly, that she thought she must give up the reading and studying for a time.

"Not for long, I hope." Stoddard received her decision with a puzzled air, turning in his fingers the copy of "Walden" which she was bringing back to him. "Perhaps now that you have your mother and the children with you, there will be less time for this sort of thing for a while, but you haven't a mind that can enjoy being inactive. You may think you'll give it up; but study — once you've tasted it — will never let you alone."

Johnnie looked up at him with a weak and pitiful version of her usual beaming smile.

"I reckon you're right," she hesitated finally, in a very low voice. "But sometimes I think the less we know the happier we are."

"How's this? How's this?" cried Stoddard, almost startled. "Why, Johnnie — I never expected to hear that sort of thing from you. I thought your optimism was as deep as a well, and as wide as a church."

Poor Johnnie surely had need of such optimism as Stoddard had ascribed to her. They were weary evenings when she came home now, with the November rain blowing in the streets and the early-falling dusk almost upon her. It was on a Saturday night, and she had been to the hospital, when she got in to find Mandy, seated in the darkest corner of the sitting room, with a red flannel cloth around her neck — a sure sign that something unfortunate had occurred, since the tall woman always had sore throat when trouble loomed large.

"What's the matter?" asked Johnnie, coming close and laying a hand on the bent shoulder to peer into the drooping countenance.

"Don't come too nigh me — you'll ketch it," warned Mandy gloomily. "A so' th'oat is as ketchin' as small-pox, and I know it so to be, though they is them that say it ain't. When mine gits like this I jest tie it up and keep away from folks best I can. I hain't dared touch the baby sence hit began to hurt me this a-way."

"There's something besides the sore throat," persisted Johnnie. "Is it anything I can help you about?"

"Now, if that ain't jest like Johnnie Consadine!" apostrophized Mandy. "Yes, there is somethin' — not that I keer." She tossed her poor old gray head scornfully, and then groaned because the movement hurt her throat. "That thar feisty old Sullivan gave me my time this evenin'. He said they was layin' off weavers, and they could spare me. I told him, well, I could spare them, too. I told him I could hire in any other mill in Cottonville befo' workin' time Monday — but I'm afeared I cain't." Weak tears began to travel down her countenance. "I know I never will make a fine hand like you, Johnnie," she said pathetically. "There ain't a thing in the mill that I love to do —

nary thing. I can tend a truck patch or raise a field o' corn to beat anybody, and nobody cain't outdo me with fowls; but the mill ——"

She broke off and sat staring dully at the floor. Pap Himes had stumped into the room during the latter part of this conversation.

"Lost your job, hey?" he inquired keenly.

Mandy nodded, with fearful eyes on his face.

"Well, you want to watch out and keep yo' board paid up here. The week you cain't pay — out you go. I reckon I better trouble you to pay me in advance, unless'n you've got some kind friend that'll stand for you."

Mandy's lips parted, but no sound came. The gaze of absolute terror with which she followed the old man's waddling bulk as he went and seated himself in front of the air-tight stove, was more than Johnnie could endure.

"I'll stand for her board, Pap," she said quietly.

"Oh, you will, will ye?" Pap received her remark with disfavour. "Well, a fool and his money don't stay together long. And who'll stand for you, Johnnie Consadine? Yo' wages ain't a-goin' to pay for yo' livin' and Mandy's too. Ye needn't lay back on bein' my stepdaughter. You ain't acted square by me, an' I don't aim to do no more for you than if we was no kin."

"You won't have to. Mandy'll get a place next week — you know she will, Pap — an experienced weaver like she is. I'll stand for her."

Himes snorted. Mandy caught at Johnnie's hand

and drew it to her, fondling it.   Her round eyes were still full of tears.

"I do know you're the sweetest thing God ever made," she whispered, as Johnnie looked down at her. "You and Deanie."   And the two went out into the dining room together.

"Thar," muttered Himes to Buckheath, as the latter passed through on his way to supper; "you see whether it would do to give Johnnie the handlin' o' all that thar money from the patent.   Why, she'd hand it out to the first feller that put up a poor mouth and asked her for it.   You heard anything, Buck?"

Shade nodded.

"Come down to the works with me after supper. I've got something to show you," he said briefly, and Himes understood that the desired letter had arrived.

At first Laurella Consadine bloomed like a late rose in the town atmosphere.   She delighted in the village streets.   She was as wildly exhilarated as a child when she was taken on the trolley to Watauga.   With strange, inherent deftness she copied the garb, the hair dressing, even the manner and speech, of such worthy models as came within her range of vision — like her daughter, she had an eye for fitness and beauty; that which was merely fashionable though truly inelegant, did not appeal to her.   She was swift to appreciate the change in Johnnie.

"You look a heap prettier, and act and speak a heap prettier than you used to up in the mountains," she told the tall girl.   "Looks like it was a mighty

sensible thing for you to come down here to the Settlement; and if it was good for you, I don't see why it
wasn't good for me — and won't be for the rest of the
children. No need for you to be so solemn over it."

The entire household was aghast at the bride's attitude toward her old husband. They watched her with
the fascinated gaze we give to a petted child encroaching
upon the rights of a cross dog, or the pretty lady with
her little riding whip in the cage of the lion. She
treated him with a kindly, tolerant, yet overbearing
familiarity that appalled. She knew not to be
frightened when he clicked his teeth, but drew up
her pretty brows and fretted at him that she wished
he wouldn't make that noise — it worried her. She
tipped the sacred yellow cat out of the rocking-chair
where it always slept in state, took the chair herself, and sent that astonished feline from the room.

It was in Laurella's evident influence that Johnnie
put her trust when, one evening, as they all sat in
Sunday leisure in the front room — most of the girls
being gone to church or out strolling with "company"
— Pap Himes broached the question of the children
going to work in the mill.

"They're too young, Pap," Johnnie said to him
mildly. "They ought to be in school this winter."

"They've every one, down to Deanie, had mo' than
the six weeks schoolin' that the laws calls for," snarled
Himes.

"You wasn't thinking of putting Deanie in the mill
— not *Deanie* — was you?" asked Johnnie breathlessly.

"Why not?" inquired Himes. "She'll get no good runnin' the streets here in Cottonville, and she can earn a little somethin' in the mill. I'm a old man, an sickly, and I ain't long for this world. If them chaps is a-goin' to do anything for me, they'd better be puttin' in their licks."

Johnnie looked from the little girl's pink-and-white infantile beauty — she sat with the child in her lap — to the old man's hulking, powerful, useless frame. What would Deanie naturally be expected to do for her stepfather?

"Nobody's asked my opinion," observed Shade Buckheath, who made one of the family group, "but as far as I can see there ain't a thing to hurt young 'uns about mill work; and there surely ain't any good reason why they shouldn't earn their way, same as we all do. I reckon they had to work back on Unaka. Goin' to set 'em up now an make swells of 'em?"

Johnnie looked bitterly at him but made no reply.

"They won't take them at the Hardwick mill," she said finally. "Mr. Stoddard has enforced the rule that they have to have an affidavit with any child the mill employs that it is of legal age; and there's nobody going to swear that Deanie's even as much as twelve years old — nor Lissy — nor Pony — nor Milo. The oldest is but eleven."

Laurella had bought a long chain of red glass beads with a heart-shaped pendant. This trinket occupied her attention entirely while her daughter and husband discussed the matter of the children's future.

"Johnnie," she began now, apparently not having heard one word that had been said, "did you ever in your life see anything so cheap as this here string of beads for a dime? I vow I could live and die in that five-and-ten-cent store at Watauga. There was more pretties in it than I could have looked at in a week. I'm going right back thar Monday and git me them green garters that the gal showed me. I don't know what I was thinkin' about to come away without 'em! They was but a nickel."

Pap Himes looked at her, at the beads, and gave the fierce, inarticulate, ludicrously futile growl of a thwarted, perplexed animal.

"Mother," appealed Johnnie desperately, "do you want the children to go into the mill?"

"I don't know but they might as well — for a spell," said Laurella Himes, vainly endeavouring to look grown-up, and to pretend that she was really the head of the family. "They want to go, and you've done mighty well in the mill. If it wasn't for my health, I reckon I might go in and try to learn to weave, myself. But there — I came a-past with Mandy t'other evenin' when she was out, and the noise of that there factory is enough for me from the outside — I never could stand to be in it. Looks like such a racket would drive me plumb crazy."

Pap stared at his bride and clicked his teeth with the gnashing sound that overawed the others. He drew his shaggy brows in an attempt to look masterful.

"Well, ef you cain't tend looms, I reckon you can

take Mavity's place in the house here, and let her keep to the weavin' stiddier. She'll just about lose her job if she has to be out and in so much as she has had to be with me here of late."

"I will when I can," said Laurella, patronizingly. "Sometimes I get to feeling just kind of restless and no-account, and can't do a stroke of work. When I'm that-a-way I go to bed and sleep it off, or get out and go somewheres that'll take my mind from my troubles. Hit's by far the best way."

Once more Pap looked at her, and opened and shut his mouth helplessly. Then he turned sullenly to his stepdaughter, grumbling.

"You hear that! She won't work, and you won't give me your money. The children have obliged to bring in a little something — that's the way it looks to me. If the mills on the Tennessee side is too choicy to take 'em — and I know well as you, Johnnie, that they air; their man Connors told me so — I can hire 'em over at the Victory, on the Georgy side."

The Victory! A mill notorious in the district for its ancient, unsanitary buildings, its poor management, its bad treatment of its hands. Yes, it was true that at the Victory you could hire out anything that could walk and talk. Johnnie caught her breath and hugged the small pliant body to her breast, feeling with a mighty throb of fierce, mother-tenderness, the poor little ribs, yet cartilagenous; the delicate, soft frame for which God and nature demanded time, and chance to grow and strengthen. Yet she knew if she gave up her wages to Pap she would be no better off — indeed, she would be helpless in his hands; and the sum of them would not cover what the children all together could earn.

"Oh, Lord! To work in the Victory!" she groaned.

"Now, Johnnie," objected her mother," don't you get meddlesome just because you're a old maid. Your great-aunt Betsy was meddlesome disposed that-a-way. I reckon single women as they get on in years is apt so to be. Every one of these children has been promised that they should be let to work in the mill. They've been jest honin' to do it ever since you came down and got your place. Deanie was scared to death for fear they wouldn't take her. Don't you be meddlesome."

"Yes, and I'm goin' to buy me a gun and a nag with my money what I earn," put in Pony explosively. "'Course I'll take you-all to ride." He added the saving clause under Milo's reproving eye. "Sis' Johnnie, don't you want me to earn money and buy a hawse and a gun, and a — and most ever'thing else ?"

Johnnie looked down into the blue eyes of the little lad who had crept close to her chair. What he would earn in the factory she knew well — blows, curses, evil knowledge.

"If they should go to the Victory, I'd be mighty proud to do all I could to look after 'em, Johnnie," spoke Mandy from the shadows, where she sat on the floor at Laurella Consadine's feet, working away with a shoe-brush and cloth at the cleaning and polishing of the little woman's tan footwear. "Ye know I'm

a-gittin' looms thar to-morrow mornin'. Yes, I am,"
in answer to Johnnie's deprecating look. "I'd ruther
do it as to run round a week — or a month —'mongst
the better ones, huntin' a job, and you here standin'
for my board."

Till late that night Johnnie laboured with her
mother and stepfather, trying to show them that the
mill was no fit place for the children. Milo was all too
apt for such a situation, the very material out of which
a cotton mill moulds its best hands and its worst citizens.
Pony, restless, emotional, gifted and ambitious, craving his share of the joy of life and its opportunities,
would never make a mill hand; but under the pressure
of factory life his sister apprehended that he would
make a criminal.

"Uh-huh," agreed Pap, drily, when she tried to put
something of this into words. "I spotted that feller for
a rogue and a shirk the minute I laid eyes on him.
The mill'll tame him. The mill'll make him git down
and pull in the collar, I reckon. Women ain't fitten to
bring up chillen. A widder's boys allers goes to ruin.
Why, Johnnie Consadine, every one of them chaps is
plumb crazy to work in the mill — just like you was —
and you're workin' in the mill yourself. What makes
you talk so foolish about it?"

Laurella nodded an agreement, looking more than
usually like a little girl playing dolls.

"I reckon Mr. Himes knows best, Johnnie, honey,"
was her reiterated comment.

Cautiously Johnnie approached the subject of pay;

her stepfather had already demanded her wages, and expressed unbounded surprise that she was not willing to pass over the Saturday pay-envelope to him and let him put the money in the bank along with his other savings. Careful calculation showed that the four children could, after a few weeks of learning, prob- ably earn a little more than she could; and in any case Himes put it as a disciplinary measure, a way of life selected largely for the good of the little ones.

"If you just as soon let me," she said to him at last, "I believe I'll take them over to the Victory myself to-morrow morning."

She had hopes of telling their ages bluntly to the mill superintendent and having them refused.

Pap agreed negligently; he had no liking for early rising. And thus it was that Johnnie found herself at eight o'clock making her way, in the midst of the little group, toward the Georgia line and the old Victory plant, which all good workers in the district shunned if possible.

As she set her foot on the first plank of the bridge she heard a little rumble of sound, and down the road came a light, two-seated vehicle, with coloured driver, and Miss Lydia Sessions taking her sister's children out for an early morning drive. There was a frail, long-visaged boy of ten sitting beside his aunt in the back, with a girl of eight tucked between them. The nurse on the front seat held the youngest child, a little girl about Deanie's age.

As they came nearer, the driver drew up, evidently

in obedience to Miss Sessions's command, and she leaned forward graciously to speak to Johnnie.

"Good morning, John," said Miss Sessions as the carriage stopped. "Whose children are those?"

"They are my little sisters and brothers," responded Johnnie, looking down with a very pale face, and busying herself with Deanie's hair.

"And you're taking them over to the mill, so that they can learn to be useful. How nice that is!" Lydia smiled brightly at the little ones — her best charity-worker's smile.

"No," returned Johnnie, goaded past endurance, "I'm going over to see if I can get them to refuse to take this one." And she bent and picked Deanie up, holding her, the child's head dropped shyly against her breast, the small flower-like face turned a bit so that one blue eye might investigate the carriage and those in it. "Deanie's too little to work in the mill," Johnnie went on. "They have night turn over there at the Victory now, and it'll just about make her sick."

Miss Lydia frowned.

"Oh, John, I think you are mistaken," she said coldly. "The work is very light — you know that. Young people work a great deal harder racing about in their play than at anything they have to do in a spooling room— I'm sure my nieces and nephews do. And in your case it is necessary and right that the younger members of the family should help. I think you will find that it will not hurt them."

Individuals who work in cotton mills, and are not

adults, are never alluded to as children. It is an offense to mention them so. They are always spoken of — even those scarcely more than three feet high — as "young people."

Miss Sessions had smiled upon the piteous little group with a judicious mixture of patronage and mild reproof, and her driver had shaken the lines over the backs of the fat horses preparatory to moving on, when Stoddard's car turned into the street from the corner above.

"Wait, Junius. Dick is afraid of autos," cautioned Miss Lydia nervously.

Junius grinned respectfully, while bay Dick dozed and regarded the approaching car philosophically. As they stood, they blocked the way, so that Gray was obliged to slow down and finally to stop. He raised his hat ceremoniously to both groups. His pained eyes went past Lydia Sessions as though she had been but the painted representation of a woman, to fasten themselves on Johnnie where she stood, her tall, deep-bosomed figure relieved against the shining water, the flaxen-haired child on her breast, the little ones huddled about her.

That Johnnie Consadine should have fallen away all at once from that higher course she had so eagerly chosen and so resolutely maintained, had been to Gray a disappointment whose depth and bitterness somewhat surprised him. In vain he recalled the fact that all his theories of life were against forcing a culture where none was desired; he went back to it with grief — he had been so sure that Johnnie did love the real things, that hers was a nature which not only wished, but must have, spiritual and mental food. Her attitude toward himself upon their few meetings of late had confirmed a certain distrust of her, if one may use so strong a word. She seemed afraid, almost ashamed to face him. What was it she was doing, he wondered, that she knew so perfectly he would disapprove? And then, with the return of the books, the dropping of Johnnie's education, came the abrupt end of those informal letters. Not till they ceased, did he realize how large a figure they had come to cut in his life. Only this morning he had taken them out and read them over, and decided that the girl who wrote them was worth at least an attempt toward an explanation and better footing. He had decided not to give her up. Now she confirmed his worst apprehensions. At his glance, her face was suffused with a swift, distressed red. She wondered if he yet knew of her mother's marriage. She dreaded the time when she must tell him. With an inarticulate murmur she spoke to the little ones, turned her back and hurried across the bridge.

"Is Johnnie putting those children in the mill?" asked Stoddard half doubtfully, as his gaze followed them toward the entrance of the Victory.

"I believe so," returned Lydia, smiling. "We were just speaking of how good it was that the cotton mills gave an opportunity for even the smaller ones to help, at work which is within their capacity."

" Johnnie Consadine said that ?" inquired Gray, startled.   " Why is she taking them over to the Victory ?"   And then he answered his own question. "She knows very well they are below the legal age in Tennessee."

Lydia Sessions trimmed instantly.

"That must be it," she said.   " I wondered a little that she seemed not to want them in the same factory that she is in.   But I remember Brother Hartley said that we are very particular at our mill to hire no young people below the legal age.   That must be it."

Stoddard looked with reprehending yet still incredulous eyes, to where Johnnie and her small following disappeared within the mill doors.   Johnnie — the girl who had written him that pathetic little letter about the children in her room, and her growing doubt as to the wholesomeness of their work; the girl who had read the books he gave her, and fed her understanding on them till she expressed herself logically and lucidly on the economic problems of the day — that, for the sake of the few cents they could earn, she should put the children, whom he knew she loved, into slavery, seemed to him monstrous beyond belief.   Why, if this were true, what a hypocrite the girl was!   As coarse and unfeeling as the rest of them.   Yet she had some shame left; had blushed to be caught in the act by him. It showed her worse than those who justified this thing, the enormity of which she had seemed to understand well.

"You mustn't blame her too much," came Lydia

Sessions's smooth voice. "John's mother is a widow, and girls of that age like pretty clothes and a good time. Some people consider John very handsome, and of course with an ignorant young woman of that class, flattery is likely to turn the head. I think she does as well as could be expected."

CHAPTER XVI

BITTER WATERS

JOHNNIE had a set of small volumes of English verse, extensively annotated by his own hand, which Stoddard had brought to her early in their acquaintance, leaving it with her more as a gift than as a loan. She kept these little books after all the others had gone back. She had read and reread them — cullings from Chaucer, from Spenser, from the Elizabethan lyrists, the border balladry, fierce, tender, oh, so human — till she knew pages of them by heart, and their vocabulary influenced her own, their imagery tinged all her leisure thoughts. It seemed to her, whenever she debated returning them, that she could not bear it. She would get them out and sit with one of them open in her hands, not reading, but staring at the pages with unseeing eyes, passing her fingers over it, as one strokes a beloved hand, or turning through each book only to find the pencilled words in the margins. She would be giving up part of herself when she took these back.

Yet it had to be done, and one miserable morning she made them all into a neat package, intending to carry them to the mill and place them on Stoddard's desk thus early, when nobody would be in the office.   Then the children came in; Deanie was half sick; and in the distress of getting the ailing child comfortably into her own bed, Johnnie forgot the books.   Taking them in at noon, she met Stoddard himself.

"I've brought you back your — those little books of Old English Poetry," she said, with a sudden constriction in her throat, and a quick burning flush that suffused brow, cheek and neck.

Stoddard looked at her; she was thinner than she had been, and otherwise showed the marks of misery and of factory life.   The sight was almost intolerable to him.   Poor girl, she herself was suffering cruelly enough beneath the same yoke she had helped to lay on the children.

"Are you really giving up your studies entirely?" he asked, in what he tried to make a very kindly voice. He laid his hand on the package of books.   "I wonder if you aren't making a mistake, Johnnie.   You look as though you were working too hard.   Some things are worth more than money and getting on in the world."

Johnnie shook her head.   For the moment words were beyond her.   Then she managed to say in a fairly composed tone.

"There isn't any other way for me.   I think some times, Mr. Stoddard, when a body is born to a hard life, all the struggling and trying just makes it that much harder.   Maybe when the children get a little older I'll have more chance."

The statement was wistfully, timidly made; yet to Gray Stoddard it seemed a brazen defence of her present course. It pierced him that she on whose nobility of nature he could have staked his life, should justify such action.

"Yes," he said with quick bitterness, "they might be able to earn more, of course, as time goes on." It was a cruel speech between two people who had discussed this feature of industrial life as these had; even Stoddard had no idea how cruel.

For a dizzy moment the girl stared at him, then, though her flushed cheeks had whitened pitifully and her lip trembled, she answered with bravely lifted head.

"I thank you very much for all the help you've been to me, Mr. Stoddard. What I said just now didn't look as though I appreciated it. I ask your pardon for that. I aim to do the best I can for the children. And I — thank you."

She turned and was gone, leaving him puzzled and with a sore ache at heart.

Winter came on, wet, dark, cheerless, in the shackling, half-built little village, and Johnnie saw for the first time what the distress of the poor in cities is. A temperature which would have been agreeable in a drier climate, bit to the bone in the mist-haunted valleys of that mountain region. The houses were mostly mere board shanties, tightened by pasting newspapers over the cracks inside, where the women of the family had time for such work; and the heating apparatus was generally a wood-burning cook-stove, with possibly an additional coal heater in the front room which could be fired on Sundays, or when the family was at home to tend it.

All through the bright autumn days, Laurella Himes had hurried from one new and charming sensation or discovery to another; she was like the butterflies that haunt the banks of little streams or wayside pools at this season, disporting themselves more gaily even than the insects of spring in what must be at best a briefer glory. When the weather began to be chilly, she complained of a pain in her side.

"Hit hurts me right there," she would say piteously, taking Johnnie's hand and laying it over the left side of her chest. "My feet haven't been good and warm since the weather turned. I jest cain't stand these here old black boxes of stoves they have in the Settlement. If I could oncet lay down on the big hearth at home and get my feet warm, I jest know my misery would leave me."

At first Pap merely grunted over these homesick repinings; but after a time he began to hang about her and offer counsel which was often enough peevishly received.

"No, I ain't et anything that disagreed with me," Laurella pettishly replied to his well-meant inquiries. "You're thinkin' about yo'se'f. I never eat more than is good for me, nor anything that ain't jest right. Hit ain't my stomach. Hit's right there in my side. Looks like hit was my heart, an' I believe in my soul it is. Oh, law, if I could oncet lay down befo' a nice, good hickory fire and get my feet warm!"

And so it came to pass that, while everybody in the boarding-house looked on amazed, almost aghast, Gideon Himes withdrew from the bank such money as was necessary, and had a chimney built at the side of the fore room and a broad hearth laid. He begged almost tearfully for a small grate which should burn the soft bituminous coal of the region, and be much cheaper to install and maintain. But Laurella turned away from these suggestions with the hopeless, pliable obstinacy of the weak.

"I wouldn't give the rappin' o' my finger for a nasty little smudgy, smoky grate fire," she declared rebelliously, thanklessly. "A hickory log-heap is what I want, and if I cain't have that, I reckon I can jest die without it."

"Now, Laurelly — now Laurelly," Pap quavered in tones none other had ever heard from him, "don't you talk about dyin'. You look as young as Johnnie this minute. I'll git you what you want. Lord, I'll have Dawson build the chimbley big enough for you to keep house in, if them's yo' ruthers."

It was almost large enough for that, and the great load of hickory logs which Himes hauled into the yard from the neighbouring mountain-side was cut to length. Fire was kindled in the new chimney; it drew perfectly; and Pap himself carried Laurella in his arms and laid her on some quilts beside the hearthstone, demanding eagerly, "Thar now — don't that make you feel better?"

"Uh-huh." The ailing woman turned restlessly

on her pallet. The big, awkward, ill-favoured old man stood with his disproportionately long arms hanging by his sides, staring at her, unaware that his presence half undid the good the leaping flames were doing her.

"I wish't Uncle Pros was sitting right over there, t'other side the fire," murmured Laurella dreamily. "How is Pros, Johnnie?"

For nobody understood, as the crazed man in the hospital might have done, that Laurella's bodily illness was but the cosmic despair of the little girl who has broken her doll. It had been the philosophy of this sun-loving, butterfly nature to turn her back on things when they got too bad and take to her bed till, in the course of events, they bettered themselves. But now she had emerged into a bleak winter world where Uncle Pros was not, where Johnnie was powerless, and where she had been allowed by an unkind Providence to work havoc with her own life and the lives of her little ones; and her illness was as the tears of the girl with a shattered toy.

The children in their broken shoes and thin, ill-selected clothing, shivered on the roads between house and mill, and gave colour to the statement of many employers that they were better off in the thoroughly warmed factories than at home. But the factories were a little too thoroughly warmed. The operatives sweated under their tasks and left the rooms, with their temperature of eighty-five, to come, drenched with perspiration, into the chill outside air. The colds which resulted were always supposed to be caught out of doors. Nobody had sufficient understanding of such matters to suggest that the rebreathed, super-heated atmosphere of the mill room was responsible.

Deanie, who had never been sick a day in her life, took a heavy cold and coughed so that she could scarcely get any sleep. Johnnie was desperately anxious, since the lint of the spinning room immediately irritated the little throat, and perpetuated the cold in a steady, hacking cough, that cotton-mill workers know well. Pony was from the first insubordinate and well-nigh incorrigible — in short, he died hard. He came to Johnnie again and again with stories of having been cursed and struck. She could only beg him to be good and do what was demanded without laying himself liable to punishment. Milo, the serious-faced little burden bearer, was growing fast, and lacked stamina. Beneath the cotton-mill régime, his chest was getting dreadfully hollow. He was all too good a worker, and tried anxiously to make up for his brother's shortcomings.

"Pony, he's a little feller," Milo would say pitifully. "He ain't nigh as old as I am. It comes easier to me than what it does to him to stay in the house and tend my frames, and do like I'm told. If the bosses would call me when he don't do to suit 'em, I could always get him to mind."

Lissy had something of her mother's shining vitality, but it dimmed woefully in the rough-and-ready clatter and slam of the big Victory mill.

The children had come from the sunlit heights and free air of the Unakas. Their play had been always out of doors, on the mosses under tall trees, where fragrant balsams dropped cushions of springy needles for the feet; their labour, the gathering of brush and chips for the fire in winter, the dropping corn, and, with the older boys, the hoeing of it in spring and summer — all under God's open sky. They had been forced into the factory when nothing but places on the night shift could be got for them. Day work was promised later, but the bitter winter wore away, and still the little captives crept over the bridge in the twilight and slunk shivering home at dawn. Johnnie made an arrangement to get off from her work a little earlier, and used to take the two girls over herself; but she could not go for them in the morning. One evening about the holidays, miserably wet, and offering its squalid contrast to the season, Johnnie, plodding along between the two little girls, with Pony and Milo following, met Gray Stoddard face to face. He halted uncertainly. There was a world of reproach in his face, and Johnnie answered it with eyes of such shame and contrition as convinced him that she knew well the degradation of what she was doing.

"You need another umbrella," he said abruptly, putting down his own as he paused under the store porch where a boy stood at the curb with his car, hood on, prepared for a trip in to Watauga.

"I lost our'n," ventured Pony. "It don't seem fair that Milo has to get wet because I'm so bad about losing things, does it?" And he smiled engagingly up into the tall man's face — Johnnie's own eyes, large-pupilled, black-lashed, full of laughter in their clear depths. Gray Stoddard stared down at them silently for a moment. Then he pushed the handle of his umbrella into the boy's grimy little hand.

"See how long you can keep that one," he said kindly. "It's marked on the handle with my name; and maybe if you lost it somebody might bring it back to you."

Johnnie had turned away and faltered on a few paces in a daze of humiliation and misery.

"Sis' Johnnie — oh, Sis' Johnnie!" Pony called after her, flourishing the umbrella. "Look what Mr. Stoddard give Milo and me." Then, in sudden consternation as Milo caught his elbow, he whirled and offered voluble thanks. "I'm a goin' to earn a whole lot of money and pay back the trouble I am to my folks," he confided to Gray, hastily. "I didn't know I was such a bad feller till I came down to the Settlement. Looks like I cain't noways behave. But I'm goin' to earn a big heap of money, an' buy things for Milo an' maw an' the girls. Only now they take all I can earn away from me."

There was a warning call from Johnnie, ahead in the dusk somewhere; and the little fellow scuttled away toward the Victory and a night of work.

Spring came late that year, and after it had given a hint of relieving the misery of the poor, there followed an Easter storm which covered all the new-made gardens with sleet and sent people shivering back to their winter wear. Deanie had been growing very thin, and the red on her cheeks was a round spot of scarlet. Laurella lay all day and far into the night on her pallet of quilts before the big fire in the front room, spent, inert, staring at the ceiling, entertaining God knows what guests of terror and remorse. Nothing distressing must be brought to her. Coming home from work once at dusk, Johnnie found the two little girls on the porch, Deanie crying and Lissy trying to comfort her.

"I thest cain't go to that old mill to-night, Sis' Johnnie," the little one pleaded. "Looks like I thest cain't."

"I could tell Mr. Reardon, and he'd put a substitute on to tend her frames," Lissy spoke up eagerly. "You ask Pap Himes will he let us do that, Sis' Johnnie."

Johnnie went past her mother, who appeared to be dozing, and into the dining room, where Himes was. He had promised to do some night work, setting up new machines at the Victory, and he was in that uncertain humour which the prospect of work always produced. Gideon Himes was an old man, pestered, as he himself would have put it, by the mysterious illness of his young wife, fretted by the presence of the children, no doubt in a measure because he felt himself to be doing an ill part by them. His grumpy silence of other days, his sardonic humour, gave place to hypochondriac complainings and outbursts of fierce temper. Pony had hurt his foot in a machine at the factory and it required daily dressing. Johnnie understood from the sounds which greeted her that the sore foot was being bandaged.

"Hold still, cain't ye?" growled Himes. "I ain't a-hurtin' ye. Now you set in to bawl and I'll give ye somethin' to bawl for — hear me?"

The old man was skilful with hurts, but he was using such unnecessary roughness in this case as set the plucky little chap to sobbing, and, just as Johnnie entered the room, got him heavy-handed punishment for it. It was an unfortunate time to bring up the question of Deanie; yet it must be settled at once.

"Pap," said the girl, urgently, "the baby ain't fit to go to the mill to-night — if ever she ought. You said that you'd get day work for them all. If you won't do that, let Deanie stay home for a spell. She sure enough isn't fit to work."

Himes faced his stepdaughter angrily.

"When I say a child's fitten to work — it's fitten to work," he rounded on her. "I hain't axed your opinion — have I? No. Well, then, keep it to yourself till it is axed for. You Pony, your foot's done and ready. You get yourself off to the mill, or you'll be docked for lost time."

The little fellow limped sniffling out; Johnnie reached down for Deanie, who had crept after her to hear how her cause went. It was evident that sight of the child lingering increased Pap's anger, yet the elder sister gathered up the ailing little one in her strong arms and tried again.

"Pap, I'll pay you for Deanie's whole week's work if you'll just let her stay home to-night. I'll pay you the money now."

"All right," Pap stuck out a ready, stubbed palm, and received in it the silver that was the price of the little girl's time for a week. He counted it over before he rammed it down in his pocket. Then, "You can pay me, and she can go to the mill, 'caze your wages ought to come to me anyhow, and it don't do chaps like her no good to be muchin' 'em all the time. Would you ruther have her go before I give her a good beatin' or after?" and he looked Johnnie fiercely in the eyes.

Johnnie looked back at him unflinching. She did not lack spirit to defy him. But her mother was this man's wife; the children were in their hands. Devoted, high-couraged as she was, she saw no way here to fight for the little ones. To her mother she could not appeal; she must have support from outside.

"Never you mind, honey," she choked as she clasped Deanie's thin little form closer, and the meagre small arms went round her neck. "Sister'll find a way. You go on to the mill to-night, and sister'll find somebody to help her, and she'll come there and get you before morning."

When the pitiful little figure had lagged away down the twilight street, holding to Lissy's hand, limping on sore feet, Johnnie stood long on the porch in the dark with gusts of rain beating intermittently at the lattice beside her. Her hands were wrung hard together. Her desperate gaze roved over the few scattered lights of the little village, over the great flaring, throbbing mills beyond, as though questioning where she could seek for assistance. Paying money to Pap Himes did no good.   So much was plain.   She had always been afraid to begin it, and she realized now that the present outcome was what she had apprehended. Uncle Pros, the source of wisdom for all her childish days, was in the hospital, a harmless lunatic.   Of late the old man's bodily health had mended suddenly, almost marvellously; but he remained vacant, childish in mind, and so far the authorities had retained him, hoping to probe in some way to the obscure, moving cause of his malady.   Twice when she spoke to her mother of late, being very desperate, Laurella had said peevishly that if she were able she'd get up and leave the house.   Plainly to-night she was too sick a woman to be troubled.   As Johnnie stood there, Shade Buck-heath passed her, going out of the house and down the street toward the store.   Once she might have thought of appealing to him; but now a sure knowledge of what his reply would be forestalled that.

There remained then what the others called her "swell   friends."   Gray   Stoddard — the   thought brought with it an agony from which she flinched. But after all, there was Lydia Sessions.   She was sure Miss Sessions meant to be kind; and if she knew that Deanie was really sick ——.   Yes, it would be worth while to go to her with the whole matter.

At the thought she turned hesitatingly toward the door, meaning to get her hat, and — though she had formulated no method of appeal — to hurry to the Hardwick house and at least talk with Miss Sessions and endeavour to enlist her help.

But the door opened before she reached it, and Mavity Bence stood there, in her face the deadly weariness of all woman's toil and travail since the fall. Johnnie moved to her quickly, putting a hand on her shoulder, remembering with swift compunction that the poor woman's burdens were trebled since Laurella lay ill, and Pap gave up so much of his time to hanging anxiously about his young wife.

"What is it, Aunt Mavity?" she asked. "Is anything the matter?"

"I hate to werry ye, Johnnie," said the other's deprecating voice; "but looks like I've jest got obliged to have a little help this evenin'. I'm plumb dead on my feet, and there's all the dishes to do and a stack of towels and things to rub out." Her dim gaze questioned the young face above her dubiously, almost desperately. The little brass lamp in her hand made a pitiful wavering.

"Of course I can help you. I'd have been in before this, only I — I — was kind of worried about something else, and I forgot," declared Johnnie, strengthening her heart to endure the necessary postponement of her purpose.

She went into the kitchen with Mavity Bence, and the two women worked there at the dishes, and washing out the towels, till after nine o'clock, Johnnie's anxiety and distress mounting with every minute of delay. At a little past nine, she left poor Mavity at the door of that wretched place the poor woman called her room, looked quietly in to see that her mother seemed

to sleep, got her hat and hurried out, goaded by a seemingly disproportionate fever of impatience and anxiety.
She took her way up the little hill and across the slope
to where the Hardwick mansion gleamed, many-
windowed, gay with lights, behind its evergreens.

When she reached the house itself she found an
evening reception going forward — the Hardwicks
were entertaining the Lyric Club. She halted outside,
debating what to do. Could she call Miss Lydia from
her company to listen to such a story as this? Was
it not in itself almost an offence to bring these things
before people who could live as Miss Lydia lived?
Somebody was playing the violin, and Johnnie drew
nearer the window to listen. She stared in at the
beautiful lighted room, the well-dressed, happy people.
Suddenly she caught sight of Gray Stoddard standing
near the girl who was playing, a watchful eye upon her
music to turn it for her. She clutched the window-
sill and stood choking and blinded, fighting with a
crowd of daunting recollections and miserable apprehensions. The young violinist was playing Schubert's
Serenade. From the violin came the cry of hungry
human love demanding its mate, questing, praying,
half despairing, and yet wooing, seeking again.

Johnnie's piteous gaze roved over the well-beloved
lineaments. She noted with a passion of tenderness
the turn of head and hand that were so familiar to her,
and so dear. Oh, she could never hate him for it, but
it was hard — hard — to be a wave in the ocean of
toil that supported the galleys of such as these!

It began to rain again softly as she stood there, scattered drops falling on her bright hair, and she gathered her dress about her and pressed close to the window where the eaves of the building sheltered her, forcing herself to look in and take note of the difference between those people in there and her own lot of life. This was not usually Johnnie's way. Her unfailing optimism prompted her always to measure the distance below her, and be glad of having climbed so far, rather than to dim her eyes with straining them toward what was above. But now she marked mercilessly the light, yet subdued, movements, the deference expressed when one of these people addressed another; and Gray Stoddard at the upper end of the room was easily the most marked figure in it. Who was she to think she might be his friend when all this beautiful world of ease and luxury and fair speech was open to him?

Like a sword flashed back to her memory of the children. They were being killed in the mills, while she wasted her thoughts and longings on people who would laugh if they knew of her presumptuous devotion.

She turned with a low exclamation of astonishment, when somebody touched her on the shoulder.

"Is you de gal Miss Lyddy sont for?" inquired the yellow waitress a bit sharply.

"No — yes — I don't know whether Miss Sessions sent for me or not," Johnnie halted out; "but," eagerly, "I must see her. I've — Cassy. I've got to speak to her right now."

Cassy regarded the newcomer rather scornfully.

Yet everybody liked Johnnie, and the servant eventually put off her design of being impressive and said in a fairly friendly manner:

"You couldn't noways see her now. I couldn't disturb her whilst she's got company — without you want to put on this here cap and apron and come he'p me sarve the refreshments. Dey was a gal comin' to resist me, but she ain't put in her disappearance yet. Ain't no time for foolin', dis ain't."

Johnnie debated a moment. A servant's livery — but Deanie was sick and ——. With a sudden, impulsive movement, and somewhat to Cassy's surprise, Johnnie followed into the pantry, seized the proffered cap and apron and proceeded to put them on.

"I've got to see Miss Sessions," she repeated, more to herself than to the negress. "Maybe what I have to say will only take a minute. I reckon she won't mind, even if she has got company. It — well, I've got to see her some way." And taking the tray of frail, dainty cups and saucers Cassy brought her, she started with it to the parlour.

The music was just dying down to its last wail when Gray looked up and caught sight of her coming. His mind had been full of her. To him certain pieces of music always meant certain people, and the Serenade could bring him nothing but Johnnie Consadine's face. His startled eyes encountered with distaste the cap pinned to her hair, descended to the white apron that covered her black skirt, and rested in astonishment on the tray that held the coffee, cream and sugar.

"Begin here," Cassie prompted her assistant, and Johnnie, stopping, offered her tray of cups.

Gray's indignant glance went from the girl herself to his hostess. What foolery was this? Why should Johnnie Consadine dress herself as a servant and wait on Lydia Sessions's guests?

Before the two reached him, he turned abruptly and went into the library, where Miss Sessions stood for a moment quite alone. Her face brightened; he had sought her society very much less of late. She looked hopefully for a renewal of that earlier companionship which seemed by contrast almost intimate.

"Have you hired Johnnie Consadine as a waitress?" Stoddard asked her in a non-committal voice. "I should have supposed that her place in the mill would pay her more, and offer better prospects."

"No — oh, no," said Miss Sessions, startled, and considerably disappointed at the subject he had selected to converse upon.

"How does she come to be here with a cap and apron on to-night?" pursued Stoddard, with an edge to his tone which he could not wholly subdue.

"I really don't understand that myself," Lydia Sessions told him. "I made no arrangement with her. I expected to have a couple of negresses — they're much better servants, you know. Of course when a girl like John gets a little taste of social contact and recognition, she may go to considerable lengths to gratify her desire for it. No doubt she feels proud of forcing herself in this evening; and then of course she knows she will be well paid. She seems to be doing nicely," glancing between the portières where Johnnie bent before one guest or another, offering her tray of cups. "I really haven't the heart to reprove her."

"Then I think I shall," said Stoddard with sudden resolution. "If you don't mind, Miss Sessions, would you let her come in and talk to me a little while, as soon as she has finished passing the coffee? I — really it seems to me that this is outrageous. Johnnie is a girl of brains and abilities, and we who have her true welfare at heart should see that she doesn't — in her youth and ignorance — fall into such errors as this."

"Oh, if you like, I'll talk to her myself," said Miss Lydia smoothly. The conversation was not so different from others that she and Stoddard had held concerning this girl's deserts and welfare. She added, after an instant's pause, speaking quickly, with heightened colour, and a little nervous catch in her voice, "I'll do my best. I — I don't want to speak harshly of John, but I must in truth say that she's the one among my Uplift Club girls that has been least satisfactory to me."

"In what way?" inquired Stoddard in an even, quiet tone.

"Well, I should be a little puzzled to put it into words," Miss Sessions answered him with a deprecating smile; "and yet it's there — the feeling that John Consadine is — I hate to say it — ungrateful."

"Ungrateful," repeated her companion, his eyes steadily on Miss Sessions's face. "To leave Johnnie

Consadine out of the matter entirely, what else do you expect from any of your protégées? What else can any one expect who goes into what the modern world calls charitable work?"

Miss Sessions studied his face in some bewilderment. Was he arraigning her, or sympathizing with her? He said no more. He left upon her the onus of further speech. She must try for the right note.

"I know it," she fumbled desperately. "And isn't it disappointing? You do everything you possibly can for people and they seem to dislike you for it."

"They don't merely seem to," said Stoddard, almost brusquely, "they do dislike and despise you, and that most heartily. It is as certain a result as that two and two make four. You have pauperized and degraded them, and they hate you for it."

Lydia Sessions shrank back on the seat, and stared at him, her hand before her open mouth.

"Why, Mr. Stoddard!" she ejaculated finally. "I thought you were fully in sympathy with my Uplift work. You — you certainly let me think so. If you despised it, as you now say, why did you help me and — and all that?"

Stoddard shook his head.

"No," he demurred a little wearily. "I don't despise you, nor your work. As for helping you — I dislike lobster, and yet I conscientiously provide you with it whenever we are where the comestible is served, because I know you like it."

"Mr. Stoddard," broke in Lydia tragically, "that is frivolous! These are grave matters, and I thought — oh, I thought certainly — that I was deserving your good opinion in this charitable work if ever I deserved such a thing in my life."

"Oh — deserved!" repeated Stoddard, almost impatiently. "No doubt you deserve a great deal more than my praise; but you know — do you not? — that people who believe as I do, regard that sort of philanthropy as a barrier to progress; and, really now, I think you ought to admit that under such circumstances I have behaved with great friendliness and self-control."

The words were spoken with something of the old teasing intonation that had once deluded Lydia Sessions into the faith that she held a relation of some intimacy to this man. She glanced at him fleetingly; then, though she felt utterly at sea, made one more desperate effort.

"But I always went first to you when I was raising money for my Uplift work, and you gave to me more liberally than anybody else. Jerome never approved of it. Hartley grumbled, or laughed at me, and came reluctantly to my little dances and receptions. I sometimes felt that I was going against all my world — except you. I depended upon your approval. I felt that you were in full sympathy with me here, if nowhere else."

She looked so disproportionately moved by the matter that Stoddard smiled a little.

"I'm sorry," he said at last. "I see now that I

have been taking it for granted all along that you understood the reservation I held in regard to this matter."

"You — you should have told me plainly," said Lydia drearily. "It — it gives me a strange feeling to have depended so entirely on you, and then to find out that you were thinking of me all the while as Jerome does."

"Have I been?" inquired Stoddard. "As Jerome does? What a passion it seems to be with folks to classify their friends. People call me a Socialist, because I am trying to find out what I really do think on certain economic and social subjects. I doubt that I shall ever bring up underneath any precise label, and yet some people would think it egotistical that I insisted upon being a class to myself. I very much doubt that I hold Mr. Hardwick's opinion exactly in any particular." He looked at the girl with a sort of urgency which she scarcely comprehended. "Miss Sessions," he said, "I wear my hair longer than most men, and the barber is always deeply grieved at my obstinacy. I never eat potatoes, and many well-meaning persons are greatly concerned over it — they regard the exclusion of potatoes from one's dietary as almost criminal. But you — I expect in you more tolerance concerning my peculiarities. Why must you care at all what I think, or what my views are in this matter?"

"Oh, I don't understand you at all," Lydia said distressfully.

"No?" agreed Stoddard with an interrogative note in his voice. "But after all there's no need for people to be so determined to understand each other, is there?"

Lydia looked at him with swimming eyes.

"Why didn't you tell me not to do those things?" she managed finally to say with some composure.

"Tell you not to do things that you had thought out for yourself and decided on?" asked Stoddard. "Oh, no, Miss Sessions. What of your own development? I had no business to interfere like that. You might be exactly right about it, and I wrong, so far as you yourself were concerned. And even if I were right and you wrong, the only chance of growth for you was to exploit the matter and find it out for yourself."

"I don't understand a word you say," Lydia Sessions repeated dully. "That's the kind of thing you used always to talk when you and I were planning for John Consadine. Development isn't what a woman wants. She wants — she needs — to understand how to please those she — approves. If she fails anywhere, and those she — well, if somebody that she has — confidence — in tells her, why then she'll know better next time. You should have told me."

Her eyes overflowed as she made an end, but Stoddard adopted a tone of determined lightness.

"Dear me," he said gently. "What reactionary views! You're out of temper with me this evening — I get on your nerves with my theorizing. Forgive me, and forget all about it."

Lydia Sessions smiled kindly on her guest, without speaking. But one thing remained to her out of it all. Gray Stoddard thought ill of her work — it carried her further from him, instead of nearer! So many months of effort worse than wasted! At that instant she had sight of Shade Buckheath's dark face in the entry. She got to her feet.

"I beg your pardon," she said wanly, "I think there is some one out there that I ought to speak to."

CHAPTER XVII

A VICTIM

IN THE spinning room at the Victory Mill, with its tall frames and endlessly turning bobbins, where the languid thread ran from hank to spool and the tired little feet must walk the narrow aisles between the jennies, watching if perchance a filament had broken, a knot caught, or other mischance occurred, and right it, Deanie plodded for what seemed to her many years. Milo and Pony both had work now in another department, and Lissy's frames were quite across the noisy big room. Whenever the little dark-haired girl could get away from her own task and the eye of the room boss, she ran across to the small, ailing sister and hugged her hard, begging her not to feel bad, not to cry, Sis' Johnnie was bound to come before long. With the morbidness of a sick child, Deanie came to dread these well-meant assurances, finding them almost as distressing as her own strange, tormenting sensations.

The room was insufferably close, because it had rained and the windows were all tightly shut. The flare of light vitiated the air, heated it, but seemed to the child's sick sense to illuminate nothing. Sometimes she found herself walking into the machinery and put out a reckless little hand to guard her steps. Sister Johnnie had said she would come and take her away. Sister Johnnie was the Providence that was never known to fail. Deanie kept on doggedly, and tied threads, almost asleep. The room opened and shut like an accordion before her fevered vision; the floor heaved and trembled under her stumbling feet. To lie down — to lie down anywhere and sleep — that was the almost intolerable longing that possessed her. Her mouth was hot and dry. The little white, peaked face, like a new moon, grew strangely luminous in its pallor. Her eyes stung in their sockets — those desolate blue eyes, dark with unshed tears, heavy with sleep.

She had turned her row and started back, when there came before her, so plain that she almost thought she might wet her feet in the clear water, a vision of the spring-branch at home up on Unaka, where she and Lissy used to play. There, among the giant roots of the old oak on its bank, was the house they had built of big stones and bright bits of broken dishes; there lay her home-made doll flung down among gay fallen leaves; a little toad squatted beside it; and near by was the tiny gourd that was their play-house dipper. Oh, for a drink from that spring!

She caught sight of Mandy Meacham passing the door, and ran to her, heedless of consequences.

"Mandy," she pleaded, taking hold of the woman's skirts and throwing back her reeling head to stare up into the face above her, "Mandy, Sis' Johnnie said she'd come; but it's a awful long time, and I'm scared I'll fall into some of these here old machines, I feel that bad. Won't you go tell Sis' Johnnie I'm waitin' for her?"

Mandy glanced forward through the weaving-room toward her own silent looms, then down at the little, flushed face at her knee. If she dared to do things, as Johnnie dared, she would pick up the baby and leave. The very thought of it terrified her. No, she must get Johnnie herself. Johnnie would make it right. She bent down and kissed the little thing, whispering:

"Never you mind, honey. Mandy's going straight and find Sis' Johnnie, and bring her here to Deanie. Jest wait a minute."

Then she turned and, swiftly, lest her courage evaporate, hurried down the stair and to the time keeper.

"Ef you've got a substitute, you can put 'em on my looms," she said brusquely. "I've got to go down in town."

"Sick?" inquired Reardon laconically, as he made some entry on a card and dropped it in a drawer beside him.

"No, I ain't sick — but Deanie Consadine is, and I'm goin' over in town to find her sister. That child ain't fitten to be in no mill — let alone workin' night turn. You men ort to be ashamed — that baby ort to be in her bed this very minute."

Her voice had faltered a bit at the conclusion. Yet she made an end of it, and hurried away with a choke in her throat. The man stared after her angrily.

"Well!" he ejaculated finally. "She's got her nerve with her. Old Himes is that gal's stepdaddy. I reckon he knows whether she's fit to work in the mills or not — he hired her here. Bob, ain't Himes down in the basement right now settin' up new machines? You go down there and name this business to him. See what he's got to say."

A party of young fellows was tramping down the village street singing. One of them carried a guitar and struck, now and again, a random chord upon its strings. The street was dark, but as the singers, stepping rythmically, passed the open door of the store, Mandy recognized a shape she knew.

"Shade — Shade Buckheath! Wait thar!" she called to him.

The others lingered, too, a moment, till they saw it was a girl following; then they turned and sauntered slowly on, still singing:

" Ef I was a little bird, I'd nest in the tallest tree,
That leans over the waters of the beautiful Tennessee.'

The words came back to Buckheath and Mandy in velvety bass and boyish tenor.

"Shade — whar's Johnnie?" panted Mandy, shaking him by the arm. "I been up to the house, and she ain't thar. Pap ain't thar, neither. I was skeered to name my business to Laurelly; Aunt Mavity ain't no help and, and — Shade — whar's Johnnie?" Buckheath looked down into her working, tragic face and his mouth hardened.

"She ain't at home," he said finally. "I've been at Himes's all evening. Pap and me has a — er, a little business on hand and — she ain't at home. They told me that they was some sort of shindig at Mr. Hardwick's to-night. I reckon Johnnie Consadine is chasin' round after her tony friends. Pap said she left the house a-goin' in that direction — or Mavity told me, I disremember which. I reckon you'll find her tha. What do you want of her?"

"It's Deanie." She glanced fearfully past his shoulder to where the big clock on the grocery wall showed through its dim window. It was half-past ten. The lateness of the hour seemed to strike her with fresh terror. "Shade, come along of me," she pleaded. "I'm so skeered. I never shall have the heart to go in and ax for Johnnie, this time o' night at that thar fine house. How she can talk up to them swell people like she does is more than I know. You go with me and ax is she thar."

The group of young men had crossed the bridge and were well on their way to the Inn. Buckheath glanced after them doubtfully and turned to walk at Mandy's side. When they came to the gate, the woman hung back, whimpering at sight of the festal array, and sound of the voices within.

"They've got a party," she deprecated. "My old dress is jest as dirty as the floor. You go ax 'em, Shade."

As she spoke, Johnnie, carrying a tray of cups and saucers, passed a lighted window, and Buckheath uttered a sudden, unpremeditated oath.

"I don't know what God Almighty means makin' women such fools," he growled. "What call had Johnnie Consadine got to come here and act the servant for them rich folks? — runnin' around after Gray Stoddard — and much good may it do her!"

Mandy crowded herself back into the shadow of the dripping evergreens, and Shade went boldly up on the side porch. She saw the door opened and her escort admitted; then through the glass was aware of Lydia Sessions in an evening frock coming into the small entry and conferring at length with him.

Her attention was diverted from them by the appearance of Johnnie herself just inside a window. She ran forward and tapped on the pane. Johnnie put down her tray and came swiftly out, passing Shade and Miss Sessions in the side entry with a word.

"What is it?" she inquired of Mandy, with a premonition of disaster in her tones.

"Hit's Deanie," choked the Meacham woman. "She's right sick, and they won't let her leave the mill — leastways she's skeered to ask, and so am I. I 'lowed I ought to come and tell you, Johnnie. Was that right? You wanted me to, didn't you?" anxiously.

"Yes—yes—yes!" cried Johnnie, reaching up swift, nervous fingers to unfasten the cap from her hair, thrusting it in the pocket of the apron, and untying the apron strings. "Wait a minute. I must give these things back. Oh, let's hurry!"

It was but a moment after that she emerged once more on the porch, and apparently for the first time noticed Buckheath.

"To-morrow, then," Miss Sessions was saying to him as he moved toward the two girls. "To-morrow morning." And with a patronizing nod to them all, she withdrew and rejoined her guests.

"I never found you when I went up to the house," explained Mandy nervously, "and so I stopped Shade on the street and axed him would he come along with me. Maybe it would do some good if he was to go up with us to the mill. They pay more attention to a man person. I tell you, Johnnie, the baby's plumb broke down and sick."

The three were moving swiftly along the darkened street now.

"I'm going to take the children away from Pap," Johnnie said in a curious voice, rapid and monotonous, as though she were reciting something to herself. "I have obliged to do it. There must be a law somewhere. God won't let me fail."

"Huh-uh," grunted Buckheath, instantly. "You can't do such a thing. Ef you was married, and yo' mother would let you adopt 'em, I reckon the courts might agree to that."

"Shade," Johnnie turned upon him, "you've got more influence with Pap Himes than anybody. I

believe if you'd talk to him, he'd let me have the children.   I could support them now."

"I don't want to fall out with Pap Himes — for
nothin'," responded Shade.   "If you'll say that you'll
wed me to-morrow morning, I'll go to Pap and get him
to give up the children."   Neither of them paid any
attention to Mandy, who listened open-eyed and
open-eared to this singular courtship.   "Or I'll get
him to take 'em out of the mill.   You're right, I ain't
got a bit of doubt I could do it.   And if I don't do it,
you needn't have me."

An illumination fell upon Johnnie's mind.   She
saw that Buckheath was in league with her stepfather,
and that the pressure was put on according to the
younger man's ideas, and would be instantly withdrawn
at his bidding.   Yet, when the swift revulsion such
knowledge brought with it made her ready to dismiss
him at once, thought of Deanie's wasted little countenance, with the red burning high on the sharp, unchildish
cheekbone, stayed her.   For a while she walked with
bent head.   Heavily before her mind's eye went the
picture of Gray Stoddard among his own people, in
his own world — where she could never come.

"Have it your way," she said finally in a suffering
voice.

"What's that you say ?   Are you goin' to take me ?"
demanded Buckheath, pressing close and reaching
out a possessive arm to put around her.

"I said yes," Johnnie shivered, pushing his hand
away; "but — but it'll only be when you can come to

me and tell me that the children are all right. If you fail me there, I ——"

Back at the Victory, downstairs went Reardon's messenger to where Pap Himes was sweating over the new machinery. Work always put the old man in a sort of incandescent fury, and now as Bob spoke to him, he raised an inflamed face, from which the small eyes twinkled redly, with a grunt of inquiry.

"That youngest gal o' yours," the man repeated. "She's tryin' to leave her job and go home. Reardon said tell you, an' see what you had to say. The Lord knows we have trouble enough with those young 'uns. I'm glad when any of their folks that's got sand is around to make 'em behave. I reckon she can't come it over you, Gid."

Himes straightened up with a groan, under any exertion his rheumatic old back always punished him cruelly for the days of indolence that had let its suppleness depart.

"Huh?" he grunted. "Whar's she at? Up in the spinnin' room? Well, is they enough of you up thar to keep her tendin' to business for a spell, till I can get this thing levelled?" He held to the mechanism he was adjusting and harangued wheezily from behind it. "I cain't drop my job an' canter upstairs every time one o' you fellers whistles. The chap ain't more'n two foot long. Looks like you-all might hold on to her for one while — I'll be thar soon as I can — 'bout a hour"; and he returned savagely to his work.

When Mandy left her, Deanie tried for a time to tend her frames; but the endlessly turning spools, the edges of the jennies, blurred before her fevered eyes. Everything — even her fear of Pap Himes, her dread of the room boss — finally became vague in her mind. More and more she dreaded little Lissy's well-meant visitations; and after nearly an hour she stole toward the door, looking half deliriously for Sister Johnnie. Nobody noticed in the noisy, flaring room that spool after spool on her frame fouled its thread and ceased turning, as the little figure left its post and hesitated like a scared, small animal toward the main exit. Pap Himes, having come to where he could leave his work in the basement, climbed painfully the many stairs to the spinning room, and met her close to where the big belt rose up to the great shaft that gave power to every machine in that department.

The loving master of the big yellow cat had always cherished a somewhat clumsily concealed dislike and hostility to Deanie. Perhaps there lingered in this a touch of half-jealousy of his wife's baby; perhaps he knew instinctively that Johnnie's rebellion against his tyranny was always strongest where Deanie was concerned.

"Why ain't you on your job?" he inquired threateningly, as the child saw him and made some futile attempt to shrink back out of his way.

"I feel so quare, Pap Himes," the little girl answered him, beginning to cry. "I thes' want to lay down and go to sleep every minute."

"Huh!" Pap exploded his favourite expletive till it sounded ferocious. "That ain't quare feelin's. That's just plain old-fashioned laziness. You git yo'self back thar and tend them frames, or I'll ——"

"I cain't! I cain't see 'em to tend! I'm right blind in the eyes!" wailed Deanie. "I wish Sis' Johnnie would come. I wish't she would!"

"Uh-huh," commented Bob Conley, who had strolled up in the old man's wake. "Reckon Sis' Johnnie would run things to suit her an' you. Himes, you can cuss me out good an' plenty, but I take notice you seem to have trouble makin' your own family mind."

"You shut your head," growled Pap.

Reardon had added himself to the spectators.

"See here," the foreman argued, "if you say there's nothing the matter with that gal, an' she carries on till we have to let her go home, she goes for good. I'll take her frames away from her."

Pap felt that a formidable show of authority must be made.

"Git back thar!" he roared, advancing upon the child, raising the hand that still held the wrench with which he had been working on the machinery down stairs. "Git back thar, or I'll make you wish you had. When I tell you to do a thing, don't you name Johnnie to me. Git back thar!"

With a faint cry the child cowered away from him. It is unlikely he would have struck her with the upraised tool he held. Perhaps he did not intend a blow at all, but one or two small frame tenders paused at the ends of their lanes to watch the scene with avid eyes, to extract the last thrill from the sensation that was being kindly brought into the midst of their monotonous toilsome hours; and Lissy, who was creeping up anxiously, yet keeping out of the range of Himes's eye, crouched as though the hammer had been raised over her own head.

"Johnnie said —" began the little girl, desperately; but the old man, stung to greater fury, sprang at her; she stumbled back and back; fell against the slowly moving belt; her frock caught in the rivets which were just passing, and she was instantly jerked from her feet. If any one of the three men looking on had taken prompt action, the child might have been rescued at once; but stupid terror held them motionless.

At the moment Johnnie, Shade and Mandy, coming up the stairs, got sight of the group, Pap with upraised hammer, the child in the clutches of imminent death.

With shrill outcries the other juvenile workers swiftly gathered in a crowd. One broke away and fled down the long room screaming.

"You Pony Consadine! Milo! Come here. Pap Himes is a-killing yo' sister."

The old man, shaking all through his bulk, stared with fallen jaw. Mandy shrieked and leaped up the few remaining steps to reach Deanie, who was already above the finger-tips of a tall man.

"Pap! Shade! Quick! Don't you see she'll be killed!" Mandy screamed in frenzy.

Something in the atmosphere must have made itself felt, for no sound could have penetrated the din of the weaving room; yet some of the women left their looms and came running in behind the two pale, scared little brothers, to add their shrieks to the general clamour. Deanie's fellow workers, poor little souls, denied their childish share of the world's excitements, gazed with a sort of awful relish. Only Johnnie, speeding down the room away from it all, was doing anything rational to avert the catastrophe. The child hung on the slowly moving belt, inert, a tiny rag of life, with her mop of tangled yellow curls, her white, little face, its blue eyes closed. When she reached the top, where the pulley was close against the ceiling, her brains would be dashed out and the small body dragged to pieces between beam and ceiling.

Those who looked at her realized this. Numbed by the inevitable, they made no effort, save Milo, who at imminent risk of his own life, was climbing on a frame near at hand; but Pony flew at Himes, beating the old man with hard-clenched, inadequate fists, and screaming.

"You git her down from thar — git her down this minute! She'll be killed, I tell ye! She'll be killed, I tell ye!"

Poor Mandy made inarticulate moanings and reached up her arms; Shade Buckheath cursed softly under his breath; the women and children stared, eager to lose no detail.

"I always have said, and I always shall say, that

chaps as young as that ain't got no business around whar machinery's at!" Bob Conley kept shouting over and over in a high, strange, mechanical voice, plainly quite unconscious that he spoke at all.

The child was so near the ceiling now that a universal groan proceeded from the watchers.   Then, all at once the belt ceased to move, and the clash and tumult were stilled.   Johnnie, who had flown to the little controlling wheel to throw off the power, came running back, crying out in the sudden quiet.

"Shade — quick — get a ladder!   Hold something under there!   She might — Oh, my God!" for Deanie's frock had pulled free and the little form hurled down before Johnnie could reach them.   But the devoted Mandy was there, her futile, inadequate skirts upheld. Into them the small body dropped, and together the two came to the floor with a dull sort of crunch.

When Johnnie reached the prostrate pair, Mandy was struggling to her knees, gasping; but Deanie lay twisted just as she had fallen, the little face sunken and deathly, a tiny trickle of blood coming from a corner of her parted lips.

"Oh, my baby!   Oh, my baby!   They've killed my baby!   Deanie — Deanie — Deanie ——!" wailed Mandy.

Johnnie was on her knees beside the child, feeling her over with tremulous hands.   Her face was bleached chalk-white, and her eyes stared fearfully at the motionless lips of the little one, from which that scarlet stream trickled; but she set her own lips silently.

"Thar — right thar in the side," groaned Mandy. "She's all staved in on the side thar — my pore little Deanie! Oh, I tried to ketch her, but she broke right through and pulled my skirts out of my hand and hit the floor."

Pap had drawn nearer on shaking limbs; the children crowded so close that Johnnie looked up and motioned them back.

"Shade — you run for a doctor, and have a carriage fetched," she ordered briefly.

"Is — Lord God, is she dead?" faltered the old man.

"Ef she ain't dead now, she'll die," Mandy answered him shrilly. "They ain't no flesh on her — she's run down to a pore little skeleton. That's what the factories does to women and children — they jest eats 'em up, and spits out they' bones."

"Well, I never aimed to skeer her that-a-way," said Himes; "but the little fool ——"

Johnnie's flaming glance silenced him, and his voice died away, a sort of a rasp in his throat. Mechanically he glanced up to the point on the great belt from which the child had fallen, and measured the distance to the floor. He scratched his bald head dubiously, and edged back from the tragedy he had made.

"Everybody knows I never hit her," he muttered as he went.

CHAPTER XVIII

LIGHT

GRAY STODDARD'S eyes had followed Lydia Sessions when she went into the hall to speak to Shade Buckheath. He had a glimpse of Johnnie, too, in the passage; he noted that she later left the house with Buckheath (Mandy Meacham was beyond his range of vision); and the pang that went through him at the sight was a strangely mingled one.

The talk between him and his hostess had been enlightening to both of them. It showed Lydia Sessions not only where she stood with Gray, but it brought home to her startlingly, and as nothing had yet done, the strength of Johnnie's hold upon him; while it forced Gray himself to realize that ever since that morning when he met the girl on the bridge going to put her little brothers and sisters in the Victory mill, he had behaved more like a sulky, disappointed lover than a staunch friend. He confessed frankly to himself, that, had Johnnie been a boy, a young man, instead of a beautiful and appealing woman, he would have been prompt to go to her and remonstrate — he would have made no bones of having the matter out clearly and fully. He blamed himself much for the estrangement which he had allowed to grow between them. He knew instinctively about what Shade Buckheath was — certainly no fit mate for Johnnie Consadine. And for the better to desert her — poor, helpless, unschooled girl — could only operate to push her toward the worse. These thoughts kept Stoddard wakeful company till almost morning.

Dawn came with a soft wind out of the west, all the odours of spring on its breath, and a penitent warmth to apologize for last night's storm. Stoddard faced his day, and decided that he would begin it with an early-morning horseback ride. He called up his stable boy over the telephone, and when Jim brought round Roan Sultan saddled there was a pause, as of custom, for conversation.

"Heared about the accident over to the Victory, Mr. Stoddard?" Jim inquired.

"No," said Gray, wheeling sharply. "Anybody hurt?"

"One o' Pap Himes's stepchildren mighty near killed, they say," the boy told him. "I seen Miss Johnnie Consadine when they was bringing the little gal down. It seems they sent for her over to Mr. Hardwickses where she was at."

Gray mounted quickly, settled himself in the saddle, and glanced down the street which would lead him past Himes's place. For months now, he had been instinctively avoiding that part of town. Poor Johnnie! She might be a disappointing character, but he knew well that she was full of love; he remembered her eyes when, nearly a year ago, up in the mist and sweetness of April on the Unakas, she had told him of the baby sister and the other little ones. She must be suffering now. Almost without reflection he turned his horse's head and rode toward the forlorn Himes boarding-house.

As he drew near, he noticed a huddled figure at the head of the steps, and coming up made it out to be Himes himself, sitting, elbows on knees, staring straight ahead of him. Pap had not undressed at all, but he had taken out his false teeth "to rest his jaws a spell," as he was in the habit of doing, and the result was startling. His cheeks were fallen in to such an extent that the blinking red eyes above looked larger; it was as though the old rascal's crimes of callous self-ishness and greed had suddenly aged him.

Stoddard pulled in his horse at the foot of the steps.

"I hear one of the little girls was hurt in the mill last night. Was she badly injured? Which one was it?" he asked abruptly.

"Hit's Deanie. She's all right," mumbled Pap. "Got the whole house uptore, and Laurelly miscallin' me till I don't know which way to look; and now the little dickens is a-goin' to git well all right. Chaps is tough, I tell ye. Ye cain't kill 'em."

"You people must have thought so," said Stoddard, "or you wouldn't have brought these little ones down and hired them to the cotton mill. Johnnie knew what that meant."

The words had come almost involuntarily. The old man stared at the speaker, breathing hard.

"What's Johnnie Consadine got to do with it?"
he inquired finally. "I'm the stepdaddy of the children
— and Johnnie's stepdaddy too, for the matter of that
— and what I say goes."

"Did you hire the children at the Victory?" inquired
Stoddard, swiftly. Back across his memory came the
picture of Johnnie with her poor little sheep for the
shambles clustered about her on the bridge before the
Victory mill. "Did you hire the children to the factory?" he repeated.

"Now Mr. Stoddard," began the old man, between
bluster and whine, "I talked about them chaps to the
superintendent of yo' mill, an' you-all said you didn't
want none of that size. And one o' yo' men — he was
a room boss, I reckon — spoke up right sassy to me —
as sassy as Johnnie Consadine herself, and God knows
she ain't got no respect for them that's set over her.
I had obliged to let 'em go to the Victory; but I don't
think you have any call to hold it ag'in me — Johnnie
was plumb impident about it — plumb impident."

Stoddard glanced up at the windows and made
as though to dismount. All night at his pillow had
stood the accusation that he had been cruel to Johnnie.
Now, as Himes's revelations went on, and he saw what
her futile efforts had been, as he guessed a part of her
sufferings, it seemed he must hurry to her and brush
away the tangle of misunderstanding which he had
allowed to grow up between them.

"They've worked over that thar chap, off an' on,
all night," the old man said. "Looks like, if they

keep hit up, she'll begin to think somethin's the matter of her."

Gray realized that his visit at this moment would be ill-timed. He would ride on through the Gap now, and call as he came back.

"I had obliged to find me a place whar I could hire out them chaps," the miserable old man before him went on, garrulously. "They's nothin' like mill work to take the davilment out o' young 'uns. Some of them chaps'll call you names and make faces at you, even whilst you' goin' through the mill yard — and think what they'd be ef they *wasn't* worked! I'm a old man, and when I married Laurelly and took the keepin' o' her passel o' chaps on my back, I aimed to make it pay. Laurelly, she won't work."

He looked helplessly at Stoddard, like a child about to cry.

"She told me up and down that she never had worked in no mill, and she was too old to l'arn. She said the noise of the thing from the outside was enough to show her that she didn't want to go inside — and go she would not."

"But she let her children go — she and Johnnie," muttered Stoddard, settling himself in his saddle.

"Well, I'd like to see either of 'em he'p theirselves!" returned Pap Himes with a reminscence of his former manner. "Johnnie ain't had the decency to give me her wages, not once since I've been her pappy; the onliest money I ever had from her — 'ceptin' to pay her board — was when she tried to buy them chaps out o' workin' in the mill. But when I put my foot down an' told her that the chillen could work in the mill without a beatin' or with one, jest as she might see and choose, she had a little sense, and took 'em over and hired 'em herself. Baylor told me afterward that she tried to make him say he didn't want 'em, but Baylor and me stands together, an' Miss Johnnie failed up on that trick."

Pap felt an altogether misplaced confidence in the view that Stoddard, as a male, was likely to take of the matter.

"A man is obliged to be boss of his own family — ain't that so, Mr. Stoddard?" he demanded. "I said the chillen had to go into the mill, and into the mill they went. They all wanted to go, at the start, and Laurelly agreed with me that hit was the right thing. Then, just because Deanie happened to a accident and Johnnie took up for her, Laurelly has to go off into hy-strikes and say she'll quit me soon as she can put foot to the ground."

Stoddard made no response to this, but touched Sultan with his heel and moved on. He had stopped at the post-office as he came past, taking from his personal box one letter. This he opened and read as he rode slowly away. Halfway up the first rise, Pap saw him rein in and turn; the old man was still staring when Gray stopped once more at the gate.

"See here, Himes," he spoke abruptly, "this concerns you — this letter that has just reached me."

Pap looked at the younger man with mere curiosity.

"When Johnnie was first given a spinning room to look after," said Gray, "she came to Mr. Sessions and myself and asked permission to have a small device of her own contrivance used on the frames as an Indicator."

Pap shuffled his feet uneasily.

"I thought no more about the matter; in fact I've not been in the spinning department for — for some time." Stoddard looked down at the hand which held his bridle, and remembered that he had absented himself from every place that threatened him with the sight of Johnnie.

Pap was breathing audibly through his open mouth.

"She — she never had nothin' made," he whispered out the ready lie hurriedly, scrambling to his feet and down the steps, pressing close to Roan Sultan's shoulder, laying a wheedling hand on the bridle, looking up anxiously into the stern young face above him.

"Oh, yes, she did," Stoddard returned. "I remember, now, hearing some of the children from the room say that she had a device which worked well. From the description they gave of it, I judge that it is the same which this letter tells me you and Buckheath are offering to the Alabama mills. Mr. Trumbull, the superintendent, says that you and Buckheath hold the patent for this Indicator jointly. As soon as I can consult with Johnnie, we will see about the matter."

Himes let go the roan's bridle and staggered back a pace or two, open-mouthed, staring. The skies had fallen. His heavy mind turned slowly toward resent-

ment against Buckheath. He wished the younger
conspirator were here to take his share. Then the door
opened and Shade himself came out wiping his mouth.
He was fresh from the breakfast table, but not on
his way to the mill, since it was still too early. He
gave Stoddard a surly nod as he passed through the
gate and on down the street, in the direction of the
Inn. Himes, in a turmoil of stupid uncertainty,
once or twice made as though to detain him. His
slow wits refused him any available counsel. Dazedly
he fumbled for something convincing to say. Then
on a sudden inspiration, he once more laid hold of the
bridle and began to speak volubly in a hoarse undertone:

"W'y, name o' God, Mr. Stoddard! Who should
have a better right to that thar patent than Buck and
me? I'm the gal's stepdaddy, an' he's the man she's
goin' to wed."

Some peculiar quality in the silence of Gray Stoddard
seemed finally to penetrate the old fellow's understanding. He looked up to find the man on horseback
regarding him, square-jawed, pale, and with eyes angrily
bright. He glanced over his shoulder at the windows
of the house behind him, moistened his lips once again,
gulped, and finally resumed in a manner both whining
and aggressive.

"Now, Mr. Stoddard, I want to talk to you mighty
plain. The whole o' Cottonville is full o' tales about
you and Johnnie. Yes — that's the truth."

He stood staring down at his big, shuffling feet,

laboriously sorting in his own mind such phrases as it might do to use. The difficulty of what he had to say blocked speech for so long that Stoddard, in a curiously quiet voice, finally prompted him.

"Tales?" he repeated. "What tales, Mr. Himes?"

"Why, they ain't a old woman in town, nor a young one neither — I believe in my soul that the young ones is the worst — that ain't been talkin' — talkin' bad — ever since you took Johnnie to ride in your otty-mobile."

Again there came a long pause. Stoddard stared down on Gideon Himes, and Himes stared at his own feet.

"Well?" Stoddard's quiet voice once more urged his accuser forward.

Pap rolled his head between his shoulders with a negative motion which intimated that it was not well.

"And lending her books, and all sich," he pursued doggedly. "That kind o' carryin' on ain't decent, and you know it ain't. Buck knows it ain't — but he's willin' to have her. He told her he was willin' to have her, and the fool gal let on like she didn't want him. He came here to board at my house because she wouldn't scarcely so much as speak to him elsewhere."

By the light of these statements Stoddard read what poor Johnnie's persecution had been. The details of it he could not, of course, know; yet he saw in that moment largely how she had been harried. At the instant of seeing, came that swift and mighty revulsion that follows surely when we have misprized and misunderstood those dear to us.

"What is it you want of me?" he inquired of Himes.

"Why, just this here," Pap told him. "You let Johnnie Consadine alone." He leaned even closer and spoke in a yet lower tone, because a number of girls were emerging from the house and starting down the steps. "A big, rich feller like you don't mean any good by a girl fixed the way Johnnie is. You wouldn't marry her — then let her alone. Things ain't got so bad but what Buck is still willin' to have her. You wouldn't marry her."

Stoddard looked down at the shameful old man with eyes that were indecipherable. If the impulse was strong in him to twist the unclean old throat against any further ill-speaking, it gave no heat to the tone in which he answered:

"It's you and your kind that say I mean harm to Johnnie, and that I would not marry her. Why should I intend ill toward her? Why shouldn't I marry her? I would — I would marry her."

As he made this, to him the only possible defence of the poor girl, Pap faltered slowly back, uttering a gurgling expression of astonishment. With a sense of surprise Stoddard saw in his face only dismay and chagrin.

"Hit — hit's a lie," Himes mumbled half-heartedly. "Ye'd never do it in the world."

Stoddard gathered up his bridle rein, preparatory to moving on.

"You're an old man, Mr. Himes," he said coldly, "and you are excited; but you don't want to say any more — that's quite enough of that sort of thing."

Then he loosened the rein on Roan Sultan, and moved away down the street.

Gideon Himes stood and gazed after him with bulging eyes. Gray Stoddard married to Johnnie! He tried to adjust his dull wits to the new position of affairs; tried to cipher the problem with this amazing new element introduced. Last night's scene of violence when the injured child was brought home went dismally before his eyes. Laurella had said she would leave him so soon as she could put foot to the floor. He had expected to coax her with gifts and money, with concessions in regard to the children if it must be; but with a rich man for a son-in-law, of course she would go. He would never see her face again. And suddenly he flung up an arm like a beaten schoolboy and began to blubbler noisily in the crook of his elbow.

An ungentle hand on his shoulder recalled him to time and place.

"For God's sake, what's the matter with you?" inquired Shade Buckheath's voice harshly.

The old man gulped down his grief and made his communication in a few hurried sentences.

"An' he'll do it," Pap concluded. "He's jest big enough fool for anything. Ain't you heard of his scheme for having the hands make the money in the mill?" (Thus he described a profit-sharing plan.) "Don't you know he's given ten thousand dollars to start up some sort o' school for the boys and gals to learn their trade in? A man like that'll do anything. And if he marries Johnnie, Laurelly'll leave me sure."

"Leave you!" echoed Buckheath darkly. "She won't have to. If Gray Stoddard marries Johnnie Consadine, you and me will just about roost in the penitentiary for the rest of our days."

"The patent!" echoed Pap blankly. He turned fiercely on his fellow conspirator. "Now see what ye done with yer foolishness," he exclaimed. "Nothin' would do ye but to be offerin' the contraption for sale, and tellin' each and every that hit'd been used in the Hardwick mill. Look what a mess ye've made. I'm sorry I ever hitched up with ye. Boy o' yo' age has got no sense."

"How was I to know they'd write to Stoddard?" growled Shade sulkily. "No harm did if hit wasn't for him. We've got the patent all right, and Johnnie cain't help herself. But him — with all his money — he can help her — damn him!"

"Yes, and he'll take a holt and hunt up about Pros's silver mine, too," said Himes. "I've always mistrusted the way he's been hangin' round Pros Passmore. Like enough he's hearn of that silver mine, and that's the reason he's after Johnnie."

The old man paused to ruminate on this feature of the case. He was pleased with his own shrewdness in fathoming Gray Stoddard's mysterious motives.

"Buck," he said finally, with a swift drop to friendliness, "hit's got to be stopped. Can you stop it?

Didn't you tell me that Johnnie promised last night to wed you? Didn't you say she promised it, when you was goin' up to the Victory with her?"

Shade nodded.

"She promised she would if I'd get you to let the children stay out of the mill. Deanie's hurt now, and you're afraid to make the others go back in the mill anyhow, 'count of Laurelly's tongue. I can't hold Johnnie to that promise. But — but there's one person I want to talk to about this business, and then I'll be ready to do something."

CHAPTER XIX

A PACT

WHILE Himes and Buckheath yet stood thus talking, the warning whistles of the various mills began to blow. Groups of girls came down the steps and stared at the two men conferring with heads close together. Mavity Bence put her face out at the front door and called.

"Pap, yo' breakfast is gettin' stone cold."

"Do you have to go to the mill right now?" inquired the older man, timorously. He was already under the domination of this swifter, bolder, more fiery spirit.

"No, I don't have to go anywhere that I don't want to. I've got business with a certain party up this-a-way, and when I git to the mill I'll be there."

He turned and hurried swiftly up the minor slope that led to the big Hardwick home, Pap's fascinated eyes following him as long as he was in sight. As the young fellow strode along he was turning in his mind Lydia Sessions's promise to talk to him this morning about Johnnie.

"But she'll be in bed and asleep, I reckon, at this time of day," he ruminated. "The good Lord knows I would if I had the chance like she has."

As he came in sight of the Hardwick house, he

checked momentarily. Standing at the gate, an astonishing figure, still in her evening frock, looking haggard
and old in the gray, disillusioning light of early morning,
was Lydia Sessions. Upstairs, her white bed was
smooth; its pillows spread fair and prim, unpressed
by any head, since the maid had settled them trimly
in place the morning before; but the long rug which
ran from her dressing table to the window might have
told a tale of pacing feet that passed restlessly from
midnight till dawn; the mirror could have disclosed
the picture of a white, anxious, and often angry face
that had stared into it as the woman paused now and
again to commune with the real Lydia Sessions.

She was thirty and penniless. She belonged to a
circle where everybody had money. Her sister had
married well, and Harriet was no better-looking than
she. All Lydia Sessions's considerable forces were
by heredity and training turned into one narrow channel
— the effort to make a creditable, if not a brilliant,
match. And she had thought she was succeeding.
Gray Stoddard had seemed seriously interested. In
those long night watches while the lights flared on
either side of her mirror, and the luxurious room of
a modern young lady lay disclosed, with all its sumptu-
ous fittings of beauty and inutility, Lydia went over
her plans of campaign. She was a suitable match for
him — anybody would say so. He had liked her —
he had liked her well enough — till he got interested
in this mill girl. They had never agreed on anything
concerning Johnnie Consadine. If that element were

eliminated to-morrow, she knew she could go back and pick up the thread of their intimacy which had promised so well, and, she doubted not at all, twist it safely into a marriage-knot. If Johnnie were only out of the way. If she would leave Cottonville. If she would marry that good-looking mechanic who plainly wanted her. How silly of her not to take him!

Toward dawn, she snatched a little cape from the garments hanging in the closet, flung it over her shoulders and ran downstairs. She must have a breath of fresh air. So, in the manner of helpless creatures who cannot go out in the highway to accost fate, she was standing at the gate when she caught sight of Shade Buckheath approaching. Here was her opportunity. She must be doing something, and the nearest enterprise at hand was to foster and encourage this young fellow's pursuit of Johnnie.

"I wanted to talk to you about a very particular matter," she broke out nervously, as soon as Buckheath was near enough to be addressed in the carefully lowered tone which she used throughout the interview. She continually huddled the light cape together at the neck with tremulous, unsteady fingers; and it was characteristic of these two that, although the woman had heard of the calamity at the Victory mill the night before, and knew that Shade came directly from the Himes home, she made no inquiry as to the welfare of Deanie, and he offered no information. He gave no reply in words to her accost, and she went on, with increasing agitation.

"I — this matter ought to be attended to at once. Something's got to be done.   I've attempted to improve the social and spiritual conditions of these girls in the mill, and if I've only worked harm by bringing them in contact with — in contact with ——"

She hesitated and stood looking into the man's face.   Buckheath knew exactly what she wished to say.   He was impatient of the flummery she found it necessary to wind around her simple proposition; but he was used to women, he understood them; and to him a woman of Miss Sessions's class was no different from a woman of his own.

"I reckon you wanted to name it to me about Johnnie Consadine," he said bluntly.

"Yes — yes, that was it," breathed Lydia Sessions, glancing back toward the house with a frightened air. "John is — she's a good girl, Mr. Buckheath; I beg of you to believe me when I assure you that John is a good, honest, upright girl.   I would not think anything else for a minute; but it seems to me that somebody has to do something, or — or ——"

Shade raised his hand to his mouth to conceal the swift, sarcastic smile on his lips.   He spat toward the pathside before agreeing seriously with Miss Lydia.

"Her and me was promised, before she come down here and got all this foolishness into her head," he said finally.   "Her mother never could do anything with Johnnie.   Looks like Johnnie's got more authority — her mother's more like a little girl to her than the other way round.   Her uncle Pros has been crazy in the hospital, and Pap Himes, her stepfather — well, I reckon she's the only human that ever had to mind Pap and didn't do it."

This somewhat ambiguous statement of the case failed to bring any smile to his hearer's lips.

"There's no use talking to John herself," Miss Lydia took up the tale feverishly. "I've done that, and it had no effect on —. Well, of course she would say that she didn't encourage him to the things I saw afterward; but I know that a man of his sort does not do things without encouragement, and — Mr. Buckheath don't you think you ought to go right to Mr. Stoddard and tell him that John is your promised wife, and show him the folly and — and the wickedness of his course — or what would be wickedness if he persisted in it? Don't you think you ought to do that?"

Shade held down his head and appeared to be giving this matter some consideration. The weak point of such an argument lay in the fact that Johnnie was not his promised wife, and Gray Stoddard was very likely to know it. Indeed, Lydia Sessions herself only believed the statement because she so wished.

"I reckon I ort," he said finally. "If I could ever get a chance of private speech with him, mebbe I'd ——"

There came a sound of light hoofs down the road, and Stoddard on Roan Sultan, riding bareheaded, came toward them under the trees.

Miss Sessions clutched the gate and stood staring. Buckheath drew a little closer, set his shoulder against the fence and tried to look unconcerned. The rising

sun behind the mountains threw long slant rays across
into the bare tree tops, so that the shimmer of it dappled
horse and man.   Gray's face was pale, his brow looked
anxious; but he rode head up and alert, and glanced
with surprise at the two at the Sessions gate.   He
had no hat to raise, but he saluted Lydia Sessions
with a sweeping gesture of the hand and passed on.   A
blithe, gallant figure cantering along the suburban
road, out toward the Gap, and the mountains beyond,
Gray Stoddard rode into the dip of the ridge and — so
far as Cottonville was concerned — vanished utterly.

Buckheath drew a long breath and straightened up.

"I'm but a poor man," he began truculently, "yit
there ain't nobody can marry the gal I set out to wed
and me stand by and say nothing."

"Oh, Mr. Buckheath!" cried Miss Lydia.   "Mr.
Stoddard had no idea of *marrying* John — a mill girl!
There is no possibility of any such thing as that.   I
want you to understand that there isn't — to feel
assured, once for all.   I have reason to know, and I
urge you to put that out of your mind."

Shade looked at her narrowly.   Up to the time Pap
gave him definite information from headquarters,
he had never for an instant supposed that there was a
possibility of Stoddard desiring to marry Johnnie;
but the flurried eagerness of Miss Sessions convinced
him that such a possibility was a very present dread
with her, and he sent a venomous glance after the
disappearing horseman.

"You go and talk to him right now, Mr. Buckheath,"

insisted Lydia anxiously. "Tell him, just as you have told me, how long you and John have been engaged, and how devoted she was to you before she came down to the mill. You appeal to him that way. You can overtake him — I mean you can intercept him — if you start right on now — cut across the turn, and go through the tunnel."

"If I go after him to talk to him, and we — uh — we have an interruption — are you going to tell everybody you see about it?" demanded Shade sharply, staring down at the woman.

She crouched a little, still clinging to the pickets of the gate. The word "interruption" only conveyed to her mind the suggestion that they might be interfered with in their conversation. She did not recollect the mountain use of it to describe a quarrel, an outbreak, or an affray.

"No," she whispered. "Oh, certainly not — I'll never tell anything that you don't want me to."

"All right," returned Buckheath hardily. "If you won't, I won't. If you name to people that I was the last one saw with Mr. Stoddard, I shall have obliged to tell 'em of what you and me was talkin' about when he passed us. You see that, don't you?"

She nodded silently, her frightened eyes on his face; and without another word he set off at that long, swinging pace which belongs to his people. Lydia turned and ran swiftly into the house, and up the stairs to her own room.

CHAPTER XX

WHEN Stoddard did not come to his desk that morning the matter remained for a time unnoticed, except by McPherson, who fretted a bit at so unusual a happening. Truth to tell, the old Scotchman had dreaded having this rich young man for an associate, and had put a rod in pickle for his chastisement. When Stoddard turned out to be a regular worker, punctual, amenable to discipline, he congratulated himself, and praised his assistant, but warily. Now came the first delinquency, and in his heart he cared more that Stoddard should absent himself without notice than for the pile of letters lying untouched.

"Dave," he finally said to the yellow office boy, "I wish you'd 'phone to Mr. Stoddard's place and see when he'll be down."

Dave came back with the information that Mr. Stoddard was not at the house; he had left for an early-morning ride, and not returned to his breakfast.

"He'll just about have stopped up at the Country Club for a snack," MacPherson muttered to himself. "I wonder who or what he found there attractive enough to keep him from his work."

Looking into Gray's office at noon, the closed desk with its pile of mail once more offended MacPherson's eye.

"Mr. Stoddard here?" inquired Hartley Sessions, glancing in at the same moment.

"No, I think not," returned the Scotchman, unwilling to admit that he did not exactly know. "I believe he's up at the club. Perhaps he's got tangled in for a longer game of golf than he reckoned on."

This unintentional and wholly innocent falsehood stopped any inquiry that there might have been. MacPherson had meant to 'phone the club during the day, but he failed to do so, and it was not until evening that he walked up himself to put more cautious inquiries.

"No, sah — no, sah, Mr. Gray ain't been here," the Negro steward told him promptly. "I sure would have remembered, sah," in answer to a startled inquiry from MacPherson. "Dey been havin' a big game on between Mr. Charley Conroy and Mr. Hardwick, and de bofe of 'em spoke of Mr. Gray, and said dey was expectin' him to play."

MacPherson came down the stone steps of the club-house, gravely disquieted. Below him the road wound, a dimly conjectured, wavering gray ribbon; on the other side of it the steep slope took off to a gulf of inky shadow, where the great valley lay, hushed under the solemn stars, silent, black, and shimmering with a myriad pulsating electric lights which glowed like swarms of fireflies caught in an invisible net. That was Watauga. The strings of brilliants that led from it were arc lights at switch crossings where the great railway lines rayed out. Near at hand was Cottonville with its vast bulks of lighted mills whose hum came faintly up to him even at this distance. MacPherson stood uncertainly in the middle of the road. Supper and bed were behind him. But he had not the heart to turn back to either. Somewhere down in that abyss of night, there was a clue — or there were many clues — to this strange absence of Gray Stoddard. Perhaps Gray himself was there; and the Scotchman cursed his own dilatoriness in waiting till darkness had covered the earth before setting afoot inquiries.

He found himself hurrying and getting out of breath as he took his way down the ridge and straight to Stoddard's cottage, only to find that the master's horse was not in the stable, and the Negro boy who cared for it had seen nothing of it or its rider since five o'clock that morning.

"I wonder, now, should I give the alarm to Hardwick," MacPherson said to himself. "The lad may have just ridden on to La Fayette, or some little nearby town, and be staying the night. Young fellows sometimes have affairs they'd rather not share with everybody — and then, there's Miss Lydia. If I go up to Hardwick's with the story, she'll be sure to hear it from Hardwick's wife."

"Did Mr. Stoddard ever go away like this before without giving you notice?" he asked with apparent carelessness.

The boy shook his head in vigorous negative.

"Never since I've been working for him," he asserted. "Mr. Stoddard wasn't starting anywhere but for his early ride — at least he wasn't intending to. He hadn't any hat on, and he was in his riding clothes. He didn't carry anything with him. I know in reason he wasn't intending to stay."

This information sent MacPherson hurrying to the Hardwick home. Dinner was over. The master of the house conferred with him a moment in the vestibule, then opened the door into the little sitting room and asked abruptly:

"When was the last time any of you saw Gray Stoddard?"

His sister-in-law screamed faintly, then cowered in her chair and stared at him mutely. But Mrs. Hardwick as yet noted nothing unusual.

"Yesterday evening," she returned placidly. "Don't you remember, Jerome, he was here at the Lyric reception?"

"Oh, I remember well enough," said Hardwick knitting his brows. "I thought some of you might have seen him since then. He's missing."

"Missing!" echoed Lydia Sessions with a note of terror in her tones.

Now Mrs. Hardwick looked startled.

"But, Jerome, I think you're inconsiderate," she began, glancing solicitously at her sister. "Under the circumstances, it seems to me you might have made your announcement more gently — to Lydia, anyhow.

Never mind, dearie — there's nothing in it to be frightened at."

"I'm not frightened," whispered Lydia Sessions through white lips that belied her assertion. Hardwick looked impatiently from his sister-in-law to his wife.

"I'm sorry if I startled you, Lydia," he said in a perfunctory tone, "but this is a serious business. MacPherson tells me Stoddard hasn't been at the factory nor at his boarding-house to-day. The last person who saw him, so far as we know, is his stable boy. Black Jim says Stoddard rode out of the gate at five o'clock this morning, bareheaded and in his riding clothes. Have any of you seen him since — that's what I want to know?"

"Since?" repeated Miss Sessions, who seemed unable to get beyond the parrot echoing of her questioner's words. "Why Jerome, what makes you think I've seen him since then? Did he say — did anybody tell you ——"

She broke off huskily and sat staring at her interlaced fingers dropped in her lap.

"No — no. Of course not, Lydia," her sister hastened to reassure her, crossing the room and putting a protecting arm about the girl's shoulders. "He shouldn't have spoken as he did, knowing that you and Gray — knowing how affairs stand."

"Well, I only thought since you and Stoddard are such great friends," Hardwick persisted, "he might have mentioned to you some excursion, or made opportunity to talk with you alone, sometime last night —

to — to say something. Did he tell you where he was going, Lydia? Are you keeping something from us that we ought to know? Remember this is no child's play. It begins to look as though it might be a question of the man's life."

Lydia Sessions started galvanically. She pushed off her sister's caressing hand with a fierce gesture.

"There's nothing — no such relation as you're hinting at, Elizabeth, between Gray Stoddard and me," she said sharply. Memory of what Gray had (as she supposed) followed her into the library to say to her wrung a sort of groan from the girl. "I suppose Matilda's told you that we had — had some conversation in the library," she managed to say.

Her brother-in-law shook his head.

"We haven't questioned the servants yet," he said briefly. "We haven't questioned anybody nor hunted up any evidence. MacPherson came direct to me from Stoddard's stable boy. Gray did stop and talk to you last night? What did he say?"

"I — why nothing in — I really don't remember," faltered Lydia, with so strange a look that both her sister and Hardwick looked at her in surprise. "That is — oh, nothing of any importance, you know. I — I believe we were talking about socialism, and — and different classes of people. . . . That sort of thing."

MacPherson, who had pushed unceremoniously into the room behind his employer, nodded his gray head. "That would always be what he was speaking of." He smiled a little as he said it.

"All right," returned Hardwick, struggling into his overcoat at the hat-tree, and seeking his hat and stick, "I'll go right back with you, Mac. This thing somehow has a sinister look to me."

As the two men were leaving the house, Hardwick felt a light, trembling touch on his arm, and turned to face his sister-in-law.

"Why — Jerome, why did you say that last?" Lydia quavered. "What do you think has happened to him? Do you think anybody — that is —? Oh, you looked at me as though you thought I had something to do with it!"

"Come, come, Lyd. Pull yourself together. You're getting hysterical," urged Hardwick kindly. Then he turned to MacPherson. As the two men went companionably down the walk and out into the street, the Scotchman said apologetically:

"Of course, I knew Miss Lydia would be alarmed. I understand about her and Stoddard. It made me hesitate a while before coming up to you folks with the thing."

"Well, by the Lord, you did well not to hesitate too long, Mac!" ejaculated Hardwick. "I shouldn't feel the anxiety I do if we hadn't been having trouble with those mountain people up toward Flat Rock over that girl that died at the hospital." He laughed a little ruefully. "Trying to do things for folks is ticklish business. There wasn't a man in the crowd that interviewed me whom I could convince that our hospital wasn't a factory for the making of stiffs which we sold to the Northern Medical College. Oh, it was gruesome!

I told them the girl had had every attention, and that she died of pernicious anæmia. They called it 'a big dic word' and asked me point blank if the girl hadn't been killed in the mill. I told them that we couldn't keep the body indefinitely, and they said they 'aimed to come and haul it away as soon as they could get a horse and wagon.' I called their attention to the fact that I couldn't know this unless they wrote and told me so in answer to my letter. But between you and me, Mac, I don't believe there was a man in the crowd who could read or write."

"For God's sake!" exclaimed the Scotchman. "You don't think *those* people were up to doing a mischief to Stoddard, do you?"

"I don't know what to think," protested Hardwick. "Yes; they are mediæval — half savage. The fact is, I have no idea what they would or what they wouldn't do."

MacPherson gave a whistle of dismay.

"Gad, it sounds like the manœuvres of one of our Highland clans three hundred years ago!" he said. "Wouldn't it be the irony of fate that Stoddard — poor fellow! — a friend of the people, a socialist, ready to call every man his brother — should be sacrificed in such a way?"

The words brought them to Stoddard's little home, silent and deserted now. Down the street, the lamps flared gustily. It was after eleven o'clock.

"Where does that boy live that takes care of the horses — black Jim?" Hardwick inquired, after they had rung the bell, thumped on the door, and called, to make sure the master had not returned during MacPherson's absence.

"I don't know — really, I don't know. He might have a room over the stable," MacPherson suggested.

But the stable proved to be a one-story affair, and they were just turning to leave when a stamping sound within arrested their notice.

"Good God! — what's that?" ejaculated Mac-Pherson, whose nerves were quivering.

"It's the horse," answered Hardwick in a relieved tone. "Stoddard's got back ——"

"Of course," broke in old MacPherson, quickly, "and gone over to Mrs. Gandish's for some supper. That is why he wasn't in the house."

To make assurance doubly sure, they opened the unlocked stable door, and MacPherson struck a match. The roan turned and whinnied hungrily at sight of them.

"That's funny," said Hardwick, scarcely above his breath. "It looks to me as though that animal hadn't been fed."

In the flare of the match MacPherson had descried the stable lantern hanging on the wall. They lit this and examined the stall. There was no feed in the box, no hay in the manger. The saddle was on Gray Stoddard's horse; the bit in his mouth; he was tied by the reins to his stall ring. The two men looked at each other with lengthening faces.

"Stoddard's too good a horseman to have done that," spoke Hardwick slowly.

"And too kind a man," supplied MacPherson loyally. "He'd have seen to the beast's hunger before he satisfied his own."

As the Scotchman spoke he was picking up the horse's hoofs, and digging at them with a bit of stick.

"They're as clean as if they'd just been washed," he said, as he straightened up. "By Heaven! I have it, Hardwick — that fellow came into town with his hoofs muffled."

The younger man looked also, and assented mutely, then suggested:

"He hasn't come far; there's not a hair turned on him."

The Scotchman shook his head. "I'm not sure of that," he debated. "Likely he's been led, and that slowly. God — this is horrible!"

Mechanically Hardwick got some hay down for the horse, while MacPherson pulled off the saddle and bridle, examining both in the process. Grain was poured into the box, and then water offered.

"He won't drink," murmured the Scotchman. "D'ye see, Hardwick? He won't drink. You can't come into Cottonville without crossing a stream. This fellow's hoofs have been wet within an hour — yes, within the half-hour."

As their eyes encountered, Hardwick caught his breath sharply; both felt that chill of the cuticle, that stirring at the roots of the hair, that marks the passing close to us of some sinister thing — stark murder, or man's naked hatred walking in the dark beside our cheerful, commonplace path. By one consent they turned back from the stable and went together to Mrs. Gandish's. The house was dark.

"Of course, you know I don't expect to find him here," said Hardwick. "I don't suppose they know anything about the matter. But we've got to wake them and ask."

They did so, and set trembling the first wave of that widening ring of horror which finally informed the remotest boundaries of the little village that a man from their midst was mysteriously missing.

The morning found the telegraph in active requisition, flashing up and down all lines by which a man might have left Cottonville or Watauga. The police of the latter place were notified, furnished with information, and set to find out if possible whether anybody in the city had seen Stoddard since he rode away on Friday morning.

The inquiries were fruitless. A young lady visiting in the city had promised him a dance at the Valentine masque to be held at the Country Club-house Friday night. Some clothing put out a few days before to be cleaned and pressed was ready for delivery. His laundry came home. His mail arrived punctually. The postmaster stated that he had no instructions for a change of address; all the little accessories of Gray Stoddard's life offered themselves, mute, impressive witnesses that he had intended to go on with it in Cottonville. But Stoddard himself had dropped as completely out of the knowledge of man as though he had been whisked off the planet.

CHAPTER XXI

THE SEARCH

THE fruitless search was vigorously prosecuted. On Saturday the Hardwick mill ran short-handed while nearly half its male employees made some effort to solve the mystery. Parties combed again and again the nearer mountains. Sunday all the mill operatives were free; and then groups of women and children added themselves to the men; dinners were taken along, lending a grotesque suggestion of picnicking to the work, a suggestion contradicted by the anxious faces, the strained timbre of the voices that called from group to group. But night brought the amateur searchers straggling home with nothing to tell. It should have been significant to any one who knew the mountain people, that information concerning Gray Stoddard within a week of his disappearance, was noticeably lacking. Nobody would admit that his had been a familiar figure on those roads. At the utmost they had "seed him a good· deal a while ago, but he'd sorter quit riding up this-a-way of late." But on no road could there be found man, woman, or child who had seen Gray Stoddard riding Friday morning on his roan horse. The whole outlying district seemed to be in a conspiracy of silence.

In Watauga and in Cottonville itself, clues were found by the police, followed up and proved worthless. All Gray's Eastern connections were immediately communicated with by telegraph, in the forlorn hope of finding some internal clue. The business men in charge of his large Eastern interests answered promptly that nothing from recent correspondence with him pointed to any intention on his part of making a journey or otherwise changing his ordinary way of living. They added urgent admonitions to Mr. Mac-Pherson to have locked up in the Company's safe various important papers which they had sent, at Stoddard's request, for signature, and which they supposed from the date, must be lying with his other mail. A boyhood friend telegraphed his intention of coming down from Massachusetts and joining the searchers. Stoddard had no near relatives. A grand-aunt, living in Boston, telegraphed to Mr. Hardwick to see that money be spent freely.

Meantime there was reason for Johnnie Consadine, shut in the little sister's sick room day and night, to hear nothing of these matters. Lissy had been allowed to help wait upon the injured child only on promise that nothing exciting should be mentioned. Both boys had instantly begged to join a searching party, Milo insisting that he could work all night and search all day, and that nobody should complain that he neglected his job. Pony, being refused, had run away; Milo the rulable followed to get him to return; and by Sunday night Mavity was feeding both boys from the back door and keeping them out of sight of Pap's vengeance. Considering that Johnnie had trouble enough, she cautioned everybody on the place to say nothing of these matters to the girl. Mandy, a feeble, unsound creature at best, was more severely injured than had been thought. She was confined to her bed for days. Pap went about somewhat like a whipped dog, spoke little on any subject, and tolerated no mention of the topic of the day in Cottonville; his face kept the boarders quiet at table and in the house, anyhow. Shade Buckheath never entered the place after Deanie was carried in from the hastily summoned carriage Thursday night.

The doctors told them that if Deanie survived the shock and its violent reaction, she had a fair chance of recovery. They found at once that she was not internally injured; the blood that had been seen came only from a cut lip. But the child's left arm was broken, the small body was dreadfully bruised, and the terror had left a profound mental disturbance. Nothing but quiet and careful nursing offered any good hope; while there was the menace that she would never be strong again, and might not live to womanhood.

At first she lay with half-closed, glazed eyes, barely breathing, a ghastly sight. Then, when she roused a bit, she wanted, not Lissy, not even Johnnie; she called for her mother.

When her child was brought home to her, dying as they all thought, Laurella had rallied her forces and got up from the pallet on which she lay to tend on the little thing; but she broke down in the course of a few hours, and seemed about to add another patient to Johnnie's cares.

Yet when the paroxysms of terror shook the emaciated frame, and the others attempted to reassure Deanie by words, it was her mother who called for a bit of gay calico, for scissors and needle and thread, and began dressing a doll in the little sufferer's sight. Laurella had carried unspoiled the faculty for play, up with her through the years.

"Let her be," the doctor counselled Johnnie, in reply to anxious inquiries. "Don't you see she's getting the child's attention? The baby notices. An ounce of happiness is worth a pound of any medicine I could bring."

And so, when Laurella could no longer sit up, they brought another cot for her, and she lay all day babbling childish nonsense, and playing dolls within hand-reach of the sick-bed; while Johnnie with Lissy's help, tended on them both.

"You've got two babies now, you big, old, solemn Johnnie," Laurella said, with a ghost of her spark-ling smile. "Deanie and me is just of one age, and that's a fact."

If Pap wanted to see his young wife — and thirst for a sight of her was a continual craving with him; she was the light of the old sinner's eyes — he had to go in and look on the child he had injured. This kept him away pretty effectually after that first fiery scene, when Laurella had flown at him like a fierce little vixen and told him that she never wanted to see his face again, that she rued the day she married him, and intended to leave him as soon as she could put foot to the ground.

In the gray dawn of Monday morning, when Johnnie was downstairs eating her bit of early breakfast, Pap shambled in to make Laurella's fire. Having got the hickory wood to blazing, he sat humped and shame-faced by the bedside a while, whispering to his wife and holding her hand, a sight for the student of man to marvel at. He had brought a paper of coarse, cheap candy for Deanie, but the child was asleep. The offering was quite as acceptable to Laurella, and she nibbled a stick as she listened to him.

The bald head with its little fringe of grizzled curls, bent close to the dark, slant-browed, lustrous-eyed, mutinous countenance; Pap whispered hoarsely for some time, Laurella replying at first in a sort of languid tolerance, but presently with little ejaculations of wonder and dismay. A step on the stair which he took to be Johnnie's put Himes to instant flight.

"I've got to go honey," he breathed huskily. "Cain't you say you forgive me before I leave? I know I ain't fitten fer the likes of you; but when I come back from this here raid I'm a-goin' to take some money out of the bank and git you whatever you want. Look-a-here; see what I've done," and he showed a little book in his hand, and what he had written in it.

"Oh — I forgive you, if that's any account to you," returned Laurella with kindly contempt. "I never

noticed that forgiving things undid the harm any;
but — yes — oh, of course I forgive you. Go along;
I'm tired now. Don't bother me any more, Gid;
I want to sleep."

The old man thrust the treasured bankbook under
Laurella's pillow, and hurried away. Downstairs in
the dining room Johnnie was eating her breakfast.

"Johnnie," said Mavity Bence, keeping behind the
girl's chair as she served the meal to her at the end of
the long table, "I ain't never done you a meanness yet,
have I? And you know I've got all the good will in
the world toward you — now don't you?"

"Why, of course, Aunt Mavity," returned Johnnie
wonderingly, trying to get sight of the older woman's
face.

Mrs. Bence took a plate and hurried out for more
biscuits. She came back with some resolution plainly
renewed in her mind.

"Johnnie," she began once more, "there's something
I've got to tell you. Your Uncle Pros has got away
from 'em up at the hospital, and to the hills, and — and
— I have obliged to tell you."

"Yes, I know," returned Johnnie passively. "They
sent me word last night. I'm sorry, but I can't do
anything about it. Maybe he won't come to any harm
out that way. I can't imagine Uncle Pros hurting
anybody. Perhaps it will do him good."

"Hit wasn't about your Uncle Pros that I was
meaning. At least not about his gettin' away from the
hospital," amended Mavity. "It was about the day

he got hurt here. I — I always aimed to tell you. I know I ort to have done it. I was always a-goin' to, and then — Pap — he ——"

She broke off and stood silent so long that Johnnie turned and looked at her.

"Surely you aren't afraid of me, Aunt Mavity," she said finally.

"No," said Mavity Bence in a low voice, "but I'm scared of — the others."

The girl stared at her curiously.

"Johnnie," burst out the woman for the third time, "yo' Uncle Pros found his silver mine! Oh, yes, he did; and Pap's got his pieces of ore upstairs in a bandanner; and him and Shade Buckheath aims to git it away from you-all and — oh, I don't know what!"

There fell a long silence. At last Johnnie's voice broke it, asking very low:

"Did they — how was Uncle Pros hurt?"

"Neither of 'em touched him," Mavity hastened to assure her. "He heard 'em name it how they'd get the mine from him — or thought he did — and he come out and talked loud, and grabbed for the bandanner, and he missed it and fell down the steps. He wasn't crazy when he come to the house. He was jest plumb wore out, and his head was hurt. He called it yo' silver mine. He said he had to put the bandanner in yo' lap and tell you hit was for you."

Johnny got suddenly to her feet.

"Thank you, Aunt Mavity," she said kindly. "This is what's been troubling you, is it? Don't worry any more, I'll see about this, somehow.   I must go back to Mother now."

Laurella had said to Pap Himes that she wanted to sleep, and indeed her eyes were closed when Johnnie entered the room; but beneath the shadow of the sweeping lashes burned such spots of crimson that her nurse was alarmed.

"What was Pap Himes saying to you to get .you so excited?" she asked anxiously.

"Johnnie, come here.   Sit down on the edge of the bed and listen to me," demanded Laurella feverishly. She laid hold of her daughter's arm, and half pulled herself up by it, staring into Johnnie's face as she talked; and out tumbled the whole story of Gray Stoddard's disappearance.

As full understanding of what her mother said came home to Johnnie, her eyes dilated in her pale face. She sank to her knees beside the bed.

"Lost!" she echoed.   "Lost — gone!   Hasn't been seen since Friday morning — Friday morning before sunup!   Friday, Saturday, Sunday.   My God, Mother — it's three days and three nights!"

"Yes, honey, it's three days and three nights," assented Laurella fearfully.   "Gid says he's going up in the mountains with a lot of others to search.   He says some thinks the moonshiners have taken him in mistake for a revenuer; and some believe it was robbery — for his watch and money; and Mr. Hardwick is blaming it on the Groner crowd that raised up such a fuss when Lura Dawson died in the hospital here. Gid says they've searched every ridge and valley this side of Big Unaka. He — Johnnie, he says *he* believes Mr. Stoddard suicided."

"Where is Shade Buckheath?" whispered Johnnie.

"Shade's been out with mighty nigh every crowd that went," Laurella told her. "Mr. Hardwick pays them wages, just the same as if they were in the mill. Shade's going with Gid this morning, in Mr. Stoddard's automobile."

"Are they gone — oh, are they gone?" Johnnie sprang to her feet in dismay, and stood staring a moment. Then swiftly she bent once more over the little woman in the bed. "Mother," she said before Laurella could speak or answer her, "Aunt Mavity can wait on you and Deanie for a little while — with what help Lissy will give you — can't she, honey? And Mandy was coming downstairs to her breakfast this morning — she's able to be afoot now — and I know she'll be wanting to help tend on Deanie. You could get along for a spell without me — don't you think you could? Honey," she spoke desperately. "I've just got to find Shade Buckheath — I must see him."

"Sure, we'll get along all right, Johnnie," Laurella put in eagerly. She tugged at a corner of the pillow, fumbled thereunder with her little brown hand, and dragging out Pap Himes's bankbook, showed it to her daughter, opening at that front page where Pap's clumsy characters made Laurella Himes free of all his savings. "You go right along, Johnnie, and see cain't you help about Mr. Stoddard. Looks like I cain't bear to think. . . the pore boy . . . you go on — me and Deanie'll be all right till you get back."

Johnnie stooped and kissed the cheek with its fever-ish flush.

"Good-bye, Mommie," she whispered hurriedly. "Don't worry about me. I'll be back —. Well, don't worry. Good-bye." She snatched a coat and hat, and, going out, closed the door quietly behind her.

She stepped out into the dancing sunlight of an early spring morning. The leafless vine on Mavity Bence's porch rattled dry stems against the lattice work in a gay March wind. Taking counsel with herself for a moment, she started swiftly down the street in the direction of the mills. In the office they told her that Mr. Hardwick had gone to Nashville to see about getting bloodhounds; MacPherson was following his own plan of search in Watauga. She was permitted to go down into the mechanical department and ask the head of it about Shade Buckheath.

"No, he ain't here," Mr. Ramsey told her promptly. "We're running so short-handed that I don't know how to get along; and if I try to get an extra man, I find he's out with the searchers. I sent up for Himes yesterday, but him and Buckheath was to go together to-day, taking Mr. Stoddard's car, so as to get further up into the Unakas."

Johnnie felt as though the blood receded from her face and gathered all about a heart which beat to suffo-cation. For a wild moment she had an impulse to denounce Buckheath and her stepfather. But almost instantly she realized that she would weaken her cause and lose all chance of assistance by doing so. Her standing in the mill was excellent, and as she ran up the stairs she was going over in her mind the persons to whom she might take her story. She found no one from whom she dared expect credence and help. Out in the street again she caught sight of Charlie Conroy, and her thoughts were turned by a natural association of ideas to Lydia Sessions. That was it! Why had it not occurred to her before? She hurried up the long hill to the Hardwick home and, trying first the bell at the front, where she got no reply, skirted the house and rapped long and loudly at the side door.

Harriet Hardwick, when things began to wear a tragic complexion, had promptly packed her wardrobe and her children and flitted to Watauga. This hegira was undertaken mainly to get her sister away from the scene of Gray Stoddard's disappearance; yet when the move came to be made, Miss Sessions refused to accompany her sister.

"I can't go," she repeated fiercely. "I'll stay here and keep house for Jerome. Then if there comes any news, I'll be where — oh, don't look at me that way. I wish you'd go on and let me alone. Yes — yes — yes — it is better for you to go to Watauga and leave me here."

Ever since her brother-in-law opened the door of the sitting room and announced to the family Gray Stoddard's disappearance, Lydia Sessions had been, as it were, a woman at war with herself. Her first impulse was of decorum — to jerk her skirts about her in seemly fashion and be certain that no smirch adhered to them.   Then she began to wonder if she could find Shade Buckheath, and discover from him the truth of the matter.   Whenever she would have made a movement toward this, she winced away from what she knew he would say to her.   She flinched even from finding out that her fears were well grounded.   As matters began to wear a more serious face, she debated now and again telling her brother-in-law of her suspicions that Buckheath had a grudge against Stoddard. But if she said this, how account for the knowledge? How explain to Jerome why she had denied seeing Stoddard Friday morning?   Jerome was so terribly practical — he would ask such searching questions.

Back of it all there was truly much remorse, and terrible anxiety for Stoddard himself; but this was continually swallowed up in her concern for her own welfare, her own good name.   Always, after she had agonized so much, there would come with a revulsion — a gust of anger.   Stoddard had never cared for her, he had been cruel in his attitude of kindness.   Let him take what followed.

Cottonville was a town distraught, and the Hardwick servants had seized the occasion to run out for a bit of delectable gossip in which the least of the horrors included Gray Stoddard's murdered and mutilated body washed down in some mountain stream to the sight of his friends.

Johnnie was too urgent to long delay.   Getting no

answer at the side door, she pushed it open and ventured through silent room after room until she came to the stairway, and so on up to Miss Sessions's bedroom door. She had been there before, and fearing to alarm by knocking, she finally called out in what she tried to make a normal, reassuring tone.

"It's only me — Johnnie Consadine — Miss Lydia."

The answer was a hasty, muffled outcry. Somebody who had been kneeling by the bed on the further side of the room sprang up and came forward, showing a face so disfigured by tears and anxiety, by loss of sleep and lack of food, as to be scarcely recognizable. That ravaged visage told plainly the battle-ground that Lydia Sessions's narrow soul had become in these dreadful days. She knew now that she had set Shade Buckheath to quarrel with Gray Stoddard — and Gray had never been seen since the hour she sent the dangerous, unscrupulous man after him to that quarrel. With this knowledge wrestled and fought the instinct we strive to develop in our girl children, the fear we brand shamefully into their natures — her name must not be connected with such an affair — she must not be "talked about."

"Have they found him?" Lydia gasped. "Is he alive?"

Johnnie, generous soul, even in the intense pre-occupation of her own pain, could pity the woman who looked and spoke thus.

"No," she answered, "they haven't found him — and some that are looking for him never will find him.

Oh, Miss Lydia, I want you to help me make them send somebody that we can trust up the Gap road, and on to the Unakas."

Miss Sessions flinched plainly.

"What do you know about it?" she inquired in a voice which shook.

Still staring at Johnnie, she moved back toward her bedroom door. "Why should you mention the Gap road? What makes you think he went up in the Unakas?"

"I — don't know that he went there," hesitated Johnnie. "But I do know who you've got to find before you can find him. Oh, get somebody to go with me and help me, before it's too late. I — " she hesitated — "I thought maybe we could get your brother Hartley's car. I could run it — I could run a car."

The bitterness that had racked Lydia Sessions's heart for more than forty-eight hours culminated. She had been instrumental in putting Gray Stoddard in mortal danger — and now if he was to be helped, assistance would come through Johnnie Consadine! It was more than she could bear.

"I don't believe it!" she gasped. "You know who to find! You're just getting up this story to be noticed. You're always doing things to attract attention to yourself. You want to go riding around in an automobile and — and — Mr. Stoddard has probably gone in to Watauga and taken the midnight train for Boston. This looking around in the mountains is folly. Who would want to harm him in the mountains?"

For a moment Johnnie stood, thwarted and non-plussed. The insults directed toward herself made almost no impression on her, strangely as they came from Lydia Sessions's lips. She was too intent on her own purpose to care greatly.

"Shade Buckheath ——" she began cautiously, intending only to state that Shade had taken Stoddard's car; but Lydia Sessions drew back with a scream.

"It's a lie!" she cried. "There isn't a word of truth in what you say, John Consadine. Oh, you're the plague of my life — you have been from the first! You follow me about and torment me. Shade Buckheath had nothing to do with Gray Stoddard's disappearance, I tell you. Nothing — nothing — nothing!"

She thrust forward her face and sent forth the words with incredible vehemence. But her tirade kindled in Johnnie no heat of personal anger. She stood looking intently at the frantic woman before her. Slowly a light of comprehension dawned in her eyes.

"Shade Buckheath had everything to do with Gray Stoddard's disappearance. You know it — that's what ails you now. You — you must have been there when they quarrelled!"

"They didn't quarrel — they didn't!" protested Miss Lydia, with a yet more hysteric emphasis. "They didn't even speak to each other. Mr. Stoddard said 'Good morning' to me, and rode right past."

Johnnie leant forward and, with a sudden sweeping movement, caught the other woman by the wrist, looking deep into her eyes.

"Lydia," she said accusingly, and neither of them noticed the freedom of the address, "you didn't tell the truth when you said you hadn't seen Gray since Friday night. You saw him Friday morning — *you — and — Shade — Buckheath!* You have both lied about it — God knows why. Now, Shade and my stepfather have taken poor Gray's car and gone up into the mountains. *What do you think they went for?*"

The blazing young eyes were on Miss Sessions's tortured countenance.

"Oh, don't let those men get at Gray. They'll murder him!" sobbed the older woman, sinking once more to her knees. "Johnnie — I've always been good to you, haven't I? You go and tell them that — say that Shade Buckheath — that somebody ought to ——"

She broke off abruptly, and sprang up like a suddenly goaded creature.

"No, I won't!" she cried out. "You needn't ask it of me. I will not tell about seeing Mr. Stoddard Friday morning. I promised not to, and it can't do any good, anyhow. If you set them at me, I'll deny it and tell them you made up the story. I will — I will — I will!"

And she ran into her room once more, and threw herself down beside the bed. Johnnie turned contemptuously and left the woman babbling incoherencies on her knees, evidently preparing to pray to a God whose laws she was determined to break.

CHAPTER XXII

THE ATLAS VERTEBRA

JOHNNIE hurried downstairs, in a mental turmoil out of which there swiftly formed itself the resolution to go herself and if possible overtake or find Shade and her stepfather. Word must first be sent to her mother. She was glad to remember that little bankbook under Laurella's pillow. Mavity and Mandy would tend the invalids well, helped by little Lissy; and with money available, she was sure they would be allowed to lack for nothing. She crossed the hall swiftly, meaning to go past the little grocery where they bought their supplies and telephone Mavity that she might be away for several days. But near the side door she noted the Hardwick telephone, and hesitated a moment. People would hear her down at Mayfield's. Already she began to have a terror of being watched or followed. Hesitatingly she took down the receiver and asked for connection. At the little tinkle of the bell, there was a swift, light rush above stairs.

"Mahala!" screamed Miss Sessions's voice over the banisters, thinking the maid was below stairs; "answer that telephone." She heard Johnnie move, and added, "Tell everybody that I can't be seen. If it's anything about Mr. Stoddard, say that I'm sick — utterly prostrated — and can't be talked to." She turned from the stairway, ran back into her own room and shut and locked the door. And at that moment Johnnie heard Mavity Bence's voice replying to her.

"Aunt Mavity," she began, "this is Johnnie. I'm up at Mr. Hardwick's now. Uncle Pros is out in the mountains, and I'm going to look for him. I'd rather not have anybody know I'm gone; do you understand that? Try to keep it from the boarders and the children. You and Mandy are the only ones that would have to know."

"Yes, honey, yes, Johnnie," came the eager, humble reply. "I'll do just like you say. Shan't nobody find out from me. Johnnie —" there was a pause — "Johnnie, Pap and Shade didn't get off as soon as they expected. Something was the matter with the machine, I believe. They ain't been gone to exceed a quarter of an hour. I — I thought maybe you'd like to know."

"Thank you, Aunt Mavity," said Johnnie. "Yes, I'm glad you told me." She understood what a struggle the kind soul had had with her weakness and timidity ere, for loyalty's sake, she was able to make the disclosure. "I may not be back for two or three days. Don't worry about me. I'll be all right. Mother's got money. You buy what she and Deanie need, and don't work too hard. Good-bye."

She hung up the receiver, went out the side door

and, reaching the main street, struck straight for the Gap, holding the big road for the Unakas. To her left was the white highway that ran along above the valley, and that Palace of Pleasure which had seemed a wonder and a mystery to her one year gone. To-day she gave no thought to the sight of river and valley and town, except to look back once at the roofs and reflect that, among all the people housed there in sight of her, there were surely those who knew the secret of Gray Stoddard's disappearance — who could tell her if they would where to search for him. Somehow, the thought made her feel very small and alone and unfriended. With its discouragement came that dogged persistence that was characteristic of the girl. She set her trembling lip and went over her plans resolutely, methodically. Deanie and Laurella were safe to be well looked after in her absence. Mavity Bence and Mandy would care for them tenderly. And there was the bankbook. If Johnnie knew her mother, the household back there would not lack, either for assistance or material matters.

And now the present enterprise began to shape itself in her mind. A practical creature, she depended from the first on getting a lift from time to time. Yet Johnnie knew better than another the vast, silent, secret network of hate that draws about the victim in a mountain vendetta. If the spirit of feud was aroused against the mill owners, if the Groners and Dawsons had been able to enlist their kin and clan, she was well aware that the man or woman who gave her smiling information as to ways and means, might, the hour before, have looked on Gray Stoddard lying dead, or sat in the council which planned to kill him. Thus she walked warily, and dared ask from none directions or help. She was not yet in her own region, these lower ridges lying between two lines of railway, which, from the mountaineer's point of view, contaminated them and gave them a tincture of the valley and the Settlement.

Noon came and passed. She was very weary. Factory life had told on her physically, and the recent distress of mind added its devitalizing influence. There was a desperate flagging of the muscles weakened by disuse and an unhealthy indoor life.

"I wonder can I ever make it?" she questioned herself. Then swiftly, "I've got to — I've got to."

Her eye roved toward a cabin on the slope above. There lived a man by the name of Straley, but he was a cousin to Lura Dawson, the girl who had died in the hospital. Johnnie knew him to be one of the bitterest enemies of the Cottonville mill owners, and realized that he would be the last one to whom she should apply. Mutely, doggedly, she pressed on, and rounding a bend in a long, lonely stretch of road, saw before her the tall, lithe form of a man, trousers tucked into boots, a tall staff in hand, making swift progress up the road. The sound of feet evidently arrested the attention of the wayfarer. He turned and waited for her to come up.

The figure was so congruous with its surroundings

that she saw with surprise a face totally strange to her. The turned-down collar of the rumpled shirt was unbuttoned at a brown throat; the face above seemed to her eyes neither old nor young, though the light, springing gait when he walked, the supple, easeful attitude now that he rested, one hand flung high on the curious tall staff, were those of a youth; the eyes of a warm, laughing hazel had the direct fearlessness of a child, and a slouch hat carried in the hand showed a fair crop of slightly grizzled, curling hair.

A stranger — at first the thought frightened, and then attracted her. This man looked not unlike Johnnie's own people, and there was something in his face that led her to entertain the idea of appealing to him for help. He settled the question of whether or no she should enter into conversation, by accosting her at once brusquely and genially.

"Mornin', sis'. You look tired," he said. "You ought to have a stick, like me. Hold on — I'll cut you one."

Before the girl could respond beyond an answering smile and "good morning," the new friend had put his own alpenstock into her hands and gone to the roadside, where, with unerring judgment, he selected a long, straight, tapering shoot of ash, and hewed it deftly with a monster jack-knife drawn from his trousers pocket.

"There — try that," he said as he returned, trimming off the last of the leaves and branches.

Johnnie took the staff with her sweet smile of thanks.

For a few moments the two walked on silently side by side, she desperately absorbed in her anxieties, her companion apparently returning to some world apart in his own mind. Suddenly:

"Can I get to the railroad down this side?" the man asked her in that odd, incidental voice of his which suggested that what he said was merely a small portion of what he thought.

"Why — yes, I reckon so," hesitated Johnnie. "It's a pretty far way, and there don't many folks travel on it. It's an old Indian trail; a heap of our roads here are that; but it'll take you right to the railroad — the W. and A."

Her companion chuckled, seemingly with some inner satisfaction.

"Yes, that's just what I supposed. I soldiered all over this country, and I thought it was about as pretty scenery as God ever made. I promised myself then that if I ever came back into this part of the world, I'd do some tramping through here. They're going to have a great big banquet at Atlanta, and they had me caged up taking me down there to make a speech. I gave them the slip at Watauga. I knew I'd strike the railroad if I footed it through the mountains here."

Johnnie examined her companion with attention. Would it do to ask him if he had seen an automobile on the road — a dark green car? Dare she make inquiry as to whether he had heard of Gray Stoddard's disappearance, or met any of the searchers? She decided on a conservative course.

"I wish I had time to set you in the right road," she hesitated; "but my poor old uncle is out here somewhere among these ridges and ravines; he's not in his right mind, and I've got to find him if I can."

"Crazy, do you mean?" asked her companion, with a quick yet easy, smiling attention. "I'd like to see him, if he's crazy. I take a great interest in crazy folks. Some of 'em have a lot of sense left."

Johnnie nodded.

"He doesn't know any of us," she said pitifully. "They've had him in the hospital three months, trying to do something for him; but the doctors say he'll never be well."

"That's right hopeful," observed the man, with a plainly intentional, dry ludicrousness. "I always think there's some chance when the doctors give 'em up — and begin to let 'em alone. How was he hurt, sis'?"

Johnnie did not pause to reflect that she had not said Uncle Pros was hurt at all. For some reason which she would herself have been at a loss to explain, she hastened to detail to this chance-met stranger the exact appearance and nature of Pros Passmore's injuries, her listener nodding his head at this or that point; making some comment or inquiry at another.

"The doctors say that they would suppose it was a fractured skull, or concussion of the brain, or something like that; but they've examined him and there is nothing to see on the outside; and they trephined and it didn't do any good; so they just let him stay about the hospital."

"No," said her new friend softly, almost absently, "it didn't do any good to trephine — but it might have done a lot of harm. I'd like to see the back of your uncle's neck. I ain't in any hurry to get to that banquet at Atlanta — a man can always overeat and make himself sick, without going so far to do it."

So, like an idle schoolboy, the unknown forsook his own course, turning from the road when Johnnie turned, and went with her up the steep, rocky gulch where the door of a deserted cabin flung to and fro on its hinges. At sight of the smokeless chimney, the gaping doorway and empty, inhospitable interior, Johnnie looked blank.

"Have you got anything to eat?" she asked her companion, hesitatingly. "I came off in such a hurry that I forgot all about it. Some people that I know used to live in that cabin, and I hoped to get my dinner there and ask after my uncle; but I see they have moved."

"Sit right down here," said the stranger, indicating the broad door-stone, around which the grass grew tall. "We'll soon make that all right." He sought in the pockets of the coat he carried slung across his shoulder and brought out a packet of food. "I laid in some fuel when I thought I might get the chance to run my own engine across the mountains," he told the girl, opening his bundle and dividing evenly. He uttered a few musical words in an unknown tongue.

"That's Indian," he commented carelessly, without looking at her. "It means you're to eat your dinner. I was with the Shawnees when I was a boy. I learned a lot of their language, and I'll never forget it. They taught me more things than talk."

Johnnie studied the man beside her as they ate their bit of lunch.

"My name is Johnnie Consadine, sir," she told him. "What shall I call you?"

Thus directly questioned, the unknown smiled quizzically, his hazel eyes crinkling at the corners and overflowing with good humour.

"Well, you might say 'Pap,'" he observed consideringly. "Lost of boys and girls do call me Pap — more than a thousand of 'em, now, I guess. And I'm eighty — mighty near old enough to have a girl of nineteen."

She looked at him in astonishment. Eighty years old, as lithe as a lad, and with a lad's clear, laughing eye! Yet there was a look of power, of that knowledge which is power, in his face that made her say to him:

"Do you think that Uncle Pros can ever be cured — have his right mind back again, I mean? Of course, the cut on his head is healed up long ago."

"The cut on his head didn't make him crazy," said her companion, murmuringly. "Of course it wasn't that, or he would have been raving when he came down from the mountain. Something happened to him afterward."

"Yes, there did," Johnnie assented wonderingly — falteringly. "I don't know how you came to guess it, but the woman who told me that she was hiding in the front room when they were quarrelling and saw Uncle Pros fall down the steps, says he landed almost square on his head. She thought at first his neck was broken — that he was killed."

"Uh-huh," nodded the newcomer. "You see I'm a good guesser. I make my living guessing things." He flung her a whimsical, sidelong glance, as, having finished their lunch, they rose and moved on. "I wish I had my hands on the processes of that atlas vertebra," he said.

"On — on what?" inquired Johnnie in a slightly startled tone.

"Never mind, sis'. If we find him, and I can handle him, I'll know where to look."

"Nobody can touch him but me when he gets out this way," Johnnie said. "He acts sort of scared and sort of fierce, and just runs and hides from people. Maybe if you'll tell me what you want done, I could do it."

"Maybe you could — and then again maybe you couldn't," returned the other, with a great show of giving her proposition serious consideration. "A good many folks think they can do just what I can — if I'd only tell 'em how — and sometimes they find out they can't."

Upon the word, they topped a little rise, and Johnnie laid a swift, detaining hand upon her companion's arm. At the roadside, in a little open, grassy space where once evidently a cabin had stood, knelt the figure of a gaunt old man. At first he seemed to the approaching pair to be gesticulating and pointing, but a moment's observation gave them the gleam of a knife in his hand — he was playing mumblety-peg. As they stood, drawn back near some roadside bushes, watching him, the long, lean old arm went up, the knife flashing against the knuckles of the clenched fist and, with a whirl of the wrist, reversing swiftly in air, to bury its blade in the soil before the player.

"Hi! Hi! Hi! I th'owed it. That counts two for me," the cracked old falsetto shrilled out.

There on that grassy plot that might have been a familiar dooryard of his early days, he was playing alone, gone back to childhood. Johnnie gazed and her eyes swam with unshed tears.

"You better not go up there — and him with the knife and all," she murmured finally. The man beside her looked around into her face and laughed.

"I'm not very bad scared," he said, advancing softly in line with his proposed patient, motioning the girl not to make herself known, or startle her uncle.

Johnnie stole after him, filled with anxiety. When the newcomer stood directly behind the kneeling man, he bent, and his arms shot out with surprising quickness. The fingers of one hand dropped as though predestined upon the back of the neck, the other caught skilfully beneath the chin. There was a sharp wrench, an odd crack, a grunt from Uncle Pros, and then the mountaineer sprang to his full and very considerable height with a roar. Whirling upon his adversary, he grappled him in his long arms, hugging like a grizzly, and shouting:

"You, Gid Himes, wha'r's my specimens?"

He shook the stranger savagely.

"You an' Shade Buckheath — you p'ar o' scoundrels — give me back my silver specimens! Give me back my silver ore that shows about the mine for my little gal."

"Uncle Pros! Uncle Pros!" screamed Johnnie, rushing in and laying hold of the man's arm. "Don't you know me? It's Johnnie. Don't hurt this gentleman."

The convulsion of rage subsided in the old man with almost comical suddenness. His tense form relaxed; he stumbled back, dropping his hands at his sides and staring about him, then at Johnnie.

"Why, honey," he gasped, "how did you come here? Whar's Gid? Whar's Shade Buckheath? Lord A'mighty! Whar am I at?"

He looked around him bewildered, evidently expecting to see the porch of Himes's boarding-house at Cottonville, the scattered bits of silver ore, and the rifled bandanna. He put his hand to his head, and sliding it softly down to the back of the neck demanded.

"What's been did to me?"

"You be right good and quiet now, and mind Johnnie," the girl began, with a pathetic tremble in her voice, "and she'll take you back to the hospital where they're so kind to you."

"The hospital?" echoed Pros. "That hospital down at Cottonville? I never was inside o' one o' them places — what do you want me to go thar for, Johnnie? Who is this gentleman? How came we-all up here on the road this-a-way?"

"I can quiet him," said Johnnie aside to her new friend. "I always can when he gets wild this way."

The unknown shook his head.

"You'll never have to quiet him any more, unless he breaks his neck again," came the announcement. "Your uncle is as sane as anybody — he just doesn't remember anything that happened from the time he fell down the steps and slipped that atlas vertebra a little bit on one side."

Again Pros Passmore's fingers sought the back of his collar.

"Looks like somebody has been tryin' to wring my neck, same as a chicken's," he said meditatively. "But hit feels all right now — all right — Hoo-ee!" he suddenly broke off to answer to a far, faint hail from the road below them.

"Pap! Hey — Pap!" The words came up through the clear blue air, infinitely diminished and attenuated, like some insect cry. The tall man seemed to guess just what the interruption would be. He turned with a pettish exclamation.

"Never could go anywhere, nor have any fun, but what some of the children had to tag," he protested.

"Hoo-ee!" He cupped his hands and sent his voice toward where two men in a vehicle had halted their horses and were looking anxiously up. "Well — what is it?"

"Did you get lost? We hired a buggy and came out to find you," the man below called up.

"Well, if I get lost, I can find myself," muttered the newcomer. He looked regretfully at the green slopes about him; the lofty, impassive cliffs where Peace seemed to perch, a visible presence; the great sweeps of free forest; then at Uncle Pros and Johnnie. And they looked back at him dubiously.

"I expect I'll have to leave you," he said at last. "I see what it is those boys want; they're trying to get me back to the railroad in time for the six-forty train. I'd a heap rather stay here with you, but —" he glanced from Johnnie and Uncle Pros down to the men in their attitude of anxious waiting — "I reckon I'll have to go."

He had made the first descending step when Johnnie's hand on his arm arrested him. Uncle Pros knew not the wonder of his own restoration; but to the girl this man before her was something more than mortal. Her eyes went from the lightly tossed hair on his brow to the mud-spattered boots — was he only a human being? What was the strange power he had over life and death and the wandering soul of man?

"What — what — aren't you going to tell me your name, and what you are, before you go?" she entreated him.

He laughed over his shoulder, an enigmatic laugh.

"What was it you did to Uncle Pros?" Her voice was vibrant with the awe and wonder of what she had seen. "Was it the laying on of hands — as they tell of it in the Bible?"

"Say, Pap, hurry up, please," wailed up the thin, impatient reminder from the road.

"Well, yes — I laid my hands on him pretty strong. Didn't I, old man?" And the stranger glanced to where Uncle Pros stood, still occasionally interrogating the back of his neck with fumbling fingers. "Don't you worry, sis'; a girl like you will get a miracle when she has to have it. If I happened to be the miracle you needed, why, that's good. As for my profession — my business in life — there was a lot of folks that used to name me the Lightning Bone-setter. For my own part, I'd just as soon you'd call me a human engineer. I pride myself on knowing how the structure of man ought to work, and keeping the bearings right and the machinery properly levelled up. Never mind. Next time you have use for a miracle, it'll be along on schedule time, without you knowing what name you need to call it. You're that sort." With that curious, onlooker's smile of his and with a nod of farewell, he plunged down the steep.

CHAPTER XXIII

A CLUE

THEY stood together watching, as the tall form retreated around the sharp curves of the red clay road, or leaped lightly and hardily down the cut-offs. They waved back to their late companion when, climbing into the waiting buggy below, he was finally driven away. Johnnie turned and looked long at her uncle with swimming eyes, as he stood gazing where the vehicle had disappeared. She finally laid a tremulous hand on his arm.

"Oh, Uncle Pros," she said falteringly, "I can't believe it yet. But you — you do understand me now, don't you? You know me. I'm Johnnie."

The old man wheeled sharply, and laughed.

"See here, honey," he said with a tinge of irritation in his tones. "I reckon I've been crazy. From what you say, looks like I haven't known my best friends for a long time. But I have got as much sense now as I ever had, and I don't remember anything about that other business. Last thing I know of was fussin' with Gid Himes and Shade Buckheath about my silver ore. By Joe! I bet they got that stuff when I was took — Johnnie, was I took sudden?"

He seated himself on the lush, ancient, deep-rooted

dooryard grass where, a half-hour gone, he had knelt, a harmless lunatic, playing mumblety peg. Half reluctantly Johnnie sank down beside him.

"Yes — yes — yes, Uncle Pros," the girl agreed, impatience mounting in her once more, with the assurance of her uncle's safety and well-being. "They did get your specimens; but we can fix all that; there's a worse thing happened now." And swiftly, succintly, she told him of the disappearance of Gray Stoddard.

"An' I been out o' my head six months and better," the old man ruminated, staring down at the ground. "Good Lord! it's funny to miss out part o' your days like that. Hit was August — but — O-o-h, hot enough to fry eggs on a shingle, the day I tramped down to Cottonville with them specimens; and here it is" — he threw up his head and took a comprehensive survey of the grove about him — "airly spring — March, I should say — ain't it, Johnnie? Yes," as she nodded. "And who is this here young man that you name that's missin', honey?"

The girl glanced at him apprehensively.

"You know, Uncle Pros," she said in a coaxing tone. "It's Mr. Stoddard, that used to come to the hospital to see you so much and play checkers with you when you got better. You — why, Uncle Pros, you liked him more than any one. He could get you to eat when you wouldn't take a spoonful from anybody else. You must remember him — you can't have forgot Mr. Stoddard."

Pros thrust out a long, lean arm, and fingered the sleeve upon it.

"Nor my own clothes, I reckon," he assented with a sort of rueful testiness; "but to the best of my knowin' and believin', I never in my life before saw this shirt I'm wearin'—every garment I've got on is a plumb stranger to me, Johnnie. Ye say I played checkers with him — and ——"

"Uncle Pros, you used to talk to him by the hour, when you didn't know me at all," Johnnie told him chokingly. "I would get afraid that you asked too much of him, but he'd leave anything to come and sit with you when you were bad. He's got the kindest heart of anybody I ever knew."

The old man's slow, thoughtful gaze was raised a moment to her eloquent, flushed face, and then dropped considerately to the path.

"An' ye tell me he's one of the rich mill owners? Mr. Gray Stoddard? That's one name you've never named in your letters. What cause have you to think that Shade wished the man ill?"

Slowly Johnnie's eyes filled with tears. "Why, what Shade said himself. He was ——"

"Jealous of him, I reckon," supplied the old man.

Johnnie nodded. It was no time for evasions.

"He had no call to be," she repeated. "Mr. Stoddard had no more thought of me in that way than he has of Deanie. He'd be just as kind to one as the other. But Shade brought his name into it, and threatened him to me in so many words. He said —"

she shivered at the recollection — "he said he'd fix him — he'd get even with him. So this morning when I found that Pap Himes and Shade had taken Mr. Stoddard's car and come on up this way, it scared me. Yet I couldn't hardly go to anybody with it. I felt as though they would say it was just a vain, foolish girl thinking she'd stirred up trouble and had the men quarrelling over her. I did try to see Mr. Hardwick and Mr. MacPherson, and both of them were away. And after that I went to Mr. Hardwick's house. The Miss Sessions I wrote you so much about was the only person there, and she wouldn't do a thing. Then I just walked up here on my two feet. Uncle Pros, I was desperate enough for anything."

Passmore had listened intently to Johnnie's swift, broken, passionate sentences.

"Yes — ye-es," he said, as she made an end. "I sorter begin to see. Hold on, honey, lemme think a minute."

He sat for some time silent, with introverted gaze, Johnnie with difficulty restraining her impatience, forbearing to break in upon his meditation.

"Hit cl'ars up to me — sorter — as I study on it," he finally said. "Hit's like this, honey; six months ago (Lord, Lord, six months!) when I was walkin' down to take that silver ore to you, Rudd Dawson stopped me, and nothing would do but I must go home with him — ye know he's got the old Gid Himes place, in the holler back of our house — an' talk to Will Venters, Jess Groner, and Rudd's brother Sam.

I didn't want to go — my head was plumb full of the silver-mine business, an' I jest wanted to git down to you quick as I could. The minute I said 'Johnnie,' Rudd 'lowed he wanted to warn me about you down in the Cottonville mills. He went over all that stuff concerning Lura, an' how she'd been killed off in the mill folk's hospital and her body shipped to Cincinnati and sold. I put in my word that you was a-doin' well in the mills; an' I axed him what proof he had that the mill folks sold dead bodies. I 'lowed that you found the people at Cottonville mighty kind, and the work good. He came right back at me sayin' that Lura had talked the same way, and that many another had. Well, I finally went with him to his place — the old Gid Himes house — an' him an' me an' Sam an' Groner had considerable talk. They told me how they'd all been down an' saw Mr. Hardwick, and how quare he spoke to 'em. 'Them mill fellers never offered me a dollar, not a dollar,' says Rudd. An' I says to him, 'Good Lord, Dawson! Never offered you money? For God's sake! Did you want to be paid for Lura's body?' And he says, 'You know damn' well I didn't want to be paid for Lura's body, Pros Passmore,' he says. 'But do you reckon I'm a-goin' to let them mill men strut around with money they got that-a-way in their pockets? No, I'll not. I'll see 'em cold in hell fust,' he says — them Dawsons is a hard nation o' folks, Johnnie. I talked to 'em for a spell, and tried to make 'em see that the Hardwick folks hadn't never sold no dead body to the student doctors; but they was all mad and out o' theirselves. I seed that they wanted to get up a feud. 'Well,' says Rudd, 'They've got one of the Dawsons, and before we're done we'll get one o' them.'

"'Uh-huh,' I says, 'you-all air a-goin' to get one o' them, air ye? Do you mean by that that you're ready to run your heads into a noose?'

"'We don't have to run our heads into nary noose,' says Sam Dawson. 'Shade Buckheath is a-standin' in with us. He knows all them mill fellers, an' their ways. He aims to he'p us; an' we'll ketch one o' them men out, and carry him off up here som'ers, and hold him till they pay us what we ask. I reckon the live body of one o' them chaps is worth a thousand dollars.' That's jest what he said," concluded the old man, turning toward her; "an' from what you tell me, Johnnie, I'll bet Shade Buckheath put the words in his mouth, if not the notion in his head."

"Yes," whispered Johnnie through white lips, "yes; but Shade Buckheath isn't looking to make money out of it. He knows better than to think that they could keep Mr. Stoddard prisoner a while, and then get money for bringing him back, and never have to answer for it. He said he'd get even — he'd fix him. Shade wants just one thing — Oh, Uncle Pros! Do you think they've killed him?"

The old man looked carefully away from her.

"This here kidnappin' business, an tryin' to get money out of a feller's friends, most generally does wind up in a killin'," he said. "The folks gits to huntin' pretty hot, then them that's done the trick gets scared, and — they wouldn't have no good place to put him, them Dawsons, and — and," reluctantly, "a dead body's easier hid than a live man. Truth is, hit looks mighty bad for the young feller, honey girl. To my mind hit's really a question of time. The sooner his friends gets to him the better, that's my belief."

Johnnie's pale, haggard face took on tragic lines as she listened to this plain putting of her own worst fears. She sprang up desperately. Uncle Pros rose, too.

"Now, which way?" she demanded.

The old hunter stood, staring thoughtfully at the path before his feet, rubbing his jaw with long, supple fingers, the daze of his recent experience yet upon him.

"Well, I had aimed to go right to our old cabin," he said finally. "Hit's little more than a mile to where Dawson lives, in Gid's old place in Blue Spring Holler. They all think I'm crazy, an' they won't interfere with me — not till they find out different. Your mother; she'll give us good help, once we git to her. There's them that thinks Laurelly is light-minded and childish, but I could tell 'em she's got a heap of sense in that thar pretty little head o' her'n."

"Oh, Uncle Pros! I forgot you don't know — of course you don't," broke in Johnnie with a sudden dismay in her voice. "I ought to have told you that mother" — she hesitated and looked at the old man — "mother isn't up at the cabin any more. I left her in Cottonville this morning."

"Cottonville!" echoed Pros in surprise. Then he added, "O' course, she came down to take care o' me when I was hurt. That's like Laurelly. Is all the chaps thar? Is the cabin empty? How's the baby?"

Johnnie nodded in answer to these inquiries, forbearing to go into any details. One thing she must tell him.

"Mother's — mother's married again," she managed finally to say.

"She's —" The old man broke off and turned Johnnie around that he might stare into her face. Then he laughed. "Well — well! Things have been happenin' — with the old man crazy an' all!" he said. "An' yit I don't know it's so strange. Laurelly is a mighty handsome little woman, and she don't look a day older than you do, Johnnie. I reckon it came through me bein' away, an' her havin' nobody to do for her. 'Course" — with pride — "she could have wedded 'most any time since your Pa died, if she'd been so minded. Who is it?"

Johnnie looked away from him. "I — Uncle Pros, I never heard a word about it till I came home one evening and there they were, bag and baggage, and they'd been married but an hour before by Squire Gaylord. It" — her voice sank almost to a whisper — "It's Pap Himes."

The old man thrust her back and stared again.

"Gid — Gideon Himes?" he exclaimed incredulously. "Why, the man's old enough to be her granddaddy, let alone her father. Gid Himes — the old —

What in the name of — ?   Johnnie — and you think Himes is mixed up with this young man that's been laywaid — him and Buckheath? Lord, what *is* all this business?"

"When Shade found I wouldn't have him," Johnnie began resolutely at the beginning, "he got Pap Himes to take him to board so that he could always be at me, tormenting me about it.   I don't know what he and Pap Himes had between them; but something — that I'm sure of.   And after the old man went up and married mother, it was worse.   He put the children in the mill and worked them almost to death; even — even Deanie," she choked back a sob.   "And Shade as good as told me he could make Pap Himes stop it any time I'd promise to marry him.   Something they were pulling together over.   Maybe it was the silver mine."

"The silver mine!" echoed old Pros.   "That's it.   Gid thought I was likely to die, and the mine would come to your mother.   Not but what he'd be glad enough to get Laurelly — but that's what put it in his head.   An' Gid Himes is married to my little Laurelly, an' been abusin' the children!   Lord, hit don't pay for a man to go crazy.   Things gits out of order without him."

"Well, what do you think now?" Johnnie inquired impatiently.   "We mustn't stay here talking when Mr. Stoddard may be in mortal danger.   Shall we go on to our place, just the same?"

The old man looked compassionately at her.

"Hold on, honey girl," he demurred gently. "We —" he sighted at the sun, which was declining over beyond the ridges toward Watauga. "I'm mighty sorry to pull back on ye, but we've got to get us a place to stay for the night. See," he directed her gaze with his own; "hit's not more'n a hour by sun. We cain't do nothin' this evenin'."

The magnitude of the disappointment struck Johnnie silent. Pros Passmore was an optimist, one who never used a strong word to express sorrow or dismay, but he came out of a brown study in which he had muttered, "Blaylock. No, Harp wouldn't do. Culp's. Sally Ann's not to be trusted. What about the Venable boys? No good" — to say with a distressed drawing of the brows, "My God! In a thing like this, you don't know who to look to."

"No. That's so, Uncle Pros," whispered Johnnie; she gazed back down the road she had come with the stranger. "I went up Slater's Lane to find Mandy Meacham's sister Roxy that married Zack Peavey," she said. "But they've moved from the cabin down there. They must have been gone a good while, for there's no work done on the truck-patch. I guess they went up to the Nooning-Spring place — Mandy said they talked of moving there. We might go and see. Mandy" — she hesitated, and looked questioningly at her uncle — "Mandy's been awful good to all of us, and she liked Mr. Stoddard."

"We'll try it," said Pros Passmore, and they set out together.

They climbed in silence, using a little-travelled woods-road, scarce more than two deep, grass-grown ruts, full of rotting stumps. Suddenly a couple of children playing under some wayside bushes leaped up and ran ahead of them, screaming.

"Maw — he's comin' back, and he's got a woman with him!"

A turn in the road brought the Nooning-Spring cabin in sight, a tiny, one-roomed log structure, ancient and ruinous; and in its door a young woman standing, with a baby in her arms, staring with all her eyes at them and at their approaching couriers.

She faltered a step toward the dilapidated rail fence as they came up.

"Howdy," she said in a low, half-frightened tone. Then to Uncle Pros, "We-all was mighty uneasy when you never come back."

Involuntarily the old man's hand went to that vertebra whose eighth-inch displacement had been so lately reduced.

"Have I been here?" he asked. "I was out of my head, and I don't remember it."

The young woman looked at him with a hopeless drawing of scant, light eyebrows above bulging gray eyes. She chugged the fretting baby gently up and down in her arms to hush it. Johnnie saw her resemblance to Mandy. Apparently giving up the effort in regard to the man, Zack Peavey's wife addressed the girl as an easier proposition.

"He was here," she said in a sort of aside. "He

stayed all night a-Saturday. Zack said he was kinder foolish, but I thought he had as much sense as most of 'em." Her gaze rested kindly on the old man. The children, wild and shy as young foxes, had stolen to the door of the cabin, in which they had taken refuge, and were staring out wonderingly.

"Well, we'll have to ask you could we stay to-night," Johnnie began doubtfully. "My uncle's been out of his head, and he got away from the folks at the hospital. I came up to hunt for him. I've just found him — but we aren't going right back. I met a man out there on the road that did something to him that — that —" she despaired of putting into words that the woman could comprehend the miracle which she had seen the stranger work — "Well, Uncle Pros is all right now, and we'd like to stay the night if we can."

"Come in — come in — the both of you," urged the woman, turning toward the cabin. "'Course, ye kin stay, an' welcome. Set and rest. Zack ain't home now. He's —" A curious, furtive look went over her round face. "Zack has got a job on hand, ploughing for — ploughing for a neighbour, but he'll be home to-night."

They went in and sat down. A kettle of wild greens was cooking over the fire, and everything was spotlessly clean. Mandy had said truly that there wasn't a thing on the farm she didn't love to do, and the gift of housewifery ran in the family. Johnnie had barely explained who she was, and made such effort as she could to enlist Mandy's sister, when Zack came tramping home, and showed, she thought, some uneasiness at finding them there. The wife ran out and met him before he reached the cabin, and they stood talking together a long time, the lines of both figures somehow expressing dismay; yet when they came in there was a fair welcome in the man's demeanour. At the supper table, whose scanty fare was well cooked, Uncle Pros and Johnnie had to tell again, and yet again, the story of that miraculous healing which both husband and wife could see was genuine.

Through it all, both Pros and Johnnie attempted to lead the talk around to some information which might be of use to them. Nothing was more natural than that they should speak of Gray Stoddard's disappearance, since Watauga, Cottonville, and the mountains above were full of the topic; yet husband and wife sheered from it in a sort of terror.

"Them that makes or meddles in such gits theirselves into trouble, that's what I say," Zack told the visitors, stroking a chin whose contours expressed the resolution and aggressiveness of a rabbit. "I ain't never seen this here Mr. Man as far as I know. I don't never want to see him. I ain't got no call to mix myself up in such, and I 'low I'll sleep easier and live longer if I don't do it."

"That's right," quavered Roxy. "Burkhalter's boy, he had to go to mixin' in when the Culps and the Venables was feudin'; and look what chanced. Nary one o' them families lost a man; but Burkhalter's boy got hisself killed up. Yes, that's what happened to him. Dead. I went to the funeral."

"True as Scriptur'," confirmed Zack — "reach an' take off, Pros. Johnnie, eat hearty — true as you-all set here. I he'ped make the coffin an' dig the grave."

After a time there came a sort of ruth to Johnnie for the poor creatures, furtive, stealing glances at each other, and answering her inquiries or Uncle Pros's with dry, evasive platitudes. She knew there was no malice in either of them; and that only the abject terror of the weak kept them from giving whatever bit of information it was they had and were consciously withholding. Soon she ceased plying them with questions, and signalled Uncle Pros that he should do the same. After the children were asleep in their trundle-bed, the four elders sat by the dying fire on the hearth and talked a little. Johnnie told Zack and Roxy of the mill work at Cottonville, how well she had got on, and how good Mr. Stoddard had been to her, choking over the treasured remembrances. She related the many kindnesses that had been shown Pros and his kinfolk at the Hospital, how the old man had been there for three months, treated as a guest during the latter part of his stay rather than a patient, and how Mr. Stoddard would leave his work in the office to come and cheer the sick man, or quiet him if he got violent.

"He looked perfectly dreadful when I first saw him," she said to them, "but the doctors took care of him as if he'd been a little baby. The nurses fed him by spoonfuls and coaxed him just like you would little Honey; and Mr. Stoddard — he never was too busy to —" the tears brimmed her eyes in the dusky cabin interior — "to come when Uncle Pros begged for him."

The woman sighed and stirred uneasily, her eye stealthily seeking her husband's.

In that little one-room hut there was no place for guests. Presently the men drifted out to the chip pile, where they lingered a while in desultory talk. Roxy and Johnnie, partly undressed, occupied the one bed; and later the host and his guest came in and lay down, clothed just as they were, with their feet to the fire, and slept.

In the darkness just before dawn, Johnnie wakened from heavy sleep and raised her head to find that a clear fire was burning on the hearth and the two men were gone. Noiselessly she arose, and replaced her outer wear, thinking to slip away without disturbing Roxy. But when she returned softly to the interior, after laving face and hands out at the wash-basin, and ordering her abundant hair, she found the little woman up and clad, slicing bacon and making coffee of generous strength from their scanty store.

"No — why, the idea!" cried Roxy. "Of course, you wasn't a-goin' on from no house o' mine 'thout no breakfast. Why, I say!"

Johnnie's throat swelled at the humble kindness. They ate, thanked Roxy and her man Zack in the simple uneffusive mountain fashion, and started away in the twilight of dawn. The big road was barely reached, when they heard steps coming after them in the dusk, and a breathless voice calling in a whisper, "Johnnie! Johnnie!"

The two turned and waited till Roxy came up.

"I — ye dropped this on the floor," the woman said, fumbling in her pocket and bringing out a bit of paper. "I didn't know as it was of any value — and then again I didn't know but what it might be. Johnnie —" she broke off and stood peering hesitatingly into the gloom toward the girl's shining face.

With a quick touch of the arm Johnnie signed to Pros to move on. As he swung out of earshot, the bulging light eyes, so like Mandy's, were suddenly dimmed by a rush of tears.

"I reckon he'd beat me ef he knowed I told," Roxy gasped. "He ain't never struck me yit, and us married five year — but I reckon he'd beat me for that."

Johnnie wisely forbore reply or interference of any sort. The woman gulped, drew her breath hard, and looked about her.

"Johnnie," she whispered again, "the — that there thing they ride in — the otty-mobile — hit broke down, and Zack was over to Pres Blevin's blacksmith shop a-he'pin' 'em work on it all day yesterday. You know Pres — he married Lura Dawson's aunt. Neither Himes nor Buckheath could git it to move, but by night they had it a-runnin' — or so hit *would* run. That's why you never saw tracks of it on the road — hit hadn't been along thar yit. But hit's went on this morning. No — no — no! I don't know whar it went. I don't know what they was aimin' to do. I don't know nothin'! Don't ask me, Johnnie Consadine, I reckon I've said right now what's put my man's neck in danger. Oh, my God — I wish the men-folks would quit their fussin' an' feudin'!"

And she turned and ran distractedly back into the cabin while Johnnie hurried on to join her uncle.

CHAPTER XXIV

THE RESCUE

JOHNNIE caught her uncle's hand and ran with him through the little thicket of saplings toward the main road.

"We'll get the track of the wheels, and when we find that car — and Shade Buckheath — and Pap Himes. . . . I . . . ." Johnnie panted, and did not finish her sentence. Her heart leaped when they came upon the broad mark of the pneumatic tires still fresh in the lonely mountain road.

"Looks like they might have passed here while we was standin' back there talkin' to Roxy," Uncle Pros said. "They could have — we'd not have heard a thing that distance, through this thick woods. Wonder could we catch up with them?"

Johnnie shook her head. She remembered the car flying up the ascents, swooping down long slopes and skimming like a bird across the levels, that morning when she had driven it.

"They'll go almost as fast as a railroad train, Uncle Pros," she told him, "but we must get there as soon as we can."

After that scarcely a word was spoken, while the two, still hand in hand, made what speed they could.

The morning waxed. The March sunshine was warm and pleasant. It was even hot, toiling endlessly up that mountain road. Now and again they met people who knew and saluted them, and who looked back at them curiously, furtively; at least it seemed so to the old man and the girl. Once a lean, hawk-nosed fellow ploughing a hillside field shouted across it:

"Hey-oh, Pros Passmore! How yuh come on? I 'lowed the student doctors would 'a' had you, long ago."

Pros ventured no reply, save a wagging of the head.

"That's Blaylock's cousin," he muttered to Johnnie. "Mighty glad we never went near 'em last night."

Once or twice they were delayed to talk. Johnnie would have hurried on, but her uncle warned her with a look to do nothing unusual. Everybody spoke to them of Gray Stoddard. Nobody had seen anything of him within a month of his disappearance, but several of them had "hearn say."

"They tell me," vouchsafed a lanky boy dawdling with his axe at a chip pile, "that the word goes in Cottonville now, that he's took money and lit out for Canada. Town folks is always a-doin' such."

"Like as not, bud," Pros assented gravely. "Me and Johnnie is goin' up to look after the old house, but we allowed to sleep to-night at Bushares's. Time enough to git to our place to-morrow."

Johnnie, who knew that her uncle hoped to reach the Consadine cabin by noon, instantly understood that he considered the possibility of this boy being a sort of picket posted to interview passers-by; and that the intention was to misinform him, so that he should not carry news of their approach.

After this, they met no one, but swung on at their best pace, and for the most part in silence, husbanding strength and breath. Twelve o'clock saw them entering that gash of the hills where the little cabin crouched against the great mountain wall. The ground became so rocky, that the track of the automobile was lost. At first it would be visible now and again on a bit of sandy loam, chain marks showing, where the tire left no impression; but, within a mile or so of the Consadine home, it seemed to have left the trail. When this point arrived, Johnnie differed from her uncle in choosing to hold to the road.

"Honey, this ends the cyar-tracks. Looks like they'd turned out. I think they took off into the bushes here, and where that cyar goes we ought to go," Pros argued.

But Johnnie hurried on ahead, looking about her eagerly. Suddenly she stooped with a cry and picked up from the path a small object.

"They've carried him past this way," she panted. "Oh, Uncle Pros, he was right here not so very long ago."

She scrutinized the sparse growth, the leafless bushes about the spot, looking for signs of a struggle, and the question in her heart was, "My God, was he alive or dead?" The thing she held in her hand was a blossom of the pink moccasin flower, carefully pressed, as though for the pages of a herbarium. The bit of paper to which it was attached was crumpled and discoloured.

"Looks like it had laid out in the dew last night," breathed Johnnie.

"Or for a week," supplied Pros. He scanned the little brown thing, then her face.

"All right," he said dubiously; "if that there tells you that he come a-past here, we'll foller this road — though it 'pears to me like we ought to stick to the cyar."

"It isn't far to our house," urged Johnnie. "Let's go there first, anyhow."

For a few minutes they pressed ahead in silence; then some subtle excitement made them break into a run. Thus they rounded the turn. The cabin came in sight. Its door swung wide on complaining hinges. The last of the rickety fence had fallen. The desolation and decay of a deserted house was over all.

"There's been folks here — lately," panted Pros. "Look thar!" and he pointed to a huddle of baskets and garments on the porch. "Mind out! Go careful. They may be thar now."

They "went careful," stealing up the steps and entering with caution; but they found nothing more alarming than the four bare walls, the ash-strewn, fireless hearth, the musty smell of a long-unoccupied house. Near the back door, at a spot where the dust was thick, Uncle Pros bent to examine a foot-print, when an exclamation from Johnnie called him through to the rear of the cabin.

"See the door!" she cried, running up the steep way toward the cave spring-house.

"Hold on, honey. Go easy," cautioned her uncle, following as fast as he could. He noted the whittling where the sapling bar that held the stout oaken door in place had been recently shaped to its present purpose. Then a soft, rhythmic sound like a giant breathing in his sleep caught the old hunter's keen ear.

"Watch out, Johnnie," he called, catching her arm. "What's that? Listen!"

Her fingers were almost on the bar. They could hear the soft lip-lip of the water as it welled out beneath the threshold, mingled with the tinkle and fall of the spring branch below.

Johnnie turned in her uncle's grasp and clutched him, staring down. Something shining and dark, brave with brass and flashing lamps, stood on the rocky way beneath, and purred like a great cat in the broad sunlight of noon — Gray Stoddard's motor car! The two, clinging to each other on the steep above it, gazed half incredulous, now that they had found the thing they sought. It looked so unbelievably adequate and modern and alive standing there, drawing its perfectly measured breath; it was so eloquent of power and the work of men's hands that there seemed to yawn a gap of half a thousand years between it and the raid in which it was being made a factor. That this pet toy of the modern millionaire should be set to work out the crude vengeance of wild men in these primitive surroundings, crowded up on a little rocky path of these savage mountains, at the door of a cave spring-house — such a food-cache as a nomad Indian might have utilized, in the gray bluff against the sky-line — it took the breath with its sinister strangeness.

They turned to the barred door. The cave was a sizable opening running far back into the mountain; indeed, the end of it had never been explored, but the vestibule containing the spring was fitted with rude benches and shelves for holding pans of milk and jars of buttermilk.

As Johnnie's hand went out to the newly cut bar, her uncle once more laid a restraining grasp upon it. A dozen men might be on the other side of the oaken door, and there might be nobody.

"Hello!" he called, guardedly.

No answer came; but within there was a sound of clinking, and then a shuffling movement. The panting motor spoke loud of those who had brought it there, who must be expecting to return to it very shortly. Johnnie's nerves gave way.

"Hello! Is there anybody inside?" she demanded fearfully.

"Who's there? Who is it?" came a muffled hail from the cave, in a voice that sent the blood to Johnnie's heart with a sudden shock.

"Uncle Pros, we've found him!" she screamed,

pushing the old man aside, and tugging at the bar which held the door in place. As she worked, there came a curious clinking sound, and then the dull impact of a heavy fall; and when she dragged the bar loose, swung the door wide and peered into the gloom, there was nothing but the silvery reach of the great spring, and beyond it a prone figure in russet riding-clothes.

"Uncle Pros — he's hurt! Oh, help me!" she cried.

The prostrate man struggled to turn his face to them.

"Is that you, Johnnie?" Gray Stoddard's voice asked. "No, I'm not hurt. These things tripped me up."

The two got to him simultaneously. They found him in heavy shackles. They noted how ankle and wrist chains had been rivetted in place. Together they helped him up.

As they did so tears ran down Johnnie's cheeks unregarded. Passmore deeply moved, yet quiet, studied him covertly. This, then, was the man of whom Johnnie thought so much, the rich young fellow who had left his work or amusements to come and cheer a sick old man in the hospital; this was the face that was a stranger's to him, but which had leaned over his cot or sat across the checker-board from him for long hours, while they talked or played together. That face was pale now, the brown hair, "a little longer than other people wore it," tossed helplessly in Stoddard's eyes, because he scarcely could raise his shackled hands to put it right; his russet-brown clothing was torn and grimed, as though with more than one struggle, though it may have been nothing worse than such mishap as his recent fall. Yet the man's soul looked out of his eyes with the same composure, the same kindness that always were his. He was eaten by neither terror nor rage, though he was alert for every possibility of help, or of advantage.

"You, Johnnie — you!" whispered Gray, struggling to his knees with their assistance, and catching a fold of her dress in those manacled hands. "I have dreamed about you here in the dark. It is you — it is really Johnnie."

He was pale, dishevelled, with a long mark of black leaf-mould across his cheek from his recent fall; and Johnnie bent speechlessly to wipe the stain away and put back the troublesome lock. He looked up into the brave beauty of her young, tear-wet face.

"Thank God for you, Johnnie," he murmured. "I might have known I wouldn't be let to die here in the dark like a rat in a hole while Johnnie lived."

"Whar's them that brought you here? The keepers?" questioned the old man anxiously, in a hoarse, hurried whisper.

"Dawson's gone to his dinner," returned Gray. "There were others here — came in an auto — I heard that. They've been quarrelling for more than an hour."

— "About what they'd do with you," broke in Pros. "Yes, part of 'em wants to put you out of the way, of course." He stooped, eagerly examining the shackles on Gray's ankles. "No way to git them things off without time and a file," he muttered, shaking his head.

"No," agreed Stoddard. "And I can't run much with them on. But we must get away from here as quick as we can. Dawson came in and told me after the other had gone that they had a big row, and he was standing out for me. Said he'd never give in to have me taken down and tied on the railroad track in Stryver's Gulch."

Johnnie's fair face whitened at the sinister words.

"The car!" she cried. "It's your own, Mr. Stoddard, and it's right down here. Uncle Pros, we can get him to it — I can run it — I know how." She put her shoulder under Stoddard's, catching the manacled hand in hers. Pros laid hold on the other side, and between them they half carried the shackled captive around the spring and to the door.

"Leggo, Johnnie!" cried her uncle. "You run on down and see if that contraption will go. I can git him thar now."

Johnnie instantly loosed the arm she held, sprang through the doorway, and headlong down the bluffy steep, stones rattling about her. She leaped into the car. Would her memory serve her? Would she forget some detail that she must know? There were two levers under the steering-wheel. She advanced her spark and partly opened the throttle. From the steady, comfortable purr which had undertoned all sounds in the tiny glen, the machine burst at once into a deep-toned roar. The narrow depression vibrated with its joyous clamour.

Suddenly, above the sound, Johnnie was aware of a distant hail, which finally resolved itself into words.

"Hi! Hoo — ee! You let that car alone, whoever you are."

She glanced over her shoulder; Passmore had got Gray to the top of the declivity, and was attempting to help him down. Both men evidently heard the challenge, but she screamed to them again and again.

"Hurry, oh hurry! They're coming — they're coming."

Stoddard had been stepping as best he could, hobbling along in the hampering leg chains, that were attached to the wrists also, and twitched on his hands with every step. His muscles responded to Johnnie's cry almost automatically, stiffening to an effort at extra speed, and he fell headlong, dragging Pros down with him. Despairingly Johnnie started to climb down from the car and go to their aid, but her uncle leaped to his feet clawing and grabbing to find a hold around Gray's waist, panting out, "Stay thar — Johnnie — I can fetch him."

With a straining heave he hoisted Gray's helpless body into his arms. The car trembled like a great, eager monster, growling in leash. Johnnie's agonized eyes searched first its mechanism, and then went to the descending figures, where her uncle plunged desperately down the slope, fell, struggled, rolled, but rose and came gallantly on, half dragging, half carrying Gray in his arms.

"Let that car alone!" a new voice took up the hail, a little nearer this time; and after it came the sound of a shot. High up on the mountain's brow, against the sky, Johnnie caught a glimpse of the heads and shoulders of men, with the slanting bar of a gun barrel over one.

"Oh, hurry, Uncle Pros!" she sobbed. "Let me come back and help you."

But Passmore stumbled across the remaining space; mutely, with drawn face and loud, labouring breath he lifted Gray and thrust him any fashion into the tonneau, climbing blindly after.

The pursuit on the hill above broke into the open. Johnnie moved the levers as Gray had shown her how to do, and with a bound of the great machine, they were off. Stoddard, dazed, bruised, abraded, was back in the tonneau struggling up with Uncle Pros's assistance. He could not help her. She must know for herself and do the right thing. The track led through the bushes, as they had found it that morning. It was fairly good, but terribly steep. She noted that the speed lever was at neutral. She slipped it over to the first speed; the car was already leaping down the hill at a tremendous pace; yet those yelling voices were behind, and her pushing fingers carried the lever through second to the third speed without pausing.

Under this tremendous pressure the car jumped like a nervous horse, lurched drunkenly down the short way, but reeled successfully around the turn at the bottom.   Johnnie knew this was going too fast.   She debated the possibility of slackening the speed a bit as they struck the highway, such as it was.   Uncle Pros, yet gasping, was trying to help Gray into the seat; but with his hampering manacles and the jerking of the car, the younger man was still on his knees, when the chase burst through the bushes, scarcely more than three hundred feet behind them.

There was a hoarse baying of men's voices; there were four of them running hard, and two carried guns. The noise of the machine, of course, prevented its occupants from distinguishing any word, but the menace of the open pursuit was apparent.

" Johnnie!"   cried Gray.   "Oh, this won't do! For God's sake, Mr. Passmore, help me over there. They wouldn't want to hurt her — but they're going to shoot.   She ——"

The old man thrust Gray down, with a hand on his shoulder.

"You keep out o' range," he shouted close to Gray's ear.   "They won't aim to hit Johnnie; but you they'll pick off as far as they can see ye.   Bend low, honey," to the girl in the driver's seat.   "But freeze to it.   Johnnie ain't no niece of mine if she goes back on a friend."

The girl in front heard neither of them.   There was a bellowing detonation, and a spatter of shot fell about the flying car.

"That ain't goin' to hurt nobody," commented

Pros philosophically. "It's no more than buck-shot anyhow."

But on the word followed a more ominous crack, and there was the whine of a bullet above them.

"My God, I can't let her do this," Gray protested. But Johnnie turned over her shoulder a shining face from which all weariness had suddenly been erased, a glorified countenance that flung him the fleeting smile she had time to spare from the machine.

"You're in worse danger right now from my driving than you are from their guns," she panted.

As she spoke there sounded once more the ripping crack of a rifle, the singing of a bullet past them, and with it the flatter, louder noise of the shot-gun was repeated. Her eye in the act of turning to her task, caught the silhouette of old Gideon Himes's uncouth figure relieved against the noonday sky, as he sprang high, both arms flung up, the hands empty and clutching, and pitched headlong to his face. But her mind scarcely registered the impression, for a rifle ball struck the shaly edge of a bluff under which the road at this point ran, and tore loose a piece of the slate-like rock, which glanced whirling into the tonneau and grazed Gray Stoddard's temple. He fell forward, crumpling down into the bottom of the vehicle.

"On — go on, honey!" yelled Pros, motioning vehemently to the girl. "Don't look back here — I'll tend to him"; and he stooped over the motionless form.

Then came the roaring impression of speed, of

rushing bushes that gathered themselves and ran back past the car while, working under full power, it stood stationary, as it seemed to Johnnie, in the middle of a long, dusty gray ribbon that was the road. The cries of the men behind them, all sounds of pursuit, were soon left so far in the distance that they were unheard.

"Ain't this rather fast?" shouted Uncle Pros, who had lifted Stoddard's bleeding head to his knee and, crouched on the bottom of the tonneau, was shielding the younger man from further injury as the motor lurched and pitched.

"Yes, it's too fast," Johnnie screamed back to him. "I'm trying to go slower, but the foot-brake won't hold. Uncle Pros, is he hurt? Is he hurt bad?"

"I don't think so, honey," roared the old man stoutly, guarding Gray's inert body with his arm. Then, stretching up as he kneeled, and leaning forward as close to her ear as he could get: "But you git him to Cottonville quick as you can. Don't you werry about goin' slow, unlessen you're scared yourself. Thar ain't no tellin' who might pop up from behind these here bushes and take a chance shot at us as we go by."

Johnnie worked over her machine wildly. Gray had told her of the foot-brake only; but her hand encountering the lever of the emergency brake, she grasped it at a hazard and shoved it forward, as the god of luck had ordered, just short of a zigzag in the steep mountain road which, at the speed they had been making, would have piled them, a mass of wreckage, beneath the cliff.

The sudden, violent check — shooting along at the speed they were, it amounted almost to a stoppage — gave the girl a sense of power. If she could do that, they were fairly safe. With the relief, her brain cleared; she was able to study the machine with some calmness. Gray could not help her — out of the side of her eye she could see where he lay inert and senseless in Passmore's hold. The lives of all three depended on her cool head at this moment. She remembered now all that Stoddard had said the morning he taught her to run the car. With one movement she threw off the switch, thus stopping the engine, entirely. They must make it to Cottonville running by gravity wherever they could; since she had no means of knowing that there was sufficient gasoline in the tank, and it would not do to be overtaken or waylaid.

On and on they flew, around quick turns, along narrow ways that skirted tall bluffs, over stretches of comparatively level road, where Johnnie again switched on the engine and speeded up. They were skimming down from the upper Unakas like a great bird whose powerful wings make nothing of distance. But Johnnie's heart was as lead when she glanced back at the motionless figure in the tonneau, the white, blood-streaked face that lay on her uncle's arm. She turned doggedly to her steering-wheel and levers, and took greater chances than ever with the going, for speed's sake. The boy they had talked with two hours before at the chip pile, met them afoot. He leaped into the bushes to let them pass, and stared after them with dilated eyes. Johnnie never knew what he shouted. They only saw his mouth open and working. Mercifully, so far, they had met no vehicles. But now the higher, wilder mountains were behind them, there was an occasional horseman. As they neared Cottonville, and teams were numerous on the road, Johnnie, jealously unwilling to slacken speed, kept the horn going almost continuously. People in wagons and buggies, or on foot, drawn out along the roadside, cupped hands to lips and yelled startled inquiries. Johnnie bent above the steering-wheel and paid no attention. Uncle Pros tried to answer with gesticulation or a shouted word, and sometimes those he replied to turned and ran, calling to others. But it was black Jim, riding on Roan Sultan, out with the searchers, who saw and understood. He looked down across the great two-mile turn beyond the Gap, and sighted the climbing car. Where he stood it was less than an eighth of a mile below him; he could almost have thrown a stone into it. He bent in his saddle, shaded his eyes, and gazed intently.

"Fo' God!" he muttered under his breath. "That's Mr. Gray hisself! Them's the clothes he was wearin'!"

Whirling his horse and digging in the spurs, he rattled pell-mell down the opposite steep toward Cottonville, shouting as he went.

"They've done got him — they've found him! Miss

Johnnie Consadine's a-bringin' him down in his own cyar!"

At the Hardwick place, where the front lawn sloped down with its close-trimmed, green-velvet sward, stood two horses. Charlie Conroy had come out as soon as the alarm was raised to help with the search. He and Lydia had ridden together each day since. Moving slowly along a quiet ravine yesterday, out of sight and hearing of the other searchers, Conroy had found an intimate moment in which to urge his suit. She had begged a little time to consider, with so encouraging an aspect that, this morning, when he came out that they might join the party bound for the mountains, he brought the ring in his pocket. The bulge of the big diamond showed through her left-hand glove. She had taken him at last. She told herself that it was the only thing to do. Harriet Hardwick, who had returned from Watauga, since her sister would not come to her, stood in the door of the big house regarding them with a countenance of distinctly chastened rejoicing. Conroy's own frame or mind was evident; deep satisfaction radiated from his commonplace countenance. He was to be Jerome Hardwick's brother-in-law, an intimate member of the mill crowd. He was as near being in love with Lydia Sessions at that moment as he ever would be. As for Lydia herself, the last week had brought that thin face of hers to look all of its thirty odd years; and the smile which she turned upon her affianced was the product of conscientious effort. She was safely in her saddle, and Conroy had just swung up to his own, when Jim came pelting down the Gap road toward the village. They could see him across the slope of the hill. Conroy cantered hastily up the street a bit to hear what the boy was vociferating. Lydia's nerves quivered at sight of him returning.

"Hurrah! Hurrah!" shouted Conroy, waving his cap. "Lord, Lord; Did you hear that, Lydia? Hoo-ee, Mrs. Hardwick! Did you hear what Jim's saying? They've got Gray! Johnnie Consadine's bringing him — in his own car." Then turning once more to his companion: "Come on, dear; we'll ride right down to the hospital. Jim said he was hurt. That's where she would take him. That Johnnie Consadine of yours is the girl — isn't she a wonder, though?"

Lydia braced herself. It had come, and it was worse than she could have anticipated. She cringed inwardly in remembrance; she wished she had not let Conroy make that pitying reference — unreproved, uncorrected — to Stoddard's being a rejected man. But perhaps they were bringing Gray in dead, after all — she tried not to hope so.

The auto became visible, a tiny dark speck, away up in the Gap. Then it was sweeping down the Gap road; and once more Conroy swung his cap and shouted, though it is to be questioned that any one marked him.

Below in the village the noisy clatter brought people

to door and casement. At the Himes boarding-house,
a group had gathered by the gate. At the window
above, in an arm-chair, sat a thin little woman with
great dark eyes, holding a sick child in her lap. The
sash was up, and both were carefully wrapped in a big
shawl that was drawn over the two of them.

"Sis' Johnnie is comin' back; she sure is comin'
back soon," Laurella was crooning to her baby. "And
we ain't goin' to work in no cotton mill, an' we ain't
goin' to live in this ol' house any more. Next thing
we're a-goin' away with Sis' Johnnie and have a fi-ine
house, where Pap Himes can't come about to be cross
to Deanie."

High up on Unaka Mountain, where a cluttered
mass of rock reared itself to front the noonday sun, an
old man's figure, prone, the hands clutched full of
leaf-mould, the gray face down amid the fern, Gideon
Himes would never offer denial to those plans, nor
seek to follow to that fine house.

The next moment an automobile flashed into sight
coming down the long lower slope from the Gap,
the horn blowing continuously, horsemen, pedestrians,
buggies and wagons fleeing to the roadside bushes as
it roared past in its cloud of dust.

"Look, honey, look — yon's Sis' Johnnie now!"
cried Laurella. "She's a-runnin' Mr. Stoddard's
car. An' thar's Unc' Pros. . . . Is — my Lord!
Is that Mr. Stoddard hisself, with blood all over him?"

Lydia and Conroy, hurrying down the street, drew
up on the fringes of the little crowd that had gathered

and was augmenting every moment, and Johnnie's face was turned to Stoddard in piteous questioning. His eyes were open now. He raised himself a bit on her uncle's arm, and declared in a fairly audible voice:

"I'm all right. I'm not hurt."

"Somebody git me a glass of water," called Uncle Pros.

Mavity Bence ran out with one, but when she got close enough to see plainly the shackled figure Passmore supported, she thrust the glass into Mandy Meacham's hand and flung her apron over her head.

"Good Lord!" she moaned. "I reckon they've killed him. They done one of my brothers that-a-way in feud times, and throwed him over a bluff. Oh, my Lord; Why will men be so mean?"

Pros had taken the glass from Mandy and held it to Gray's lips. Then he dashed part of the remaining water on Stoddard's handkerchief and with Mandy's help, got the blood cleared away.

From every shanty, women and children came hastening — men hurried up from every direction.

"Look at her — look at Johnnie!" cried Beulah Catlett. "Pony! Milo!" turning back into the house, where the boys lay sleeping. "Come out here and look at your sister!"

"Did ye run it all by yourself, Sis' Johnnie?" piped Lissy from the porch.

The girl in the driver's seat smiled and nodded to the child.

"Are you through there, Uncle Pros?" asked

Johnnie. "We must get Mr. Stoddard on to his house."

The women and children drew back, the crowd ahead parted, and the car got under way once more. The entire press of people followed in its wake, surged about it, augmenting at every corner.

"I'm afraid my horse won't stand this sort of thing," Lydia objected, desperately, reining in. Conroy glanced at her in surprise. Bay Dick was the soberest of mounts. Then he looked wistfully after the crowd.

"Would you mind if I —" he began, and broke off to say contritely, "I'll go back with you if you'd rather." It was evident that Lydia would make of him a thoroughly disciplined husband.

"Never mind," she said, locking her teeth. "I'll go with you." One might as well have it done and over with. And they hurried on to make up for lost time.

They saw the car turn in to the street which led to the Hardwick factory. Somebody had hurried ahead and told MacPherson and Jerome Hardwick; and just as they came in sight, the office doors burst open and the two men came running hatless down the steps. Suddenly the factory whistles roared out the signal that had been agreed upon, which bellowed to the hills the tidings that Gray Stoddard was found. Three long calls and a short one — that meant that he was found alive. As the din of it died down, Hexter's mills across the creek took up the message, and when they were silent, the old Victory came in on their heels, bawling it again. Every whistle in Cottonville gave tongue, clamouring hoarsely above the valley, and out across the ranges, to the hundreds at their futile search, "Gray Stoddard is found. Stoddard is found. Alive. He is brought in alive."

MacPherson ran up to one side of the car and Hardwick to the other.

"Are you hurt?" inquired the Scotchman, his hands stretched out.

"Can you get out and come in?" Hardwick demanded eagerly.

On the instant, the big gates swung wide, the factory poured out a tide of people as though the building had been afire. At sight of Stoddard, the car, and Johnnie, a cheer went up, spontaneous, heart-shaking.

"My God — look at that!" MacPherson's eyes had encountered the shackles on Stoddard's wrists.

"Lift him down — lift him out," cried Jerome Hardwick. With tears on his tanned cheeks the Scotchman complied; and Hardwick's eyes, too, were wet as he saw it.

"We'll have those things off of him in no time," he shouted. "Here, let's get him in to the couch in my office. Send some of the mechanics here. Where's Shade Buckheath?"

A dozen pairs of hands were stretched up to assist MacPherson and Pros Passmore. As many as could get to the rescued man helped. And when the crowd saw that shackled figure raised, and heard in the tense silence the clinking sound of the chains, a low groan went through it; more than one woman sobbed aloud. But at this Gray raised his head a bit, and once more declared in a fairly strong voice:

"I'm not hurt, people — only a little crack on the head. I'm all right — thanks to her," and he motioned toward the girl in the car, who was watching anxiously.

Then the ever thickening throng went wild; and as Gray was carried up the steps and disappeared through the office doors, it turned toward the automobile, surging about the car, a sea of friendly, admiring faces, most of them touched with the tenderness of tears, and cheered its very heart out for Johnnie Consadine.

CHAPTER XXV

THE FUTURE

G RAY!" it was Uncle Pros's voice, and Uncle Pros's face looked in at the office door. "Could I bother you a minute about the sidewalk in front of the place up yon? Mr. Hexter told me you'd know whether the grade was right, and I could let the workmen go ahead."

Stoddard swung around from his desk and looked at the old man.

"Come right in," he said. "I'm not busy — I'm just pretending this morning. MacPherson won't give me anything to do. He persists in considering me still an invalid."

Uncle Pros came slowly in and laid his hat down gingerly before seating himself. He was dressed in the garb which, with money, he would always have selected — the village ideal of a rich gentleman's wear — and he looked unbelievably tall and imposing in his black broadcloth. When the matter of the patent was made known to Jerome Hardwick, a company was hastily formed to take hold of it, which advanced the ready money for Johnnie and her family to place themselves. Mrs. Hexter, who had been all winter in Boston, had decided, suddenly, to go abroad; and when her husband wired her to know if he might let the house to the Consadine-Passmore household, she made a quick, warm response.

So they were domiciled in a ready-prepared home of elegance and beauty. Though the place at Cottonville had been only a winter residence with Mrs. Hexter, she was a woman of taste, and had always had large means at her command. With all a child's plasticity, Laurella dropped into the improved order of things. Her cleverness in selecting the proper wear for herself and children was nothing short of marvellous; and her calm acceptance of the new state of affairs, the acme of good breeding. Johnnie immediately set about seeing that Mavity Bence and Mandy Meacham were comfortably provided for in the old boarding-house, where she assured Gray they could do more good than many Uplift clubs.

"We'll have a truck-patch there, and a couple of cows and some chickens," she said. "That'll be good for the table, and it'll give Mandy the work she loves to do. Aunt Mavity can have some help in the house — there's always a girl or two breaking down in the mills, who would be glad to have a chance at housework for a while."

Now Pros looked all about him, and seemed in no haste to begin, though Gray knew well there was something on his mind. Finally Stoddard observed, smiling:

"You're the very man I wanted to see, Uncle Pros. I rang up the house just now, but Johnnie said you had started down to the mills. What do you think I've found out about our mine?"

Certainly the old man looked very tall and dignified in his new splendours; but now he was all boy, leaning eagerly forward to half whisper:

"I don't know — what?"

Stoddard's face was scarcely less animated as he searched hastily in the pigeon-holes of his desk. The patent might have a company to manage its affairs, but the mine on Big Unaka was sacred to these two, in whom the immortal urchin sufficiently survived to make mine-hunting and exploiting delectable employment.

"Why, Uncle Pros, it isn't silver at all. It's —" Gray looked up and caught the woeful drop of the face before him, and hastened on to add, "It's better than silver — it's nickel. The price of silver fluctuates; but the world supply of nickel is limited, and nickel's a sure thing."

Pros Passmore leaned back in his chair, digesting this new bit of information luxuriously.

"Nickel," he said reflectively. And again he repeated the word to himself. "Nickel. Well, I don't know but what that's finer. Leastways, it's likelier. To say a silver mine, always seemed just like taking money out of the ground; but then, nickels are money too — and enough of 'em is all a body needs."

"These people say the ore is exceptionally fine." Stoddard had got out the letter now and was glancing over it. "They're sending down an expert, and you and I will go up with him as soon as he gets here. There are likely to be other valuable minerals as by-products in a nickel mine. And we want to build an ideal mining village, as well as model cotton mills. Oh, we've got the work cut out for us and laid right to hand! If we don't do our little share toward solving some problems, it will be strange."

"Cur'us how things turns out in this world," the old man ruminated. "Ever sence I was a little chap settin' on my granddaddy's knees by the hearth — big hickory fire a-roarin' up the chimbly, wind a-goin' 'whooh!' overhead, an' me with my eyes like saucers a-listenin' to his tales of the silver mine that the Injuns had — ever sence that time I've hunted that thar mine." He laughed chucklingly, deep in his throat. "Thar wasn't a wild-catter that could have a hideout safe from me. They just had to trust me. I crawled into every hole. I came mighty near seein' the end of every cave — but one. And that cave was the one whar my Mammy kept her milk and butter — the springhouse whar they put you in prison. Somehow, I never did think about goin' to the end of that. Looked like it was too near home to have a silver mine in it; and thar the stuff lay and waited for the day when I should take a notion to find a pretty rock for Deanie, and crawl back in thar and keep a crawlin', till I just fell over it, all croppin' out in the biggest kind of vein."

Gray had heard Uncle Pros tell the story many times, but it had a perennial charm.

"Then I lost six months — plumb lost 'em, you know. And time I come to myself, Johnnie an' me was a-huntin' for you. And there we found you shut in that thar same cave; and I was so tuck up with that matter that I never once thought, till I got you home, to wonder did Buckheath and the rest of 'em know that they'd penned you in the silver mine. I ain't never asked you, but you'd have knowed if they had."

"I should have known anything that Rudd Dawson or Groner or Venters knew," Gray said, "but I'm not sure about Buckheath or Himes. However, Himes is dead, and Buckheath — I don't suppose anybody in Cottonville will ever see him again."

Pros's face changed instantly. He leaned abruptly forward and laid a hand on the other's knee.

"That's exactly what I came down here to speak with you about, Gray," he said. "They've fetched Shade Buckheath in — now, what do you make out of that?"

Stoddard shoved the letter from the Eastern mining man back in its pigeon-hole.

"Well," he said slowly, "I didn't expect that. I thought of course Shade was safely out of the country. I — Passmore, I'm sorry they've got him." After a little silence he spoke again. "What do I make of it? Why, that there are some folks up on Big Unaka who need pretty badly to appear as very law-abiding citizens. I'll wager anything that Groner and Rudd Dawson brought Shade in."

Uncle Pros nodded seriously. "Them's the very fellers," he said. "Reckon they've talked pretty free to you. I never axed ye, Gray — how did they treat ye?"

"Dawson was the best friend I had," Stoddard returned promptly. "When I got to the big turn on Sultan — coming home that Friday morning — Buckheath met me, and asked me to go down to Burnt Cabin and help him with a man that had fallen and hurt himself on the rocks. Dawson told me afterward that he and Jesse Groner were posted at the roadside to stop me and hem me in before I got to the bluff. I've described to you how Buckheath tried to back Sultan over the edge, and I got off on the side where the two were, not noticing them till they tied me hand and foot. They almost came to a clinch with Buckheath then and there. You ought to have heard Groner swear! It was like praying gone wrong."

"Uh-huh," agreed Pros, "Jess is a terrible wicked man — in speech that-a-way — but he's good-hearted."

"That first scrimmage showed me just what the men were after," Stoddard said. "Buckheath plainly wanted me put out of the way; but the others had some vague idea of holding me for a ransom and getting money out of the Hardwicks. Dawson complained always that he thought the mills owed him money. He said they must have sold his girl's body for as much as a hundred dollars, and he felt that he'd been cheated. Oh, it was all crazy stuff! But he and the others had justified themselves; and they had no notion of standing for what Buckheath was after. I was one of the cotton-mill men to them; they had no personal malice.

Through the long evenings when Groner or Dawson or Will Venters was guarding me — or maybe all three of them — we used to talk; and it surprised me to find how simple and childish those fellows were. They were as kind to me as though I had been a brother, and treated me courteously always.

"Little by little, I got at the whole thing from them. It seems that Buckheath took advantage of the feeling there was in the mountains against the mill men on account of the hospital and some other matters. He went up there and interviewed anybody that he thought might join him in a vendetta. I imagine he found plenty of them that were ready to talk and some that were willing to do; but it chanced that Dawson and Jesse Groner were coming down to Cottonville that morning I passed Buckheath at the Hardwick gate, and he must have cut across the turn and followed me, intending to pick a quarrel. Then he met Dawson and Groner and framed up this other plan with their assistance.

"Uncle Pros, I want you to help me out. If Buckheath has to stand trial, how are we — any of us — going to testify without making it hard on the Dawson crowd? I expect to live here the rest of my days. Here's this mine of ours. And right here I mean to build a big mill and work out my plans. I think you know that I hope to marry a mountain wife, and I can't afford to quarrel with those folks."

Uncle Pros's chin dropped to his breast, his eyes half closed as he sat thinking intently.

"Well," he said finally, "they won't have nothing worse than manslaughter against Shade. It can't be proved that he intended to shoot Pap — 'cause he didn't. If he was shootin' after us — there's the thing we don't want to bring up. You was down in the bottom of the cyar, an' I had my back to him, and so did Johnnie, and we don't know anything about what was done — ain't that so? As for you, you've already told Mr. Hardwick and the others that you was taken prisoner and detained by parties unknown. Johnnie an' me was gettin' you out of the springhouse and away in the machine. Then Gid and Shade comes up, and thinkin' we're the other crowd stealin' the machine — they try to catch us and turn loose at us — that makes a pretty good story, don't it?"

"It does if Dawson and Groner and Venters agree to it," Stoddard laughed. "But somebody will have to communicate with them before they tell another one — or several others."

"I'll see to that, Gray," Pros said, rising and preparing to go. "Boy," he looked down fondly at the younger man, and set a brown right hand on his shoulder, "you never done a wiser thing nor a kinder in your life, than when you forgave your enemies that time. I'll bet you could ride the Unakas from end to end, the balance o' your days, the safest man that ever travelled their trails."

"Talking silver mine?" inquired MacPherson, putting his quizzical face in at the door.

"No," returned Stoddard. "We were just mentioning my pestilent cotton-mill projects. By this time next year, you and Hardwick will be wanting to have me abated as a nuisance."

"No, no," remonstrated MacPherson, coming in and leaning with affectionate familiarity on the younger man's chair. "There's no pestilence in you, Gray. You couldn't be a nuisance if you tried. People who will work out their theories stand to do good in the world; it's only the fellows who are content with bellowing them out that I object to."

"Better be careful!" laughed Stoddard. "We'll make you vice-president of the company."

"Is that an offer?" countered MacPherson swiftly. "I've got a bit of money to invest in this county; and Hardwick has ever a new brother-in-law or such that looks longingly at my shoes."

"You'd furnish the conservative element, surely," debated Stoddard.

"I'd keep you from bankruptcy," grunted the Scotchman, as he laid a small book on Gray's desk. "I doubt not Providence demands it of me."

Evening was closing in with a greenish-yellow sunset, and a big full moon pushing up to whiten the sky above it. It was late March now, and the air was full of vernal promise. Johnnie stepped out on the porch and glanced toward the west. She was expecting Gray that evening. Would there be time before he came, she wondered, for a little errand she wanted to do? Turning back into the hall, she caught a jacket from the hook where it hung and hurried down to the gate, settling her arms in the sleeves as she ran. There would be time if she went fast. She wished to get the little packet into which she had made Gray's letters months ago, dreading to look even at the folded outsides of them, tucking them away on the high shelf of her dress-closet at the Pap Himes boarding-house, and trying to forget them. Nobody would know where to look but herself. She got permission from Mavity to go upstairs. Once there, the letters made their own plea; and alone in the little room that was lately her own, she opened the packet, carrying the contents to the fading light and glancing over sheet after sheet. She knew them all by heart. How often she had stood at that very window devouring these same words, not realizing then, as she did now, what deep meaning was in each phrase, how the feeling expressed increased from the first to the last. Across the ravine, one of the loom fixers found the evening warm enough to sit on the porch playing his guitar. The sound of the twanging strings, and the appealing vibration of his young voice in a plaintive minor air, came over to her. She gathered the sheets together and pressed them to her face as though they were flowers, or the hands of little children.

"I've got to tell him — to-night," she whispered to herself, in the dusky, small, dismantled room. "I've got to get him to see it as I do. I must make myself worthy of him before I let him take me for his own."

She thrust the letters into the breast-pocket of her

coat and ran downstairs.   Mavity Bence stood in the hall, plainly awaiting her.

"Honey," she began fondly, "I've been putting away Pap's things to-day — jest like you oncet found me putting away Lou's. I came on this here." And then Johnnie noticed a folded bandanna in her hands.

"You-all asked me to let ye go through and find that nickel ore, and ye brung it out in a pasteboard box; but this here is what it was in on the day your Uncle Pros fetched hit here, and I thought maybe you'd take a interest in having the handkercher that your fortune come down the mountains in."

"Yes, indeed, Aunt Mavity," said Johnnie, taking the bandanna into her own hands.

"Pap, he's gone," the poor woman went on tremulously, "an' the evil what he done — or wanted to do — is a thing that I reckon you can afford to forget.   You're a mighty happy woman, Johnnie Consadine; the Lord knows you deserve to be."

She stood looking after the girl as she went out into the twilit street.   Johnnie was dressed as she chose now, not as she must, and her clothing showed itself to be of the best.   Anything that might be had in Wautaga was within her means; and the tall, graceful figure passing so quietly down the street would never have been taken for other than a member of what we are learning to call the "leisure class."   When the shadows at the end of the block swallowed her up, Mavity turned, wiping her eyes, and addressed herself to her tasks.

"I reckon Lou would 'a' been just like that if she'd

'a' lived," she said to Mandy Meacham, with the tender fatuity of mothers. "Johnnie seems like a daughter to me — an' I know in my soul no daughter could be kinder. Look at her makin' me keep every cent Pap had in the bank, when Laurelly could have claimed it all and kep' it."

"Yes, an' addin' somethin' to it," put in Mandy. "I do love 'em both — Johnnie an' Deanie. Ef I ever was so fortunate as to get a man and be wedded and have chaps o' my own, I know mighty well and good I couldn't love any one of 'em any better than I do Deanie. An' yet Johnnie's quare. I always will say that Johnnie Consadine is quare. What in the nation does she want to go chasin' off to Yurrup for, when she's got everything that heart could desire or mind think of right here in Cottonville?"

That same question was being put even more searchingly to Johnnie by somebody else at the instant when Mandy enunciated it. She had found Gray waiting for her at the gate of her home.

"Let's walk here a little while before we go in," he suggested. "I went up to the house and found you were out. The air is delightful, and I've got something I want to say to you."

He had put his arm under hers, and they strolled together down the long walk that led to the front of the lawn. The evening air was pure and keen, tingling with the breath of the wakening season.

"Sweetheart," Gray broke out suddenly, "I've been thinking day and night since we last talked together about this year abroad that you're planning. I certainly don't want to put my preferences before yours. I only want to be very sure that I know what your real preferences are," and he turned and searched her face with a pair of ardent eyes.

"I think I ought to go," the girl said in a very low voice, her head drooped, her own eyes bent toward the path at her feet.

"Why?" whispered her lover.

"I — oh, Gray — you know. If we should ever be married — well, then," in answer to a swift, impatient exclamation, "when we are married, if you should show that you were ashamed of me — I think it would kill me. No, don't say there's not any danger. You might have plenty of reason. And I — I want to be safe, Gray — safe, if I can."

Gray regarded the beautiful, anxious face long and thoughtfully. Yes, of course it was possible for her to feel that way. Assurance was so deep and perfect in his own heart, that he had not reflected what it might lack in hers.

"Dear girl," he said, pausing and making her look at him, "how little you do know of me, after all! Do I care so much for what people say? Aren't you always having to reprove me because I so persistently like what I like, without reference to the opinions of the world? Besides, you're a beauty," with tender brusqueness, "and a charmer that steals the hearts of men. If you don't know all this, it isn't from lack of telling. Moreover, I can keep on informing you. A year of European travel could not make you any more beautiful, Johnnie — or sweeter. You may not believe me, but there's little the 'European capitals' could add to your native bearing — you must have learned that simple dignity from these mountains of yours. Of course, if you wanted to go for pleasure —" His head a little on one side, he regarded her with a tender, half-quizzical smile, hoping he had sounded the note that would bring him swift surrender.

"It isn't altogether for myself — there are the others," Johnnie told him, lifting honest eyes to his in the dim moonlight. "They're all I had in the world, Gray, till you came into my life, and I must keep my own. I belong to a people who never give up anything they love."

Stoddard dropped an arm about his beloved, and turned her that she might face the windows of the house behind them, bending to set his cheek against hers and direct her gaze.

"Look there," he whispered, laughingly.

She looked and saw her mother, clad in such wear as Laurella's taste could select and Laurella's beauty make effective. The slight, dark little woman was coming in from the dining room with her children all about her, a noble group.

"Your mother is much more the fine lady than you'll ever be, Johnnie Stoddard," Gray said, giving her the name that always brought the blood to the girl's cheek and made her dumb before him. "You know your Uncle Pros and I are warmly attached to each other.

What is it you'd be waiting for, girl? Why, Johnnie, a man has just so long to live on this earth, and the years in which he has loved are the only years that count — would you be throwing one of these away? A year — twelve months — three hundred and sixty-five days — cast to the void. You reckless creature!"

He cupped his hands about her beautiful, fair face and lifted it, studying it.

"Johnnie — Johnnie — Johnnie Stoddard; the one woman out of all the world for me," he murmured, his deep voice dropping to a wooing cadence. "I couldn't love you better — I shall never love you less. Don't let us foolishly throw away a year out of the days which will be vouchsafed us together. Don't do it, darling — it's folly."

Hard-pressed, Johnnie made only a sort of inarticulate response.

"Come, love, sit a moment with me, here," pleaded Gray, indicating a small bench hidden among the evergreens and shrubs at the end of the path. "Sit down, and let's reason this thing out."

"Reasoning with you," began Johnnie, helplessly, "isn't — it isn't reasonable!"

"It is," he told her, in that deep, masterful tone which, like a true woman, she both loved and dreaded. "It's the height of reasonableness. Why, dear, the great primal reason of all things speaks through me. And I won't let you throw away a year of our love. Johnnie, it isn't as though we'd been neighbours, and grown up side by side. I came from the ends of the earth to find you, darling — and I knew my own as soon as I saw you."

He put out his arms and gathered her into a close embrace.

For a space they rested so, murmuring question and reply, checked or answered by swift, sweet kisses.

"The first time I ever saw you, love. . . . "

"Oh, in those dusty old shoes and a sunbonnet! Could you love me then, Gray?"

"The same as at this moment, sweetheart. Shoes and sunbonnets — I'm ashamed of you now, Johnnie, in earnest. What do such things matter?"

"And that morning on the mountain, when we got the moccasin flowers," the girl's voice took up the theme. "I — it was sweet to be with you — and bitter, too. I could not dream then that you were for me. And afterward — the long, black, dreadful time when you seemed so utterly lost to me ——"

At the mention of those months, Gray stopped her words with a kiss.

"Mine," he whispered with his lips against hers, "Out of all the world — mine."

THE END